Praise for Terri Reed
and her novels

"In *Love Comes Home*, Terri Reed tells
the touching story of a couple whose faith
must help them overcome past hurts."
—*Romantic Times BOOKreviews*

"Terri Reed's *A Sheltering Love* beautifully
combines the development of love with enough
conflict to keep the reader guessing about the
outcome. God's ability to repair relationships is
tenderly depicted."
—*Romantic Times BOOKreviews*

"Reed's characters are warm, true to life
and imperfect."
—*Romantic Times BOOKreviews* on *A Time of Hope*

"*Giving Thanks for Baby* has a nice twist that
readers are certain to enjoy. Terri Reed does an
exceptional job blending deeper issues with her
story to bind a well-written book."
—*Romantic Times BOOKreviews*

TERRI REED

Love Comes Home

A Sheltering Love

Steeple
Hill®

Published by Steeple Hill Books™

STEEPLE HILL BOOKS

Steeple
Hill®

Recycling programs
for this product may
not exist in your area.

ISBN-13: 978-0-373-65128-3
ISBN-10:   0-373-65128-7

LOVE COMES HOME AND A SHELTERING LOVE

LOVE COMES HOME
Copyright © 2004 by Terri Reed

A SHELTERING LOVE
Copyright © 2005 by Terri Reed

CONTENTS

Books by Terri Reed

Love Inspired

Loves Comes Home
A Sheltering Love
A Sheltering Heart
A Time of Hope
Giving Thanks for Baby

Love Inspired Suspense

Strictly Confidential
Double Deception
Beloved Enemy
*Double Jeopardy
*Double Cross
*Double Threat Christmas

*The McClains

TERRI REED

At an early age Terri Reed discovered the wonderful world of fiction and declared she would one day write a book. Now she is fulfilling that dream and enjoys writing for Steeple Hill. Her second book, *A Sheltering Love,* was a 2006 RITA® Award finalist and a 2005 National Reader's Choice Award finalist. Her book *Strictly Confidential,* book five of the Faith at the Crossroads continuity series, took third place in the 2007 American Christian Fiction Writers Book of the Year Award. She is an active member of both Romance Writers of America and American Christian Fiction Writers. She resides in the Pacific Northwest with her college-sweetheart husband, two wonderful children and an array of critters. When not writing, she enjoys spending time with her family and friends, gardening and playing with her dogs.

You can write to Terri at P.O. Box 19555, Portland, OR 97280, visit her on the Web at www.loveinspiredauthors.com or leave comments on her blog at http://ladiesofsuspense.blogspot.com/.

LOVE COMES HOME

For I know the plans I have for you,
declares the Lord, plans for welfare and not for
calamity, to give you a future and a hope.
—*Jeremiah* 29:11

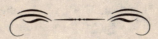

I want to dedicate this book
to everyone who has struggled to pursue a dream.
Keep believing. Faith and perseverance do pay off.

There are so many people to thank, who,
in one way or another, have touched my life
as a writer. I apologize if I've forgotten anyone
and ask for your forgiveness.

First and foremost, thank you to my husband and
children. I could never have done this without your
love and support. Thank you to my mother-in-law
for urging me to follow my dream. Thank you to
my mother for always believing in me.

A big thanks to my critique partners, Leah Vale and
Lissa Manley, for encouraging me, challenging me
to grow and never letting me quit.

Thank you to my writerly friends:
Melissa McClone, Delilah Ahrendt,
Tina Bilton-Smith, Amy Danicic, Carolyn Zane,
Susan Alverson, Cynthia Rutledge
and Lenora Worth. I have learned
and grown from knowing you.

And a heartfelt thanks to my spirit-filled sisters
who've been my cheering section as well as my
friends: Tricia, Sherry B., Sheri S., Deanna, Debbie
and all the ladies at Southlake Foursquare Church.
But mostly, I thank my Savior Jesus,
for all the blessings.

Chapter One

She was home.

Inhaling deeply the fresh scent of pine and exhaust-free air, Dr. Rachel Maguire stared at the seven-story redbrick building, the words Sonora Community Hospital spelled out in bright blue letters across the side. A strange tightness pulled at her chest. As a child, this had been the first hospital she'd ever entered.

Her gaze dropped to another set of letters above the door in front of her. Her breath froze. The emergency entrance.

She shied away from using the double sliding doors,

and instead followed the tidy walkway, carpeted on either side by lush green lawns, leading to the main entrance. The early-June sun warmed her face, and from high in the branches of a towering pine an unseen bird chirped a melodic tune. Off in the distance to the east, the peaks of the Sierra Nevadas rose to meet the clear blue sky. Even to her untrained eye, the vibrant greens and hues of brown and gold dotting the hillside were a painter's dream.

She paused, alert to the eerie peacefulness and serenity around her. With no outside noise to blend with, the unsettled, restless feelings she constantly lived with clamored for attention. She closed her eyes and willed the chaos to subside. She missed the pulsing beat of Chicago.

But not returning to California hadn't been an option.

Mom G. needed her.

Rachel took a deep breath, adjusted her grip on her small suitcase and walked through the sliding doors of the main hospital entrance. Even inside the hospital, tranquillity reigned. People waiting in the lobby area spoke in lowered tones and soothing, classical music played from somewhere overhead. She stepped briskly up to the administration desk.

"I'm looking for Mrs. Olivia Green's room."

The woman behind the desk smiled. "Hello, Rachel."

"Hello." She struggled to put a name to the round, wide-eyed face.

"Polly Anderson, now Campbell. You were a year ahead of me in school."

"Oh." Rachel didn't remember her, but smiled politely. "Hello, Polly."

"Your mom is on the fifth floor, room six. She'll be glad to see you. Welcome home."

Rachel blinked, surprised that anyone here would remember her after all this time and that there would be such open friendliness. Her fast-paced world had little time for niceties.

"Thank you, Polly," she said, and hurried to catch the elevator.

The doors opened on the fifth floor. Emotionally steeling herself, she stepped out. With a purposeful stride, she headed down the corridor. Overhead, the fluorescent lights glowed bright. A distinctive, familiar antiseptic smell assaulted her senses and settled in the back of her throat, offering her a measure of comfort.

Strange, she'd never before noticed how the quiet hum and soft beeping of machines coupled with the rumble of hushed voices lent the air a surreal quality. She'd spent so many years working in hospitals that her senses had grown accustomed to the surroundings. She couldn't remember ever noticing the atmosphere of her work. It was all part of being a doctor.

Only, this wasn't her hospital and she wasn't here as a doctor. She was a visitor. A chill ran down her spine. Someone she loved lay in one of these rooms. Even though she'd reviewed Mom G.'s chart and knew her prognosis, the older woman's condition didn't seem real. Rachel didn't want it to be real.

She stopped. Her breathing turned shallow. A long-suppressed memory surfaced, and her mind reeled.

Memories of walking down a similar corridor. She'd been six years old, her hand held firmly in the grasp of Nurse Claire, the woman who'd taken charge of her after they'd arrived at the hospital.

"Is my mommy all right?"

The woman's kind gaze regarded her steadily. "I don't know, honey."

Not much comfort there. There'd been no daddy to run to, either. After her mother had died, no man had come forward claiming her as his daughter. No one had wanted her.

Until years later, when her foster mother, Olivia Green, legally adopted her. But she'd insisted that Rachel keep her last name in honor of her mother.

Mom G. gave Rachel not only a place to belong but reason to hope. The generous woman's loving nature had stirred up Rachel's pain of losing her mother. And Rachel had finally given in to the tears she'd held so long. In her gentle wisdom, Mom G. had suggested Rachel channel her grief into making a difference in the world.

God had handed her a purpose in that moment. She would become a doctor so she could improve and change the triage techniques used in emergency rooms, procedures that had cost her mother her life. That was Rachel's life goal, her focus, never to be forgotten nor sidetracked from.

She squared her shoulders and continued walking.

Standing outside of room 6, she whispered, "Lord, I need Your strength."

When she pushed open the door, the fragrant scent

of gardenias greeted her and she smiled, pleased to know the flowers she'd ordered had arrived. She wanted Mom G. to be surrounded by the things she loved.

Rachel stepped inside the cheery private room, her gaze taking in the woman she loved so dearly. She'd seen thousands of patients hooked up to IVs, heart rate and blood pressure monitors, and machines that helped the body function, but seeing the once-vibrant and beautiful Olivia Green hooked up accordingly made Rachel's knees wobbly. She quelled the uncharacteristic sensation by sheer will. She wouldn't give in to any weakness.

Remember your purpose.

But she hated seeing Mom G. so still and quiet. Rachel's gaze swung to the monitors. Heart rate, steady. Blood pressure, within a reasonable range.

Then her mind focused on the complete picture. A man sat beside the bed holding one of Mom G.'s hands. His bent head caused his tawny hair to fall forward over his brow. Dark blond lashes rested against bronze skin. His mouth moved with silent words.

Rachel swallowed. Agitated butterflies performed a riotous dance in the pit of her stomach. She blinked several times, hoping the man would disappear.

Josh Taylor. What was he doing here?

As though he'd heard her question, he opened his eyes and lifted his head. Their gazes locked. A smoldering blaze ignited and heat shimmered between them. Rachel drew in a cooling breath. She wouldn't allow this man to burn her again.

He slowly stood, his towering frame dwarfing the room.

Emotions churned and bubbled like a whirlpool inside her. They moved like running water through her consciousness so quickly she couldn't grasp one long enough to use as a defense against his presence. Her pulse leapt with unexpected pleasure, her heart ached with the sting of rejection and her cheeks flamed with sudden anger. She wasn't ready for this—for seeing Josh, feeling emotions she'd long ago buried. She hated being vulnerable and unsure.

So she did what had become natural—she cloaked herself in professionalism. She was a doctor. She'd come to help Mom G., not stir the embers of a past love.

She inclined her head. "Josh."

He followed suit. "Rachel." His deep voice brushed over her, making her shiver with surprising awareness.

Uncomfortable with her response, she set her suitcase by the door and went to the bed, focusing her attention on Mom G. Her color looked good. Rachel picked up a hand. Veins showed through the near-translucent skin. Warm. Her hands were still warm. So many times Mom G.'s gentle hands had wiped a tear, clapped at an accomplishment, held hers when she needed comfort.

"I'm surprised to see you here, Rachel." Josh's softly spoken words broke the silence.

She lifted her gaze to his intense, gold-specked eyes and cocked her head to one side. "Why?"

"I never thought you'd come back."

His comment stung. "She needs me."

Josh nodded, his expression closed. "She does." He shrugged. "Still, I didn't really think you'd come."

Hurt burrowed in deep. Her spine straightened. "I guess that says a lot about what you think of me."

"You have no idea what I think of you."

The look in his vibrant gaze caught her off guard. If she didn't know better, she'd swear that beneath the disdain, she saw longing. But that couldn't be. Not after what had happened. He'd made his feelings clear years ago. With a mental tug she pulled her protective cloak tighter around her heart.

She pursed her lips. "You're right, Josh. I have no idea what you think of me. And I'd just as soon keep it that way."

"So would I." His expression hardened. "So would I."

What he thought of her didn't matter. Not in the least. What they'd had once was long over.

Ignoring his overwhelming presence and the commotion going on inside her, she picked up the chart hanging behind the bed and studied the notes. She clenched her teeth as she read. Mom G.'s condition had worsened in the last twenty-four hours. They'd prescribed Mannitol, a drug meant to prevent herniation of the brain stem, an extreme complication of a glioblastoma multiforme.

Josh shifted, drawing her attention. "What's that say?"

She quickly looked away, avoiding his intent gaze, and replaced the chart. "What have they told you about her condition?"

Josh let out a weary breath. "She has a brain tumor with a long, fancy name. They operated but couldn't remove the full mass because of the risk of complications. Dr. Kessler said she's deteriorating rapidly and time's short."

Rachel didn't want to hear those words, wouldn't allow her mind to register such dire news. A flush of anger ran through her. Dr. Kessler shouldn't have said that to Josh. The doctor shouldn't have ruled out hope.

"Yes, well." She glanced down at Mom G. Fear stabbed at her, making her edgy. "We'll see about that."

She wasn't about to give up. They'd barely started the chemotherapy, and other treatment options had yet to be explored. She'd find a way to help Mom G. She had to.

"She'll be happy to see you when she wakes up."

"How long has she been asleep?"

"She was sleeping when I arrived. And that was about thirty minutes before you. Why?"

Rachel kept the little burst of panic in check. Just because Mom G. lay sleeping didn't mean anything other than she was tired. The rational side of Rachel's brain warned that when the type of tumor Mom G. developed became severe enough, sleepiness eventually led to coma, then death. Rachel's emotional side that deeply loved her adoptive mother refused to acknowledge the information. "We should wake her."

"You should ask the doctor."

She bristled. "I *am* a doctor."

"But not *her* doctor," he gently reminded.

She couldn't refute that, though she was licensed to

practice in the state of California as well as several other states. Her teaching schedule required traveling and being hands-on in other E.R.s around the country. But out of respect for Mom G.'s doctor, she said, "I'll go find Dr. Kessler."

Josh stepped around the bed and placed a hand on her arm. "You stay. I'll go find him."

Moved by his thoughtfulness, Rachel stared at his big, tanned hand where it rested against the lightweight blue fabric of her suit coat. Through the thin material, his warmth seeped into her skin. The touch evoked memories of younger days. Days when they'd been happy and in love, walking the school halls, side by side, Josh's arm casually draped about her shoulders or their fingers intertwined.

Days long gone.

"All right." Anything to create distance between them.

Josh moved past her. His long legs carried him with confidence. As the door swung shut behind him, the room suddenly seemed lonely and cold even though the warmth of the sun streamed through the window. She rubbed her arm where his touch lingered and went to the chair where he'd sat. Mom G. still slept. Rachel gathered one of the older woman's hands in her own and with the other hand smoothed back a faded blond curl. "Oh, Mom G., I'm so sorry this is happening to you. But I'm here now. I'll take care of you."

Oh, God. Please show me how to help her.

Unlike the doctors who couldn't save her mother, Rachel would do *anything* for Mom G. Even if that meant dealing with Josh, who was the last person she needed in her life. She had no intention of allowing the pain of the past to repeat itself.

"Sure thing, Josh." Dr. Kessler set the chart in his hand down on the counter of the nurses' station. "I'll speak with her right now."

"Thank you, Doctor." Josh liked the man and Mrs. G. trusted him.

Dr. Kessler stuck a pen into the breast pocket of his white coat. "Are you coming?"

"No. I'm going to get some coffee." He wasn't ready to see Rachel again just yet. Being near her, able to touch her, hear her voice after all these years had brought back so many memories of when they were teens. It was too much to deal with in such a short time.

As Dr. Kessler disappeared into the elevator, Josh headed for the hospital chapel. He slipped into a pew. The quiet serenity of the room eased some of the turmoil within.

Almost twelve years. Twelve years since she'd walked out of his life, choosing her career, her dream of being a doctor, over their love—his love.

I love you, Josh, but I can't stay. I have to do this.

As he ran a hand through his thick hair, jagged pain engulfed him. Pain as fresh now as it had been then. As it had been when he was fourteen and his mother's words to his father mirrored Rachel's.

Sharon Taylor had decided being a mother and wife wasn't fulfilling enough. She'd left to pursue a career in the art world and never came back. She'd tried to contact Josh, had wanted to see him, but at fourteen, he'd been too hurt, too angry to welcome her overtures. He'd hardened his heart to her and refused to listen when his father tried to talk to him about her. Josh could never accept his father's claim that he'd loved her enough to let her go. After a time she'd stopped trying. And Josh tried to forget her.

It seemed the Taylor men were under a curse. Destined to love women who had no use for marriage, commitment or family.

Josh prayed fervently that when the time came, his son would find love with a woman committed to her family. A woman passionate about marriage and motherhood.

A woman nothing like Rachel Maguire.

He closed his eyes and rubbed his forehead.

He'd forced his feelings for Rachel aside and moved on with his life. He'd married and had a son whom he loved beyond anything he thought possible.

Josh opened his eyes and glanced at his watch. School would let out soon. He hoped Griff remembered Grandpa was picking him up today. If he took the bus home, no one would be there. Thankfully Mrs. G's surgery and subsequent critical condition hadn't happened a week later since summer vacation would start on Monday.

Until her sickness, Mrs. G. had watched Griff after school. But when Mrs. G. had gone into the hospital, Josh had made it a point to be home from work when his son got there. But today, with Mrs. G.'s condition so critical, he needed to be at the hospital.

And now Rachel was here, too.

So much the same, yet so different. The once-pretty teen had grown into a beautiful woman. Her shoulder-length ebony hair framed her face and made the most of her startling blue eyes. He drew in a deep breath and could have sworn her scent clung to his clothes. She still smelled of a flowered meadow on a summer's day. Fresh, alive and invigorating.

That's what had first alerted him to her presence in the hospital room. The familiar and alluring scent of Rachel.

Contrary to what he'd said, he'd known she would return. He just hadn't realized how hard seeing her again would be. All the agony of having loved and lost, which he'd hidden away, was simmering and working its way through his heart. He didn't like it one bit.

He didn't need to remind himself that he wasn't enough, that his love wasn't enough. The knowledge was branded across his soul.

Yet this Rachel was different. As a teen she'd been warm and lively, full of laughter. Now she was so calmly cool and in control. She was like an exquisitely designed ice sculpture. Each angle and curve perfectly cut, the sleek and smooth surface beckoning to be touched. Yet to the one who dared, the scar of freezer burn would be their reward. This Rachel wasn't the woman he'd fallen in love with all those years ago. He took comfort in that. Finally something that didn't remind him of the past.

Staring up at the window, he watched sunlight splinter through the various colors of the beautiful stained-glass cross. He wanted to pray for himself, wanted to lay his troubles at the feet of Jesus. But he couldn't. Oh, he could pray for others—Mrs. G., Griff, his dad. Even strangers. But not himself.

Anger lay between him and Jesus like a desolate wasteland. No way around it, no way across it.

Abruptly he stood and walked away, leaving behind the chapel and the peace that God could offer.

He wound his way through the hospital to the cafeteria where he ordered two cups of coffee to go. Not knowing how Rachel took hers, he stuck packets of sugar and cream in his pocket. As the elevator doors opened and he stepped into the hall, he saw Rachel and Dr. Kessler talking outside Mrs. G.'s door.

Josh walked forward, sympathy stirring as he watched Rachel pace, her arms wrapping and unwrapping about her middle. Her normally creamy complexion had gone pasty white and the small splattering of freckles across the bridge of her nose stood out in stark contrast. The agitation so obvious in her posture belied her coldness, and Josh fought the urge to enfold her in his arms. He approached, stopping a few paces away.

"You can't rule out NDGA. There've been tremendous results with the use of chaparral tea in persons with cancerous tumors."

"I'm not denying that, Dr. Maguire. But I don't believe it will help Olivia."

Rachel stopped her pacing and glared at Dr. Kessler. "But it could help. We have to at least try."

"The best we can do for Olivia is make her comfortable."

"The *best* we can do is make her better."

"She's entered the last stages. Even the chemo's questionable at this point."

Sharp, ugly pain gripped Rachel's insides. It was her mother's plight all over again. Everything they knew to do was being done, but they held little hope. Helplessness clawed its way to the surface. She wanted to cry, to find a dark place and curl into a tiny ball to escape this nightmare. She gritted her teeth and fought for composure. Mom G. needed her to be strong and she *would* be strong, because the alternative was breaking down in hysterics and that was unacceptable. There had to be hope. "But you'll continue with the chemo?"

"For now."

"Then the tea could make her more comfortable."

A sad, patronizing smile touched Dr. Kessler's lips. Rachel wanted to scream. The man didn't get it. They couldn't just give up on Mom G.

"All right, Dr. Maguire. I'll see what we can do about getting some chaparral tea."

The small victory did nothing to dispel the ache in Rachel's heart. Deep down, she knew he was agreeing for her sake, not Mom G.'s. But she didn't care if it meant Mom G. had a chance to live a little longer.

"Now, if you'll excuse me. I'll go check on Olivia." Dr. Kessler retreated into Mom G.'s room.

Rachel stared at the closed door, feeling as though her universe had been knocked off-kilter. She should be the one checking on the patient, the one in control. But here, in this hospital, she was a loved one, not a doctor.

"Rachel."

She braced herself and turned to find Josh's expressive hazel eyes regarding her with compassion. Her arms dropped to her sides and she resisted clenching her fists. She wouldn't let him see how scared and uncertain she felt. She didn't need his pity.

And his comfort would ultimately only harm her.

He held out a steaming cup of coffee and she relaxed slightly.

His square, blunt fingers engulfed the disposable cup and thin white scars stood out against his tanned skin. As she took the drink she noticed her own hand, the skin pale and smooth from years of being scrubbed and encased in rubber gloves. How different their lives had become.

The brush of his fingers scorched her skin. A splash of coffee wouldn't have been as hot. Or as painful. She steadied herself. "Thank you. That was very thoughtful."

Just as she feared, his presence *was* comforting. Like a solid oak tree in a windstorm. Able to sway and bend but never break.

"You're welcome." He stuck his hand into the pocket of his casual khaki slacks and pulled out packets of sugar and cream. "I didn't know…"

"Black," she said, moved by his concern.

Josh returned the items to his pocket.

Rachel took a fortifying swig from the cup and savored the robust flavor, until the hot liquid hit her empty stomach with an acidic thud. She grimaced. She'd forgotten to eat again.

"That bad, huh?" Josh asked, his expression softening as he gave a small laugh.

She sucked in a quick breath and could only stare. This man standing before her may be the boy she'd loved in high school but he'd matured into an appealing man she didn't know. A man who made her want to believe a dancing hot flame could heal as well as harm.

And she had no intention of playing with fire, no matter how fascinating the blaze.

The moment stretched to an almost unbearable ache, then abruptly Josh asked, "So, what's chaparral tea?"

Rachel blinked, but took her cue and slipped easily into her professional demeanor. "The tea leaves come from the creosote bush, which is found in the southwestern states. The healing properties of the tea have been used by Native Americans for centuries."

"And the ND…?"

"NDGA—nordihydroguaiaretic. It's the proponent in the plant that seems to help in reducing cancerous mass."

"You think this tea will help Mrs. G.?"

Her poise slipped a notch as she stared down at her coffee. She wanted to believe it would help, but the doctor in her knew the chances at this point were slim to none, just as Dr. Kessler had said. But she refused to give up and reject *anything* that might help. She hated this feeling of helplessness.

She shrugged. "At this point, it's hard to know what will help and what won't."

"That's a typical doctor answer," he said with the slightest trace of teasing in his tone.

She glanced up. "Pretty vague, huh?"

The corners of his generous mouth tipped upward and he sipped from his coffee.

"Habit, I suppose. As a doctor, you try not to give false hope or bad news before you're absolutely sure."

"Rules of the trade," he remarked dryly.

"I suppose."

They lapsed into silence again. Rachel drank from her cup and watched Josh. She tried to view him objectively. Adulthood had etched lines around his eyes, and the outdoors had weathered his skin to a burnished sheen. His broad shoulders looked as though they could carry heavy burdens. Sometimes she wished she had someone to share her load with, but her life didn't have room for sharing.

"So, Rachel—" Josh broke the silence "—I hear you recently got a promotion."

She met his gaze, expecting to be assaulted by the disdain she'd seen earlier, but his expression was curiously friendly, as if he'd just asked if she liked rainbows and sunshine instead of probing at an old wound. A wound inflicted by the choice she'd had to make.

Josh had offered her a different path, one so inviting that she'd begun to doubt God's plan for her life. But, no matter how tempting, it would have been selfish of her to choose Josh over what she knew to be her purpose. No matter how much it hurt.

Chapter Two

"Yes. Yes, I did," Rachel replied, proud that her voice didn't betray her feelings.

"Good for you."

Uncomfortable with the thought that he'd discussed her with Mom G., she wondered what else he knew about her. He certainly didn't know what was between her and God. No one knew how emotionally crippled she was because of the way her mother had died. If anyone found out then she would be perceived as weak. And if she were viewed as weak then she wouldn't be able to achieve her goal of making sure her mother hadn't died in vain. No one would take her seriously. "I've worked extremely hard to get where I am."

"The fast track to success," he stated, his voice devoid of inflection and his eyes now remote.

She narrowed her gaze. "I'm on the fast track. This recent promotion will be one of many. But it's not about success. It's about changing the way things are done so no one else needlessly dies. My ultimate goal is to be chief of staff in a prestigious hospital where I can further the research in new and innovative triage techniques."

"That's certainly ambitious."

"That's the only way things get done."

He shrugged. "Is being a doctor everything you thought it would be?"

Irritation flared at his casually asked question. She'd had to make a tough choice all those years ago. He'd forced her to make the choice. It was all or nothing with him. "Yes, I love being a doctor."

He nodded, but made no comment. He shouldn't be so calm and collected, not when her world was spinning out of her control. She wanted to shake a few leaves off his tree.

"It's who I am." She couldn't help the defensiveness in her voice.

A tawny brow arched. "Must be very fulfilling."

"What's that supposed to mean?"

Anger stirred in his eyes. "Nothing." A leaf fell.

Something inside Rachel made her want to pick a fight. Anything to distract herself from what lay ahead with Mom G. "You obviously meant something by that remark, Josh. If you've something to say to me, then say it."

"You've changed," he stated matter-of-factly, his gaze assessing.

She almost smiled. Almost. The woman she'd become was very different from the young girl who'd left. "What? I'm not mousy like you remember?"

"You were never mousy."

She chose to ignore the compliment in his tone. "My job's very satisfying. What's wrong with that?"

"Nothing." The tension visible in his jaw claimed he was far from the ambivalence suggested in his tone. "But it doesn't leave much room for anything else, does it?"

"I've never wanted anything else." She narrowed her gaze. "Why are you still so angry?"

"I'm not angry." His denial rang false. Leaves fell all over the place.

"Yes, you are." She put voice to the suspicion she'd always had. "You're angry not because I became a doctor, but because you didn't get what you wanted."

He looked her square in the eye, his expression derisive and taut. "You're right, Rachel. I didn't get what I wanted. I wanted *you.*"

"You didn't want me," she scoffed. "You wanted a *wife.*"

"I wanted *you* to be my wife."

"No, Josh. You wanted a cookie-cutter wife. Someone you could put in a box and mold to your specifications. And it didn't take you six months after I left to find one, did it?" Her own anger and pain reared up, making her chest ache. "That only proves how deep your undying love went, doesn't it?"

He drew back. Hurt—desolate and unmistakable—darkened his hazel eyes. "I did love you, Rachel."

He sounded sincere. But then, he'd always sounded sincere. "Oh, save it, Josh. I'm not buying it this time."

"What did you expect? You left and made it very

clear you weren't coming back." The sarcasm in his tone dug at her heart.

"But I hadn't given up hope that we'd work things out once I finished school." Hurt-filled tears burned behind her eyes, making her more angry that she was losing her control. Shaking her head, she admitted, "I lay in my dorm room every night and agonized over my decision. Was being a doctor worth the risk of losing you?" She gave a bitter laugh. "But I never really had you."

Josh opened his mouth, but no words came. His perplexed expression galvanized her into adding, "You never once checked on me. No phone call. No letters. Nothing."

He shook his head. "I was hurt and angry, Rachel. You chose your dream of being a doctor over my love. I certainly didn't think you wanted to hear from me." His tone seethed with anger and resignation.

"No, you were too busy planning your wedding." Thinking about the blonde who'd been after him all through high school made her insides twist with... jealousy? No, never. "And how's dear Andrea?"

A spasm of pain, or perhaps guilt, crossed his features. "Andrea's dead." He stepped around her and walked toward the elevators.

Shock doused her anger like a swollen rain cloud emptying itself. "Oh, no." Sympathy and regret tore through her, and she hurried after him. "Wait. I'm sorry. I didn't know."

He jabbed his finger on the elevator call button. "Not your problem."

She reached out, wishing she could retract her words. Josh reared away as if she were contaminated. Stung, she let her hand drop to her side. Feeling small and petty, she said softly, "I'm truly sorry."

The elevator doors opened and he stepped in. He turned and stared at her, his eyes cold with fury and his face a hard mask of stone. An oak tree never looked so intimidating.

"Josh, please," she implored, wanting somehow to make amends.

He looked away and the elevator doors slid shut in her face, leaving her alone.

Should she go after him?

Rachel took a deep, shuddering breath. Her unruly tongue had caused enough damage for one day. Leaving Josh alone and staying as far away from him as possible while she was in town was the best thing she could do for him…and herself.

Andrea was dead.

Compassion filled her heart to overwhelming proportions. She ached for what Josh had lost. His wife, his helpmate, his dream.

How long ago had Andrea died? How did she die? Did they have children? Goose bumps of remorse tightened Rachel's skin.

Years ago, she'd made it clear to Mom G. the subject of Josh and his bride was off-limits. She hadn't wanted her assumptions of his picture-perfect life confirmed. How arrogant she'd been.

The resentment she'd used to close off the pain of

Josh's marriage deteriorated, exposing her to fresh wounds.

Slowly she walked back down the hall, rubbing away the goose bumps from her arm.

How had Josh taken the news of Andrea's death? Had he been with her at the end? Or had he been at work and received a call? How had the doctor told him? With compassion? Coldness? Understanding? Detachment?

The questions plagued her mind. And she welcomed them as she stopped in front of Mom G.'s door. As painful as it was, thinking about Josh kept her from worrying about Mom G.

Rachel leaned against the wall and closed her eyes. *Lord, why does life have to hurt so badly?*

She hoped, when all was said and done, she'd have enough mortar left in her to repair the crumbling wall around her heart.

"Dr. Maguire?"

Rachel's eyelids jerked open. She pushed away from the wall. "Dr. Kessler?"

He smiled kindly, his big gray eyes peering at her through his glasses. "Olivia's asking for you."

Relief surged in her chest. "How—how is she?"

"Holding her own for the moment."

Relief gave way to a dull ache at the words meant to give comfort but not false hope. She nodded her thanks and stepped into the room. Her footsteps faltered slightly as she approached the bed.

A nurse hovered over Mom G. For a panicked moment Rachel feared something was wrong, that she wouldn't have a chance to tell Mom G. how much she loved her, how much she appreciated her.

The nurse straightened and moved away, a reassuring smile on her face. Rachel resumed walking, her heart rate slowing to normal. As she reached the bedside, Mom G.'s eyes opened and she smiled. "I'm so happy to see you."

Rachel winced at how weak and breathless her mother sounded. Taking her hand, Rachel held on tight. "I'm sorry I wasn't here sooner." She wanted to say she should have been called right away but she didn't want to lay guilt on Mom G. It would serve no purpose.

"You're here, now. There's so much to say before—"

"Don't even go there," Rachel interjected. "We're going to make you well. I'm going to make you well."

Mom G. shook her head. "I'm dying, dear. We must accept that."

"Nooo!" Tears clogged her throat. She didn't like constantly being on the verge of tears. Even when she'd bounced from foster home to foster home, she'd never been this scared or so close to the breaking point. She wanted to draw into herself as she'd done as a child. But she couldn't. Mom G. needed her. And she needed Mom G.

"Rachel, please, don't cry. Let's use this time as best we can."

Rachel wiped at the tears unceremoniously slipping down her cheeks. She nodded. There was so much to say. "I love you. I want you to know how much you mean to me. I wouldn't be who I am today if you hadn't taken me in."

Mom G. squeezed her hand. "I hadn't ever planned on having kids, but when I was asked if I'd take on one child…I prayed and God urged me to say yes. I remember the first time I saw you. So skinny and scared. And you tried so hard not to show it. Now look at you. You're a grown woman and a wonderful doctor. Just like you'd planned. Are you happy, Rachel?"

Taken off guard by the question—surely Mom G. knew how much medicine meant to her—Rachel nodded. "Of course."

Mom G.'s eyes narrowed. "Really? For a long time I've had the sense that something's missing from your life. You've never talked about a man, or friends, even. Your phone conversations are always about your work. Work can't be the only thing in your life, Rachel."

"It's not. I…" But try as she may, she couldn't come up with an example. She worked six, sometimes seven days a week. Her apartment was small and cozy, but not a place she'd feel comfortable inviting anyone to visit. When she wasn't working she went to movies by herself or rented videos. She attended a Bible study through her church, but outside of class, she didn't socialize with any of the other participants.

When she wasn't knee-deep in research, sometimes she'd go to the library and read the latest medical journals and texts. Occasionally she'd dated. There'd been a fellow med student in school and a real nice guy from church a while ago, but over the years she hadn't met anyone she particularly wanted to pursue a relationship with. Besides, she didn't have time for men. Her life was the way she wanted it. No attachments. No hassles. No pain.

"Have you seen Josh?" Mom G. asked.

"Yes." Remembering their meeting made her skin heat with embarrassment. She'd acted very badly, nothing like how she'd expected to act. Calm and cool, showing him that he couldn't affect her, which was how she'd dreamed their reunion would be. "He was here when I arrived."

Mom G.'s expression became wistful. "It seems like only yesterday I was watching you go off to the prom with him. You two made such a handsome couple."

A shiver of vivid recollection raced through Rachel. Her beautiful dress, Josh's tux. The excitement, the anguish. "I haven't thought about that night in years."

"The king and the queen of the ball," Mom G. teased lightly.

Rachel laughed, remembering the almost giddy feeling she'd had when they'd placed the gold crown on her head. "It was a perfect evening." At first.

"That was the night Josh proposed."

Rachel slid her gaze away from the intense look in Mom G.'s eyes. Her mind burned with the unwanted memories of that night. Josh had looked so handsome wearing that crown. They'd been dancing when he'd pulled her out onto the balcony and asked her to be his wife.

She'd been torn between her love for him and the path God had chosen for her. At the time she naively thought she could have both. She'd asked Josh for time, for him to be patient. Had expected they'd find a way to work it out that she could become a doctor and his wife.

But when it came down to accepting his proposal and his condition of staying in Sonora or the full scholarship to Northwestern, she'd chosen medicine because her soul would die if she didn't.

At that moment she'd known that God's plan for her didn't include the kind of love she'd have only with Josh.

"That was a long time ago and has no bearing on my life now."

Sadness filled Mom G. eyes. "I've respected your wish not to talk about him. But, dear, we need to have this talk."

"Why?"

"Because I love you both."

Rachel drew in a deep breath. She'd learned long ago it was better to meet a challenge head on rather than flee from it. "All right, if that's what you wish." She didn't want to have this conversation while standing. She sat down. "I know about Andrea."

Mom G.'s eyes widened. "Then you've talked with Josh."

"A little."

Mom G. shook her head; her wispy blond hair stuck to the pillow. "Such a waste."

"How—how did she…?" Rachel wanted to know, yet she knew sometimes there was protection in ignorance.

Mom G. pursed her lips. "An awful, awful car accident."

Rachel winced in sympathy. She shuddered slightly and suppressed the image of the last car accident victim she hadn't been able to save. "It must have been hard on Josh."

"Oh, honey, it was in so many ways." Mom G. stared into space for a heartbeat then turned to Rachel. "Do you have someone in your life?"

She blinked. "Uh…you mean a man?"

"Are you involved in a relationship?"

"No."

"I didn't think so. Good." Mom G. seemed to relax.

Rachel narrowed her eyes. "What do you mean 'good'?"

Mom G. gripped Rachel's hand tight. "Is your hope still in Jesus?"

Rachel gently patted the frail hand encased within her own. "Yes, my hope's in Jesus. He's my strength. You showed me that—you and Josh."

Mom G. nodded. "God loves you."

"I know. He's blessed me greatly. He brought me to you. Without Him and you in my life I'd…be lost. I'm doing what He wants with my life."

Mom G.'s brows drew together. "But He wants so much more for you."

More? She'd tried to have more once and she'd ended up with nothing but pain. Loving was a risk she was no longer willing to take. She shook her head. "I have everything I need. There couldn't possibly be more."

"What about love? Aren't you lonely?"

Mom G.'s words struck a cord within Rachel. She tugged at her bottom lip, loath to admit that there had been times over the years she'd watched couples, families, and felt an ache she couldn't explain. Was it loneliness?

Maybe.

But loneliness was a small price to pay to fulfill God's plan and to protect her heart.

"My life's very full. I might not have as many friends as I could…" Rachel frowned at the direction of her thoughts. Friends couldn't help in her quest to change emergency room procedures. "I just don't have time for relationships."

"Don't grow old alone. Believe me, it's not fun."

Guilt reached up and slapped Rachel. "I'm sorry I haven't been here for you."

Mom G. touched Rachel's cheek. "No, honey, you had to do what you needed to do. I regret that I never remarried after Frank died. I don't want you to make the same mistake."

Rachel nuzzled into the touch. She hadn't known Mr. Green. He'd been gone long before she'd come to live with Mom G. His picture graced the nightstand in Mom G.'s bedroom. "I'll be fine, I promise," Rachel assured her.

"Don't you think you'd be better with Josh in your life?"

Rachel schooled her features. She didn't want Mom G. to know how upsetting she found the subject of Josh. She didn't want her to know she still hurt deep inside her heart, in a far corner she pretended didn't exist.

"Don't avoid this Rachel."

Rachel met Mom G.'s gaze straight on. "There's

nothing to avoid. Josh isn't a part of my life and he's not going to be."

Tears gathered at the corners of Mom G.'s eyes. "He needs you."

Mom G.'s sadness tore at Rachel. She wouldn't be able to make Mom G. happy. Not if her happiness involved Josh. "This is upsetting you."

"He needs you," Mom G. insisted.

Slowly Rachel shook her head. "He's never needed *me.*"

"But he does. Rachel, he's always loved you and you still love him."

A double-edged sword of hurt and anger sliced through her. Her heart raced and her blood pounded in her ears. Josh didn't love her. She doubted he ever had.

As for her loving him… She closed her eyes briefly and hardened her heart. Been there, done that. Not doing it again. Emotions would not control her actions. Her goal in life was to make sure her mother hadn't died in vain, not to resurrect her relationship with Josh.

She opened her eyes and took a calming breath, regaining her composure. "It's not a matter of love. Josh had an idea of what he wanted in a wife and I wasn't it. He wanted someone I couldn't be."

"But that was then."

Rachel lifted one shoulder. "Nothing has changed. I'm still who I am."

"But they need you."

They? Rachel figured she must mean Josh and his father, Rod.

Mom G. dropped her gaze and sighed, but not before

Rachel saw the disappointment in her eyes. She wouldn't say anything to encourage Mom G. She and Josh were history. And nothing could change that.

"Tell me about your new position."

Rachel nodded, thankful for a subject she'd have no trouble discussing, a subject that didn't make her suffer deep in her soul.

Because no matter how she looked at it, the subject of Josh would only bring her heartache.

The late-afternoon sun began to make its descent behind the mountain range, the fading light casting long shadows across the yard and backlighting Josh's Victorian house. Coming home at the end of the day always gave him a sense of satisfaction and peace. He'd worked long and hard refurbishing the broken-down Victorian, preserving as much of the original woodwork as possible. The overgrown land and swamp of a built-in pool had required hours of grueling labor to bring out the potential he'd known lay underneath. He'd created a stable sanctuary for his son and managed to ignore the vague feeling of incompleteness that plagued him at night.

Josh eased open the large solid-oak front door far enough to squeeze through. He didn't want a squeak of the hinge to herald his arrival. He wasn't ready to see his family, whom he could hear in the kitchen. He needed time, time to sort out the struggle going on inside of him.

He took the hardwood stairs slowly, placing each foot carefully in the spots where they wouldn't creak. In his room he closed the door and sat on the bed. With his elbows on his knees, he dropped his head into his hands.

All the way home he'd kept the thoughts at bay, forcing his mind into a blank numbness. But now they wouldn't be held back. Had Rachel really not known about Andrea? She'd seemed genuinely surprised, and remorseful. His heart told him she hadn't known, which only confirmed his belief that once she'd left town she'd never looked back.

Just like his mother.

Andrea. Sweet Andrea. Guilt engulfed him. He groaned, a deep, gut-wrenching sound that echoed in the quiet of his room.

Lord, it's too much to bear. Please take my guilt.

The plea went up as it had a hundred times before, but Josh snatched his plea back before he could feel any relief. He didn't deserve God's attention and mentally flogged himself with the pain of his guilt.

He hadn't loved Andrea enough. Not the way she'd needed to be loved. He'd tried to be a good husband. He'd encouraged her, supported her, provided for her. He'd given her everything he could but not the one thing she'd wanted—all of his heart.

Josh scrubbed at his face, trying to wipe away the sting of his self-loathing.

It was his *fault* Andrea was dead.

Because he couldn't erase Rachel from his heart.

Rachel. Was she right that he'd only wanted a wife, any wife? Had he been that arrogant and selfish? He'd tried to love Andrea with the same intensity he'd loved Rachel, but it had never happened.

Should he have pursued Rachel after she left? According to her, yes. But would his pursuit have changed anything? Would she have come back to the mountains to be his wife?

No, she wouldn't have.

And he couldn't have lived in the city playing second fiddle to her career.

Josh stood and paced, the leather soles of his shoes leaving indents in the dark green carpet. In the back of his mind a thought crept up, making him pause. Had he held his heart from Andrea because he was afraid to love her too deeply?

He clenched his jaw. It didn't matter now.

What he'd had to give hadn't been enough for Andrea. He'd lost her, just as he'd lost Rachel and his mother. Because he was not enough. And he was never going to make the mistake of trying to love again.

Now Rachel was back. He had every intention of not seeing her again before she left. He would have to plan his visits to Mrs. G. for when Rachel wouldn't be around.

Because this time he wouldn't be left behind with a broken heart.

Silvery light filtered into the hospital room, filling in the shadows created by the bedside lamp.

"In the emergency room we…" Rachel paused as she noticed Mom G. fighting to keep her eyes open. "Here, now. I've talked enough. You should rest."

Mom G. smiled slightly. "Your life sounds very interesting, dear."

"It can be." Satisfaction in her career grew through the research she'd done and the triage techniques she'd implemented so far. But so much more could be done to improve the quality of patient care, and every day she spent in the emergency room was a new adventure.

She liked delivering babies the best. Liked the amazing miracle of life. God's wondrous process for continuing humanity. Sometimes she'd thought about switching gears and going into obstetrics or pediatrics, but she didn't want the emotional attachments those specialties would bring. In the E.R., patients came, they left. Her heart wasn't at risk and her mind stayed focused on her goal.

"Rachel, would you read to me for a bit?"

"Of course. What…?"

Mom G. pointed to the small bedside table. "My Bible's in the drawer."

She pulled out the black Bible, the same Bible that Mom G. had read to her from years ago. The worn black leather grew warm beneath her hands. "I remember this Bible." She glanced at Mom G. For a moment it appeared Mom G. had fallen asleep. Then she opened her eyes and smiled. Rachel looked questioningly at her.

Mom G. sighed. "I think the Psalms would be soothing."

Rachel opened the book and the once-familiar scent of Mom G.'s soft, powdery perfume wafted from the yellowed pages. A pang of nostalgia tugged at her heartstrings.

"Rachel?"

She paused and glanced up. "Yes?

"Would you do something for me?"

"Anything."

Mom G. gazed at her intently. "Would you call Josh?"

Rachel drew back. She didn't want to talk with Josh. "Call him?"

"I want to talk to you both."

"I'm sure he'll come tomorrow." Rachel would make sure she took the opportunity to speak with Dr. Kessler in his office while Josh visited so they wouldn't have to see each other.

Mom G. nodded. "Yes, but I want to make sure. I want to see you both together."

She lifted her brows. "Together?" Inside, she cringed. She'd come to town for Mom G., not to spend time with Josh.

"Please," Mom G. implored.

Rachel couldn't deny her the request. If Mom G. wanted to see them together then they'd be here together. Even if seeing Josh was painful, Rachel would do it, for Mom G. "I'll call him." So much for keeping her distance.

Mom G. relaxed. "Thank you."

Her chest hurt with love for Mom G. She leaned over and kissed her cheek. "You're welcome."

She sat back and stared at the open Bible in her lap. She didn't like the quiver of anticipation racing along her limbs at the thought of seeing Josh again. It was a purely physical reaction. Just because she found him attractive meant nothing.

She read King David's Psalms. *Lord, speak to me. I need Your guidance.* After all, she was who she was and the past was the past. There was only now, for Mom G. But Rachel didn't feel comforted by that thought.

A familiar sense of hurt filled her, reminding her of the pain loving Josh had caused. She would keep her focus on her path in life and fortify the fortress around her heart. She refused to allow him back in because once there he would make her want something she wasn't able to have—a life with him.

Chapter Three

Moonlight bathed the old Victorian in a soft glow as the community of Sonora settled down to enjoy another peaceful night nestled at the foot of the Sierra Nevadas. The Taylor men relaxed together in the cozy warmth of the living room. Josh had read in some parent-oriented magazine that children needed a calming home environment. He'd tried to make the inside of the house as comfortable and welcoming as possible with furniture that, in soothing greens and blues, invited relaxation yet was durable for a growing boy like Griff.

Josh liked this time of evening. He could talk to his son and find out about his day. What he'd done, seen, learned. And Josh would tell about his own day. Only, tonight he left out seeing Rachel. She wasn't a part of their lives and never would be.

Josh glanced at his watch. "Time for bed, kiddo."

"Aw, Dad. Come on. Just a little longer, please?"

Josh ruffled his son's hair. "Nope. It's time for bed."

"Will you read to me?" Griff asked as he slowly got off the couch.

He nodded. "Go get ready for bed, then pick out your book. I'll be up soon."

Griff walked to the bookcase where Rod Taylor stood with a book in hand. He kissed the older man's leathery cheek. "Good night, Grandpa."

Rod gave the boy a hug. "Night, pipsqueak."

Josh's heart swelled with love for his boy. Some said Griff looked like Josh. Josh didn't see it. His son had lighter hair, his eyes were more the color of moss than hazel and he had his mother's smile. Sadly Josh hadn't seen Andrea smile much toward the end. He should have tried harder to make her happy. A well-aimed stab of guilt twisted in his gut.

The phone rang.

Rod suggested, "Probably the station again. David Mackafee called earlier, wondering when you were coming back in."

Josh shrugged. He'd written out his schedule for the crew. Because of Mrs. G.'s illness, he'd been taking some personal leave from his duties as District Ranger for the Forestry Service of Tuolumne County. He would be going into the station in the morning, after he checked on Mrs. G.

He picked up the phone. "Hello?"

"Hello, Josh."

His brows rose in surprise to hear the female voice on the other end of the line. "Rachel?" His heart contracted painfully in his chest. There could only be one reason she would call him. "Is Mrs. G.....?"

"No, no," she said quickly. "She's holding her own."

The tightness in his chest eased. He glanced at his father and son who both stared at him with anxious expressions. "Hold on," he told Rachel. "She's fine," he said to his family. Both Griff and Rod sagged in relief.

Then Rod arched a brow. "Rachel Maguire?"

"Who's that?" Griff questioned and moved to stand next to Josh, the top of his head reaching the middle of Josh's chest.

Josh shook his head and pointed upward.

Griff groaned and shuffled out of the room. As for his father, Josh said, "Do you mind?"

Rod grinned. "Not at all." And he sat back down in his recliner.

Josh rolled his eyes. Talking to Rachel on the phone while his father casually listened from his chair took him back to the past. But back then they'd had plenty to talk about—school, love, their future. The only thing they had in common now was Mrs. G.

"Sorry about that," he said into the receiver as he turned his back to his father.

"That's all right." Her voice sounded hesitant. "Mom G. would like to see you in the morning."

"I'd planned on coming by."

"But she wanted me to call and make sure. She… uh…hmmm…well, she wants to see us together."

Josh frowned. "Really?" He didn't want to see Rachel again.

"Yes. I don't know why, but I hope we can be civil to make her happy."

"I've never been uncivil to you, Rachel."

A moment of silence passed.

"Well, I mean, we could refrain from fighting. I—I want to apologize for earlier," she said in a rush.

The corner of his mouth lifted. At least one part of her hadn't changed. The old Rachel had always accepted responsibility for her actions.

"Forget it." He didn't need her apology. He thought about what she'd asked, then made a decision. "I'll be there tomorrow morning and I can be friendly for Mrs. G.'s sake."

"Excellent." She sounded pleased, but he couldn't be sure. "Goodbye, Josh."

"Bye." He slowly replaced the receiver. He hadn't wanted to see her, but he couldn't let Mrs. G. down. He'd tolerate Rachel if it killed him.

And when he thought about it, the best way to annihilate any feelings he harbored for Rachel was to be around the woman she'd become. She was so aloof and distant. Much different than she'd been in high school. Then she'd been open and friendly. Always looking for someone she could help. She'd needed to be of use.

Being a doctor must fulfill that need for her. But had becoming a doctor made her so cold? He supposed life in the big city could change a person, take warm people and turn them into an icy reflection of their former selves.

"You're going to be friendly with Rachel, huh?" Rod broke into his thoughts.

Josh shrugged. "Mrs. G. wants to see us both."

Rod looked pleased. "I might come with you."

"Fine." He didn't want to discuss Rachel with his dad. Didn't want to hear Rod's opinion that he shouldn't have let her slip out of his life. He'd had no choice. She was determined to go. "I'll see you in the morning." Josh turned to leave but stopped at Rod's soft chuckle. "What's so funny?"

"I have a pretty good idea what Olivia is up to."

"You want to let me in on the secret?"

Rod smacked his lips and grinned. "No. I'll let this one play itself out."

Josh frowned. His father and Mrs. G. were up to something. Rachel was the only girl Rod had ever approved of and Mrs. G., of course, loved her. But no amount of matchmaking was going to work. "You're a nut."

Rod wiggled his brows. "Takes one to know one."

Josh smiled. He loved his father and was thankful he'd agreed to live with him and Griff when they moved into this house. "Dad, what am I going to do with you?"

Rod laughed. "Hey, don't forget to call the station."

"Thanks."

"Sleep well, son. I have a feeling you'll need your strength tomorrow."

Josh shook his head in exasperation. He didn't relish disappointing Mrs. G. and his father, but nothing could bring him and Rachel back together. Their needs, their wants in life were too different. Rachel wanted success, prestige and a position of power. He wanted a stable, secure life with a woman who loved him enough to commit to him.

And Rachel wasn't that woman.

* * *

Rachel shielded her eyes against the sunlight streaming through the curtains of Mom G.'s hospital room. She blinked several times, trying to moisten her gritty eyes. She'd spent the night sitting beside Mom G.'s bed, too afraid to leave. She didn't want to get a middle-of-the-night call or find an empty bed in the morning. By staying, Rachel hoped she could keep death from claiming Mom G.

She listened to Mom G.'s labored breathing. Helplessness swamped her, making her head pound and her chest hurt. There had to be something more she could do.

She heard the door open. Expecting Josh, she fortified her nerves against his powerful presence and slowly turned around. The sight of a tall, older gentleman dressed in faded jeans and a dark patterned flannel shirt sent surprised pleasure coursing through her.

"Rod," she exclaimed softly. She glanced at Mom G., who still slept, then stood and went to the man who, for a time, had been the closest she'd ever come to having a father.

His infectious grin filled her with fondness. He hugged her for a long moment and she savored the steady comfort.

"Here, now." He drew back to look at her. "It's good to see you."

"And it's good to see you." She noticed his hair had turned a very distinguished gray and the crinkles around the corners of his hazel eyes had deepened. "How are you?"

"As ornery as ever."

"Some things never change," she teased.

He looked past her toward the bed. "How's she?"

"She had a rough night. The chemo took a lot of her strength."

He shook his head. "Such a shame."

"It is." Rachel knew Mom G. would be going on to a better place, but she didn't want her to go. She didn't want to think about the hole Mom G.'s death would leave in her life. Even though they'd been physically apart, Rachel took strength from both the knowledge that Mom G. loved her and from her weekly phone calls. Mom G. had always been there for her.

"Olivia's very proud of you, Rachel."

His words brought her pleasure. Mom G. had always encouraged and supported her goals. But the little girl she kept locked inside shook with dread. She was scared to be alone. "What am I going to do, Rod?"

He hugged her close again. "What are we all going to do? She's been a rock in all of our lives."

Rachel nodded, remembering how fond Mom G. was of Rod. Rachel had always wondered if their relationship went beyond friendship. Neither would admit—at least not to anyone else—to anything deeper nor act on it.

Speculatively she glanced at Rod. "You two are close, aren't you?"

His eyes twinkled despite an obvious sadness. "Yes, we are."

"How close?"

"Close enough." He winked.

"You…" A noise from the bed made her pause. Mom G.'s eyes were open.

"She's awake." Rachel breathed out a sigh of relief, thankful sleep hadn't turned into a coma. Each time Mom G. closed her eyes, the chance she wouldn't reopen them increased.

"She is indeed." Rod sat next to the bed and took Mom G.'s hand in his. "Olivia, my dear. I'm glad to see you. I came by early yesterday but you were sound asleep."

Mom G. smiled and her eyes glowed with affection. Rachel swallowed back the sadness that threatened to choke her. Mom G. and Rod obviously cared for one another, but now Mom G.'s illness was robbing them of their happiness.

"Time's…short," Mom G. said softly. "There's much to do."

Rod nodded. "Yes, Olivia. It'll all work out, don't you worry."

Rachel had no idea what they were talking about, and felt like an intruder.

"Rachel's…"

"Here," Rod interjected.

Mom G. shifted her gaze and Rachel stepped forward. "I'm right here."

"She's all grown up, Rod. All grown up."

Rachel savored the motherly words, tucking the tender feelings they evoked away in her heart for safekeeping.

Rod grinned. "That she is, my dear. And a doctor, to boot."

The praise in Rod's voice pleased Rachel.

For a brief space of time, Rod and Mom G. silently communicated. Rachel watched, growing decidedly uncomfortable. The look in Rod's eyes as he gazed at Mom G. was more than affection.

He loved her.

A funny ache throbbed within Rachel's chest.

She refused to call it yearning.

But even if it was, she wasn't stepping off God's chosen path for her life. No matter what the cost to her heart.

Wanting to give Mom G. and Rod some privacy, and needing a moment to cool her thoughts, Rachel went to the window. The dew on the needles of the pines glinted in the sunshine like little teardrops.

"Rachel, would you mind getting me a cup of coffee?" Rod asked.

"Not at all." Rachel headed for the door, grateful for the task.

"Cream and sugar," Rod called after her.

She stopped at the nurses' station and smiled at the four nurses who bustled about. "Where could I get a cup of coffee?"

"I'll get you one," said a red-haired nurse who looked vaguely familiar.

"Do I know you?" Rachel tried to remember where she'd seen the striking woman.

The nurse smiled. "My name's Jamie. You were in my older brother's class. Bob Forbes."

"Okay, I remember him." She smiled back, remembering the red-haired boy who'd been the class clown.

"I'll be right back with your coffee, Rachel." Jamie walked away.

"Cream and sugar, too, please," Rachel called after the retreating nurse.

It was strange being in a place where people knew her. Not the doctor she'd become but the girl she'd been. That girl was gone, replaced by the professional woman who knew exactly what her life was meant to be. Giving hope and health to those who needed it. She never pretended to think she could save their minds or their souls. That wasn't her calling.

But their bodies she could fix by making sure the care in the E.R. was better so no one else would needlessly lose a mom. Yet a wave of helplessness swept through her. The one person most important to her needed her skills as a doctor and she didn't know how— She cut that thought off abruptly. She'd find a way to help Mom G. She had to.

Dr. Kessler came down the hall. "Dr. Maguire."

She tensed. "Doctor."

"I was hoping to see you before I made my rounds. We found some chaparral tea."

"Good." It may be a long shot but it was all she had.

"You realize the use of this tea is only effective when used regularly over a period of time."

She shot him a hard glare. She didn't need the reminder that time was an issue. "I'm well aware of the situation, Doctor."

She gritted her teeth against the gentle, pitying look in his eyes.

"Here you go." Jamie sailed up and handed her a disposable cup. Steam billowed from the milky, brown liquid.

"Thank you, Jamie. Doctor." She headed back to Mom G.'s room. She opened the door and slowly walked in, hovering just inside the room. Her throat tightened. Rod leaned in close to Mom G., still holding her hand. They talked in quiet tones. Rachel stepped back, intending to give them more time, but her elbow bumped the wall, making a dull thud. Rod glanced at her, and the corner of his mouth lifted before he turned back to Mom G.

Rachel continued forward. As she approached the bed, she heard Rod say, "I will do my best, my dear. I promise."

Mom G. nodded. "We have to try."

Rod stood. "Here's Rachel, back just in time. I have to take off, but I'll return this evening."

"Your coffee."

"Thank you." He took the cup and walked from the room.

"Such a nice man." Mom G. stared after him.

"He is." Rachel lifted a brow. "You and Rod have become close. You never said anything in your letters or phone calls."

Mom G. smiled slightly and a blush brightened her pale cheeks. Rachel laughed, loving the life shining from Mom G.'s eyes. If only she could hold on to that.

"Where's Josh?" Mom G. asked.

Rachel sat in the chair. "He said he'd be here."

Mom G. took her hand. "I'm going to rest until he arrives. Please wake me."

"Of course."

Mom G. closed her eyes. Rachel listened, thankful Mom G. breathed easier than she had earlier, but she couldn't shake the fear Mom G. might not reawaken.

Dropping her head onto the side of the bed, Rachel squeezed her eyes shut. *Lord, Your word says to count it all joy when we fall into various trials. This sickness is a trial that affects so many people. Mom G., Rod, Josh, me. Where's the joy, Lord? Show me, teach me. I don't understand.*

The low beeping of the machines, combined with Mom G.'s soft breathing, lulled Rachel's senses. Heart heavy with concern, she allowed herself to rest.

Josh pushed opened the door to Mrs. G.'s hospital room and stepped in. He stopped short when he saw Rachel sitting in the chair, her body bent forward and her head resting against the blue covers of the bed. He could see the steady rise and fall of the blankets over Mrs. G.

They were both resting. He started to leave, but found himself staring into Rachel's crystal-blue gaze. She straightened and her black hair brushed loosely across her shoulders. She wore the clothes he'd seen her in yesterday. She hadn't left and he doubted she'd had more than a few moments of rest.

She blinked several times. "Hi," she said softly.

She sounded young and vulnerable, more like the girl he'd known. His heart twisted with longing. He pushed the unwanted emotion aside and told himself he felt sympathy for her for what was to come. Nothing else. "Where's my dad?"

"He left."

Josh frowned. "We came together, but he sent me to get coffee for him."

Rachel smiled ruefully. "With cream and sugar."

"Yes." He smiled and held out one of the cups in his hand. "I brought you one, too."

She stood and took the cup from him. Her hands shook slightly.

"Have you eaten?" He didn't appreciate the sudden need to take care of her.

"No." She sipped from the coffee cup.

He watched her press the cup to her mouth. He remembered kissing those lips so many years ago. Remembered her soft, pliant mouth beneath his, the way she'd felt in his arms.

Angry at the unwanted course of his thoughts, he averted his gaze. "You shouldn't drink that on an empty stomach. Why don't we go to the cafeteria and get some breakfast?"

She shook her head. "She wanted me to wake her when you got here."

Even though Mrs. G. lay a few feet away, being this close to—this intimate with—Rachel troubled him. It was too easy to remember the past, to remember how he'd once loved her, how she'd looked at him with love in her blue eyes. Too easy to remember that she'd wanted to be a doctor more than she'd wanted to be with him. And being a doctor had changed her. The woman standing before him set his nerves on edge.

"I'll let you do the honors." He took her cup and set it, along with his own, on the side table.

Rachel lay a hand on Mrs. G.'s shoulder. "Mom G., Josh is here."

Mrs. G. stirred. Her eyelids fluttered.

Josh's chest tightened. Mrs. G. had been such a godsend to him and his family. They'd kept in touch after Rachel left town, and when Andrea died, Mrs. G. had insisted on keeping Griff while Josh had dealt with the funeral arrangements. Then she'd insisted on continuing to care for his son while he worked. She'd become the grandmother that Griff needed.

And now they were losing her. Josh didn't know if his heart could take much more loss, and he worried what the loss would do to his son.

Mrs. G.'s eyes opened fully and she smiled weakly. "Thank you, Josh, for coming."

Josh moved closer. "Of course I'm here. I'll always be here," he said softly. From the corner of his eye he saw Rachel glance at him.

"We're both here, Mom G.," she said softly.

Mrs. G. lifted her hand from the bed and held it out. Rachel immediately wrapped her own hand around Mrs. G.'s.

"Josh." Mrs. G.'s intent was clear. He hesitated before he slowly lifted his own hand and placed it over Rachel's. He kept his gaze trained on Mrs. G. and ignored the cool hand beneath his palm.

"I need a promise from…you both."

He glanced at Rachel. Her gaze met his. The wariness in her eyes reflected his own. Whatever Mrs. G. wanted, they would do everything in their power to make it happen.

As if she'd heard his thoughts, Rachel nodded imperceptibly and turned to Mrs. G. "Yes, of course, we'll promise you anything."

"Of course." Josh murmured his agreement.

His brows drew slightly together as he met the older woman's gaze. A mischievous glint twinkled in Mrs. G.'s eyes. Josh dismissed it as a trick of the light. Then she said, "Promise me that you two will take care of each other when I'm gone."

Josh stilled. Mischief nothing, the woman was bent on matchmaking! And he'd just given his word he'd do anything for her.

He hoped that wasn't a mistake he'd come to regret.

Chapter Four

Dismay sat heavy on Josh's chest, but he saw the fledgling hope in Mrs. G.'s expression and determination set in. He would do anything it took to fulfill her dying wish.

Hers would be one grave he wouldn't stand over with regret.

His gaze slid to Rachel. A slow red stain spread over her cheeks. She shook herself, glanced at him with wide, panicked eyes and then began to sputter, "Mom G. I…can't— You can't possibly expect…"

Josh tightened his fingers around Rachel's.

She ignored him. "We can't make a promise like that."

Josh applied more pressure. "Rachel, we can do this," he said with deliberate slowness.

Her head snapped toward him, her expression thunderous. "What?"

He was not going to argue with her in front of Mrs.

G. It was bad enough that she was balking. He refused to subject Mrs. G. to the tempest that was about to explode. Because, like it or not, he was going to make sure she agreed. He couldn't let her live with the kind of regret that plagued him. He lifted Rachel's hand away from Mrs. G.'s. "We need to discuss this outside."

Rachel stared at him mutinously. "There's nothing to discuss. It can't be done. I live thousands of miles away, Josh."

He smiled tightly at Mrs. G. "We'll be right back." He tugged on Rachel's hand. She pulled against him but finally stood and jerked her hand from his grasp.

"Fine," she snapped, her expression softening as she looked at Mrs. G. "You'll be okay?"

Mrs. G. blinked. "Of course."

Rachel strode out of the room. Josh watched her go. She'd become quite a formidable woman. He normally chose to defuse confrontational situations long before they came to a head. That skill made him a good manager of the forestry team he was responsible for. But he found a part of himself looking forward to seeing the sparks fly, to being a part of the controlled energy that was Rachel.

Filled with anticipation, he winked at Mrs. G. before following in Rachel's wake, confident he could manage her.

Rachel's head was going to explode. Anger raged, pounding at her temples. She couldn't make such a promise. She wouldn't lie to Mom G. How dare Josh even consider promising something he had no intention of fulfilling?

She rubbed at her temples, trying for a calm that was proving elusive. She could control her emotions. She was a doctor, a professional, standing in a hospital corridor, after all. She wouldn't cause a scene.

But the second Josh stepped into the hall radiating confidence, she whirled on him, her vow to remain calm pushed aside. "What was that all about? What are you trying to do?"

Rachel paced away from Josh in an effort to cool her temper.

Unruffled, he stated, "Trying to make Mrs. G. happy."

She screeched to a halt. "By lying to her? You think that's going to make her happy? Is your conscience out to lunch?"

Josh held up a hand. "Whoa, you need to calm down."

"Calm down?" She didn't appreciate him pointing out the obvious. Unfortunately her reserve of cool and collected was suddenly lacking. And it was Josh's fault. Something about the man he'd become caused her to lose her self-restraint. She didn't like being this out of sorts. It was too much; she felt too vulnerable.

She needed calm. She needed to breathe. *In slow, out slow, find the calm.* "We can't make that promise."

The dark green of his button-down shirt magnified the intent look in his eyes. "We said we'd do anything for her."

"But…not this. Are you out of your mind?"

"No." He shook his head. "I don't want to live regretting that I didn't do everything I could to make Mrs. G. happy."

His words struck her with sharp bites of guilt. "I want to make her happy, too, but I can't do this."

His expression hardened. "How difficult would it be for you to set your feelings aside for a moment and do something for her?"

She drew back, stung. "I'm not being selfish, Josh. I'm being realistic."

His look said he didn't believe her.

"Think for a second, Josh." Her hand gesturing wildly. "Your life's here. My life's in Chicago. And I'm leaving as soon as Mom—"

She froze. She widened her eyes and she covered her mouth with her hand as she realized what she'd almost said. A tremor assaulted her body. The reality of the situation hit her full force. No matter how good the medical care, Mom G. was going to die. Sooner rather than later.

Just like her mother had.

No! This was different. Her mother hadn't received the best care possible. Mistakes had been made, inadequate procedures followed. None of that was happening with Mom G. It was God's decision. *He* was in control.

She squeezed her eyes tight and fought the tears building, clogging her throat. She didn't want Josh to see her like this. She hated this feeling of utter helplessness.

God, I need you. I can't face this on my own.

She heard Josh let out an exasperated groan. Then his arms came around her, pulling her to his chest. She stiffened in shock. The odd combination of his woodsy-

and-spice scent filled her head, evoking images of Christmastime. She longed to melt into his big broad chest and partake of the comfort being offered.

She didn't want his comfort. It hurt too much because it came from pity, not affection, but she couldn't deny the warmth soaking her through, making her conscious of every point of contact between them, every bunching muscle, every beat of his heart.

She swallowed her tears and broke away from him before she gave in to the attraction building between them.

Bereft of his warmth, she wrapped her arms around her middle. *Focus, Rachel, focus.* "What had Mom G. asked us to promise? To take care of each other. It wasn't like she was asking us to get married."

"Right." Josh's voice drew her attention.

She hadn't realized she'd spoken her thoughts out loud. "But how?"

"I don't know, but we'll figure out a way."

She stared down the hall. Maybe Josh had a point. It could be done. Through telephone calls, Christmas cards, e-mail. They could take care of each other long-distance. In ways that wouldn't wreak havoc on her life. Or his.

She straightened to her full height, still only barely reaching his shoulders. "You're right. We'll find a way. We can do this."

He smiled approvingly. "Yes, we can."

She resented how good his approval felt.

As Rachel swept by him and back into Mrs. G.'s room, Josh took a moment to recover from the shock of seeing Rachel almost shatter. It tore him up inside to know she hadn't completely accepted the eventuality of Mrs. G.'s death. Rachel was trying so hard to be strong. Behind her controlled exterior was a woman struggling against death and grief. He understood why Mrs. G. wanted his promise. When Mrs. G. died, Rachel was going to need an anchor to hold on to because the arctic storm brewing within her would be overwhelming. Whether he liked it or not, he would be there for Rachel because he'd promised.

Mom G. stared up at Rachel with anxious eyes. Taking her hand, Rachel sought to reassure her. "We promise to take care of each other." Rachel glanced at Josh next to her. His smile was pensive.

"Thank heaven." Mom G. relaxed into the pillow for a moment and then looked at them with worried eyes. "I need one more thing from you both."

Rachel braced herself. What more could she want from them? What more anguish would she have to suffer in Josh's presence?

Josh chuckled softly. "Whatever you need, Mrs. G."

"Rachel, you need to eat. You're too thin. Josh take her to get something to eat."

The motherly words touched Rachel deeply. "I'm okay, really."

"Please, Josh, make her go," Mom G. implored.

Rachel had had enough of Josh, thank you very much. "I'm not leaving you."

"I don't want you to get sick, honey."

A flutter of panic hit Rachel. What if she left and

Mom G. died before she returned? Rachel knew she couldn't live with that. "Josh can bring something here."

"I want to sleep, Rachel. I'll rest better knowing you're letting Josh take care of you. As you promised."

Josh reached out and took her hand. She swallowed back the shiver of comfort in his heated touch. "Rachel, you need a break. We'll be back in a hour."

"Anything could happen in an hour," she whispered and pulled her hand free. Tears once again burned at the edges of her eyes.

"Do you trust God?"

She gazed into his warm hazel eyes. "Of course." Her answer was automatic. There was no question in her mind she trusted God. He'd seen her through so much and had given her the direction for her life.

Josh placed his hand on her shoulder; heat spread out from the point of contact. "Then let's entrust her to His care and ask for Him not to take her until you've returned."

This was a test of her faith and she hated the sudden hesitation gripping her soul. She wanted to know where Josh stood. Had his faith survived the death of his wife? "Is your faith that strong?"

Something akin to anguish flittered across his face, but then it was gone, replaced by determination. "Right now it is."

She had her answer. His relationship with Christ had suffered. She understood. To lose the one you loved so suddenly, without having a chance to say goodbye, would be enough to rock the most solid of foundations.

Mom G. squeezed her fingers. The weight of Josh's hand on her shoulder imprinted her skin. Her gaze darted between the two. Did she have enough faith? A still, quiet moment slipped by and Rachel was filled with a comforting peace. She nodded. *Please, God, let there be time for me to say goodbye.*

Rachel listened to Josh's words of prayer, felt them reverberate within her heart, filling her with comfort she gladly accepted. She'd always loved the sound of his resonant voice, could listen to him talk for hours. Time had only deepened the timbre, matured it in a way that was very appealing. And his words of faith were a balm to her weary soul.

"Thank you, Josh," Rachel murmured.

"Shall we?" He gestured toward the door.

Rachel kissed Mom G. goodbye, noting how drawn and exhausted she looked. Mom G. had expended a great deal of energy in securing the promise she wanted. It made Rachel more determined to comply.

Josh led the way out of the room. Rachel walked to the nurses' station, where she gave them her beeper number and elicited a promise from Jamie to make sure Mom G. received some tea before her next chemo session, which she was scheduled for within the hour.

"Everything okay?" Josh asked as they boarded the elevator.

"Yes." She followed him to the cafeteria.

Josh held open the door for her to pass through. The rattle of dishes and the rumble of voices greeted them. In one corner, a young mother spoon-fed a fussy toddler, while doctors and nurses, their white coats or green scrubs distinguishable, relaxed at several tables.

With metal trays in hand, Rachel and Josh went through the food line.

Even though it was only midmorning, Rachel chose a salad. She didn't want the heaviness of breakfast fare. Josh picked a hamburger and fries. "That food's going to sit in your stomach like a rock," she commented.

He grinned. "I'm a meat-and-potatoes kind of guy."

"Apparently."

At the cashier, Josh insisted on paying. Though she was used to taking care of herself, Rachel didn't argue. She needed to think about something else. Anything. She searched her mind for a topic of conversation, but unfortunately with Josh, all they had was the past.

"Whatever happened to your '65 Chevy?" she asked as they took their seats at a table near the floor-to-ceiling window. The warm sun fell on her back and she shrugged out of her jacket.

"I still have her." Josh sat opposite her.

"She runs? You were always tinkering with the engine, replacing one thing or another."

The corner of Josh's mouth twitched. "Sort of."

"Do you ever drive her out to the lake?" Now why'd she go and ask that? Cherry Lake had been a special place for them. A place to go when the world was too hectic and intrusive. It occurred to her that there at the lake, alone with Josh, she'd never experienced that trapped, restless sensation. She mentally shrugged the notion off, attributing the lack of restlessness to being a teenager in love.

Any semblance of a smile vanished from his face. "No," came the terse answer.

Silence, dense and thick, filled the air between them.

Pushing her Cobb salad around with her fork, she searched for a neutral topic. "Does your dad still work for the forestry service?"

"He's semiretired." He picked up his hamburger and took a bite.

"That's nice for him."

"Uh-huh."

Frustrated that he wasn't being cooperative with small talk, she watched him drown his French fries in ketchup. The red gooey mess didn't look healthy.

She ate slowly, her body recognizing the need for sustenance, but her mind rebelled, urging her back to Mom G. After a long moment of silence she tried again. "And you, Josh? What do you do?"

"I'm a ranger."

"You are?" Surprise echoed in her voice.

He glanced at her sharply. "I wouldn't lie."

"I didn't mean to suggest you would." She softened her voice. "You used to talk about going into the forestry service. I didn't think…" She trailed off, not wanting to offend him.

"You didn't think I would." He sounded amused.

"No, truth be told, I figured when you married Andrea you'd settle into a nine-to-five job and have a picture-perfect life." She'd imagined him living the fantasy. The fantasy they'd dreamed together those days long ago. An old Victorian house, the dog, the picket fence. Those were the things they'd wanted.

Only, as a doctor she didn't fit into his cookie-cutter world and she couldn't do what needed to be done from this hospital. The place where her mother had died.

Rachel noticed the ticking muscle along Josh's strong jaw. "I'm sorry. If you'd rather not talk about Andrea, I understand."

"Do you?"

The intensity in his voice made her wince. He was still grieving for his wife but she didn't know what to say or do to help him. The usual words of condolence she'd deliver to a family member of a patient didn't seem appropriate here. This was Josh.

"Dr. Maguire, Josh." Dr. Kessler approached the table.

"Doctor," Josh said.

Rachel rose, gripping the edge of the table, panic pounding in her veins. "Mom G.?"

Dr. Kessler held up a reassuring hand. "I'm on my way to see her. Just stopped in to grab a coffee."

She released her white-knuckled grip and sat down again. Josh reached across and took her hand, giving it a gentle squeeze. Comforted by his gesture, she gave him a grateful smile before slipping her hand away. His touch was too warm, too welcome. She couldn't allow herself the luxury of wanting his touch because wanting something she couldn't have was not her style.

"Dr. Maguire, our E.R. attending was very excited to learn you were here. I hope you'll take a moment and stop by the E.R. to introduce yourself."

Fat chance. She wasn't going anywhere near that

E.R. Too many of her nightmares involved that place. Careful to keep her thoughts from showing, she smiled. "If I have time."

Behind his wire-rimmed glasses, Dr. Kessler's eyes showed disappointment. "I'll check on Olivia now."

Rachel watched the doctor leave. "What do you think of him?"

"He's a good doctor."

Josh's tone rang with certainty and she accepted his pronouncement.

She finished the last of her salad, then picked up her tray and stood. "I'm going back upstairs now."

Josh rose, taking her tray from her. "I've got it." He took their trays and deposited them in the dirty dish bin before coming back to stand beside her. "We could go down to the emergency room. We haven't been gone very long."

Slipping her jacket back over her silk, short-sleeve top, Rachel shook her head. "I'm not here to work."

He arched a brow. "Too small-town for you?"

"No. I wouldn't be able to stay focused."

"Right. Focused."

The beeper attached to Rachel's waistband sent a shrill alarm ringing through the cafeteria. Her heart slammed against her chest. Mom G. Rachel couldn't make her feet move; panic gripped her, clogging her throat. Josh moved to her side, his big, warm hand cradling her elbow. "Josh, Mom G...."

"Let's go." The urgency in his tone clutched at her throat. She gratefully leaned on him as he propelled her out of the cafeteria and through the hospital.

Rachel and Josh stepped off the elevator and onto the fifth floor and sprinted down the corridor to Mom G.'s room. They skidded to a halt as a nurse emerged out the door.

"Is she…?" Rachel couldn't say the words.

The nurse smiled at her kindly. "She's waiting for you."

"Oh, thank you, God," Rachel breathed out. She swept past the nurse and into the room, aware that Josh followed closely behind.

Dr. Kessler stood at the foot of the bed, writing on the chart. He turned as Rachel approached. There was relief in his sympathetic eyes. "Her vitals are erratic. She's slipping away fast. It'll be only a matter of hours."

A heaviness settled on Rachel as she moved to the side of the bed and took Mom G.'s hand.

Mom G. stirred and opened her eyes. Her gaze focused on Rachel. "I love you."

Rachel swallowed the huge, burning lump in her throat and tried to smile, but could only manage a slight lifting of the corners of her mouth. Agony and grief gnarled in her heart. "I love *you*."

"You're my daughter. And I thank God every day that He brought you into my life." Her voice was weak, strained with the effort to talk.

Rachel let the tears slipping down her cheeks fall into her lap. She couldn't fight the pain of losing the only person who really cared about her.

"Rachel, happiness lies beyond what you think's possible. It's there waiting for you. You only have to have faith."

"I don't want you to leave me," Rachel whispered, shuddering with the intensity of her grief.

Mom G.'s grip tightened ever so slightly. "It's time for me to go be with my Savior. I've had a good life." She shifted her gaze away from Rachel. "Josh, you'll keep your promise?"

Josh's deep voice filled the room. "Yes, I promise."

Mom G. nodded and then seemed to shrink within herself.

Rachel pressed Mom G.'s hand to her cheek. Wanting to hang on, to somehow, with the force of her love, keep her from slipping away.

"I'll wait for you in heaven." Mom G. breathed the words with a smile and then her eyes closed.

Rachel refused to budge from Mom G.'s side. The hospital staff went about their business and Josh pulled up a chair beside her. Even though he didn't touch her, she felt his presence like a soft covering. Two hours ticked by in agonizing slowness as Mom. G's breathing slowed to small hiccups of air.

Mom G.'s heartbeat fell, then stopped. Machines sounded a strident warning. Rachel instinctively reacted by rising, ready to begin resuscitation. She looked wildly at the others filing into the room. Everyone stood quietly by as Mom G.'s life ebbed away. "Why aren't you doing something?" she sobbed. "Let's bring her back!"

Dr. Kessler stepped forward and lay a gentle but firm hand on her arm. "She has a standing DNR. She was in great pain. She wanted to go."

Rachel looked down at her mother. *Peaceful* was the

only word she could use to describe her. She was at peace with God.

Slowly Rachel sat back in the chair. A cold numbness seeped into her heart, spreading throughout her body. The two most important people in the world—her mother and Mom G.—had left her behind.

The weight of Josh's hand on her shoulder brought a fraction of solace to her restless thoughts. But that was an illusion, she reminded herself. A momentary respite from the grief welling up inside.

As soon as possible, she would return to her life and Josh would stay here.

Now she was truly alone on this earth.

Rachel sat near the window and surveyed the crowded church reception room. Among the various flower arrangements and tables filled with food, there were so many people. So many lives touched by Mom G. Some of the faces she recognized, others were new to her. Everyone had expressed his or her grief over Mom G.'s passing and then wandered off to talk among themselves.

Her gaze dropped to the taupe carpet and the polite smile she'd worn all day faltered. She was out of place among these people. Without Mom G. she didn't belong.

A slight film of dust covered her black pumps. Though she'd numbly stood by the grave with eyes blurry from tears, the graveside service had been beautiful. Pastor Larkin had delivered a lovely eulogy and Josh had spoken, giving a sentimental testament to Mom G.'s memory.

He'd grown so close to Mom G. while Rachel had been so far away. She was glad the funeral was over. After the reception, she would meet with the lawyer, Mr. Finley, to discuss Mom G.'s estate and then she wouldn't have any reason to stay. She'd be free to return to the life she'd carved out for herself, the life God wanted for her. Strangely there was no peace in that thought.

Constrained laughter caught her attention and she looked up. Across the room Josh held a captivated audience as he talked.

She sighed. He looked handsome in his dark navy suit and tie, looking more like he belonged in a board-room than out fighting fires. He stood tall and carried himself with a confidence that she envied. He was a part of these people. He belonged here. She didn't.

A young boy moved to stand beside Josh. Shock momentarily wiped away the numb ambivalence that had taken ahold of her the moment Mom G. died. Rachel's heart pounded as she looked from the boy to Josh and back to the boy.

Even as Josh put his arm around the child and hugged him, Rachel realized that this boy with his light-colored hair and expressive eyes could only be Josh's son. The "they" Mom G. had been talking about.

The child could have been *her* son.

She blinked and turned to stare out the window at the little town of Sonora. The quaint, turn-of-the-century homes, the cute little café that hadn't been there when she'd lived in the town and the gas station where Josh had worked during high school turned blurry through fresh tears.

Josh had a son. Why hadn't Josh mentioned him? Why did she care?

She realized she didn't know that much about Josh and his life. She didn't want to know, she told herself. She couldn't change the past, could only accept it.

There was so much to accept.

The quicker she left Sonora and the memories behind, the easier the past would be to accept—and forget.

Chapter Five

Josh hugged his son close. He was grateful his father had had the foresight to take Griff to the hospital before school the day before Mrs. G. died. He hated to think of the pain Griff would have suffered had he not had the chance to say goodbye to the woman who had helped raise him.

Thankfully Rachel had been able to say goodbye, too. He scanned the crowd. He'd seen her earlier talking with Mr. and Mrs. Poe, then he'd lost sight of her.

She was putting on a good show of strength. Though her complexion was ghostly pale and her eyes were a little glazed, she'd smiled and moved gracefully through the funeral service and the reception.

She looked very mature and womanly in her black tailored suit with her hair pulled up into a fancy twist. When they'd talked briefly at the cemetery, she'd been distant and polite, but he could see by the tiny lines bracketing her mouth and the way she had to blink constantly to fight tears, that she was struggling to keep her composure.

Where was she? He frowned. She shouldn't have to deal with her grief alone. He started to usher his son toward the door in search of Rachel when he saw her sitting by the window. She looked composed and serene, but he knew inside she had to be crumbling. He steered Griff toward the window.

As they approached, she turned and he saw a flicker of an emotion he couldn't identify in her eyes. But then it was gone and she smiled with distant, polite interest.

"Rachel, I'd like you to meet my son, Griff. Griff, this is Rachel Maguire."

Rachel held out her hand. "It's nice to meet you, Griff."

Griff took her hand. "You're in the picture with my dad at Mrs. G.'s house."

Her eyes widened with surprise. "Yes, I am. How did you know?"

"Mrs. G. takes care of me when Dad and Grandpa work."

Rachel fought the burning behind her eyes at the boy's use of the present tense. She could only imagine the grief the child would suffer when he realized that Mom G. wasn't coming back.

Josh cleared his throat. She saw the same concern in his eyes.

"When you're ready to leave, let me know and we'll give you a ride to your hotel," he said.

"That won't be necessary." She didn't want to rely on anyone, especially Josh, for anything.

He gave her a pointed look. "Yes, it is."

Annoyance arced though her. Their promise to Mom G. didn't include his services as chauffeur.

He set his jaw and grated out a warning, "Rachel."

From across the room, Rod called out Josh's name.

Rachel turned her attention to Griff. "So who's your favorite baseball team?"

"The Mariners."

"Seattle fan, huh?" She nodded sagely. "I'm a Cubs fan myself."

"They're in Chicago."

Rachel laughed softly. "That's right, they are."

Josh placed a hand on Griff's shoulder. "Come on, Griff. Let's give Rachel some space. Let's go find Grandpa."

Griff gestured with his thumb. "He's over there."

"I know he's over there, son. I need you to come with me. We'll come back and take Rachel home when she's ready."

Rachel ground her teeth, but didn't say anything. She wouldn't argue with Josh in front of his son.

"Aw, Dad. I wanna stay here and talk to her."

"He can hang with me." Rachel blinked up at Josh, half expecting him to say no way.

"Okay. Then we'll take you home," he said firmly.

Their promise didn't give him a license to try to control her, but she didn't have the energy to point that out to him. "Fine."

Josh nodded and moved away, sapping the air of its heat and leaving her chilled.

"I have a baseball card collection."

Rachel turned her attention back to Griff. "You do?" An unfamiliar yearning crowded her senses. She supposed she was drawn to him because this boy was so like his father.

"It used to be Dad's, but he gave it to me. Now I collect them."

"How old are you, Griff?"

"I'm eight."

Rachel absorbed that information with a bit of shock. Josh and Andrea had waited before having a child. She'd expected them to start a family right away because that was what he'd wanted. "You look like your dad."

Griff grinned. "Everybody says that."

"I see your mother in you, too." His hair was more the color of Andrea's and the shape of his nose favored her, as well.

"You knew my mom?"

Rachel smiled compassionately. "We all went to high school together."

"What was she like?"

She blinked. "Don't you remember her?"

He shook his head. "She died in a car accident when I was a baby."

This news carried the weight of a punch to the solar plexus. Andrea had died nearly eight years ago. Rachel had assumed because Josh was still grieving that she'd died fairly recently.

Griff had grown up without a mother. Josh had raised his son from infancy all by himself. She had no doubts that Rod helped, but that Josh took on the responsibility made her admire him in a way she hadn't before. And made her ache for both Josh and his son. Ached for what they'd lost.

"Why are you crying?"

Rachel wiped at the tear coursing down her cheek and gave a shaky laugh. "I…don't know."

"Are you sad because Mrs. G. died?"

She nodded, surprised and relieved he understood that Mom G. was gone. She'd underestimated the child.

"She's in a better place now, where there's no pain."

"Did your daddy tell you that?"

"Yes. Mrs. G.'s in heaven with my mom."

Rachel hurt for this little boy, for what he'd miss. She hurt for herself, for the hole Mom G. left in her life. She hurt for Josh.

In an unfamiliar moment of need, Rachel hugged the boy. He smelled clean, like sunshine and fresh air. And when his little arms wrapped around her neck, she couldn't stop the sob that broke free.

"Shh, its okay," Griff said, his voice so grown up, so like Josh's.

Rachel forced herself to let go. "I'm sorry. That was inappropriate."

Griff cocked his head to one side. "Why?"

"You don't know me."

"Sure I do. You're Mrs. G.'s daughter. She talked about you all the time."

She swallowed past the lump in her throat. "Did she?"

"Yep. Hey, will you come to church tomorrow?"

That the next day would be Sunday hit her like a

blast of cold air. Her normally ordered and scheduled life was in disarray. With all the emotional stress of the past few days, she'd lost track of time. Attending a church service would be soothing. Josh would be there, but she could handle that. "Yes, I will."

"Will you sit with us?"

Taken aback by the invitation, she struggled for an answer. "I don't know. We'll see."

"Aw, that usually means no. Please? You can sit next to me."

"Well..." She bit her lip. She didn't want to disappoint Griff, but...

"Griff, don't badger her." Josh's voice interrupted her thoughts and warmed her senses.

"He's not badgering me," she said.

"But he will until you say yes," he countered with an amused twinkle in his eyes.

"Aw, Dad."

Josh raised a brow and Griff rolled his eyes. Rachel smiled at the father-son exchange. Josh was a good father. His love for his son was evident in the way he looked at the boy, the way he displayed affection to Griff so freely. She'd always known Josh would be a good dad.

She sighed, feeling suddenly more alone and lonely than she'd felt in years. Josh had his son; she had no one. But she'd made her choice. A family wasn't part of her world, couldn't be a part of her world. Her job came first, would always come first. She doubted any man would accept that.

"You look tired," Josh said abruptly. "We should take you to the hotel."

Rachel stood. "You really don't have to do that. I'm sure Mr. Finley can take me there." She glanced around for the balding lawyer.

"No, we will," he stated. "Mr. Finley can stop by later after you've had a chance to rest."

She didn't like being told how she felt. "I'm not tired."

His expression became speculative and his tone softened. "Humor me, okay? Let us take you."

Griff slipped his hand into hers. "You can sit with me."

"Now how can you refuse an offer like that?" Josh asked.

She was sunk. How could she refuse Griff anything?

But Josh was another story. She couldn't decipher what she felt for him. The confusion left her wary and upset.

She wanted to go back to Chicago, far away from Josh and the jumbled mess of emotions he so easily stirred.

"Fine," she relented, only to have her nerves strung taut by the pleased look on Josh's face. Pleasing him shouldn't feel so good.

The tall, white-tipped, pointed steeple of the historic Red Church, its red paint gleaming in bright contrast to the clear blue sky, rose high above the maple and oak trees in the parklike setting of the church grounds. White-painted woodwork outlined beautifully etched stained-glass windows. The melodic strain of the church organ drifted out with the people as they exited through the open, wide double doors.

Rachel made her way toward the street, intent on walking back to her hotel without being waylaid by Josh.

The sound of pounding feet behind her drew her attention. She turned to see Griff skid to a halt before grabbing her hand. "Will you go get ice cream with us?"

Rachel laughed. "Don't you mean lunch?"

Griff shook his head. "Nope, ice cream."

His little face beamed and she felt tightness in her chest she'd never experienced before. He looked so adorable in his navy slacks with a checkered button-down shirt coming untucked at the waist.

She glanced up as Josh approached. His tawny hair was combed back and the green stripe in his tie brought out the green in his eyes. A warm flush flowed over her skin. "Ice cream after church?" she asked.

He shrugged sheepishly. "It's tradition."

"Will you come? Will you, huh?" Griff tugged on her hand.

"I don't think so." The numbness she'd allowed to seep into her soul after Mom G.'s passing seemed to retreat every time this child was present, only to be replaced with a tender yearning.

The new feeling worried her; confusion was not something she allowed herself. She always knew exactly what she wanted and how to get it. Except when it came to Josh and now his son. She didn't like the out-of-her-control feelings spinning around her heart and mind.

"Please," he wheedled. "You can get any flavor you want. Right, Dad?"

"Sure she can." She heard the challenge in his tone.

Rachel tried to discern what was going on inside Josh's head. His expression gave nothing away. He looked decidedly…neutral, but his voice told her otherwise.

"I have things to do…." She stopped as Josh cocked one brow and Griff tightened his grip on her hand.

"You have all day to do stuff," Griff complained. "Please, please? I really want you to come with us."

Her mouth twisted in a half smile. She understood now what Josh had meant about being badgered. Ice cream did sound good, if only because it was a decadence she rarely indulged in. "Well…"

Griff pounced on her momentary indecision. "Yay!"

To Josh's amused expression, she said, "What? I like ice cream. Besides, he can be convincing."

"There's no doubt about that." Josh's mouth quirked up at the corners. His gaze narrowed slightly. "I went to the hotel this morning to pick you up."

"I told you not to," she countered.

He smiled with wry humor. "I went anyway."

She'd hoped he wouldn't. She didn't want him to think she'd deliberately stood him up. "I came early to spend a few moments of quiet before the service."

He nodded, but she could tell he wasn't truly convinced.

"Rachel?" a female voice called.

She turned to a see Jennifer Martin hurrying toward her. They'd been best friends in high school. Very different, not only in looks—Jennifer, blond and olive-skinned contrasted to Rachel's own dark hair and fair skin—but also in temperament. Jennifer was outgoing and confident. Rachel had envied that about her friend.

They'd spoken briefly at the funeral, but Rachel hadn't been in the mood to play catch-up on the locals. Jennifer had understood.

"Hi, Jennifer."

To Rachel's surprise, Jennifer hugged her again, as she had the day before at the graveside. Rachel wasn't accustomed to displays of affection from anyone other than Mom G. And Josh. Though she couldn't say that he'd held her at the hospital with any amount of affection, more like obligation. She stiffly hugged Jennifer back.

"We're going to get ice cream," Griff piped up.

Jennifer's speculative gaze traveled from Griff, to Josh and then settled on Rachel. "That's wonderful."

Rachel smiled tightly.

"I'm so glad to see you here," Jennifer said with a bright smile. "You'll have to come for dinner and spend time with my family. I can't wait for you to meet Paul and the kids."

"That would be nice," Rachel replied politely, feeling a pang of guilt. She wouldn't be in town long enough to make it to her friend's house, but now was not the time to say so.

"Good. Tonight then."

Before Rachel could protest, Jennifer turned to Josh. "You two come along."

"Sure, we'd love to," Josh replied.

"Great. It's settled then." Jennifer beamed. "Why don't you pick up Rachel and you can all come together?"

"We can do that."

"Hey, wait," Rachel interjected, hating the maddening way they were arranging her life. "I have things to do. I've got to organize Mom G.'s house, pack things up. I don't have time for dinner. I…" Her protest faded as disappointment clouded Jennifer's eyes.

Josh nudged her with his elbow and the look he gave her was a clear signal that she was blowing it and about to hurt Jennifer's feelings. "I suppose I can take care of everything tomorrow. Dinner would be great. Thank you."

The sparkle returned to Jennifer's eyes. "I'll see you all about five."

"Can we go now?" Griff asked, and gave Rachel's hand another tug.

Swallowing back the trepidation that she was getting in too deep, Rachel nodded and allowed Griff to pull her along.

The local ice-cream parlor was packed. The old-fashioned decor with its mahogany tables and soda fountain counter always gave Josh the impression of stepping back in time. He waved at several people and endured the assessing glances as he herded Griff and Rachel toward the back where he spotted a table being vacated by two teens. His gaze strayed over Rachel's long floral skirt, appreciating the curves and the way the hem flirted with her trim ankles.

"I want strawberry with caramel sauce on a waffle cone," Griff said as soon as his bottom hit the chair.

Josh raised a brow, not sure overloading his son on sugar was such a good idea.

"Awww." A fleeting expression of disappointment crossed Griff's face. "Okay, no sauce."

"What? No sauce? Outrageous." Rachel's light laughter captured Josh's gaze. She blinked up at him, her blue eyes full of merriment. "We gotta have caramel sauce on strawberry waffle cones."

"Yeah, that's right," Griff chimed in eagerly.

She raised her dark winged brows, daring Josh to say no. He didn't want to spoil the air of fun surrounding them. "All right, caramel sauce it is." So much for any semblance of nutrition.

Griff's exuberance exploded in a loud "Yeah!"

Rachel's pleased smile sent ripples of pleasure down Josh's spine. Right now there wasn't anything remotely cold in her gaze. Her eyes were alive and warm, drawing him in, making him wish for the impossible, wish for a way to be enough for this woman. And wish the three of them could be a family. His stomach dropped. Abruptly he stood and headed to the counter. What was he doing having Rachel join them as if they *were* a family?

She's a friend, Josh admonished himself. Friends could have ice cream together. Friends could sit and have a decent conversation without their emotions being strung out to dry. Friends could laugh and enjoy each other's company without risking heartbreak.

His mouth twisted wryly. He was going to have to find a different category in which to place Rachel, because "friend" wasn't the correct one.

He paid and walked back to the table with three cones in hand.

At Rachel's appraising look he muttered, "It sounded good."

She laughed again. Josh liked her laugh. He'd forgotten how lyrical the sound could be, how her laugh wrapped around his senses. When they were in high school, Rachel's laugh was what had gained his attention.

As they ate their cones, Josh saw a side of Rachel he'd thought long gone. Here was the girl he'd been so crazy about in high school but there was so much more to her now. She'd seen things, experienced things that had changed her, given her depths that hadn't been there before.

Yet she was capable of an easy wit and gentle nature that made the time fly by. And Griff hung on every story coming from her lovely lips. How could his son help but fall for Rachel who at turns made Josh crazy with frustration and longing?

"Wow." Rachel sighed. "That was delicious. I haven't had ice cream in ages."

"Why not?" asked Griff.

"You know, I don't know."

She looked genuinely puzzled. Like the thought of enjoying something as simple as ice cream was foreign to her. What was her life like in the big city of Chicago? Did she have many friends? What did she do for fun? Was there a man in her life?

That last thought stopped him cold. He had no business even caring, let alone being tempted to ask if she had someone waiting for her return. Even so, curiosity about every facet of Rachel's life hounded him, made him want to know why the woman she'd become drew him to her despite his resistance.

They left the parlor and stepped into the sunshine. The parking lot hummed with the rumble of cars on the highway as well as the many entering and leaving the parking lot. The newly developed strip mall with the drugstore, bookstore, several specialty stores and two restaurants buzzed with activity as people meandered about, busy shopping and such on Sunday afternoon.

At the curb, Rachel touched his arm. "Thank you. I really enjoyed this morning."

He stared into those crystal-blue eyes and found he couldn't speak. The softness he saw spoke of caring and affection.

Her touch remained icy hot on his arm. An innocent touch that shouldn't cause such a riot inside.

He shouldn't let this get too personal, let the easy companionship of the morning cloud reality with wanting more from her. Yet he couldn't stop himself from covering her hand with his.

He told himself she needed comfort whether she wanted to admit to the need or not. She'd lost Mrs. G. The least he could do was offer some solace. Her eyes widened, and he was gratified to see a bit of the same chaos he felt reflected in her gaze.

She slipped her hand away. He wasn't surprised.

"We'll take you back to the hotel."

She drew herself up. The composed politeness he was beginning to detest settled over her lovely face and her petite form stiffened. Gone was the congenial woman of moments before. Now he was faced with the

Rachel she'd become, the one he didn't understand or know how to deal with.

"That would be fine. I have things that need to be taken care of before we go to Jennifer's," she said stiffly.

And he would be there to help her take care of things, because of his promise, not because he wanted to. At least that's what he tried to convince himself of as he headed them out of the parking lot and drove them to the hotel.

When they arrived at the gray motel lodge consisting of ten single units, Rachel slid from the truck.

"Can I stay with you?" asked Griff, his little face full of eager anticipation.

Josh swallowed past the lump in his throat. His son's eagerness to be with Rachel was touching.

Rachel smiled, her blue eyes twinkling. "You're going to get sick of me if we spend too much time together."

"Naw, couldn't happen," Griff scoffed.

Josh ruffled Griff's hair. "We'll be seeing Rachel tonight, buddy." He turned his attention to her. "I'll be back in a while to help you with things."

Her brows drew together. "You don't need to."

"But I will," he insisted.

"Josh, I'm going to rest for a while. Please don't come back until it's time to leave for Jennifer's."

The edge to her tone conveyed the subtle message: *You're not wanted.* Well, too bad. She was stuck with him for the duration of her stay because that's what Mrs. G. wanted.

And he always honored his promises.

He chose to ignore the little voice in his head that wondered why it seemed like so much more. He didn't want more. Rachel would be leaving soon and he'd be safe to remember that spending time with her was for now only. There could never be a forever for them.

Chapter Six

Rachel was ready and fresh from a nap when the boys arrived to pick her up. She was thankful Josh had honored her wishes and not returned earlier. She'd needed the time to get herself refocused on her mission: See to Mom G.'s affairs and then head back to Chicago. She'd made an appointment with Mr. Finley to go over the terms of the will and sign the necessary papers.

The drive to Jennifer's went smoothly with Griff chattering away about an upcoming Boy Scout trip. The only trouble she had was keeping her pulse from racing every time she met Josh's gaze. He'd grown more handsome since morning. He wore dark denim jeans, a light blue chambray shirt with a white T-shirt peeking out at the V where the first three buttons were undone.

She forced herself to look straight ahead at the scenery going by as he drove, in an effort to keep herself from overheating. They turned onto a gravel driveway where Josh pulled the truck to a stop beside a white minivan.

The large, yellow with white trim A-frame stood on the top of a rise on the north side of the county. The wraparound porch cluttered with a smattering of toys added charm to the house. The laughter of children reached her ears and she couldn't tell if the sound came from inside the house or from the back where she'd glimpsed a lawn with a wooden swing set. On the evening breeze the scent of barbecue drifted past.

Griff bounded up the porch stairs while she and Josh followed at a more sedate pace.

"This is lovely," Rachel commented as they stopped in front of the large oak door. Sandwiched between Josh, his muscular body pressing into her as he reached to press the doorbell, and Griff, his small hand tucked tightly within her grip, she felt oddly out of place, yet not. It was a very strange feeling.

Heavy footfalls approached the door and it opened to reveal a man, average in height, with dark, short hair and a clean-shaven face. She kept her surprise in check. This man with his pressed khakis and white button-down shirt didn't match the type she'd always pictured with Jennifer. She'd figured Jennifer for the bohemian type of man willing to ramble around the world with his photojournalist wife.

The man smiled, his warm brown eyes crinkling at the corners. "Welcome. Hey, we're still on for bowling next Saturday?"

Josh flexed his fingers. "You bet. We'll whip up on Larry and Stan like last time."

"That we will." Paul ruffled Griff's hair. "Griff, the kids are around somewhere. Why don't you go find them?"

Griff didn't needed to be asked twice. He disappeared from sight without a backward glance.

The man turned his attention to her. "You must be Rachel."

"Yes. And you must be Paul."

"I am indeed. Please, come in."

He stepped aside, allowing Josh and Rachel to enter. The comfortable coziness of the house surrounded her with peace. Even the clutter of toys couldn't diminish the rustic beauty of Jennifer's home.

The dining area directly across from the entryway held a large oval table set for dinner, surrounded by high-backed chairs and a high chair. In the living room to her right, Rachel noted the furniture was an eclectic mix of old and new. A huge stone fireplace dominated one wall.

"Jen's changing the baby. She'll be out in a sec."

"Great." *Baby?* How many children did Jennifer have? Rachel tried to remember what Mom G. had said the last time she'd given her an update.

An enlarged photograph on the living room wall caught her attention. She moved to get a closer look. The peaceful serenity of the meadow scene struck a familiar chord. Bright yellow monkey flowers, indigenous in the Sierras, carpeted the sides of a meandering stream. The petals, which resembled the face of a grinning ape, were captured in vivid detail. Off in the distance mountains rose in majestic splendor meeting the sky in sharp lines.

"Jen took that." Pride rang in Paul's tone.

"That's why it looked familiar. Jennifer and I spent

many summer hours in that meadow." She'd planned her life as a doctor and Jennifer had dreamed of photographing the world.

What happened to Jennifer's dream?

The sound of running footsteps echoed through the quiet of the house as Griff and three children of various ages and genders came skidding to a halt in the archway of the living room.

"Kids." Paul's deep voice brought the children to attention. "Meet Mom's friend Rachel. Introduce yourselves."

The tallest boy, close to Griff's age, smiled, showing even white teeth. "Hi, I'm Will."

Next to him a girl, younger and smaller, peered at her through a veil of blond hair. "I'm Krissy."

The youngest of the three, another girl with short, light brown curly hair blinked up at Rachel. "I'm Linnea. I'm four." She held up four fingers.

"Hello, Will, Krissy and Linnea. I'm pleased to meet you."

The three stared at her silently, assessing her. She smiled reassuringly, hoping she met with their approval.

"You're pretty," Linnea said, her little round face breaking into a grin.

Beside her Josh made a noise of agreement. When she met his gaze, his eyes were dancing with mirth.

Griff sidled up to her and took her hand.

"Okay, kids." Paul clapped his hands. "Go wash up for dinner. We eat in five."

The four kids turned and vanished down the hall just as Jennifer sailed in, carrying an infant on one hip.

"Hi. I'm so glad you could come." Jennifer gave Rachel an one-armed hug. And then she gave Josh one.

"Me, too." She hoped her friend didn't hear her hesitancy. Though Rachel had worked with children often at the hospital, being in the midst of such a large brood was overwhelming. How did Jennifer juggle four kids?

"The barbecue's just about ready," Paul said. "It shouldn't be more than a few minutes."

"Need some help?" offered Josh.

"Yeah, come on back." Paul and Josh disappeared behind a swinging door.

"He cooks?" Rachel quipped.

"One of the perks of our marriage." Jennifer studied her with curious intensity. "Josh is a really good cook, too."

Hoping to distract Jennifer from the subject of Josh, Rachel held a hand out to the baby in Jennifer's arms. The little angel wrapped a chubby hand around one finger and pulled it toward his mouth. "Who's this?"

"Oh, honey, I'm sure Rachel doesn't want to become a pacifier." Jennifer extracted Rachel's finger from the child's grip. "This is Bobby. He's teething and everything goes in the mouth right now."

"Hey, Bobby." Rachel held out both hands. "May I?"

Surprise flickered in Jennifer's eyes. "Of course."

She passed the baby over and Rachel took him, loving the slight weight in her arms, enjoying the fresh, powdery scent coming from the baby's soft, downy hair.

"You're a natural," Jennifer declared.

Rachel laughed. "I'm a doctor. I get to do this occasionally."

"Dinner's served," Paul announced as he and Josh came through the swinging door carrying two large platters.

On cue the children raced down the hall and straight to their chairs. Griff took the empty seat next to Will. Rachel handed the baby back to Jennifer and then slowly moved to an empty chair. She sat with Jennifer on her right and Linnea on her left. Across from her sat Josh.

When Linnea's hand slipped into hers, Rachel blinked with surprise, but then she realized that Jennifer's hand was extended toward her. Around the table hands were held, forming a circle. Rachel took Jennifer's hand, completing the ring. As Paul said the blessing, Rachel felt a stab of longing for Josh. For the family with him that would never be. She forced herself not to open her eyes and look at him.

The meal progressed in a chaotic whirl. Rachel fielded questions about her life and in turn she asked about their lives. She found out Paul was a bank executive, Will liked basketball as did Griff, Krissy was passionate about horses and Linnea loved to have tea parties.

The children all had something to say, and the volume rose as they talked over each other. Jennifer fed the baby with intermittent comments and Paul listened attentively to each person while exchanging loving glances with his wife.

Rachel glanced at Josh occasionally and would catch him staring at her, heating her with the almost tender expression in his eyes. She smiled at him and felt like such a fake. She wasn't cut out for this kind of scene. Yet she couldn't deny the stirrings of need for such a life, for a family to call her own. She watched Jennifer. Her friend's eyes lit with joy and her smile came readily. Did she regret not pursuing her dreams? Could Rachel ever hope to have what her friend had?

Even if she could, that kind of life would never include Josh. His life was here; hers was in Chicago. A ribbon of sadness wound its way through her. She accepted it because she had no choice. She had to keep focused on God's plan for her.

After the table was cleared, Paul hefted Bobby into his arms. "Why doesn't Griff stay the night?" he asked Josh. "We have extra toothbrushes and he can sleep in a pair of Will's pj's."

"Can I, Dad? Can I?" Griff hopped in excitement.

"Sure, I suppose that would be okay since school's out now," Josh replied, earning himself a big hug from Griff.

"I'll get these rugrats settled in," Paul said as he ushered the kids down the hall.

Josh's gazed darted between the two women and then he called after Paul, "I'll help you."

"Chicken," Rachel teased.

He glanced over his shoulder. "I know to retreat when I'm outnumbered." He winked and then disappeared.

"Coffee or tea?" Jennifer asked once they were alone.

"Herbal tea would be nice."

Rachel followed Jennifer into the kitchen. The white-tile countertops, light oak cabinetry and blue-and-white gingham window coverings created an inviting and soothing atmosphere. Rachel dismally recalled her own kitchen with its harvest-gold counters, bare walls and dark cabinets.

She watched Jennifer go about the task of making tea, her movements fluid and natural.

"How are you really doing, Rachel?"

The intensity in Jennifer's voice grabbed Rachel's attention. Sliding onto a stool at the wide, white-tiled island in the center of the kitchen, she replied, "I'm hanging in there."

Jennifer's clear eyes searched Rachel's face. "I'm worried about you."

Rachel tilted her head, touched by her concern. "Why?"

Jennifer took the remaining stool. "Nothing specific. I just want you to be happy."

Rachel put her hand on her friend's hand. "Are *you* happy?"

Jennifer's smile brightened the room. "Yes."

"But you gave up your dream."

Confusion dampened Jennifer's smile. "What dream was that?"

"Traveling the world, taking pictures."

Jennifer laughed softly. "Dreams change."

Rachel sat back with a frown. "But you were so set on photojournalism."

Jennifer went to the stove. She was silent as she poured the tea. Carrying two mugs, she handed one to Rachel and then resumed her seat. "You know, I envied you so much when we were young. You always knew who you were and what you wanted out of life."

Rachel wrapped a hand around her mug. "So did you."

Jennifer shook her head. "I didn't have the conviction you did. It sounded good. Photojournalism." She gave a wry laugh. "That would've been a lonely life. I was afraid to tell you my real dream was to have a family."

"Why?"

Jennifer shrugged. "Your dream was so lofty, so ambitious. I didn't want you to think less of me."

Stung by that revelation, all Rachel could say was "Wow."

Something deep inside Rachel shifted and an uncomfortable, wholly strange sensation filled her. For a pregnant, silent moment she stared at her friend, then comprehension dawned. She was envious. Envious of Jennifer's freedom to choose.

But Rachel had been given a choice once. Marry Josh or pursue medicine. She'd made the only choice she could.

A sharp pain banged behind Rachel's eyes. She pinched the bridge of her nose.

Her stirrings of longing for a family intensified, but along with that came the reality of what having a family for her would mean. The sacrifices and compromises that would need to be made. And the greatest sacrifice—the risk of loving and hurting.

Could she make those sacrifices, those compromises? And in doing so, would she be going against God's plan? How could she ever make that choice?

"Rachel, are you okay?"

"I'm getting a bad headache." She could hear the strain in her voice, feel the weight of her future crushing her heart.

Jennifer touched her arm. "I'm sorry if I upset you."

With practiced effort, Rachel forced the pain to recede. "It's not you, Jennifer. It's everything. Losing Mom G., seeing Josh..." The loneliness, the confusion. "Away from the hospital, I feel like I'm losing myself."

"Or finding yourself."

Jennifer's verbal arrow quivered in the center of the bull's-eye. "Maybe," Rachel scoffed lightly, trying to ignore the well-aimed words.

"I watched Josh tonight. He cares for you."

"Nothing could ever come of it. Josh and I both know that."

"We both know what?" Josh asked as he and Paul entered the kitchen.

Heat flushed her cheeks. "Nothing."

He arched a brow. "Looking pretty guilty for nothing."

Rachel threw a panicked glance to Jennifer, looking for help.

Jennifer flipped her curls and smiled serenely. "Coffee or tea, gentlemen?"

Rachel was thankful the conversation turned to world news events. She relaxed as the light banter among the four of them stayed on subjects that didn't include her and Josh in the same sentence.

She was painfully aware of Josh leaning against the

counter beside her. His big hands toyed with a napkin, distracting her. He had nice strong hands. When he touched her hand, it seemed natural for her to curl her fingers around his.

"You tired?" he asked.

"Yeah, a little." She stared into his eyes. *He cares for you.* She was getting in way too deep. She slipped her hand away.

They said their goodbyes to Griff, who was snuggled in a sleeping bag on the floor of Will's room.

After promising Jennifer she'd see her again before leaving town, she followed Josh to the truck. He helped her in, his hand hot on her elbow, a shiver prickling her skin.

Alone with him in the truck, Rachel was acutely conscious of his masculine appeal. His muscled thighs and wide shoulders took up room, making her feel feminine in contrast. "It was a nice evening."

"You surprised?" He slanted her a quick glance.

She shrugged. "I didn't know what to expect."

Josh pushed a button on the dash and soft country music filled the cab. She couldn't tear her gaze from his profile. She liked the strength of his jaw and the line of his nose. Her gaze landed on his mouth, his lips. She clamped her jaw shut and turned away. She had no business fostering her attraction to him. No business wanting to kiss him.

They arrived at the hotel and Josh cut the engine. He shifted on the seat to face her, his arm stretching across the back of the seat, his big body leaning close. The tips of his fingers made little swirls on the top of her shoulder, setting off little sparks through her bloodstream. The light coming from the moon bathed his ruggedly handsome face in a soft glow, but couldn't disguise the magnetic pull of his eyes. She clenched her fist to keep from reaching for him.

"I have to go to the station tomorrow but I'll come back to help you at Mrs. G.'s as soon as I can."

"That's not necessary." It wasn't a good idea to keep seeing him when she knew it would only make leaving harder.

"I know it's not. But I want to." The husky timbre of his voice slid along her limbs like a smooth caress.

"What are we doing, Josh?" she asked, hoping to bring some perspective into the intimate atmosphere surrounding them.

His fingers stopped. He drew back slightly. "I don't know. Taunting disaster?"

"I'd say so," she whispered, striving for calmness when her heart was beating wildly.

His mouth quirked up in a self-effacing way as he stared out the front window for a heartbeat. "I'll walk you to the door."

He climbed out and came around the truck to open her door. As she slid out, his arm encircled her waist, drawing her up against the length of his solid body. She tipped her head and the smoldering blaze she saw in his gaze ignited an answering flame inside.

She felt exposed, vulnerable to the attraction coursing through her. But it was so much more than purely physical and it scared her because any way she examined it, they had no future together. Giving in to this thing arcing between them would only spawn more regret and heartache. She deliberately shut down her feelings and pulled away from him.

On unsteady legs she moved up the stairs of her unit and unlocked and opened the door. She turned to say good-night, expecting he'd be where she'd left him by the truck, but found herself staring at his broad chest. She quickly stepped inside, keeping the threshold between them.

"It's best if you don't come tomorrow, Josh."

A look of implacable determination settled on his face. "Sleep well, Rachel. And I *will* see you tomorrow."

She watched him stride away and climb back into his truck.

"Sleep well?" she muttered as she closed the door and listened to him drive away. He might as well have told her she could perform surgery with her arms tied behind her back.

Josh drove home on autopilot. He was all tied up inside. Hanging out at Jennifer and Paul's with Rachel at his side—as if they were a couple, a family—had felt right and natural. He'd liked it way too much. He'd let it go to his head. Let his guard down and had been tempted to act on the attraction building between him and Rachel.

She'd relaxed a bit tonight, as she had earlier at the ice cream parlor. When she wasn't all frosty and controlled, he really liked her.

But liking her and letting himself fall for her were two very different things. He was grateful she'd turned on the ice and reminded him how painful freezer burn could be. He'd be more careful in the future. He had a promise to fulfill, and as long as she was within his reach he'd do what he could to take care of her. But that's as far as he could let it go without costing him his heart.

Chapter Seven

Rachel wiped perspiration from her brow with the corner of her oversize T-shirt and surveyed the pile of boxes filling the back of Mom G.'s car. Driving again had felt strange after living in a city where she utilized public transportation every day. She made a mental note to contact Pastor Larkin and see if he knew of a family in need to whom she could donate Mom G.'s car.

"That should do it," she told the grocery clerk who'd come out to help.

"All right, you have a good day. And if you need any more boxes, you're welcome to come back and get them." The young man smiled and disappeared back into the grocery store.

She closed the back hatch and moved around Mom G.'s station wagon to the driver's side. Thankfully she'd left the windows down. The high sun raged like an inferno, letting everyone know that summer had officially arrived in the Sierras.

Driving along the pine-tree-lined streets, seeing the houses of those she'd once called neighbors, Rachel shrugged off the feeling of isolation. This wasn't her life and this wasn't how she wanted to live. But as she pulled into the driveway of Mom G.'s ranch-style house, a wave of loneliness swept through her and she realized with a start that the sensation was all too familiar.

She felt the loneliness at night when she headed home from the hospital, she felt it on Sundays when she attended her church in Chicago and saw families sitting in the pews. She felt it every time she left Josh and Griff.

She was lonely. There, she'd admitted it. But she couldn't do anything about it. Not now, not until she returned to Chicago. Then she'd be able to formulate a plan on how to end her loneliness. Maybe a dog or cat would help.

After dragging the boxes into the stuffy, closed-up house, she faced the task of sorting through all of Mom G.'s items and packing what she wanted to ship to Chicago. The rest would be donated to Goodwill. Forcing her tears away, she walked through the house, and with each step, with every effort to keep grief from overtaking her, the numbness returned.

"Might as well start in the family room," she muttered, wanting to work up to the rooms that would be more emotionally difficult to face.

As she worked, her mind kept turning to Josh.

His steady strength appealed to her. Even when his overbearing behavior grated on her nerves, she found him compelling. Found comfort in his presence and in his sense of duty and honor. He was a man worth admiring. Worth loving. If only…

She ached for his loss, ached that he grieved for the wife he'd obviously loved. Would Andrea always hold his heart? Or would he heal from her death someday and try to love again? What would it be like to be really loved by Josh, to have his stoic presence filling her life, balancing the irregularity of the E.R. with his unwavering strength?

Shaking her head at her own foolishness, she chided herself for thinking of Josh in terms of the future. His life was here—raising his son, working for the forestry service. Her life was across the country where her newest ideas in triage treatment were waiting to be implemented.

She reached for a platter from the cupboard and paused, remembering with vivid clarity the look in Josh's eyes the night before. He'd looked at her with such yearning and need. As if he wanted the relaxed and intimate atmosphere that had enveloped their time together to continue. As if somehow the past didn't matter, only the present. As if he could finally accept her for who she was. As if—

She slammed her thoughts down. Getting caught up in the moment was foolish. For both of them. Josh would never accept her for who she was. He would never accept that medicine was important to her and he would never leave Sonora. Allowing even a brief hope that somehow they could make a life together was beyond absurd.

She forced herself to concentrate on the job at hand. She moved with renewed purpose, her mind so focused that at first she thought a loud pounding on the door was merely an echo of the pounding in her head. She started out of her single-minded drive to get the job done. Hours had passed and dusk had fallen, creating shadows along the walls. She made her way through the house turning on lights as she went. She peered out the peephole and froze.

Josh.

If she didn't answer the door, would he go away?

The loud knocking persisted. No, he wouldn't. She took a deep, shaky breath, opened the door and drank in the sight of him in faded denim jeans and navy polo shirt that revealed muscled biceps. His hair looked slightly damp as if he'd recently showered, and the clean scent of soap and man filled her senses.

"You okay?" he asked, concern etched in the lines on his face.

Under his considerate regard, her heart raced and her body heated. With more effort than it should have taken, she composed herself. "I'm fine. Just working on getting things packed. What can I do for you?"

His brows shot up. "You could let me in."

"I don't think so. I asked you not to come."

"And I told you I would."

She couldn't argue that. She tried a different tactic. "I appreciate your trying to fulfill your promise to Mom G., but this is a little extreme. Honestly, Josh, the best thing you can do for me is leave."

He stepped closer, consuming the air, making breathing suddenly difficult. She involuntarily stepped back, trying to allow more oxygen to come between them. "Josh, please."

In a low, subdued voice he said, "Let me help. The quicker you're done, the quicker you can leave."

So that was it. Never mind that his words reflected her own thoughts. All his offers of help were to hurry her along her way. She shouldn't feel this bubble of disappointed hurt choking her. Shouldn't feel betrayed that he'd want her gone. She should be glad of the help, glad to move things along so she could leave and resume her life once again. A life without him.

The tumultuous conflict going on inside nearly made her stagger. But she drew herself up, arranging her features into what she hoped would appear as a polite, unaffected smile. "Of course. Leaving's my priority. But I don't need your help."

"I'd think that you'd want the packing done quickly," he grated out.

She bristled. "Am I not moving fast enough for you?"

"Frankly, no."

She couldn't let him in. She'd put off working on her old room and Mom G.'s room for fear of being swamped by her grief. *Lord, I need Your strength.* She was almost done with the rest of the house. "I can do this on my own."

He let out an exasperated breath. "Rachel, you shouldn't be doing this alone." His voice softened, wrapping her up in its even tones.

She resented how much she suddenly wanted him to help, wanted him to take her in his arms and make all the grief disappear. "I've done perfectly well alone for years. What makes you think I need you now?"

His quick intake of air was unmistakable. She peered up into his face, trying to discern his expression in the porch light. A shadow obscured his features, frustrating her attempt to decipher why her words would cause him distress.

"I can't believe you're going to renege on your promise so easily. Let me take care of you."

Stabbing guilt made her open the door wider and step back. He stepped in, engulfing the house with his presence.

She hastily closed the door then moved to a stack of empty boxes and watched him survey the piles she'd scattered about the living room. "I've boxed up what I'm having shipped and the rest will be donated to Goodwill."

He nodded, his piercing, gold-specked gaze making a fire rise in her cheeks. She swallowed, fighting the attraction that always hovered close to the surface. He was a big, handsome man and it was natural for her to find him attractive.

Get a grip. She picked up a box and held it out to him. "We can finish the kitchen."

In two long strides, he came toward her and took the box. "After you."

She could do this. She marched past him and into the kitchen. They worked together in tense silence. Rachel found it hard to concentrate with only a few feet separating them. She'd catch herself watching his hands as they wrapped newspaper around dishes, those large masculine hands that with the slightest touch brought her comfort she'd never experienced with anyone else. She forced her mind to focus on her task. Soon the kitchen was packed.

"That's done." Josh stretched, his navy blue shirt pulling taut across his shoulders, emphasizing the broad width.

Rachel blinked and quickly turned away as she rose from her position on the floor where she'd finished taping closed the last box. Her stiff legs ached, reminding her she'd hadn't exercised in a while.

"Now where?"

Her stomach clenched in nervous agitation. "The bedrooms."

She hoped she could make it through this without breaking down. She didn't want Josh to witness any weakness.

Josh followed her down the hall to her old room. She pushed open the door, expecting Mom G. had already boxed most of her things and would have used the room for her own purposes, and was surprised to find it much as she'd left it. The frilly white bed coverings were neatly made, the shelves lining the walls held the various books and dolls she'd left behind.

Josh peered over her shoulder. "It's like walking back in time."

She closed her eyes against the sudden images of herself as a teenager. With graphic clarity, she saw herself sitting at the desk beneath the window doing her homework, her hair held high in a ponytail, her feet tucked beneath her.

She could still remember the night Mom G. had opened her door and said she had a visitor.

Josh had walked in with his easy grin and gentle manners. She'd secretly had a crush on him since the first day of high school. She hadn't known he'd noticed her. She hadn't known that one day he'd break her heart.

She opened her eyes and deliberately stepped forward and began pulling books and dolls from the shelves.

Without further comment, Josh dragged in several empty boxes and placed them at her feet.

"Thanks," she muttered, grateful for his thoughtfulness.

After a moment she paused and noticed his perplexed expression. The big, strapping male looked wholly out of place in the little girl's frilly room and clearly he didn't know what to touch and what not to.

Rachel stifled a smile. "You could strip the bed and pile it with the Goodwill items."

He flashed a relieved grin that hit Rachel with the shock force of a defibrillator. Quickly she turned back to her shelves. *Focus, focus,* she chanted inside her head.

After those first few awkward moments, they worked together like a tenured surgical team. She'd load a box, he'd tape it closed and fill out the address label.

Slowly conversation started, tentative at first. Rachel sought for neutral subjects and Josh seemed eager to keep their talk light.

As teens they'd had similar tastes in movies and books. Rachel was mildly surprised to discover that as adults they still shared many common interests.

They relaxed into a sort of rhythm, where one thread of conversation quickly led to another and another. They laughed and companionably argued over politics, choices for the Oscars and which authors should appear on the *New York Times* bestseller list.

In an amazingly short amount of time, they had her old room boxed up. "Thank you, Josh, for your help," Rachel said as they finished dragging the boxes into the living room.

"Sure thing." He held out his large hand. "Just one room left. You ready?"

She swallowed back the sudden tears that burned at the edges of her eyes. His offer of support nearly undid her. Clearly they both knew how hard this was going to be. She shored up her defenses. She couldn't show weakness, but she took his offered hand and allowed his warm palm to give her strength as they headed down the hall.

Mom G.'s room also was as she remembered. The double bed with its fluffy pink comforter, the dresser cluttered with trinkets and jewelry. The bedside table still held the picture of Mr. Green as a young man.

Rachel headed toward the closet, then stopped as she noticed the new pictures hanging on the wall. They took her breath away.

There were pictures of herself in beautiful frames. School pictures, pictures of her with Mom G., at the prom with Josh at her side, her graduation pictures from high school, college and medical school.

"She was very proud of you."

Josh's softly spoken words sent shivers of fire down

her spine. If only he could be proud of her. She frowned at the thought and began pulling the pictures from the wall.

Lovingly she wrapped each frame in paper and stacked them in a box Josh had carried in. This time they worked in reverent silence, occasionally sharing memories of Mom G. Rachel kept more of the items from Mom G.'s room than she had from any other.

The large armoire that graced the wall next to the closet drew her attention. She'd find a place for it in her apartment. She ran her hand over the gleaming wood.

"When I first came to live with Mom G. I was a very scared little girl," she commented aloud. "Once again frightened by a new place, a new parent and a new set of rules to learn. One day I hid inside this chest."

"What happened?" Josh asked as he came to stand beside her, his presence comforting.

She smiled up at him, liking the way his interest was centered on her. "Mom G. found me. Instead of the anger I had expected, she lovingly held me and told me stories until the fear went away. She was an awesome woman."

Josh reached out and tucked a strand of hair behind her ear. His touch was electrifying as his knuckles grazed her cheek. "She was."

His gaze trapped hers. She was letting him get too close both physically and emotionally. She didn't want that, couldn't allow it. Only pain would result. She stepped back out of reach and gulped for air. "I'll have the shipping company pack up the armoire."

One corner of Josh's mouth tipped up as if he knew

how he was affecting her. Disconcerted, she turned her focus to the closet. She touched each garment and Mom G.'s scent wafted up from the clothes, tugging at Rachel, making her ache.

"What's that?"

She wiped away a tear before facing Josh. "What?"

He tilted his head upward. "There."

She followed his gaze. A white box on the top shelf of the closet bore her name. She glanced at him. "Would you mind?"

Josh squeezed beside her, eating up space, and Rachel stepped back, nearly falling into the clothes piled on the floor. He reached out to steady her, his huge, strong hand closing around her forearm, sending hot sparks shooting up her arm.

"Thanks." She extracted herself from his grip and moved a safe distance way. Josh's proximity and his touch did funny things to her insides and she didn't want funny things going on inside. It made staying focused difficult.

He easily retrieved the box. "The living room?"

"Please." She headed down the hall. Josh set the box on the coffee table. She opened the lid and widened her eyes in pleasure. A tattered teddy bear lay on top of a scrapbook.

"Yours?"

"Yes." She picked up the bear and ran a hand over it. "My mother gave him to me before she died. I'd thought I'd lost him. Mom G. must have packed him up to preserve him." A lump rose in her throat. She held the bear close to ease the tightness in her chest.

Setting the bear aside, she picked up the scrapbook and laid it on the table. She sat on the sofa and flipped through the pages. Josh took the seat beside her, distracting her.

"Mrs. G. put effort into this," he remarked.

"It's wonderful." She couldn't believe how much she enjoyed looking at the pictures and the little anecdotes written beside the frames. The book chronicled her life with Mom G., starting with the first day she'd arrived to the last picture Rachel had sent. On the last line in the book Mom G. had written, "The rest of the book is for you to fill with pictures of your family."

Rachel stared at the words. Mom G. was her family. Without her, Rachel was alone.

As if he'd heard her thoughts, Josh asked softly, "Are those pages going to be filled, Rachel? Do you have someone waiting for you in Chicago?"

She slanted him a glance, aware of the anger stirring in her chest. Anger because he had no right to ask her that, anger because the answer was no.

"What do you think? No, wait." She held up a hand before he could respond. "What was it you said? 'No man would want to marry a woman whose priority in life was her career.' My priority is my career."

His words still haunted her. Every time a man had shown interest in her, she'd remember those words, remembered the pain of loving only to have to make a choice between the man and her God-given path. And her choice would always be the same.

Her life was about making a difference, about being a doctor.

"Rachel, I'm—"

"You're what? Sorry?" Rachel scoffed, her strength rapidly depleting. "Don't be. You were right. I wouldn't have accomplished what I have if I'd married or stayed in this town." She couldn't stand the pity in his eyes but hated even more that she'd validated his position on her career.

She closed the book.

Josh tipped the box forward. "There's something else in here."

She watched as he pulled a large manila envelope from the box and handed it to her. Anxious to get through this, she broke the seal and grabbed an official-looking file. Her name stared at her from the tab.

Ignoring the prickling awareness of Josh's gaze, she flipped open the file. The contents marked her progress through the Department of Child Services, starting with the day she became a ward of the state and continued on, noting every foster home with comments by the foster parents. She quickly read and absorbed the words. For out of the five homes she'd lived in, the comments were nearly the same: *"The child cooperates well, is very quiet and insecure."*

Rachel's mouth twisted. More like scared to death.

Mom G.'s name appeared as the last foster home. The remarks made by Mom G. touched Rachel deeply. To Mom G. she wasn't "the child," she was Rachel. A little girl who needed love and affection.

With a snap, she closed the file. She wasn't a little girl anymore, but a grown woman who just lost the last bit of family she'd ever known.

The hospital. The people there would be her family now. Her focus would be entirely on the patients, and their care, with no distractions.

Impatiently she dumped out the rest of the manila envelope. A hospital bracelet with her mother's name and the blue and white insignia of Sonora Community Hospital, a birth certificate and a small grouping of photos fell out.

Her breath caught in her throat. With shaky hands, she reached for the top snapshot. The woman in the picture had curly hair, which framed her face, and blue eyes sparkling with intelligence.

"Is this your mother?"

She nodded, afraid that if she spoke he'd hear her anguish. She had one picture of her mother that the social worker had given to her. It sat on her bedside table in a crystal frame.

"You look like her."

The compliment nearly shattered her composure.

Gathering every vestige of her control, she spread the rest of the photos out on the table. Five in all. "I've never seen these. I wonder why Mom G. never gave them to me."

"Maybe she thought they'd make you sad."

In one frame, her mother stood on a beach staring out at the waves, her expression pensive. In another, her mother held a tiny baby wrapped in a pink blanket. The next was a park setting. A two-year-old Rachel sat on a swing, her mother behind her, joyous smiles on both of their faces. The last photo was of her mother, dressed up and looking like a princess.

"I wonder if my father took these?" Everything hurt inside and she willed the pain away.

Josh took her hand. His fingers wrapped around hers, anchoring her as the tide of grief began to rise within her.

"I don't even know who he was, Josh. What he'd been like. Why he'd left."

"I didn't know," he responded softly. "You'd said he was gone. I'd assumed he was dead."

"He was gone before I was born." She picked up the birth certificate. Her own. She pointed to the line where her father's name should have been. "'Unknown'?" Her voice rose, betraying the anguish building in her chest.

At sixteen she'd needed her birth certificate for her driver's license. Any hopes or plans she had of seeking her father out died when she'd seen that one word. "I can't accept he was some stranger my mother hadn't loved. Some one-night-stand type of deal."

"Maybe he hadn't known she was pregnant when they broke up."

Josh's compassionate reasoning left her with more questions. "Were they even married? Or just dating? Did they fight? Is that why she didn't want him to be a part of my life?" She suppressed a shuddering breath. "I'll never know. The answers died with her."

Rachel's heart throbbed with longing. She had spent such a short part of her life with the woman in the photos. "I don't even know what she was like. What had been her dreams, her struggles? There's no one for me to ask. She hadn't had any family that I could find."

A tear slipped down her cheek and landed on the corner of one picture. The wetness distorted the film, like the tears in her eyes distorted her vision. Josh's arm came around her shoulders and a distressed moan escaped her lips.

Rachel didn't want him to witness her private breakdown. She didn't want to need his strength, his warmth. She tried to pull away but he wouldn't let go. His grip tightened and he eased her back against his solid chest. She resisted by leaning away from him.

"Rachel," he coaxed, his voice tender, caressing.

Everything inside screamed for her to protest, to run and seek solitude for her grief. She didn't need anyone. Yet his steadfast, comforting presence beckoned to her. She sniffed and shuddered as she tried to keep control of the tears.

When he turned her around, she dropped her gaze to the front of his shirt. She couldn't look into that handsome face and see the sympathy in his eyes. His hand reached out and gently lifted her chin. She almost died to see the tender caring in his hazel eyes. Everything inside melted liked chocolate over an open flame.

"It's okay to cry, Rachel."

His compassionate words brought fresh tears. "No. I'm not crying," she sniffed.

"Stubborn woman," he muttered softly as he pulled her to him. "You have to let it out or it will eat away at you."

Rachel held herself stiff against his chest, but as his hand caressed her hair, and his heart beat a steady cadence against her cheek, her staid control slipped away. She wrapped her arms around him and a tremor worked its way through her body and a deep sob broke free.

She cried for the two mothers she'd lost.

As her sobs receded and the tears dried, she became acutely aware of Josh's arms holding her tight. The once-familiar pressure of his embrace made her snuggle closer. His woodsy, clean scent filled her senses. She clung to him.

She should let go. She should find her composure and graciously extract herself from his embrace. But she didn't want to, couldn't because of an inner need beyond her stalwart control.

Chapter Eight

Rachel eased back and looked up at him. He stared down at her with careful regard. How could he look at her with such tenderness when the heat in his eyes threatened to singe?

Her clinical mind registered that focusing on Josh kept her from dwelling on her mother's life so tragically cut short. Focusing on Josh kept the overwhelming grief of Mom G.'s death from engulfing her. Focusing on Josh made her heart pound and her limbs tingle with anticipation. Anticipation for what she didn't know. It went beyond the physical, to a heart-rending level. And it scared her.

She hated being scared.

In defense, her mind focused on the obvious—the awareness that overtook her every time he was near. As foolish as it was, she wanted to know what it would be like to kiss him as an adult, as a woman.

Before her brain could protest, she leaned forward and touched her lips to his.

An electric jolt sizzled between them.

Josh flinched.

Rachel tightened her hold around his waist and continued the kiss. Slowly, gently, he responded. His lips moved over hers with drugging intensity and she realized immediately she'd made a mistake.

Kissing him was far more potent than she'd imagined. She wouldn't just be burned, she'd turn to ash.

As Josh broke the kiss with a tortured sound, rejection settled at the bottom of Rachel's heart like a rock in a pool. Of course he didn't want her. He never really had.

She pulled away from him and took a deep breath, collecting herself. "I'm sorry. That was totally inappropriate."

His jaw clenched. "Why did you kiss me?"

"I—to distract myself from the pain," she admitted and wiped at her damp cheeks.

His guarded expression ripped at her insides.

She quickly gathered the photos and slid them back into the envelope.

A gigantic boulder lodged itself in the middle of Josh's chest as he watched Rachel. Taut lines of anxiety tightened around her mouth. Her struggle to maintain control was painful to watch. He hurt for her, could only imagine the depth of torment she carried. He'd never realized how devastating her mother's death had been to her. And to find out she didn't know her father's name—it blew his mind. His own mother had abandoned them, but at least at one time he had belonged to her. Rachel didn't even have that. His heart twisted with sympathy and a protectiveness surged through him. Mrs. G. had fulfilled the roles of both mother and father for Rachel, but now she was gone. It was up to him to be there for Rachel. If she'd let him.

She'd already expressed that she didn't want his comfort and he'd tried to give her space. But when she'd cried, his promise came slamming back to him. Mrs. G. had known what they'd find. That was why she'd insisted on their promise. He was honor-bound to offer his comfort and protection regardless of the cost to himself.

And cost him it did.

In the past few hours he'd glimpsed another facet of Rachel. She was a woman of strong opinions and tastes. Funny and charming when the wall of ice was down. So in need of care and compassion.

Then to hold her, to feel the luxury of her arms wrapped around his waist, had made his soul ache with longing for what might have been. For what would never be.

He sternly reminded himself that he wasn't enough for this woman. What he had to offer hadn't been enough twelve years ago and it wouldn't be enough now.

Her career was on the fast track. Onward and upward. She'd made it clear her life held no room for marriage, no room for commitment. Her career was her priority. That seemed such a joyless and lonely existence.

But when she'd kissed him and he'd felt the splendid caress of her lips against his own, he'd known that keeping his heart safe from Rachel while trying to be there for her was going to take every ounce of strength he could muster, and then some. He sorely wished he could find strength in God, but he'd lost the right to ask for God's help.

So instead he decided to take the high road. "It's late."

Rachel replaced the lid to the box. "Yes. It's been a long day."

Josh stood. "You should get some rest."

A little crease appeared between her blue eyes. A wry chuckle escaped. "I don't think I'll get much sleep tonight."

"Do you want to take the box back to the hotel with you?"

She chewed her bottom lip and stared at the box. Tears glistened in her eyes, making the blue brighter. She didn't answer. He couldn't stand to see her in such pain.

He reached for her, pulling her in again to the shelter of his arms. She wasn't nearly as resistant, and his blood surged at how right it felt to hold her close. "Leave the box. It'll be here tomorrow."

She nodded and allowed him to lead her to his truck. They drove to the hotel in silence. He felt protective of her and didn't like the idea of her alone with only her memories for company. "I'll stay. I can sleep on the floor."

Her gaze jumped to his. "No. That won't be necessary."

"Maybe not necessary, but the right thing to do." And the hardest thing.

She gave him a small, gentle smile. "I always liked that about you."

"What?"

She touched her hand to his jaw, the touch feather light yet searing. "Your sense of honor."

His chest swelled from her compliment. "I try."

She cleared her throat. "You should go home."

She was right, because staying might lead to someplace neither one wanted to go. "You sure you'll be okay?"

She shrugged. "It's better this way. I really did appreciate your help tonight. I'm glad you insisted."

"Just keeping my promise," he said evenly, but deep down a voice whispered it was so much more than that.

Her mouth twisted. "Well, it's still appreciated." She pushed open the door of her unit. "Good night."

He stepped back. "I'll have Dad check in on you tomorrow."

Rachel hated the little spurt of hurt his words caused. A foolish part of her wanted him to check on her. "Fine. Great."

He touched her cheek, the slight pressure like a brand against her skin. She swallowed and forced herself not to lean into his touch.

"Call if you need anything."

She lifted her chin. "Of course."

His hand dropped away. "Good night, then."

And he walked away.

Rachel couldn't bear to watch his departure. She closed the door and slowly sank to her knees. She heard the roar of an engine turning over then the spray of gravel as he left the parking lot and drove away.

She hadn't felt this bereft since the day she'd learned he'd married Andrea. Mistakenly she'd thought focusing on her career had plugged the hole in her heart where her love for him had lived. But now she was left with a gaping abyss she didn't know how to heal.

And even if by some miracle she and Josh could find their way back to each other, she couldn't give up on the quest that had consumed her all her life, the task God had entrusted her with—to change the way things were done in the E.R. so that patients weren't needlessly lost.

And she couldn't do that in Sonora. She couldn't go into the E.R. where her mother had died. Not even God would ask that of her.

A line of Scripture came to mind and she clung to the promise in the simple words.

He heals the brokenhearted, binding up their wounds.

Peace and comfort would be hers, for God so promised. Her wounds would heal and she would return to her life, accepting the past and looking only to the future.

Without Josh.

The jingle of the phone roused Rachel from a fitful slumber. She opened eyes, gritty from crying herself to sleep, and glanced at the clock. Who would call at seven in the morning? Flipping to her back, she stared at the ceiling. Her body felt bruised, her eyes scratchy and she felt totally drained.

The phone jingled again. Rachel threw an irritated glance at the instrument sitting on the bedside table.

Even as depleted as her body and her emotions were, the steps of mourning that she'd gone through last night were necessary. She wasn't so presumptuous as to think she'd made it through the whole gamut of emotions that the grieving process produced, but her soul felt cleansed. She was ready to move on with her life. There were a few loose ends that needed her attention; then she could leave. Closure. Isn't that what they called it?

"You better not be bearing bad news," she muttered to the ringing phone, and picked up the receiver. "Hello."

"Is that you, Rachel?" a hesitant young boy's voice asked.

All irritation fled. "Yes. Griff, is that you?"

"It's me." His youthful exuberance returned full force into his voice. "Did I wake you?"

"Mmm-hmm," she answered on a yawn, and relaxed back on the pillow.

"Sorry, but I wanted to see if you'd go to Columbia with me today."

"Columbia?" The historic state park on the outskirts of Sonora was one of the finest restored mining towns in the county. She'd spent many weekends exploring the town. Once, in high school, her government class had held a mock trial in the old justice building. She'd been one of twelve students who sat in the old wooden chairs as jurors.

"Yeah, we could go gold-panning. Dad has to work and Grandpa doesn't want to go."

"Well…" she hedged. She'd love to spend time with Griff. She didn't have to be anywhere until later in the afternoon, when she signed the necessary paperwork to sell the house. She did have to call the shippers and Goodwill to arrange for the various boxes to be taken care of, but that wouldn't take long. And she loved to gold-pan. She and Josh had spent many hours at the task when they'd been younger.

"Will you go? Huh?" Griff's eager voice snagged her attention.

"Your dad's at work?"

"Yep, and summer vacation started yesterday. Grandpa has business in town and he said we could pick you up then he'd drop us off in Columbia."

It would be nice to see Rod again before she left. With Josh at work all day there wouldn't be any surprise meetings.

"I have to get up and dressed, then make a few phone calls."

"So you'll come with me?"

She laughed. "Yes. I'll go gold panning with you."

"Yahoo!"

Rachel held the phone away from her ear and grinned. Her mood lightened as energy seeped back into her body. Spending the day with Griff would make a good memory to take with her when she returned to Chicago.

"You sure you won't join us?"

"No, no. I gave up my gold-panning days long ago.

But I sure appreciate you taking Griff. He's been wanting to do this for some time." Rod's gold-specked eyes sparkled with life. Even in his sixties he was a good-looking man with his thick graying hair and ready grin.

Rachel smiled. "It's really great to see you."

Rod reached out and patted her arm. "Now, don't you worry none. We'll spend some time together before you head back to your big-city life."

The way he said it, her life in Chicago sounded glamorous. Too bad there wasn't anyone there waiting to spend time with her. A familiar sense of loneliness gnawed at the edges of her mind.

A warm smile creased Rod's weathered face. No one smiled at her with real affection in the big city.

"I'll be back in time to get you to your appointment. Don't you worry about that," he said.

"I'm not." She turned to Griff. "All set to hit the gold?"

Griff scrambled out of the car in answer. He looked adorable in his loose, navy cotton athletic shorts and yellow-and-red striped shirt. By the size of his once-white sneakers, Rachel knew he'd grow tall like his father. Her heart pinched a little every time she looked at Griff. He resembled his father so much.

She turned back to Rod. "What will you do with yourself now?"

"I'm meeting with Pastor Larkin today about some renovations the church council wants done to the building."

"Tell him hello for me. And thanks for driving."

"No problem. You guys have fun and I'll see you in a few hours."

Rachel slid from the car and watched Rod drive away, his old white Buick ambling down the road. Tenderness filled her. For the first time she acknowledged to herself that she'd missed out by not having a father figure in her life. Rod was as close as she'd ever come and she loved him for that.

Griff danced from one foot to the other with anticipation, drawing her attention. "Let's go." His eyes widened and he pointed. "There's the stagecoach. Can we take a ride on that, too?"

The jangle of the harnesses on two big chestnut horses and the crunching of large wooden wheels over the loose dirt road heralded the coach's arrival.

Catching the boy's enthusiasm, she laughed. "We can do anything your little heart desires."

"Yahoo!" He tugged her along eagerly.

Rachel was glad she'd worn her running shoes. She'd forgotten that the streets were unpaved, and dust clung to her feet. And she had a feeling Griff intended to run her feet off. She couldn't think of a better exercise. The wooden sidewalks creaked as they stepped up onto the planks and headed to the stagecoach office.

Rachel paid for their tickets and they walked back outside to wait for the stage.

"I'm so excited," Griff whispered, loud enough that several people smiled.

In a stage whisper, Rachel replied, "Me, too."

The coach arrived and let off its passengers. Rachel and Griff climbed aboard. Griff scrambled to sit by the window and Rachel took the seat next to him. Soon the coach was filled and they were off. A speaker in the side of the rig showed the only sign of modernization.

The driver's voice filled the stage.

"Welcome to Columbia State Park. In 1850 gold was discovered and the mining town exploded with activity."

Rachel's mind wandered as she watched Griff, excitement danced in his eyes as he pointed out the window at various passing interests. She hadn't thought much about having kids of her own, not after Josh had married Andrea. Having a family had been relegated to "someday." "Someday" had always seemed far away, though looking at Griff she couldn't stop the maternal stirring in her spirit. She would have liked to have seen Griff as an infant, a toddler and a preschooler. To watch him discover the world and to teach him all the wonders of life.

A knot formed in her stomach. Could she be a good mom and still make a difference?

There were female doctors at the hospital who had families. They managed to be both. Though men dominated the upper management of the hospital, she would find one of her female peers and discover the secret to having a successful career and family. Finding a man to have a family with wouldn't be as easy. Especially not after seeing Josh, feeling his touch, his kiss—

Thankfully, the voice of the driver interrupted her thoughts.

"In the 1940s, the Parks and Recreation Department acquired the downtown district and restored it to its

1850-to-1870-era appearance. You'll find many of the shopkeepers dressed in nineteenth-century garb."

The coach came to a rambling halt.

"We hope you enjoyed your ride," the driver said. "Have a fun time in town."

Rachel and Griff disembarked.

A flash of awareness whispered down her spine like a warm breeze. Puzzled by the strange sensation, she glanced around then asked, "Where to now?"

"Gold-panning."

"Mind if I join you?"

Rachel started at the familiar voice and turned to find Josh leaning against a wooden railing that once had served as the hitching post for horses. Today he wore black shorts, showing off his strong muscular legs, and a red T-shirt emphasizing his broad chest. He looked virile and handsome, making her feel self-conscious in her khaki shorts and scoop-necked blue T-shirt. She hadn't expected to see him and was shamefully pleased.

"Dad! 'Course we don't mind." Griff rubbed his hands together. "This is going to be so fun."

"I thought you were working today." Why did she sound so breathless?

He pushed away from the railing and strode toward her. A grin flashed, revealing his white teeth. "I decided to play hookey."

"What's hookey?" Griff asked.

Rachel met Josh's gaze and grinned, waiting to see how he'd explain that.

"Something we'll talk about when you're older."

"Aw, Dad. You always say that."

He gave her a pained look over Griff's head. She laughed, liking the shared moment.

"I thought we were gold-panning?" she said.

"Race you," shouted Griff as he tore down the road toward the end of town.

Josh let out a breath. "Sometimes being a parent keeps me on my toes."

"Blunder often, do you?" she teased.

"Only when I'm distracted by a pretty girl." He waggled his blond brows at her.

A blush crept into her cheeks. "Bad habit to have."

"Oh, I don't know." He put his arm around her shoulders and propelled her forward. "This is one habit I probably could get used to."

He was flirting with her and she liked it, even though it wasn't a good idea. He was still grieving and she lived thousands of miles away. She slanted him a glance and caught his gaze. The banked fire swirling in the depths of his eyes knocked the breath from her lungs. The day seemed suddenly ten degrees warmer as she felt an answering spark within her.

"Come on, you guys!" Griff yelled from the miner's shack front porch.

She blinked. A slow smile tipped one corner of Josh's mouth. He leaned close. She swallowed. Was he going to kiss her, here in front of everyone?

"Race ya," he whispered, and then started running.

"Hey," she shouted with a laugh as she made her legs go. They reached Griff at the same time, laughing and breathing hard. "I haven't felt like this in years."

Not since she'd left Josh behind.

His steady gaze bore into her in silent knowledge as if he'd heard her thought. She quickly glanced away, unwilling to confirm his suspicion.

Josh went inside and a few moments later returned with pans for each of them. They walked together to the small creek where the pleasant smell of pines mingled with the scent of wet earth.

For what seemed like hours they sifted through mud and dirt for any sparkling specks.

As they worked, Rachel enjoyed the natural way the three of them talked. She found out Griff dreamed to one day be a forest ranger like Josh and Rod. Griff's admiration for his father and grandfather was obvious.

Josh told stories about Rod and Mom. G. He spoke about his job and she could tell how much he liked the forestry service. She talked about being a doctor, but was careful to keep the focus light. She didn't want to ruin the easy camaraderie of the day with reminders of what her career meant to Josh.

At one point, she stopped to watch Josh help Griff with a big hard chunk of dirt. Their heads were bent together, their hands chipping away at the dirt. Would Josh ever remarry? She felt a little stab of jealousy for the woman who would capture his heart. She only hoped, for Griff's sake, Josh chose wisely.

"Well," Josh finally stood and stretched. "There's no getting rich quick for us." He glanced up at her. "Rachel, you okay?"

"Yes." She was determined to enjoy this time and not dwell on what couldn't be.

Griff stared at his empty pan with disappointment. "I thought for sure we would find some gold."

"How about finding some lunch?" Rachel suggested.

The pan forgotten, Griff's eyes lit up. "That sounds good. I'm starved."

"Me, too," Josh stated, his eyes trained on her.

She tugged on her bottom lip with her teeth and repressed a shiver as a charged current passed between them.

Feeling a little dazed, she followed the Taylors to a little deli that had been added to the storefront shops since the last time that Rachel had visited Columbia. They grabbed sandwiches and old-fashioned cream sodas.

When finished with their meal, they walked along the plank sidewalk, ducking into first a jewelry shop where they examined different sizes and shapes of gold nuggets. They continued on through town, looking at the antiques in one store, the tourist items in another. Then even went into the old jailhouse and marveled at the open jail cell with its thick black bars and single cot.

"This is what we need at home," Josh mused with a teasing glint in his eyes. "A barred cell for when you misbehave."

"Dad," Griff squeaked.

A rhythmic pulse bounced off the stone walls. Josh pulled a tiny flip phone from his shorts pocket. After a brief conversation, he hung up. "I need to go to the station."

To hide her disappointment that the day was coming

to an end, Rachel placed a hand on Griff's shoulder. "We'll be okay. Rod will be here shortly to pick us up."

"Right." His gazed searched her face. "This was fun, Rachel. I'm glad we were able to spend this time together."

"It *was* fun." More fun than she could remember having in years.

Josh hugged Griff and then sauntered away. Rachel stared after him, memorizing the way he walked, the way he carried himself. She didn't know when she'd see him again. And she didn't want to analyze how that made her feel.

"I know what we need," she said to Griff. "Candy."

His eyes grew wide. "That's right. We need candy."

The candy store was just as she remembered. Large glass cases filled to the brim with sweets. She recognized the sandy-blond-haired girl behind the counter as the younger sister of one of her old classmates. She surprised herself by asking, "Are you Kate?"

The girl cocked her head and squinted her brown eyes. "Do I know you?"

"I went to school with your brother Craig. My name's Rachel Maguire."

Recognition dawned in her eyes. "Hi, I remember you. You used to date Josh Taylor. Everyone was surprised when he married Andrea Marsh instead."

Rachel sucked in a breath. She placed her arm protectively around Griff's shoulders. "This is Josh and Andrea's son."

Kate smiled apologetically. "Oh, sorry."

Rachel wanted out of the store as quickly as

possible. "We'd like some taffy, please." She hoped Griff hadn't caught the meaning of the exchange. She felt a tug on her hand. "Hmmm?"

"Chocolate?" Griff whispered.

"Some chocolate, too, please."

Taking their candy, they sat under a tree on a wooden bench. They sat in silence for a few minutes as they savored their stash. She realized with a start that she was content, relaxed. For the moment she felt comfortable in her own skin. The only thing missing was Josh.

"You were supposed to marry my dad?"

Rachel swallowed the suddenly sticky taffy. Tensing, she chose her words carefully. "At one time we thought we'd get married."

"Why didn't you?"

She tried to explain. "Sometimes we make choices in our lives that take people in opposite directions. I had to make one of those choices."

"Why?"

"Because ever since I was a very little girl I wanted to be a doctor, and the school I wanted to go to was far away. Your dad wanted to stay here." Rachel hoped that answer appeased Griff's curiosity and he'd let the matter drop.

Silence stretched out between them. Griff turned solemn eyes upon her and Rachel braced herself.

"Would you marry my dad now and be my mom?"

Chapter Nine

Rachel's heart threatened to splinter into a million pieces. He didn't understand the impact or the impossibility of his question. "Honey, I don't need to be your mother to love you."

"But being my mom would be better."

But if she gave up on what she was doing, more children might lose their mothers. Rachel sighed. "Your dad and I aren't getting married."

"How come?"

"We have very different lives. I live in Chicago where I'm a doctor and your dad has a very important job here. It just wouldn't work out."

"You could be a doctor here," he pointed out with a stubborn tilt of his chin. The gesture, so similar to his father's, caused a pang of tenderness to shoot through her.

Even if she could make the changes that needed to be made, while working from a smaller hospital, it wasn't possible for her at Sonora Community. Her mother had died there. She couldn't work there. Josh would never accept the importance of her career and she couldn't give up what God wanted her to do.

In a gesture that was becoming less awkward, she put her arms around Griff's thin shoulders. "I'm flattered you want me to be your mom. That makes me very happy."

He relaxed into her embrace for a moment before pulling away to stare up at her. His earnest expression was breaking her heart. "Do you love my dad?"

"I…" Rachel didn't have the words to explain her feelings for Josh.

She supposed she'd always love him with one tiny corner of her heart. The tiny corner that housed her girlish dreams. The tiny corner where there once was a wound so big she'd thought she'd never survive the pain. Today that part of her had seemed whole and complete. But that tiny corner didn't matter because in their situation, love wasn't enough. It never had been and nothing had changed.

Searching for words, she settled for a simple truth, even though she knew it was a cop-out. "God teaches us to love everyone."

Griff nodded thoughtfully. "That's true, because God's love and He loved us so much He sent His only Son to die for us so that we can go to heaven to be with Him."

Rachel smiled at Griff. "Did you learn that in Sunday School?"

"Yes and no. Dad taught me about God's love first, then I heard it in Sunday school."

"Your dad's a smart man." She was glad to see Josh had imparted to his son the wonder of God's love. She could still vividly remember the first time she'd heard the gospel message and the impact it had had on her life once she really owned the promise in the words.

Mom G. had taken her to the Red Church right after she came to live in Sonora. The pastor had talked about Jesus and His death. She'd understood it, but hadn't really felt its connection to her.

Later, as she and Josh became close, he'd convinced her to join the youth group at church. There she began to comprehend the significance of God's mercy and grace and His redeeming love.

Glancing up from Griff, Rachel saw Rod walking toward them. "Here's your grandpa."

They stood and hurried to meet him.

"Hi. Did you have a good time?" Rod hugged his grandson and smiled over his head at Rachel.

"We sure did. Dad came to help, except we didn't find any gold," Griff told him.

If Rod was surprised that Josh had shown up, he didn't comment. Rachel suspected Rod had had a hand in Josh's appearance.

"Some days are like that. You'll find gold another time," Rod stated. "Right now, we'd better scoot or Rachel will be late."

Sitting inside Rod's car as it rambled away from Columbia, Rachel stared out the window. The smattering of huge white limestone boulders which miners, looking for gold, had once dredged out of the earth, stretched along the road between Sonora and the state park. Rachel knew that though the stones looked like a fun place to explore, the area was home to a large rattlesnake population. She'd found that out once the hard way.

Griff's continuous dialogue to Rod about their adventures drew Rachel's attention away from the countryside. As she listened to Griff recount the day, a stitch of sadness crept over her. It was the only time in her life she'd been a part of a child's adventures.

Rod pulled up in front of the brick law office of Mr. Finley. "We'll wait for you."

"You don't have to do that," Rachel replied as she climbed from the car, but secretly hoped they would wait. She really didn't want to be alone.

"Now, what kind of gentleman would I be if I didn't wait?" Rod grinned.

Rachel laughed with relief. "I shouldn't be too long." She hurried inside the old brick law firm.

For the sake of Griff and Rod, she blocked the swirling grief and sadness that hovered over her as she signed the necessary papers that established her as owner of Mom G.'s house and the papers that allowed the lawyer to act in her stead in the sale of the house.

She thanked Mr. Finley and quickly left. Sure enough, Rod and Griff were waiting. With a sense of homecoming that warmed and confused her, she climbed in the car and settled back against the seat. As Rod headed into the late afternoon downtown traffic, Rachel realized they were traveling in the opposite direction of her hotel. "Rod, where are we going?"

"I need to make a quick stop."

Rachel glanced at him sharply and caught the twinkle in his eye. What mischief was he up to?

He turned the car off the main street and onto a dirt road. Over a slight rise, a two-story Victorian house came into view. A large lush lawn stretched around the towering gray-and-white-trimmed house, an oak tree with a homemade wooden swing dangled from a low-hanging branch and cheery flowers grew in wooden flower beds along the porch. Everything looked well kept and cared for.

A black-and-white border collie came racing around the front of the old '65 Chevy pickup sitting off to the side of the driveway. Josh's house. The dog's welcoming barks and wagging tail told Rachel this was the family dog.

A flutter of nerves sent rippling waves across her skin.

"I just need to check something," Rod explained as he cut the engine and left the car.

"Want to see my garden?" Without waiting for an answer, Griff jumped from the car. With the dog barking a welcome at his heels, he disappeared behind the house.

Left alone, Rachel slowly emerged from the confines of the suddenly suffocating car. Her gaze took in the obvious love that had gone into the upkeep of the house and yard.

In the back of her mind a voice taunted her. *This is the house he'd shared with Andrea. The kind of house you could have had.*

Rachel pushed the thought away. She didn't regret the

choice she'd made; she loved being a doctor. But a sudden desire for more crept in, making her wonder what their life would have been like had she chosen differently.

"Rachel!"

She followed the sound of Griff's call to the backyard, which proved to be as closely tended as the front. Griff waved from the middle of a large patch of freshly tilled earth and a few rows of green plants. She skirted around a built-in pool and across another nicely mowed expanse of lawn to stand beside the raised garden bed. "Wow, Griff. This is great." She breathed deeply of the sweet country air.

"This is my garden and I'm the farmer," he said proudly.

"Looks wonderful, Farmer Griff. What have you planted?"

She listened patiently as he explained about the types of vegetables he'd planted. He seemed quite versed in the care and feeding of his plants. Was that Josh's doing or Rod's?

After a while, Rod appeared from around the house. "We better get you home. It's almost supper time."

"Could Rachel have dinner with us?" Griff asked as he wiped his hands on his shorts, leaving stripes of smeared dirt.

"Sure she can. That's a great idea." Rod turned his gaze on her. "You don't want to eat alone when you could dine with us handsome men, now, do you?"

She laughed, charmed. "Thank you, but..."

He looked at her intently. "You already have plans?"

"No. I don't want to intrude. I'm sure Josh wouldn't want to come home to find company for dinner." The excuse sounded lame, especially after the day they'd shared, but she couldn't stay. She couldn't see Josh again. She wasn't ready for another ride on the emotional roller coaster that she rode every time he was near. "I really must leave." She headed toward the car.

"But Dad won't mind." Griff and Rod fell into step with her. "He won't get home until late anyway."

Rod gave an assessing look. "We can take you home right after we eat."

"We can pick green beans from my garden. They taste so much better than the ones you get from the can," Griff added, his expression so earnest that Rachel stopped walking.

She bit her bottom lip. She didn't relish being alone any more than she had to. A problem she'd never experienced in Chicago. But she wasn't in Chicago, where her fast-paced world kept her from dwelling on things like loneliness and isolation. She decided to go with her current need. Besides, she wasn't ready for her time with Griff to end. She wanted to make the most of the memories.

"All right, let's go pick us some green beans."

Rod smiled with approval. She blushed and hurried after Griff, ignoring the certainty that leaving had just become that much harder.

Oh, Rachel. What are you doing?

The aroma of spaghetti sauce and warm bread greeted Josh when he walked through the front door.

Laughter drifted in from the kitchen. Feminine laughter.

His brows snapped together. His father had left a message saying they needed Josh home right away.

As he made his way through the house, he could hear voices. His father's, Griff's and then a voice he'd thought he'd never hear in his home: Rachel's.

His father, it seemed, had taken up the matchmaking business where Mrs. G. had left off. But their efforts would never pay off, regardless of how easy and natural it felt to be in her company.

When his dad had told him that Griff and Rachel were at Columbia, all he could think about were the times they'd spent there years ago and how much he wanted to spend the day with Rachel and his son.

He'd wanted to make sure she was okay after the revelations of the day before; at least that's how he'd rationalized his need to be with them. It had been sweet torture. He hadn't wanted it to end. Reality really stank at times.

Rounding the corner to the kitchen, he stopped in the doorway. Griff stood on a chair in front of a large pot on the stove with a spoon in his hand. Rachel was leaning over his shoulder, his father's barbecue apron double-wrapped around her slim waist. One of Josh's old bandanas held back her ebony hair.

For a moment, dizziness swept through him. Seeing Rachel and Griff together, their heads bent close, made his heart ache. This was what he wanted. A wife to raise his son and a woman who would be passionate about their family, about him. A warm woman to love, who would want his love.

He gave himself a shake.

Rachel was not that person. Her career was her priority. She'd made that perfectly clear. She would never be content living here with them no matter how much fun they had together.

He exhaled slowly, finally remembering to breathe, and met his father's knowing gaze. Josh narrowed his eyes with silent reprimand. Rod shrugged, but his eyes held mirth and mischief.

"I didn't know we were having company tonight," Josh commented as he stepped fully into the room.

Rachel turned quickly toward him, her eyes wide. Obviously she wasn't a willing participant in his father's matchmaking scheme. Not that she'd ever agree to such a thing. She'd claimed she didn't need anyone and Josh pitied her for that. He'd have self-destructed long ago if not for his father, Griff and Mrs. G.

Sadness for Rachel, for the blows she'd sustained in the past few days and for her insistence of a solitary life, weighed heavily on his heart. She deserved his compassion and understanding. He'd made her laugh today. He'd do what he could to keep things light between them.

Griff waved the spoon, sending red sauce spraying everywhere. "Hi, Dad. What are you doing home so early? We didn't think you'd be home 'til late."

A splatter of sauce landed on Rachel's cheek but she didn't seem to notice. Her gaze pierced him. Her blue eyes darkened and her lips parted slightly. He recognized that look. The same one she'd had before she'd kissed him. It was a look that told him she saw him as a man in the here and now, not just as some guy from her past.

The uncomfortable pounding of his heart made thinking difficult. He broke the eye contact with Rachel and forced himself to answer his son. "I got a message—"

Rod cleared his throat, cutting him off. Josh shook his head at his father's antics. This had to stop. He and Rachel weren't going to get back together. The sooner his father accepted reality the better.

In a sudden flurry of activity, Rachel pulled off the apron, moved to the sink and washed her hands. "I think I should be leaving now. You gentlemen enjoy your dinner." She moved to the back door and then stopped. Slowly she turned around. "Uh, Rod, would you mind taking me back to the hotel?"

Eyebrows raised in innocent surprise, Rod asked, "Couldn't we wait until after we eat? I'm hungry." He deliberately moved to the table and sat down.

Her gaze darted between the men. She swallowed. "I don't want to intrude."

Josh moved to the sink and washed his hands. Her gaze remained on him and he sensed her reluctance. "I'll take you back after dinner, Rachel."

She pulled her lip between her teeth, looking a little forlorn and uncertain. Surprise flickered through him. Seeing the moment of vulnerability touched him, making him want to take her in his arms and hold her. If they could recapture a fraction of the comfortable and easy atmosphere they'd shared earlier in the day, then he could let her go.

"Stay and eat, please." He smiled reassuringly and stepped closer.

She stepped back, bumping into the door. She gazed up at him and blinked. Slowly, so to not send her running, he reached out and wiped the red smear of sauce from her cheek with his index finger. She swallowed. He held up his finger. "Sauce," he said, his voice low.

She nodded, her lips parted. Josh fought the urge to kiss her. To recapture the blissful torture she'd inflicted upon him the other day. Abruptly he stepped back. Kissing her in front of his son and father was not a good idea. In fact, kissing her at all was a very bad idea. It would only heighten his attraction to her and complicate an already complicated situation.

He held out a chair at the table. "Sit, Rachel."

A mutinous expression came over her lovely face. "You sit." A spark of spunk flashed in her bright blue gaze.

"Are you going to serve us?" he teased, and liked the way she flushed in response.

She squared her shoulders and drew herself up, once again appearing cool and aloof. "No, I'm not going to serve you. You can set the table and get some serving dishes." Her tone softened as she looked at Griff. "You can come down from there and join your grandfather at the table." She threw Rod a murderous look before moving to the stove.

Josh hid his amused smile. She was something special. Running cold yet she could send his blood pressure skyrocketing with one smoldering glance. He staunchly forced himself to squelch the fierce need welling inside. He had no business allowing his feelings to run amok. She would be leaving soon, and he was not going to pine away for her a second time in his life.

He set the table and then tried to help her transfer the food onto the dishes, but she batted him away. "Utensils?" she asked.

"Yes, ma'am." He gave her a mock salute. She rolled her eyes but a smile played at the corners of her mouth, softening her features, reminding him of their day together. He'd liked the way they'd teased and flirted, like the way being with her had felt so right.

When all was ready, they sat. Josh took Griff's hand and then held out his other hand to Rachel.

She blinked.

Josh raised a brow. "For grace."

"Oh," she murmured before slipping her hand into his.

"Dad, would you do the honors?"

His father said the blessing over their food and thanked God for His abundance. In unison they agreed, "Amen."

Rachel gently tugged her hand from Josh's grip. He missed the contact and called himself a fool for wanting more.

Silence filled the kitchen as all four went about the business of eating.

"Yum," said Griff around a mouthful of spaghetti.

"This is delicious," agreed Rod.

"Wonderful," Josh added with approval.

Rachel blushed becomingly. "Thank you."

Josh couldn't take his eyes off her. Sitting with Rachel in his kitchen, at his table, as if they were a family, squeezed his chest. A shiver tripped down his spine, reminding him that letting down his guard, letting their relationship become something personal and intimate, was dangerous.

This woman had broken his heart once. He didn't want the past to repeat itself. He didn't want to be faced with not being enough.

His gaze swung from his son to Rachel and back. The look of adoration in Griff's eyes hit Josh in the gut. He had to protect his son from a broken heart. Rachel was good at breaking hearts. He cleared his throat. He decided to get things out in the open. Leave no illusions for Griff or himself. "When are you leaving, Rachel?"

She stilled. "After dinner."

He shook his head. "I mean leaving town. Going back to Chicago."

"Oh." She picked up her glass and sipped the water, her gaze chilly over the rim. "In a day or two. I have a shipping company coming tomorrow and Goodwill's also sending out a truck, but they weren't sure of the time. Why?"

"Just curious."

Her look said she didn't believe him, but he didn't elaborate. Two days. Two days and then she'd go back to her life, leaving him behind again. Only this time he wouldn't ache and hurt like he had the first time. This time he wouldn't allow himself to feel the emptiness that had engulfed him years ago. And bigger mountains had been moved before.

Griff stabbed a forkful of green beans and waved them toward Josh.

He raised a brow. "Yes?"

"Rachel and I picked these out of the garden."

At the tender smile she gave Griff, a shaft of envy shot through Josh, surprising him with its intensity. He longed to have her smile at him in such a way that would soften the lines around her mouth and make her blue eyes glow with affection.

The look of respect and admiration in her eyes sent him reeling. "A garden's a good thing for a child to have. To eat from the plants that he takes care of. You're a good father, Josh."

A slow rush of heat spread up his neck. "Thank you," he said quietly.

Awkward silence arced between them. Josh caught his father's knowing, pleased smile and quickly looked away. He didn't want to see the hope flaring behind the amusement.

"When I bought this house, I told Griff he could plant anything he wanted."

"That's right," Griff piped in. "I chose the green beans, cantaloupe and watermelon. The corn and the tomatoes were Grandpa's idea."

"Well, what's a garden without corn or tomatoes?" Rod interjected.

"When did you buy this place?" Rachel asked in a tight voice.

Josh shrugged. "About four years ago."

Her mouth went slightly slack. Josh waited for her to explain her obvious surprise. Instead, she bit into her bread and concentrated on chewing.

"Dad, after dinner can I show Rachel the pictures of you guys in the attic?"

Her head snapped up.

Josh frowned and shook his head. "No, I'm sure she isn't interested in going down memory lane. Those pictures are for us, son."

That Griff knew about the box of pictures tucked away upstairs surprised Josh, and he made a mental note to ask his son how he'd discovered them when he wasn't allowed in the attic. Josh hadn't realized until they'd all moved into this house together that his father had kept Josh's yearbooks and memorabilia from high school, including pictures of him and Rachel.

He noted with interest the flare of curiosity in Rachel's eyes before she averted her gaze and studied her near-empty plate.

As they finished the meal and cleared the table, Rachel touched Rod's arm. "I'm ready to go."

Josh leaned against the sink and exchanged a look with his father. "I'll take you."

She barely glanced at him. "I don't think—"

"Dad's eyesight at night isn't what it used to be." Josh received a pained look from his father. Though it was true his father did have to wear glasses to drive at night, he could have driven her back, but Josh wanted the opportunity to make sure they agreed on keeping their promise to Mrs. G.

Rachel sent Rod a questioning look. He held up his hands in a gesture of "What can I say?"

Griff bounced from his chair. "Can I go, too, Dad?"

"Yes," Rachel said a little desperately.

"No," Josh said just as quickly.

Griff's gaze swung between the two adults.

"No," Josh repeated. "You need to stay and help Grandpa clean up."

Rod put a hand on Griff's shoulder. "I'll wash, you dry."

Josh opened the door for Rachel. "After you."

Rachel gave Griff a hug. "Thanks for today. I really enjoyed it."

He hugged her back fiercely. "Will I see you before you leave?"

Josh's heart twisted. His son needed a mother. If only— He broke the thought off. God would provide what Griff needed.

As for himself...

Heaven only knew what God had planned for him. But Josh was sure it didn't include Rachel.

Chapter Ten

"I don't know if you'll see me again." Rachel kissed the top of Griff's head and Josh could have sworn she had tears in her eyes. "I'll at least call you to say goodbye if you don't."

Griff smiled sadly. "Okay."

She gave Rod a peck on the cheek. Josh inclined his head as she moved past him and left the house.

"Dad?"

Josh paused. "Yes, son."

"I like Rachel."

His heart stalled for a moment and he nodded, not sure what to say.

Griff cocked his head. "Do you?"

Everything stilled inside Josh. At Griff's intent expression, he stepped closer and knelt down so they were at eye level. The innocently asked question deserved a truthful, uncomplicated answer. "Yes."

"You used to love her, right?"

Josh swallowed as his heart began to thud erratically in his chest. Warily he nodded again.

"Do you still?"

He couldn't go there right now. That question couldn't be answered in uncomplicated terms. "Griff, this isn't the time for this discussion."

"But, Dad, do you?" Griff insisted, his expression earnest and unshakable.

"I…why?"

Griff launched himself at Josh, his small arms encircling his neck. "I don't want her to go." Griff buried his face into Josh's shoulder.

Pain sliced a jagged tear through Josh as he held his son and closed his eyes. He should have seen this coming. He couldn't do anything about what was done, but there was no way he could allow it to happen again.

They would get through this together, he and his son. Just as he and his father had made it through his mother's departure from their lives.

"Shh now." He wiped Griff's tears away. "When I get home we'll talk some more. I need you to be strong now."

Griff nodded. Rod came and placed an arm around the boy's shoulders as Josh stood. "You go on. Rachel's waiting. We'll be just fine, won't we, Griff?"

Wiping at his nose, Griff mumbled, "Sure."

With a heavy heart Josh left the house. He was determined to protect his son, even if it meant breaking his promise to Mrs. G.

Rachel pushed away from the truck and allowed Josh to unlock the passenger door. She noticed there was a distance in his eyes that hadn't been there before, and tiny lines framed the corners of his mouth.

She climbed into the cab. With a decisive snap he shut the door he'd held open for her. She flinched.

In the setting sun, she watched him walk around the front of the truck. His honey-blond hair shone in the sun's waning rays and her heart skipped a beat. He was handsome in a rugged, outdoorsy sort of way that she found very appealing.

Since the moment he'd walked into the kitchen in his ranger's uniform, she'd been having trouble remembering that nothing good would come of getting close to him. Instead, her fanciful mind skipped off with thoughts of what it would be like to live in that house and wait for him to come home from work every night. In the house he *hadn't* shared with Andrea.

She couldn't explain why that news had sent such pleasure ricocheting through her.

Josh climbed in and started the engine. He eased the truck out of the driveway and onto the road. They rode in unsettling silence until Rachel couldn't stand it. "You've done a fine job with Griff."

"So you said," he replied tersely.

They lapsed back into silence. Where was the fun and teasing man she'd spent the day with?

"Rachel."

His tone set her on wary alert. She studied his profile. His jaw tightened into a grim line. She waited. The silence stretched out. She watched his expression shift ever so slightly, as if he was struggling for the words. Finally he let out a quick breath. "I can't do this."

His words were so quiet, she might have missed what he'd said if she hadn't been anticipating something. "What can't you do?"

He took a deep breath and exhaled slowly. "I'm not going to be able to keep my promise. Not at the expense of my son."

She blinked. "I don't understand."

"Griff's the most important thing in my life. I have to protect my son."

"What do you have to protect him from?" She held her breath, not sure where he was going with this.

"I have to protect him from you."

She drew back, stung. "Me? You're not making sense."

"He likes you and he's becoming too attached to you. Today wasn't a good idea. It would be best if you kept your distance from him until you leave."

His words were a slap across the face. What had she done to warrant such a warning? She quickly thought back over the day. Nothing justified Josh's attitude. She liked Griff and the boy liked her. What was wrong with that?

She stared at Josh in speculation. Why was he reacting like this? Did Josh think Griff wouldn't understand why she had to go back to Chicago? "I think you underestimate your son. I explained to him about my leaving. He understands why I can't stay."

"You've discussed this with him?" His voice sounded strained.

"Yes. He's a sweet child and I was touched he'd want to have me as a mother, but we talked about why that was impossible and he understood the situation."

Josh slowed the truck and pulled to the side of the road. He gripped the steering wheel tightly. "He asked you to be his *mother?*"

Uh-oh. She shouldn't have said anything. But he should know what was going on inside his son's head. "Well, yes. Though I think his asking has more to do with losing Mom G. than with me. A boy needs a mother, and he's just lost the only mother figure he's known."

Josh's jaw tightened, and his displeasure surged toward her in waves. She empathized with his need to safeguard his son's well-being, but Josh also had to understand that the boy needed more in his life. "Griff's starved for female attention. You know what it's like to grow up without a mother."

"I turned out fine," he said between clenched teeth.

"Like you're not full of anger and bitterness," she tossed out, shaking her head in disbelief. "I know how hard it was on you to grow up without your mother."

His eyes narrowed, and the angles in his face hardened. She wondered why he didn't crack under the strain of controlling his temper.

"We're talking about Griff," he grated out, the words harsh and low. "I don't want you to break his heart."

She exhaled a breath in exasperation. "I'm not going to break his heart. Why would you think I'd do such a thing?"

"Because you're good at it," he barked. "Really, really good at it."

Rachel gaped. "Excuse me? I think you need a history lesson, buddy."

"Yeah, right. You're the one who left me, remember?"

"Whoa." She held up a hand. She couldn't believe he had the audacity to suggest she'd broken his heart. "You knew from the day you met me where my life was headed."

He stared out the front window, his expression no less hard than before.

She should let it drop and leave as quickly as possible, and never look back. She knew she should. But she couldn't. She always met a challenge head-on. "You knew I wanted to be a doctor, but you thought our love should be enough for me. Sorry to burst your bubble. This is the twenty-first century, Josh. Women aren't expected to be content barefoot, pregnant and in the kitchen. Your archaic ideas of what a wife and mother should be need an update."

Josh closed his eyes as if in pain. If what she'd said got him thinking, then the twinge of guilt she felt for hurting him was worth the price.

"You need a wake-up call. If not for yourself, then for Griff. I dread thinking Griff will grow up believing that women shouldn't have a life outside of family. I don't want Griff to end up alone and lonely like his father."

He flinched, and with a little shock, she realized that was exactly how she saw Josh. Alone and lonely, a lot like her, yet he was so stubborn that he probably didn't realize how miserable he was.

She didn't want to care, fought against the softening in her heart. The tiny corner where her teenage fantasies lived seemed to expand, making her chest hurt. Letting any amount of feeling grow was not smart.

And she was a smart woman.

So why did she find it so hard to stop the unwanted emotions from bouncing around, wreaking havoc with her resolve not to care, not to wish there were some way she could help him to find happiness?

He faced her, his expression haggard. "What's wrong with wanting to be the priority in someone's life?"

She sighed. "Nothing. I'm sure Andrea fit the bill perfectly."

He froze, the light of anger in his eyes turned into a raging inferno. "I don't want to talk about her."

Rachel regretted her biting words that stirred up his grief. "I'm sorry. That was uncalled for. I wish you luck in finding the next perfect woman."

"I'm not looking for perfection. I want someone whose priority will be her family. I want…" He shook his head and made a dismissive gesture with his hand. "It doesn't matter."

It doesn't matter. She stiffened. He might as well have said, "you don't matter." Because what he wanted they both knew she couldn't deliver. "My career's my priority. It will always be my priority. It has to be. I have no choice. Can't you see that?"

He surprised her by running a knuckle gently down her cheek, the heat of his touch like a brand.

"I do see. But at what cost?"

"Cost?" She drew away from him. "There's no cost. This is what God wants of me. Making a difference is what my life's about. Why can't you understand that?"

"But life has so much more to offer than work. I can't believe that's all God has planned for you."

His words brought reverberations of her conversation with Mom G. slamming into her consciousness. She hated the little flutter of…hope…battering around her heart because it threatened her career. But more importantly, she wanted to believe in the hope. "'More' as in you?"

He sat back, his hands once again tightly gripping the steering wheel. "No."

That one simple word sliced through her like an out-of-control surgeon slicing a vital organ with a scalpel. Swallowing a gasp of pain, she stared at his strong profile. Shadows deepened the contours and accentuated the angles. Her heart bled.

"No, I am quite aware that the time we've shared these past few days has led us to a dead end," he stated, his tone less harsh. "'More' as in enjoying life. Where's the joy in your life?"

She closed her eyes against the certainty that there would never be a future for them and asked, "What makes you think I don't enjoy my life?"

Staring straight ahead, he sighed. "Your intentions are honorable, I'll give you that."

She opened her eyes and raised her chin. "But…?"

He turned to stare at her, his eyes burning like hot coals in the dark. "There are other ways of making a difference."

"Not for me. There's no other option." She couldn't go against what God wanted, any more than she could stop breathing.

Without further comment he started the engine and drove to the hotel. She was thankful for the reprieve from her own torturous thoughts, and when the truck swung into the parking lot, she had the door partly opened before they came to a stop. She hopped out and turned to say goodbye. Discomfited, she watched Josh open his door and climb out.

"You don't have to walk me to the door, Josh. This isn't a date." She walked past him and up the stairs.

He stopped at the foot of the steps. "You're right, Rachel, this isn't a date. It's a goodbye."

Her heart twisted at the finality in his words. But saying goodbye now was for the best. She didn't think her heart could stand this emotional upheaval anymore. She wanted her nice, controlled existence back. Wanted to be back where she knew what was what and had everything lined up with no risk of heartache. She needed the detachment that had served her well over the years. With supreme effort, she managed to sound cool. "Goodbye."

Josh crossed his arms over his broad chest. "You'll let me know how you're doing when you get back?"

She arched a brow. "I thought you'd decided you couldn't keep your promise?"

"Not while you're in town."

Her gaze lifted away from him standing there so closed off, and settled on the half-moon high in the sky. "I see."

But she didn't really. Was he having as much trouble keeping his heart from aching for her as she was for him? A small wry laugh escaped. Who was she kidding? Josh had made it abundantly clear he didn't want her. Two days at the most and she could resume her life. "Goodbye, Josh." She fumbled for her key.

Josh approached and she braced herself.

He laid a hot hand on her shoulder. "I didn't mean to hurt your feelings."

She closed her eyes against the soul-searing pain of his touch. "You didn't."

The denial rang false as she sniffed back tears. Where was her composure, her resolve not to allow him to affect her? She'd been away from her job too long. She wasn't herself. This person who always seemed on the verge of tears wasn't her. She feared she'd lose her effectiveness as a doctor if this penchant for emotions continued. She didn't want to feel. She didn't want to want him.

He turned her around. "Rachel, I'm sorry."

She wouldn't ever be able to forget him. He'd always been in her life, a shadowy figure that other men had fallen short of. Too bad it had taken until today for her to realize it. All this time she hadn't wanted him to take root in her heart when he'd already been there. Angry with him, angry with herself, her temper rose. "Sorry you made a promise you don't want to keep?"

His gaze narrowed before his face settled into that neutral expression she hated. He stepped back. The two-foot distance between them seemed as wide as California. He didn't deny her accusations, didn't defend himself. "God go with you, Rachel. I hope you find peace in your life."

He walked down the stairs and was halfway to his

truck before she managed to react. How dare he be magnanimous and wish her well. She'd find peace all right. God would see to that. *As long as you aren't in my life, Josh Taylor, I'll be just fine.*

As she watched him drive his truck away, she prayed she wasn't deluding herself. She *would* be fine without Josh Taylor. She had to be.

The next morning as she watched the moving van being loaded with the items she'd chosen to keep, stark reality hit. With Mom G.'s passing, she mattered to no one. Rachel was truly on her own.

Who would claim any of her possessions as mementos of her life when she was gone? Sadly, no one. No one who would care. No one would mourn her passing. A desolate and vacant hole formed in her heart, making her acutely aware of how alone in life she really was.

After the van disappeared down the driveway, she entered the house to stare at the piles of stuff that would be donated to Goodwill.

So many things accumulated over a lifetime and yet, what value did possessions really have? Mom G. would be in heaven now; her reward for living a life expressing Jesus' love would be a beautiful crown with many jewels upon her head. One of those jewels would be for Rachel, for taking in and loving an unwanted child.

What treasure was she laying for herself up in heaven? Saving the lives of people she didn't know and didn't love? There was merit in her work. But where was the love?

The stillness of the house, the tomblike quiet, made Rachel edgy. Even the exercises that normally calmed her mind and body did little to offer rest for her harried thoughts. She missed Griff, missed his generous affection and easy laughter.

She could admit that easily enough, though thoughts of Griff always led back to Josh. To the miniscule area that harbored feelings that weren't wanted. To his stubborn refusal to give an inch toward accepting her need to be a doctor.

She resigned herself to knowing he would never comprehend what her career meant to her. And she accepted that Josh wasn't to be a part of her life.

The next day, after the Goodwill truck had left and Mom G.'s house was empty, Rachel returned to her hotel. Restless, and needing to get out of the quiet hotel room, she donned the running shoes she'd packed and set out.

She worked up a sweat running on the country roads that wound around the town of Sonora. Her lungs filled with the smog-free air and her senses took in the scenic tranquillity of the verdant trees, foliage and quaint homes along the way.

She ran for hours, occasionally slowing to a walk to sip from the water bottle attached to her fanny pack, before resuming her heart-pounding pace, trying to outrun the memory of Josh's goodbye.

Late in the afternoon, with muscles quivering, Rachel's pace became a brisk stroll as she talked with God, asking for wisdom and guidance. *Josh, doesn't want me and I can't walk away from the work I'm doing. Lord, I don't understand. What is it You want from me?*

Her heart beat wildly though the adrenaline from her run had long dissipated. She felt as if she stood on the brink of understanding and one little nudge...

She raised her gaze heavenward hoping for enlightenment and noticed that in the distance a discernible gray trail of smoke wound its way toward the sky. She frowned. Fire season had started early this year.

The beep of a horn drew her attention. Rod's Buick pulled to the side of the street. He gestured to her.

"Hi." The pleasure of seeing a friendly face gladdened her heart.

"Griff's in trouble," Rod stated tersely.

Apprehension uncoiled in her veins. "What's wrong?"

"He got separated from his Boy Scout troop. They went hiking up at the lake and I'm worried." Rod pointed toward the front window.

She lifted her gaze toward the rising smoke over the mountain ridge. Her heart pounded in her ears. "He's out there?"

Rod nodded. "Will you come?"

Without answering she opened the door and climbed in. *Dear Lord, put Your angels around Griff and keep him safe.*

As the car sped away, Rachel tried not to think what would happen to Josh if he lost Griff, too.

Josh stared at the map hanging on the wall of the ranger's station conference room. Several red thumbtacks stuck out, indicating the locations of his crews. They'd been working furiously to contain the sudden heat fire that engulfed the woods around Cherry Lake.

He hated to think of the damage being done. The acres of trees and wildlife being destroyed. Beyond the destruction of the forest, he knew the fire might cause human fatality. The beauty of the lake attracted day hikers and backpackers alike. The search and rescue teams had been deployed.

These situations were never good when people could be trapped. Families out for the day, overnight hikers, scout troops—thank goodness Griff's troop went to Pine Mountain Lake today—and teens. Teens like he and Rachel had been, seeking privacy for hot kisses and carving names into trees. Hopefully the fire wouldn't destroy their tree. He grimaced at the use of the pronoun. There was no "their" anymore.

Back when life had seemed full of possibilities, they'd found a plateau overlooking the lake where a lone oak tree stood. Their spot, their tree. He'd carved their initials into the trunk.

The memory was bittersweet. He shook his head. He had no business letting thoughts of Rachel crowd his mind. They'd said their goodbyes. He doubted they'd see or hear from her again.

Explaining to his son why he wouldn't be seeing her again had been one of the hardest things Josh had ever done. Confessing to his boy that he'd basically forbid Rachel to have any more contact with Griff had put a wedge between father and son.

Josh could have blamed Rachel, could have told his

son that she didn't keep her promises, but he couldn't. Not only was that untrue, but for reasons he refused to examine, he'd preferred his son be angry with him rather than with Rachel.

Griff would get over his anger and they'd repair their relationship. Someday he hoped Griff would understand why not having Rachel in their lives was for the best. Someday Josh would tell his son to be careful when he fell in love. He didn't want Griff to make the same mistake of finding someone who would only commit to one thing—her career.

Rachel had called him chauvinistic. Was it chauvinistic to want to be loved passionately? To want to know that the woman he loved wouldn't up and leave one day? He just wanted a wife whose love he would be sure of. He would never be sure of Rachel's feelings because her devotion to medicine was all consuming. And even understanding her belief that she was doing God's will didn't make letting her go any easier. It made him admire her for her faith and obedience, and made him aware of his unworthiness to receive anything from God.

A commotion in the outer office brought his mind back to the problem at hand. Abruptly he turned from the wall and headed out of the conference room into the large lobby of the log-cabin-style ranger's station. He stopped short.

Amid the chaos of people doing their jobs stood Rachel, wearing nylon jogging shorts and a tank top, talking quickly and gesturing wildly to Joe Leads, Timber Manager.

"What are you doing here, Rachel?"

At the sound of his voice her attention snapped to him. Her big blue eyes looked panicked.

Warily Josh moved toward her as she rushed to him. What would make her seek him out? Dread knotted his muscles. What would make her lose her control?

Chapter Eleven

She grabbed his arm, her grasp fierce and biting. "Josh, you have to come quick."

Josh frowned. Concern overrode the shock of seeing her again. He fought it back. "Rachel, we're in the middle of fighting a fire—"

"Griff's out there," she gasped.

Fear, stark and choking, seized Josh's heart, but he tried to rationalize it away. "They're miles from the fire. His troop went to Pine Mountain Lake."

"No. Rod said there'd been a last-minute change in plans and he dropped Griff off at Cherry Lake this morning." Cool, collected Rachel sounded scared. "The troop leader called and said Griff and another boy got separated from the group. Your dad went in after them."

For a dizzying moment Josh fought the panic threatening to cut off his air supply. The world narrowed down to one terrorizing thought: *I can't lose Griff, too.*

He recovered his equilibrium and forced his mind

to concentrate on what needed to be done. In long strides he crossed the room, grabbed his keys and coat. "Connie, call George. Tell him what's happening. Tell him I'm going in to find my son and that my dad's on his way in.

"Joe, you take over here and call the sheriff's department with this update. See if they've already located Griff. Call me on my cell." He shouted the commands as he grabbed two walkie-talkies from a cabinet. His heart pounded in his ears, but he kept moving, kept focused on the details.

"You, Chris—" he pointed to a startled young ranger "—you're going in with me."

"But he hasn't—" Joe began.

Josh cut him off with a glare. "I need you here." He stated the obvious. Joe nodded sharply, acknowledging one of the prime rules: Go in with a buddy.

Josh hurried toward the door with Chris right on his heels. He didn't even stop when he heard Rachel's cry of "What about me?"

"Go home," he growled over his shoulder, and then he was out the door.

Rachel stared at the door as it slammed shut behind Josh's retreating back. *Go home.* Like she could go home now. Not with Griff missing and a fire blazing. Her feet were moving before she'd even thought about commanding them to. She rushed out the door and watched Josh's truck speeding away.

She ignored the bite of rejection at Josh's harsh command and ran for Rod's Buick. *He's going to need you, Rachel. Whatever happens today, Josh is going to need you.* Rod's words echoed inside her head as she drove after Josh.

Yeah, well, tell him *that, why don't you?* she thought sourly. She pressed harder on the gas pedal. The Buick shook with the speed, but she didn't let up as she turned off Highway 120 and headed up the gravel road that would lead her to the lake.

Josh's truck had long since disappeared ahead of her. But she knew where he'd start. Not at the usual visitors' trailhead. No, he'd take the fire road until it ended miles up the trail. She didn't question her certainty, she just knew. She almost missed the turn for the fire road but the faint cloud of dust clinging to the air pointed the way.

Josh and Chris were already out of sight by the time she parked the Buick behind Josh's truck. A fallen log blocked the way. They'd have to hike up the fire road to where it converged with the main trail. She ran to catch up to them, grimacing at the awful smell of smoke. Her approaching footsteps gave away her arrival before she had thought of what to say.

Josh's head whipped around, his eyes widened for a fraction of a second before narrowing to burning slits. "Go back, Rachel. I don't want you here. You'll just get in the way."

Her heart tore at the pain visible beneath his obvious irritation. "You might need me. I'm a doctor, remember."

His feet still moved at a rapid pace—she had to take three steps to his one—but his eyes remained on her for a long moment. His lip curled into a nasty sneer. "A city doctor."

"A doctor just the same," she retorted between gulps of air, the smoke burning her lungs. "I'm coming with you. Get over it."

"Rachel, you're a civilian. I—"

"Which means you can't order me around," she interrupted tersely.

He snorted at her over his shoulder, his pace never slowing. "If you think you can handle it."

She noticed Chris kept glancing at her but she didn't feel inclined to appease his curiosity.

Being behind the two men, Rachel got a good dose of dust kicked up into her face. She tried to stifle her coughs because every time she coughed loud enough for Josh to hear, he'd turn and glare at her. She could feel his animosity toward her, claiming he found her presence a nuisance. But Griff was the one out there, maybe hurt, needing help. And if she could help, then angering Josh was a small price to pay.

When the fire road met with the main trail, Josh stopped abruptly. Chris smoothly sidestepped him, but Rachel had her head down and didn't realize he'd stopped until she ran smack into his broad back, knocking her off her feet.

She glared up him. He stared back dispassionately.

"You could help me up," she groused, her bottom aching from the impact with the ground.

For a tense moment Rachel thought he wouldn't help her. Finally he stuck out a hand and swiftly pulled her to her feet. He dropped her hand quickly and turned to Chris. "Take the trail down to the visitors' center. You should meet my father. When you do, contact me." He turned a knob on one of the walkie-talkies before handing it over to the bemused youth.

"I thought we were to stay together?" Chris questioned, his young face creasing with anxiety.

Josh flipped the knobs on his own walkie-talkie. "Take her with you."

"No," Rachel said immediately. If Griff or the other boy were hurt... She didn't even want to think about that. They had to find the two boys before it got dark.

"It's safer if you go with Chris," he replied without looking at her.

Anger that he'd dismiss her so readily gave her words a cutting edge. "Safer for whom?"

He glanced at her sharply. Then gave a wry twist of his lips. "For both of us." With that left between them, he turned and headed up the trail.

Rachel stared after him for a moment, wondering what he meant by that remark. Then she turned to the kid beside her. "You go on, Chris. I'll stay with Josh."

At the young man's hesitancy, she nodded. "It's okay. Go find Rod."

Chris shrugged and headed in the opposite direction. Rachel trudged after Josh. She wasn't sure if he knew that she followed several feet behind him, until his voice came at her tight and clipped. "You could easily make it back to the car before dark."

"I'm coming with you," she declared through ragged breaths.

"Suit yourself," he grumbled.

A dull ache throbbed in her side. She ignored her fatigued body's protest against the extra exercise.

The trail narrowed. Tree branches brushed across her legs, biting into her skin. Wryly she glanced down at her slick running shoes, made for smooth paved track, not rugged dirt trails. Her gaze lifted to Josh. His uniform and work boots were much better suited for the trek.

They hiked to the clanking rhythm of Josh's fire ax hanging from his gear belt. The smoke grew thicker by the minute. In the distance she could hear the crackling and hissing of trees burning. Somewhere out there men were fighting the fire. Somewhere out there was Griff.

Josh stopped in his tracks. Rachel ran headfirst into his back again. He put out a steadying hand. "Pay attention," he snapped.

He called for Griff, his voice loud and booming through the trees. They waited, but only the sounds of the flaming forest answered.

He started forward again. Rachel followed, aware of the fear in Josh's eyes, aware of the panic building within her chest. She'd been panicked when she'd arrived at the station, but once she'd seen Josh, the panic had given way to an assurance that he would make things right. He'd find his son and the world would go on. It shook her to the core to see Josh so scared.

The third time Josh stopped abruptly, Rachel managed not to ram into him. Her tennis shoes skidded on the loose dirt, raising a murky cloud of dust.

Their fruitless cries for Griff echoed back at them through the tree. Josh's gaze traveled over her with concern. "You're not dressed for this."

"I didn't plan on going for a hike in the wilderness today." She tried for some levity, but failed.

He rubbed a hand over his face. "I should have grabbed some gear out of the truck for you. I wasn't thinking."

She caught his hand in hers. "You were worried about Griff. Besides, you didn't know I'd follow you."

Josh's gaze moved away from her and to the wooded trail. "He should have been headed back down by now. He knows how to pace himself, how to gauge his time and distance so that at any given point he could turn back and know exactly how much time the return would take." He held her hand tightly. "What am I going to do if anything happens to my son?" His voice was ragged and his face in the dusky light showed the signs of the terrible thoughts running through his head.

"Josh, don't. You can't assume anything. We'll find him. We have to trust that God will protect him."

"I know. I know. But the fire…"

"Remember what you asked me in the hospital? You asked if I trusted God. Now, I'm asking you, Josh. Do you trust Him? Is your faith strong enough?"

She held her breath. The last time she'd asked he'd seemed to struggle for his answer. On some level, she knew he was at a turning point in his relationship with God. Choosing to trust when things were going your way was easy, but trusting in the midst of a crisis, when only the Almighty was in control, took a step in faith.

"'Faith's being sure of what we hope for and certain of what we do not see,'" she quoted softly.

He closed his eyes. Rachel could only guess he was

searching his own heart for the answer, desperately trying not to let his fear overwhelm him. He breathed out and his eyes opened.

They were clearer, less panicked, more focused. "I do trust Him."

He held out his other hand. Rachel slipped her free hand into his. She garnered comfort from his touch. He bowed his head and prayed aloud, a simple, heartfelt plea for God's protection and direction.

When he'd finished, he slipped out of his jacket and wrapped it around her shoulders. "Thank you, Rachel."

She looked up at him in surprise. "I should be the one thanking you for the coat."

In the fading light she saw a soft smile curve his lips. "Thank you for reminding me where my strength lies."

His smile made her heart quicken. His eyes, hot with intensity, locked with hers. She swallowed.

A static beep drew their attention, breaking the momentary spell.

"Son, come in." Rod's voice came from the little box that Josh had secured to his belt.

He grabbed the instrument. "Copy, Dad."

"Have you found them?"

"Negative, Dad. We're almost to the summit and we'll head down to the shoreline."

"We'll head toward you then." Rod's voice sounded strained.

Josh frowned. "Copy, Dad. Be careful."

"You too, son. Take care of Rachel, too."

"Copy that, Dad. Out."

"Will your dad be okay?" Rachel asked, thinking about Rod's age and Josh's frown.

"Yes. He has years of experience and Chris with him. They'll be fine. How about you? How are you doing?"

Her feet hurt and her muscles were cramping, but adrenaline kept the pain from overwhelming her. "I'm fine. Let's keep moving."

His expression said he didn't quite believe her, but he gave a sharp nod and they continued on. Rachel noticed that Josh adjusted his stride so she didn't have to jog.

She knew what that little concession must cost him in anxiety. She could feel his restrained power as his long legs ate up the ground beside her. Soon they reached the top of the small summit where the trail began to head down toward the lake.

The sight stole her breath. On the far side of the lake the fire burned hot and bright. Tall trees glowing like eerie specters rising from the ground sent a shiver sliding over her arms. Standing at the top like this, the smoke was thick and burning to her lungs.

Below them the water reflected the red glow of the flames, making the blaze overwhelming. Where could Griff be? Surely at this frightening sight he'd have headed back, unless he were hurt. Her throat constricted at the thought.

Josh yelled for Griff and she added her own cries to his. Their voices echoed across the water. Below, nothing moved; there wasn't any sign of life.

"Where could they be?" she wondered aloud, her eyes scanning the darkness.

"I don't know. Unless—" He broke off. His gaze traveling from the lake to the left, down an incline to the plateau where the top of an oak tree jutted out above the other trees.

She followed his gaze. "The tree?"

"Maybe." He looked thoughtful. "Worth a chance."

The implication that he'd told Griff about their tree left her reeling. The memories of that last visit to the old oak were etched firmly in her heart. It was the day she'd told Josh goodbye. Leaving him had been the hardest thing she'd ever done.

They left the trail and started down the hill. Rocks slid beneath Rachel's feet. Josh grabbed her arm and steadied her. As they neared the bottom, Josh yelled for Griff again.

A faint noise from below them paused Rachel's heart. Josh halted and called again. An answering cry filled the air. Spurred on by the tiny voice, she scrambled behind Josh. As they came out of the brush and into the clearing, a small boy came running forward. "Mr. Taylor."

Josh ran to the dark-haired boy and gathered him in his arms. "Ben, are you okay? Where's Griff?"

She watched as he checked the boy for injuries. Josh's compassion for the frightened child touched her deeply.

Ben dissolved into tears, and Josh put his big, strong arms around the small boy. "Shh, it's all right. You're safe now. Where's Griff?"

Over the boy's head Rachel met his gaze. She saw fear, stark and vivid, in his hazel eyes. She stepped closer and laid a hand on his shoulder.

Ben gulped, his body shaking. "He—he fell. I didn't

know what to do. I didn't want to leave him. And the fire…the forest's b-burning."

"Show me where Griff is," Josh said in a tight, strained voice.

The boy took Josh's hand and pulled him toward the lone tree. Rachel saw two legs jutting out from the other side. The side that bore the marks that Josh had carved into the trunk. Was that what lured him from his troop?

Quickly they rounded the tree and stopped short.

Griff lay prone and still. Rachel rushed past a frozen Josh to kneel at Griff's side. She fought a moment of alarm and forced her mind to focus. She immediately checked his pulse, which was strong, his breathing and then searched for injuries.

Josh knelt down beside her and very carefully took Griff's hand. "Griff, Griff." His voice broke.

"He's breathing and his heartbeat's good," she said.

"He's alive," Josh breathed out, his relief evident.

"Yes, he's alive." She laid a reassuring hand on his arm and blinked back sudden tears. She gained control of herself and turned to the boy. "Ben, how long has he been unconscious?" Her tone was amazingly cool, despite the hammering in her chest.

"I—I don't know. For a while." The boy burst into fresh tears.

She looked up to see Josh staring at her intently. "His ankle's swollen, probably broken. He has a contusion on his head. We need to get him out of here."

"I'll carry him back." Josh moved to pick up his son.

Rachel squeezed his arm tightly. "You need to call for the rescue team to come take him out on a backboard."

"No. That will take too long. You said he was okay, just a broken ankle."

"Josh, my evaluation's superficial. We won't know if he has internal injuries until we can get him to the hospital. You could do more damage by moving him."

Her stern and uncompromising tone rang with familiarity in her own ears. This was the voice that got things done in the E.R. How easily and comfortably she slipped back into her doctor persona.

She could see he didn't want to comply with her assessment, but after a moment's hesitation, he acquiesced. From the pocket of the coat that she'd laid over Griff he pulled out a cellular phone and dialed. He quickly and tersely explained their situation.

Next he grabbed his walkie-talkie. "Dad, come in."

"Here, son. Have you found Griff?" Rod's voice sounded breathless.

"Yes. Where are you?"

"Just cresting the summit now."

"Take the incline to your left. We're here. Griff's unconscious, but alive. Rachel wants us to wait to move him. I've called for the rescue team. They should arrive shortly."

"Copy that, thank God. Out."

"Copy, out." He turned to her, his expression grim and full of worry. "What can we do?"

"Wait." The one word that was so hard to do. Part of the practice of medicine consisted of waiting and seeing. Sometimes God worked miracles where a doctor never could.

Josh stood and paced. "How did he fall, Ben?"

"He was trying to climb the tree."

Josh groaned. "He knows better than to do that by himself. How many times have I told him that without supervision he could get hurt?"

"He's a boy exploring his world, Josh," she stated quietly.

He whirled on her. "What do you know about it? You're not a parent."

She drew back at his angry outburst, hurt by his harsh words.

Immediately his expression turned contrite. "I'm sorry. That was uncalled for. I didn't mean—"

She held up a hand. "You're right, Josh. I'm not a parent. I can only imagine the torment you're feeling right now."

Though she'd only known Griff a short time, she loved the boy and had felt the same fear as Josh. She'd glimpsed the battle Josh fought every day with fear, the fear that something would happen to his son, one of the risks of family she wasn't sure she was up for. She forgave him his painful words. But the sting reminded her she wasn't welcome in Josh's life.

The sound of voices carrying down the hill was a welcome relief. Rod and Chris charged through the brush, quickly followed by three uniformed rescue personnel. Josh hastily detailed the situation.

"They snuck away from the rest of the troop and came up the hill from the shoreline," Rod explained to Rachel as he came to kneel by Griff's feet.

A member of the rescue team knelt beside Rachel. She gave him her evaluation. The man, named Brian, placed a neck brace on Griff. The other two members of the team brought over a backboard.

Efficiently they secured Griff to the board and splinted his ankle, then lifted him and cautiously headed up the hill. Rachel picked up Josh's jacket and watched as Josh disappeared with the rescue team.

Rod's arm came around her shoulders. "Shall we?"

She nodded, feeling suddenly exhausted. They followed Chris and Ben up the hill moving at a good clip.

"There'll be an ambulance meeting us at the fire road," Rod explained.

"That's good."

"Thanks for staying with Josh. I know he appreciated your presence."

Rachel gave Rod a sidelong glance. "I probably slowed him down."

Rod shrugged. "You two worked together and found Griff. That's what matters."

They'd worked together. Like a team. A couple. The pang that thought brought made Rachel stumble. Rod's hand on her arm steadied her. They weren't a couple. She would be leaving in the morning, going back to her life where she needed to stay focused on her goal. But the enthusiasm for the task didn't come, didn't fill her with the peace it usually did.

Rod cleared his throat. "You know, Josh still needs you."

"Hardly."

"The fire's still blazing. He's got a job to do. He's going to need your help."

Rod's softly spoken words echoed inside her head. "My help?"

"With Griff, while he fights the fire."

She doubted Josh would recant his demand for her to stay away from his son. He hadn't wanted her to come on the search. He surely wouldn't want her to stay with Griff. "They have you."

"I'm needed out here, too. We're going to need every hand available to stop this blaze."

In anxiety-ridden silence, Rachel digested her conversation with Rod. Josh had needed her, but did he still? *Lord, show me what to do.*

At the head of the fire road, lights blazed. Two people came rushing forward from one of the vehicles.

"Ben!" called Ben's mother. Ben hurried to meet his parents.

Rachel smiled to see the three hugging and kissing. Until recently, she hadn't known what that would feel like. To be so glad to see someone, to hold them close and be thankful for their existence.

But she'd felt that with Griff. She loved Josh's son, and she intended to continue to be there for him somehow, some way. Even if that meant staying a few days longer in Josh's world where she wasn't welcome.

Chapter Twelve

With Rod at her side, she headed toward his car.

"Rachel." Josh's voice brought her to a halt. He stood at the open doors to the ambulance. Inside, a paramedic worked on Griff. She knew he'd hook him up to an IV to keep him hydrated.

"Go on," Rod urged.

She moved forward on wooden feet. "Yes?"

"Ride with us," Josh said abruptly.

She was astonished by Josh's request and by the thrilling glow that flowed through her in response. "Of course." She climbed in and sat on the narrow bench next to Griff. She heard Josh tell his dad they'd see him at the hospital. The two men hugged. Josh climbed in and sat next to her.

When he gathered her hand in his, her brows rose in stunned surprise. Heat embraced her palm and traveled to her heart, making her aware of Josh's close proximity and of the need she felt in his touch. He *did* need her for Griff's sake.

"Thank you for being here." His voice was thick and unsteady.

Her heart went out to him and a calming peace settled over her. "You're welcome."

What would he think when he learned that she intended to keep her promise to Mom G., and that for the next few days it wasn't going to be from long distance?

"Can't you go any faster?" Josh grumbled, anxiety twisting in his chest.

"We're going as fast as we can, sir," the ambulance driver replied with curt politeness.

Josh stared at his unconscious son. He looked so little and helpless lying on the backboard. Love swelled to overwhelming proportions, making Josh aware of how vulnerable his heart was where his son was concerned. If he lost Griff, he didn't know if he could survive life in one piece.

Do you trust Him? Rachel had asked. Such a simple question yet not easily answered.

In placing his trust in the Lord, Josh was admitting he had no control over life. No control over whether his son lived or died. The out-of-control feeling nagged at his soul with frightening intensity. He'd had to call on every bit of knowledge he possessed about God to say yes with any conviction.

God was not some powerful being who took joy in His creations' pain, but rather a Heavenly Father who suffered with His children.

Faith, Rachel had reminded him, was more than just

believing. Faith was trusting in something intangible, placing your life in God's care and being assured that He would work all things out for your own good.

The comforting pressure of Rachel's hand in his reminded him of her presence. He looked up to meet her gentle, blue gaze. There was nothing icy in the subtle look of understanding in her eyes.

This woman amazed him. She'd been there for him when he needed her quiet strength, her steady, reassuring presence. She'd kept her cool. Her doctorly, professional cool. And he was grateful.

Why she had insisted on coming to help search for Griff, he could only guess at the answer. He supposed the bond she and his son had formed had prompted her assistance.

Any other reason… He wouldn't go there, couldn't go there. Surely her determination to help had only stemmed from her love of his son and her experience as a doctor, not from feelings for him. Yet, as he held her gaze, he couldn't stop the ache that suddenly consumed his heart.

To divert his uneasy thoughts, he said, "You think he'll be okay?"

Her expression didn't change. "The fracture in his ankle seems to be a clean break but only an X ray will tell for certain."

His gaze moved to the purple bruise on Griff's forehead. "What about his head?"

"Head injuries are tricky. We won't know what damage, if any, he has sustained until we run tests and he wakes up. But the size of the lump and the location indicate to me that at worst he may have a pretty good concussion. The forehead's the thickest part of the skull."

Her soft voice worked like a balm to his tightly strung nerves. Just as she'd calmly soothed his panic when they'd found Griff and for that agonizing moment when he'd thought his son was dead.

"I froze." The admission tore from him.

She blinked. "What?"

He couldn't meet her gaze now. If he saw disdain in her eyes it would kill him. But he needed to get the words out. His self-loathing wouldn't permit him not to. "I froze. I saw him lying there and couldn't function."

He rubbed the back of his neck. "Even though I know what to do. I've been trained by the best. I've worked Search and Rescue. But when it mattered the most, I froze."

"Don't blame yourself, Josh." With her free hand, she drew his face toward her. When he met her gaze, he didn't see the reproach he'd anticipated. Instead he saw understanding and compassion.

"When it's someone you love who's hurt, it makes a difference. I can't tell you how many times I've seen the most competent doctors turn into a mass of jelly when their child or spouse is injured. Don't beat yourself up about something that happens to everyone in your situation. Doctors don't treat their own for that precise reason."

He wanted to believe her. To believe *in* her. Her hand stroked his cheek. He'd willingly endure frostbite for her precious touch. He pressed a kiss to her palm. Her eyes widened but she didn't withdraw. "Thank you," he whispered.

Her tender smile sent a deep yearning screaming through his tension-filled body. A yearning for what could never be: Rachel loving him and being his wife.

Rachel's career was important to her, so important he couldn't ask her to give it up. And he knew she never would for him.

He frowned at the turn of his thoughts. She dropped her hand away and loosened her hold on him, as if giving him a chance to withdraw if he wanted. He tightened his hold.

He didn't want to go through this alone. He didn't like living a life by himself, not having someone to share the heartache and the joy with. He wanted a helpmate. He wanted Rachel, needed her, if only for now.

He forced his thoughts away from dangerous ground and onto the one love that he was sure of—his son.

What had Griff been thinking, wandering off from the troop like that? And going to that tree? He glanced up at Rachel. Their tree. Her eyes were trained on Griff, but she was miles away, lost in her thoughts.

"You know, I have no idea how Griff knew about the tree," he said softly.

Her brows rose in response to his statement but she didn't turn toward him.

"Dad could have told him," Josh said aloud, more to keep the silence from filling his head with far-fetched thoughts he had no business thinking than from wanting any more of a response from her.

Thoughts like how much he admired and respected Rachel for pursuing her dreams, even at the cost to him, and about how good a doctor she must be if what he'd glimpsed today was any indication. She'd known what to do, had been efficient, yet caring.

When they arrived at the hospital, Josh jumped out before the vehicle stopped completely. Rachel's restraining hand kept him from pulling the stretcher out himself. He wanted to help, to do something other than stand by helplessly and watch. He didn't like being pushed aside. He didn't like the images hovering at the sidelines of his consciousness, taunting him.

"Josh, let them do their jobs."

Rachel's authoritative tone brought a halt to his chaotic mind. She was right. He was getting in the way. He stepped back and allowed the EMTs to do their job. They transferred Griff to a gurney and rushed toward the emergency room entrance.

He took Rachel's hand and followed the gurney into the hospital. An orderly moved forward, blocking the way. "Are you the boy's parents?"

"Yes." Josh looked past the man to where they'd wheeled Griff behind a curtain. "I need to be with my son."

"You can't go back there, sir. The doctors will take good care of your boy." The orderly gestured toward the administration desk. "If you could step over to the counter and fill out some standard forms...sir?"

Josh ignored the young man. He couldn't see his son, couldn't see what was happening. He pulled

Rachel forward. "This is Dr. Maguire. She's my son's doctor. She needs to be with him."

The man frowned. "I thought you—"

Josh turned to Rachel and pleaded, "Please, go be with Griff. At least until I can call his pediatrician."

She stared up at him, her complexion a pasty white. Something akin to fear shifted in her gaze. Josh didn't understand. She was an E.R. doctor and he was asking her to do her job.

The young orderly puffed himself up. "Sir, she can't. She's not part of our staff."

Josh waited, ignoring the man's pronouncement. There was a struggle going on in Rachel. He could see the flicking emotions in her blue eyes. He didn't understand why she was hesitating.

Finally she blinked and straightened. Steely determination filled her gaze, crowding the fear to the edges. She focused on the orderly. "I'd like to speak to the attending."

The man frowned. "He's unavailable. You can leave a message—"

"I'd like to speak to him *now*," she demanded, her voice strong and cold.

The young man flushed and seemed to look around for help. "Uh, well. I—I think…"

Rachel started walking, her steps decisive. "Lead the way."

The man stared at her retreating back, speechless for a second, then hurried after her.

Josh could understand the orderly's reaction. Rachel's cool, commanding tone was formidable.

Clearly she was a woman used to being in charge. There was a remarkable strength in her petite form. He took a deep breath and the tightness in his chest eased somewhat, secure in knowing she'd take care of his son, though the fear he'd seen in her eyes nagged at him. What was that about?

As each step forward drew Rachel closer to the place where her mother died, her spirit groaned in agony. She didn't want to do this, she'd stayed away from this place since that day, but now she had to walk in there. For Griff's sake.

She pursed her lips tightly. *Be honest with yourself, Rachel. This is for Josh.* Because he needed her to go in there. She couldn't explain how deeply his trust overwhelmed her and filled her with strength she'd not thought possible.

She approached the metal swinging doors leading to the restricted emergency care area and her steps faltered. A chill ran down her arms raising pinpricks of dread. Lifting her chin, she vowed to face the demons haunting her even if they destroyed her.

For Josh.

Josh was determined to do something, anything, to keep from rushing back to where they'd taken Griff. Nervous energy flowed through him as he moved to the administration desk. "What papers do you need filled out?"

The woman behind the desk smiled and handed him a clipboard and pen. "Here, sir. Fill in both sides, please."

Taking the clipboard, Josh sat in the waiting area and filled out the forms. He focused on the papers in front of him, fighting off the memories of the last time he'd been in the emergency room filling out similar forms.

As the minutes turned into what seemed like hours, a feeling of helplessness settled over him like a blanket of fog. Pacing the waiting room like a caged tiger didn't help. Nothing did. All he could do was wait. He hated to wait.

Rod, who had arrived shortly after Rachel disappeared with the orderly, sat in one of the stiff chairs, his legs stretched out in front of him. "Sit down, son. You're making me more nervous."

With an exasperated glance, Josh stopped and stared out the window. His reflection looked back at him, accusingly.

Remembrance seeped in—memories and images of the night his wife had died. The gruesome reality of her death and his guilt struck at him, battering his already-weakened sense of self.

They'd brought her here to the emergency room; she'd undoubtedly disappeared down the hall on a gurney much the same way Griff had. She hadn't survived. He shuddered with the sense of loathing and uselessness that had plagued him for years. He couldn't change what had happened. No amount of penitence would bring her back.

He had to focus on Griff. That was the only thing that kept him sane, that kept him going. He had to be the best father he could be for Griff.

Abruptly he turned from the window and resumed pacing. It shouldn't take so long. Why hadn't Rachel come to tell him how Griff was?

"Josh." A dark-haired man with gentle brown eyes walked into the waiting area.

"Dr. Michaelson." Josh hurried over to Griff's pediatrician. Though the doctor was only a few years older than Josh, he exuded an aura of maturity and quiet compassion that appealed to Josh. Josh felt comforted by Dr. Michaelson's presence. "How is he?"

"He's awake and asking for you. Hi, Rod." The doctor acknowledged Rod, who came to stand beside them.

"Doc." Rod's good-natured reply elicited a smile from the doctor.

"And he's okay?" Josh asked, holding a breath.

"He'll have a nasty bruise and headache to match for a few days. We set his ankle in a cast, but it's a fairly minor break. He'll need to stay off his feet for a while, but other than that he's fine." Dr. Michaelson smiled.

Josh let out his breath. "Thank you, God."

Rod clapped Josh on the back. "Let's go see the little tiger."

Dr. Michaelson led the way to the elevators and stepped in with them. "He's been moved upstairs to a private room. He'll be released in the morning."

When the elevator doors closed, Josh stuck out his hand. "Thank you, Dr. Michaelson."

The doctor shook Josh's hand and gave a small chuckle. "You're welcome. Though I didn't do much.

Dr. Maguire had everything under control when I arrived."

Josh breathed a grateful sigh of relief to know that Rachel had taken good care of his son.

The three men arrived at Griff's room and heard laughter. Josh stepped in, followed closely by Rod and Dr. Michaelson, to see his son smiling and chuckling at Rachel as she made funny faces while telling him a story.

"So you see—oh, here's your dad." Rachel hastily stood; a hesitant smile played at the corners of her mouth. She'd acquired a pair of green scrubs, which hugged her form attractively.

"Dad," Griff exclaimed, his eyes lighting up.

Josh rushed to his son's side and gave him a fierce hug. Overwhelmed by love and relief, his voice broke. "I'm so thankful you're okay."

Griff sniffed. "I'm sorry, Dad. I shouldn't have left the group."

"No, you shouldn't have. But we can talk about that later." He put his heart in his smile as he gazed with love at his boy. He was aware of Rachel as she walked around the bed and hugged Rod. Annoyed that she hadn't reacted that way with him, Josh said stiffly, "Thank you, Rachel, for everything."

She turned startled eyes on him. "You're welcome, Josh."

He held her gaze for a long moment, craving for her to show him the same affection she so easily doled out to the rest of his family. *Get a grip, man. You'll never be a priority in her life.* Chief of staff. That was her goal, not him.

He broke the eye contact because it was too painful to get lost in her winter-blue gaze.

He smoothed back a lock of Griff's hair that had fallen over the awful goose egg on his forehead. "Good thing you have such a tough noggin," he teased, trying to distract himself from the allure of Rachel's presence.

Behind him, he heard Rachel murmur something to his father and then she left along with Dr. Michaelson. Some of the energy in the room left with her and Josh sagged into a chair, acknowledging how much he'd depended on her today. That had to end here and now. She would leave in the morning. And with her she would take a piece of his heart, just as she'd done the first time she'd left.

All that had transpired in the past few hours hit Rachel with the force of a dump truck, and a quiver shook her bottom lip. She staggered to the wall.

She'd worked in the E.R. where her mother had died.

And she had survived.

Her mind was a jumbled, chaotic mess. And her emotions were riding a runaway roller coaster.

The first few moments after she'd walked through the swinging doors, choking memories had reared to life. But then she'd realized that nothing was as she remembered it. The tall doctor with the sad, brown eyes, who'd informed her that her mother was dead, wasn't there.

Logically she acknowledged he'd be past retirement age by now. But his face had haunted her nightmares.

But the biggest difference and the greatest healing came when she noticed that many of the triage techniques she'd implemented in her own hospital and others around the country had been duplicated at Sonora Community.

The attending had been more than gracious and overflowing with compliments as he'd explained how the papers she'd written and had published in popular medical journals over the past few years had changed the procedures of Sonora Community's E.R.

Tears welled in her eyes and a cleansing sob broke free as a huge weight was lifted from her chest. Her mother hadn't died in vain. Knowing that helped her to release the anger and bitterness she'd harbored toward the doctors and staff of the hospital.

And she wouldn't have ever had that confirmed if Josh hadn't asked her to stay with Griff. *Thank you, God, for using Griff and Josh to heal me.*

Josh's trust meant so much, yet his harsh words came floating back: *I have to protect him from you.*

He trusted her as a doctor but not as a woman. She supposed she should be thankful that at least he'd acknowledged her capabilities as a physician. There was a measure of comfort in his acknowledgment.

She shuddered as she recalled the panic and fear in his eyes out at the lake. When he'd first seen Griff lying there on the ground, she'd seen the flash of agony in his face and had known he'd thought for an instant that his son was dead. His relief was tangible.

His admission that he'd froze came as a surprise. Not that he'd recognized his reaction but that'd he'd admitted as much. She could only imagine what saying those words to her had cost him, showing any weakness to the person he'd accused of breaking his heart. Compassion and tenderness had welled up inside her. Josh was mature enough to expose his fallibility.

But when he'd taken her hand in the ambulance and held on as if she were his lifeline, her already tightly strung nerves nearly shattered, leaving her a bit dizzy with… She couldn't grasp what she'd felt in those moments.

Hunger for more, a certain amount of pride that he'd needed her, hope that maybe he could begin to accept her and her drive to make a difference. She didn't know which emotion was prominent or if they'd just bunched together into a single, unidentifiable glob.

Then he'd done something that had made even that jumbled-up mess of emotions pale in comparison. He'd said yes when asked if they were Griff's parents.

He couldn't possibly know the deep, soul-piercing pain he'd caused her.

The kicker had come when he'd entered the room after Griff had awakened. His very polite and indifferent thank-you had warred with the look in his eyes.

For a long, tense moment there'd been a yearning she hadn't seen in a very long time. An answering need had awakened in her, a longing to reach out to him and hold him close, only to be shot down as the look in his eyes shifted to something hostile and dangerous. As if he'd just remembered who and what she was. The woman he didn't want in his life, the woman he'd accused of breaking his heart. The woman he didn't love.

She'd have to remember that. He didn't love her. His heart mourned for his wife. Thinking him a wounded soul kept her from indulging in self-pity. She couldn't compete with a dead woman. She couldn't compete with his ideals. She didn't want to, she told herself sternly.

She'd made a promise and she intended to keep her side of the deal, for Griff's sake and to prove to Josh she could be a part of Griff's life without causing him irreparable damage. Through Griff she could take care of Josh and fulfill her promise to Mom G. That was the only way it was going to happen.

With that thought solidly established, Rachel headed for the one place that had always made her feel needed, the one place she could lose herself and calm her own frazzled nerves. She headed for the E.R. in hopes they could use some help.

Hours later, Rachel rolled her shoulders to relieve the tension in her bunched-up muscles. The clock on the E.R. wall read twelve-thirty in the morning. She slipped into the elevator, pushed the button for Griff's floor and leaned against the metal wall.

She'd been working for a long time and she was exhausted, but calmer. These hours spent doing what she'd been trained to do reminded her how much she loved her job, how much meaning her life held. And knowing that she'd conquered her demons lifted her spirits in a way she hadn't felt before.

The elevator opened and she exited. The dimly lit hall revealed a lone nurse sitting at the nurses' station. The woman smiled at Rachel. Rachel pointed down the hall. The nurse nodded and resumed whatever she'd been doing.

Rachel moved soundlessly to Griff's room. She wanted to check on him and make sure he slept comfortably. She was almost certain to find Josh in the room, as well, and she hoped he'd found some rest, too.

As she eased open the door, a muffled sound met her ears. She frowned and stepped into the room. Griff slept peacefully, his face young and innocent in repose. In the chair next to the bed sat Josh. His head was bowed and one of his hands held Griff's hand.

Josh was crying.

Chapter Thirteen

Tears streamed down Josh's cheeks and his breathing came shallow and fast. Immediately Rachel's gaze jumped back to Griff. Her heart pounded with dread until she saw the gentle rise and fall of his chest. She let out a relieved breath. He was sound asleep.

Her attention turned back to the big man sitting there weeping and her heart contracted painfully in her chest. She tried to reconcile this hurting man to the strong man who'd anchored her when her own torrent of tears threatened to sweep her away. The need to comfort, the need to help, propelled her forward. She reached his side and laid a hand gently on his shoulder. "Josh?"

He stiffened. The feel of him recoiling hurt, but she held her ground just as he had when she'd needed to grieve. She owed him this kindness and she stayed because her very essence wouldn't permit her to retreat. She was a healer; she couldn't walk away from someone in need.

Especially if that someone was Josh.

Rachel squeezed Josh's shoulder, the muscles beneath her palm rock hard and solid. He raised his head; the ragged expression on his strong, handsome face tore at her heart. He stared straight ahead.

"What are you doing here?" His lowered voice rang with harshness.

"I came to check on you both."

"We're fine."

Right. "It shows."

He flinched and wiped his eyes with the back of his free hand.

"Josh, what's wrong?"

A long silent moment passed. He was fighting to stay in control. She understood what that was like, the energy and the concentration it took to keep from being vulnerable to the emotions that threatened to overwhelm and destroy. She took a deep breath, wanting to help, to take away whatever it was that was eating at him, even if he didn't want her to. "Remember what you said to me?"

He didn't respond.

She kneeled next to the chair and turned his face toward her with her hand, his stubbled jaw prickly to her touch. His tortured eyes, looking bleak and lost, ripped at her soul. She had to help him.

"'You have to let it out or it will eat away at you.'" She quoted the words he'd spoken to her that day when she'd cried in his arms. "Josh, whatever it is, you can tell me."

"I can't. You don't want to know."

The suffering in his voice brought fresh tears to clog her throat. She laid her hand on his cheek, her thumb gently caressing.

His eyes closed briefly, accepting her offer of solace. Satisfaction flowed through her. Empathy for his pain tightened her chest. Such a strange mix of emotions.

He pulled away. "I don't deserve your comfort or your concern."

The utter lack of emotion in his hushed voice sent a shiver down her spine and started the reconstruction of the wall around her heart. She withdrew her hand, stung that even now he would push her away. At least she'd tried. "Don't deserve or don't want?"

"There's no absolution for what I've done."

The self-recriminations in his tone made her shake her head. "Griff's accident was not your fault. He's going to be okay."

He gave a short, humorless laugh. "I know that. Griff's the only thing I've done right in my life."

His cryptic remarks confused her. "That's not true. You help people every day doing your job."

He shot her a sharp glance. "Yeah, well. A career doesn't make up for a lost life."

"A lost life…" Realization dawned. "Andrea."

His gaze grew distant; his body drew inward, closing Rachel out. She'd known Josh mourned his wife, but she hadn't really understood how deep his grief went.

"You must have loved her a great deal," she whispered past the lump in her throat.

She didn't know what to say to ease his pain. Or her own. Behind her wall of defense, the tiny corner of her heart that held the dream of Josh's love withered. Even if she could stay longer than she intended, she didn't stand a chance against the memory of the love he and Andrea had shared.

He glanced at Griff, then gave a sharp negative shake of his head before abruptly standing and moving by the window.

Rachel rose. Her heart hammered in her chest. What had he meant? That he hadn't loved Andrea or that he wasn't going to talk to Rachel about his wife? She watched him for a long, tense moment. His rigid stance screamed isolation, but the agony marring his handsome features belied his body language.

She'd promised Mom G. she'd take care of Josh. She'd wanted to fulfill the promise through Griff. But she needed to reach out to Josh. He'd unknowingly helped heal her scarred soul. It was her turn to help him.

Grim determination straightened her spine. She didn't want Griff to wake up and see his father so distressed. She closed the distance between them and laid a hand on Josh's arm.

He looked down at her hand, then met her gaze. She sucked in a breath at the torment in his eyes. "For Griff's sake, please let me help."

His jaw tightened.

"Stubborn man," she muttered with frustration.

The corner of his mouth quirked up, reminding her of when he'd said the same thing about her. Rachel narrowed his gaze on him as an idea formed. He'd wrapped her in his arms and had refused to let go when he'd said those words.

Not taking the time to rationalize why what she was about to do was dangerous to her heart, she stepped closer and slipped her arms around his waist. His breath hitched and she tightened her hold.

"Rachel," he groaned, his tone full of warning and longing.

"It's okay. Everything will be okay," she said into his shirt.

"No." His hands came down on her shoulders and tried gently to push her away. She refused to budge.

"Everything will never be okay," he stated in a shattered voice.

"Why?"

He stopped pushing. She leaned back to look up at him. "Why, Josh? Why won't everything be okay?"

"You don't want to know." His hands dropped away from her and he shifted within the confines of her loosened hold.

Suddenly, holding him seemed awkward and inappropriate. She stepped back and let her arms fall to her side. "Tell me."

A noise broke from him. Agonizing to hear, full of misery and torture. He didn't answer. He walked to Griff's bedside and stared down at his son. Rachel was almost relieved that he wanted to back away from the heartache of his story, but she could see the suffering in his eyes.

She walked to stand beside him.

He sighed. "You're not going to let this lie, are you?"

"No," she said softly.

He ran a finger down Griff's cheek. "I love him, you know. More than I love my own life."

"I know." She slipped her hand into his, wanting to share her strength. "Let's take a walk so we don't disturb him."

Josh swallowed and then nodded. They left the room and walked down the corridor. She wasn't sure where to go, but then she realized that Josh had taken the lead. He led them to the hospital chapel. The softly lit sanctuary was empty. They slid into the back pew.

"Tell me what's eating at you," she gently prodded.

His gaze shifted from her face to the stained glass window. The misery so clear in his expression tore at her heart. She didn't know what memory was playing behind his glazed, wide-eyed stare, but whatever images he saw were harrowing. His pain made her ache in a way she never had before. *Lord, give me strength to help him.*

He closed his eyes, and a violent shudder wracked his body. When he opened his eyes and turned to stare down at her, she drew back at the blank, desolate look.

"I killed my wife."

Shock reverberated through Rachel. He wasn't serious. He couldn't be. He was only trying to scare her, drive her away. Josh would never kill anyone. She was as sure of that as she was that God loved her and had a plan for her life. Neither belief was tangible, but true just the same.

"Were you driving the car?" she asked, prepared for his answer to be yes.

"No."

She blinked. "But Mom G. said she'd died in a car accident."

"She did."

Those two words left her more confused. "Then how can you be responsible?"

"Because," he responded fiercely, "she was in that car because of me."

She frowned. That was so like a guy to not come out with a straight answer. She contemplated him a moment. Her instincts told her he wouldn't respond to her coddling him, but he would respond to logical and rational reasoning.

Succeeding in a male-dominated profession had taught her to draw her male counterparts out with challenging questions delivered unemotionally. The men in her world wouldn't tolerate an emotional female. She schooled her features into impassivity and said, "But it was an accident, right? How can you be at fault?"

"We'd argued."

For Josh's marriage to be suddenly cut short in the midst of an argument was undoubtedly a hard blow.

"I should've stopped her. I shouldn't have let her get in the car. I should've never kept…" His voice trailed off and he suddenly looked angry.

"That's a lot of *should have*s," Rachel stated quietly. "Did you somehow become omnipotent? Do you believe you could have stopped something out of your control?"

His scathing look was razor sharp. "It wasn't out of my control."

"How could you control an accident?"

"It wasn't just an accident, Rachel. It was so much worse." He turned back toward the window and fisted his hands. "So much worse."

Frustrated with him and aching for him all at the same time, she touched his arm. "Tell me what happened."

"That night I was working late, a double shift. Something I'd been doing a lot then. The nanny called. Said Andrea had locked herself in the bedroom and she could hear things crashing."

He shook his head as if trying to deny what he was remembering. "I had to break down the bedroom door. She had torn the place apart. I was…shocked. She threw shoes at me and punched me. I grabbed her and shook her, demanding to know why she was behaving like a lunatic."

He closed his eyes, and she could only guess at the images in his mind. "She'd been crying. Her eyes were swollen and red, her cheeks stained with her tears. She jerked out of my grasp, screaming at me."

"Oh, Josh," Rachel whispered, her chest tightening with anguish for him. "Why was she so angry?"

The misery etching lines in his face made her want to hold him. "She'd found a picture I'd hidden away."

"A picture?"

With extreme effort she refrained from flinching at the guilt and self-loathing emanating from his eyes.

"The picture of us by our tree," he said, his voice painful to listen to, the tone ravaged and scarred.

Then the meaning in his words hit Rachel full force and the breath left her body in a rush. He'd saved something of *their* past together. She knew which picture he meant. *The picture of us by our tree.* The tree where they'd found Griff. The tree Josh had carved their initials in, surrounded by a heart.

The week before she'd left for college, they'd driven up to the lake wanting to spend as much time together as possible. Those last few weeks were tense because Josh had been hurt by her refusal of his marriage proposal. That day had been no different.

The entire drive to the lake, they'd fought about her need to become a doctor. He wouldn't compromise. She'd tried to tell him of her mother's death and the effect it had had on her, but he hadn't wanted to hear.

Finally, in desperation, she'd asked if they could spend a few hours together without thinking about anything but the here and now. And they had. For a few short hours no one else existed. Only their love mattered.

They'd propped the camera on a rock and used the timer to record the moment. But as dusk came, so had reality. They'd driven home in silence, the tension returning. One week later she'd left.

Josh had hidden away that picture. She didn't understand, couldn't begin to make sense of this.

And Andrea... Rachel imagined the pain Andrea had felt, the jealousy she'd experienced when she found her husband had saved a memento of his ex-girlfriend. A sick feeling moved through her. "She drove off in a rage?"

He nodded. The deep grooves around his eyes showed the strain of loss.

"You can't take responsibility for that."

"It was my fault," he insisted.

Hurting for him and Griff, she tried to make him see reason. "She was a grown woman. She made the choice to drive while upset. That's not your fault." Rachel could see the disbelief in the depths of his hazel eyes.

"You don't understand, Rachel. She wrapped her car around that tree on purpose." He shuddered as if haunted by the memory. "I saw the finality in her eyes as she tore out of the driveway."

Her mind recoiled from accepting that thought. "You don't know that as fact. Why didn't you tell her the picture didn't mean anything?"

He closed his eyes. His mouth tightened into a grim line as if somehow he could stop the words from coming. She'd pushed him this far; she wasn't going to let him back away from letting out whatever was destroying him inside.

Even as her hand reached for him, she acknowledged that in touching him, she felt connected to him in a way she'd never felt with anyone else.

She rubbed his arm until his hand captured hers. Fascinated, she watched as he brought her palm to his lips. He kissed the tender flesh, then slid his lips to her fingertips before replacing her hand in her lap. She shivered with the impact of those gentle kisses.

"You didn't answer my question," she stated, her voice shaky.

When he looked at her, the tenderness swirling in the hazel depths of his eyes sent her heart racing. When he spoke, his words made her breathing screech to a halt.

"Because it would've been a lie."

Josh waited for Rachel to say something, anything. Instead, he watched the coldness come over her, seeping into her glacier-blue gaze. The doctor was back.

"Well, I can certainly understand how that would've made your wife more unhappy," she said dryly.

He blinked.

A little crease appeared between her dark brows. "That still doesn't give you the right to own all the guilt for Andrea's death."

"What do you mean? Of course I'm guilty. She wouldn't have been in the car if she hadn't found that picture I'd kept and she wouldn't have driven away if I'd stopped her. If I'd been a better husband, none of this would have happened. If I'd loved her enough. Been enough..." The words broke from him in an anguished rush.

She shook her head. "Wow, I thought doctors were the only ones susceptible to God complexes."

He rubbed his face wearily. "When did you develop such a biting wit?"

"Josh, listen to me." Her authoritative tone demanded attention. "I have no doubt you were a good husband. But you're right, Josh, you weren't enough."

Shocked, the air left his body as if he'd been pushed off a cliff and was free-falling without a parachute.

Josh looked into her eyes, expecting to see condemnation but instead saw cool compassion.

"Only God's enough. And you aren't God. He gives each of us free will. Andrea could have chosen to handle the situation differently. Unfortunately, you have to live with the results of her choice." Her gaze shifted away. "We all have to live with the results of others' choices and...our own. Some good, some bad. Some necessary, others optional."

The wisdom in her words touched him deeply. Did she regret the choices she'd made? "You're an amazing woman, Rachel Maguire."

She raised a brow at him, a joking glint in her blue eyes. "You're just now figuring that out?"

"I've always known. I'm just starting to appreciate it more." And it was true. He did appreciate her strength, her compassion and her wit.

A faint tinge of pink brightened her cheeks but the look in her eyes turned impossibly colder before she quickly checked her watch. "It's, uh, late. Or early, depending on your frame of reference. You—you should check on Griff. Yes, that's what you should do." She stood, her spine rigid and straight.

Was she flustered? She rambled as if she was, but her body language said otherwise. He'd like to be able to figure her out. But he would never get the chance.

Slowly he stood. "And you have a plane to catch."

A hollow feeling settled in the pit of his stomach. He hated the thought of her leaving, of never seeing her again, but he knew it was for the best. His heart couldn't take much more damage.

"Oh, yes. I do have to take care of my flight." She walked out of the chapel and to the elevators.

Josh followed. His heart twisted in his chest at her cold and unemotional acknowledgment of her departure.

Once they were inside the elevator, she pushed the button for Griff's floor and then the lobby.

Josh frowned. "You're not coming to see Griff?"

She didn't look at him. "I need to use the phone. Dr.

Hunford, the E.R. attending, said I could use the doctor's lounge in the E.R."

"You could use the phone in Griff's room."

She glanced at him. "I don't want to disturb him."

"Griff will be upset if he doesn't get to see you before you leave." Just thinking about having to tell his son she'd left for good made his stomach churn.

She turned her crystal gaze on him and cocked her head speculatively. "What about your request that I stay away from him?"

Josh ran a hand through his hair. "I overreacted. I shouldn't have said that."

"No, you shouldn't have." Her expression softened slightly. "But I understand."

He touched her cheek, enjoying the softness of her skin beneath his callused hand. "Do you?" he asked quietly, wondering if she really understood she had the power to destroy all of their hearts.

She swallowed. His eyes were drawn to the slender column of her neck, to the visible pulse point in her creamy skin. He leaned toward her with every intention of kissing her.

Then the elevator doors opened.

Rachel stepped back, her eyes wide and cool.

Reining in his attraction, he asked, "We'll see you later?"

She nodded and the elevator doors slid shut, leaving Josh to deal with the sad ache gripping his heart. Resignation lay heavy on his shoulders. She'd leave and he's miss her.

Again.

Chapter Fourteen

As soon as the doors closed and she was alone in the elevator, Rachel slumped against the cool surface of the wall. Josh had almost kissed her. And she'd have let him. She wanted him to, actually.

Josh and his son had demolished the barricade she'd placed around her heart. She felt beat-up and bruised. But recuperation would have to wait until she returned to Chicago. Which meant if she were truly committed to staying a few more days, she'd have to shore up her defenses and guard her heart and her emotions like a fortress.

But not tonight. She ached too much to do anything. Everything Josh had revealed left her reeling.

Andrea's tragic death made Rachel's insides quiver with sadness and guilt.

Sadness for what Josh had lost—his wife, his complete family and his dream. Sadness for Griff who lost his mother before he ever got a chance to know her.

Guilt. No, she wouldn't own the guilt. It was not her fault that Andrea drove into that tree. Nor was it Josh's, regardless of what he believed.

The man was too honorable, too generous and caring to be burdened with such guilt. She wanted to protect him, to make his life better. These feelings were so different, so much more than what she'd felt for him in high school. More intense, deeper. Based not on the fantasies of a starry-eyed teenager but on the reality of loving the man Josh had become.

The admission made her already-weak knees tremble as the elevator door slid open. Placing one foot in front of the other and walking out into the hall took a great deal of concentration.

She loved Josh.

Not with a girl's infatuation but with a grown woman's love. And not only with a tiny corner of her heart, but with the whole kit and caboodle. Every defense she had crumbled to smithereens, laying her heart and emotions exposed and vulnerable.

Lord, what do I do now?

Telling him served no purpose. Her life was in Chicago, his here in Sonora.

But thinking about the small apartment she called home filled her with emptiness. Even thinking about Cook County Hospital, her prestigious position and the tremendous accomplishments in triage care, working to prevent a repeat of her mother's experience, didn't fill the vacant spots. Only thoughts of Josh, Griff and the big Victorian house caused warmth to spread through her and pushed away the empty coldness.

She entered the deserted lounge and put her hand on the phone. She'd thought the decision to stay was for Griff's sake, but the decision had been for Josh and herself, as well. He needed her even if he didn't know it.

And she needed him.

She'd never realized how much until now.

She'd thought she was getting along fine in life alone, when in actuality she'd had Mom G. as a safety net. Now that she was in reality alone, with no family, she didn't want to be alone.

She wanted more. Mom G. had said God wanted more for her. More than a career. She couldn't discount the satisfaction that came from her work, but the long lonely years ahead stretched out before her, making her want to find the *more* that God had waiting for her.

She hoped it was Josh. She needed his steady presence, his solid strength. She needed his force of character, honest and fair, though at times misguided in his attempts to protect himself and those he loved. Could he love her? The question bounced around her head and her pulse sped up.

Then another thought came slamming home. She could live in Sonora and still practice medicine because the hospital no longer held the haunting specter of her mother's unnecessary death. Her mother hadn't died in vain. Rachel had made a difference and could continue on in this hospital.

With her heart beating in her throat, she quickly made her calls, leaving her return to Chicago open-ended.

She would stay and see if there was any hope for her

and Josh. She prayed that this was part of God's plan because it was now part of hers.

Josh stepped out of the elevator and into the E.R. People milled through the waiting area and he felt a pang of sympathy. He remembered all too well what it was like waiting to find out if your life would ever be the same again. He suppressed the shudder that rippled over him and searched for the doctors' lounge.

Not seeing any marked doors, he headed toward a man in a white coat. The name tag on the man's breast pocket identified him as Dr. Hunford. He remembered Rachel mentioning him. "Excuse me, Doctor. Could you point me toward the doctors' lounge?"

Bushy black brows rose over dark eyes. "Can I help you with something?"

Josh smiled politely. "I'm looking for a friend who was going to use the lounge phone."

Dr. Hunford returned his smile. "You mean Dr. Maguire?"

"Have you seen her?"

"Come with me."

Dr. Hunford led the way down a hallway. "Do you know Dr. Maguire well?"

He answered, "Yes."

Did he know her well? Josh considered the question. He knew many things about Rachel. She was generous with her time, affectionate and loving toward his son, full of compassion and strength, a competent doctor, authoritative and challenging until he thought he'd howl with frustration, and yet, she remained a mystery to him. The thoughts that accompanied those sparkling blue eyes, eyes that at times turned to cold ice, were hidden from him.

"It was a good thing for us that Dr. Maguire has a license to practice in the state of California. We were in quite a pickle last night with the pileup on Highway 108. We appreciated all her help," Dr. Hunford said.

Josh frowned. She'd helped in the E.R. last night? When he'd thought she'd gone back to her hotel, she'd been down here. She must be exhausted.

As they approached a room marked Doctors' Lounge, Rachel stepped out. She smiled when she saw the two men. Josh sucked in a breath. She hadn't smiled like that since… He couldn't remember seeing her smile with that much warmth since she'd returned. At least not at him. His son received smiles like that but Josh didn't. He narrowed his eyes. He didn't get it. What did she have up her sleeve?

"Here she is," Dr. Hunford said unnecessarily.

"Dr. Hunford, Joshua. You were looking for me?" she said, her tone cheery.

Josh's suspicions deepened. She never called him Joshua. He thought back through the years. The only time he could recall her using the formal form of his name was… His eyes widened and his gaze jumped to her face.

When they'd been at their tree. She'd wanted to stop fighting and had distracted him with his name on her lips and that glorious mouth drove all arguments from his head.

What was going on?

Dr. Hunford smiled. "I wanted to say thank you for pitching in last night."

"You're welcome. I enjoyed working alongside your staff. They're very good."

Dr. Hunford puffed with pride. "They are. But we could sure use more people like you around here. Any chance you'll be sticking around?"

The subtle glance the man gave Josh was rife with meaning. Josh suppressed the urge to roll his eyes and say, "Yeah, when gold flows freely through the Mother Lode again."

Her smile faltered slightly. "I'll be in town for at least a few more days."

Okay. As announcements went, it was like a good sock in the stomach. His brows rose as wariness twisted in his chest. What sweet torture was she planning now? "You will?"

She tugged on her bottom lip. The subtle sign of uncertainty rocked Josh. Even when she'd broken down, she hadn't been unsure of herself. Dr. Hunford's gaze bobbed between Josh and Rachel with great interest. Josh wished the man would go away.

"Because…ummm…Griff." Her gaze slid away and then back again. Gone was the hesitancy. Cold determination filled her eyes and her chin went up. "Because you need me to help out with Griff."

Josh gaped at her. "Excuse me?"

Rachel smiled patiently. "Griff's being released today and you still have a fire to deal with."

Oh, man. Rachel staying to help him would only prolong the agony for him and Griff. "I've got my dad."

She arched a black brow. "Your dad has already gone to help with the fire."

He narrowed his gaze. "I'll manage. We've done perfectly well for years without you." He threw her words back at her, not caring that Dr. Hunford was really interested now.

He felt the pierce of her narrowed gaze. "You always had Mom G. to help. Now you have me."

Anger flared hot. Until she got bored and decided the hospital was where she'd rather be. "I don't need you."

Dr. Hunford chose that moment to interrupt. "Well, I do."

Josh swung his angry gaze to the doctor, who blinked owlishly.

Rachel smiled that annoying polite, professional smile. "I'll let you know if I have time to help out."

Dr. Hunford began to back up. "Wonderful. We're shorthanded for the next week or so and I'd love the opportunity to discuss your innovative techniques I've read so much about." He disappeared around the corner.

A week or so. Josh fumed. She would not be staying a week or so. He couldn't take having her in town any longer, not when all he wanted to do was kiss that calm-and-collected look off her beautiful face. He fisted his hands. "You are not staying."

"Yes, I am."

"Why?"

Her smile never changed. "I told you why. You have a fire to deal with. I'm staying until you put it out."

He didn't know if he'd ever be able to put out the

fire she'd ignited in his blood. He'd seen the damage a
fire could cause. He didn't intend to get burned. Again.
"I'll figure something out. Leave as planned."

She shrugged. "I've already changed my plans."

"Unchange them."

"No." The stubborn tilt to her chin didn't bode well.
"You're wasting time. Let's get Griff home."

He gritted his teeth. There had to be another way. He
could call Jen and see if she'd take care of Griff. No,
he couldn't add to her already-busy life. Griff was
going to need a lot of attention at first. Josh would tell
his father to go home. That's what he'd do.

"Josh, the fire."

"All right, all right," he said, irritated by her
reminder. What choice did he have? He would have to
allow her to come to the house and stay with Griff until
he could send Dad home from the fire. And then he'd
send Rachel packing, boxing up his hopes and wishes
to be shipped along with her.

Josh pulled the truck to a halt in front of his house.
Fury churned and twisted in his chest, mingling with
worry. His father had refused to leave the station and
return home to relieve Rachel of her charge. In fact, his
father had elected to sleep at the station. Rod's misguided attempts at matchmaking were wearing thin.

To make matters worse, the blaze had jumped the
fire line.

Josh hadn't been able to even think about going
home until well past dark, which left his son with
Rachel for hours. Oh, he knew she'd take good care of

him. Too good of care. She'd be affectionate and funny with Griff. She probably had tons of stories to tell and would make his son's heart swell with love. Which would make her leaving that much harder.

He opened the front door. The house was quiet. A single light from the family room lent its glow to guide him. He stopped inside the doorway, his breath trapped somewhere between his lungs and his heart.

Rachel sat on the couch. She'd changed from the green scrubs into—he blinked, stunned—his sweat suit.

Her eyes were closed, dark lashes rested against her milky complexion and her lustrous hair spread across the cushions. Her crossed ankles were propped up on the coffee table. He dragged his eyes away from her red-tipped toes to Griff. His small, round head rested on Rachel's lap and his broken ankle lay resting on another pillow.

Bittersweet longing hit him square between the eyes. If only this scene were real. He longed for Rachel to be his wife, for her to be his son's mother. He longed to come home from work like this and see her here waiting for him. To hear her voice filling the house with love and laughter. He longed for nights spent in her arms and to awaken in the morning light with her beside him.

He longed for a life that would never be.

She would never be content to be his wife. To live a simple life. To live again in this small town when the big city beckoned her away with excitement, when the hospital she worked at provided her the fulfillment she craved: a high-powered position with upward career possibilities. He couldn't compete with what she believed God had planned for her.

Just as he and his father hadn't been able to compete with the life his mother had wanted.

He must never forget that the most important thing to Rachel would always be her career. He hadn't been enough then, and he wouldn't be now.

And the quicker he got her out of his house the better. So Griff wouldn't be hurt like he'd been hurt.

But what was he to do with her tonight? He couldn't leave Griff to take her to the hotel and he couldn't leave her on the couch. She'd have to sleep in the guest room upstairs. Down the hall from his room.

He gulped.

Taking a deep breath, he moved to the couch and gingerly lifted Griff from her lap and carried him upstairs, careful of his ankle. Once his son was settled, Josh went to the guest room and turned down the bed.

He ignored the hammering in his chest at the thought of her beautiful dark hair spilling across the white pillow. He quickly spun away from the choking image.

Back downstairs, he contemplated how best to move Rachel upstairs. He rapidly dismissed the idea of waking her because facing a sleepy and cute Rachel was something he'd rather not do.

Cautiously he slipped a hand under her head and the other under her knees. He slowly lifted her, testing her weight. She barely weighed anything. Easily he raised her up in his arms and held her to him. She stirred, sighing slightly.

"Shh, its okay," he whispered.

Her arms slid around his neck and she nuzzled closer, her cheek warm against his chest. She'd showered, and the scent of Griff's shampoo clung to her soft hair. He'd never considered the smell of green apples an aphrodisiac.

Thinking himself insane for putting himself through such torture, he hurried upstairs with her. By the light of the moon coming through the window he laid her down gently on the soft bed and rested her head on the pillow. Her arms tightened around his neck and she made a soft sound of protest deep in her throat as he tried to extract himself.

He leaned in a little, his face close to hers, her arms allowing some slack. Her breath teased the hair at his temple. He closed his eyes against the zing of pleasure ricocheting through his veins and crippling his heart.

Every instinct urged him to gather her close and give in to the feminine allure of Rachel. To abandon all thought, all conscience and reasoning, for one precious moment in her arms.

God help me.

By strength drawn only from his faith, Josh gently pried her arms lose and laid them beside her. She snuggled into the bed and turned on her side. He swallowed and quickly pulled up the lightweight blanket, covering her slender curves.

He backed out of the room, very much aware that Rachel Maguire slept in his house. He doubted he'd get any sleep tonight.

Rachel bolted upright. She blinked, her eyes adjusting to the darkness broken slightly by the moonlight seeping through the crack of the curtain. She was in an unfamiliar room in a strange bed. Then it hit her. She smiled with pleasure. She was in Josh's house, apparently in the guest room.

She pushed the button on her watch and the circular dial lit up with a green glow. Two-forty in the morning.

The last thing she remembered was sitting on the couch with Griff, telling him the funnier stories from the E.R. The time was precious and she'd never felt so wanted or so satisfied. She belonged here with this family. Griff had finally dozed off and she must have, as well.

Tugging on the too-big sweatshirt she'd confiscated from Josh's dryer, pleasure welled up at the thought of Josh carrying her upstairs. With the way he'd reacted when she'd stated she was staying, it was little wonder he hadn't carted her back to the hotel. But he hadn't. He'd made her comfortable. He'd taken care of her. She liked the idea of Josh caring for her.

Yawning sleepily, she slid her feet off the bed and onto the floor. She stood, swaying slightly as blood rushed to her head. When her equilibrium returned, she shuffled to the door and peeked into the dark hall. She bit her lip trying to remember which way to the bathroom. She shrugged and started out to her left. Her big toe connected with something hard and solid which in turn connected with the wall.

"Ouch," she muttered at the small table, and steadied it with her hands, hoping the noise from the table scraping the wall hadn't disturbed anyone.

She tried the first door she came to, peering in.

Griff's room. Pale moonlight shone on the sleeping boy. Rachel stood watching Griff sleep for a moment. He'd become so dear to her. Quietly she closed the door.

She turned to head the other way and ran into a big, firm mass. A small yelp escaped her.

"You okay?" Josh's groggy voice swept over her in the darkness, chasing away the last vestiges of sleep.

"Josh, you scared me," she whispered back.

"Sorry. Heard a noise. Wanted to make sure you were okay."

His sleep-husky voice sent a thrill down her spine. He was worried about her. "Just looking for the bathroom."

"Over here." His hand reached out and found her shoulder. Bits of fire raced along her arm and she trembled under the onslaught of emotions the heat sparked.

He guided her toward another door, opened it, flipped the switch and stepped back.

Rachel blinked in the sudden light. When she was able to focus, her heart twisted with tenderness. Josh looked so adorable standing there in his plaid flannel boxers and T-shirt, his hair mussed from sleep, his eyes drowsy and his expression unguarded. "Thank you for letting me sleep here tonight."

He smiled a sweet, boyish smile that melted her heart. "Anytime." He stepped forward and placed a feather-light kiss on her lips. "G'night." He turned and shuffled down the dark hall.

Rachel's breath caught and held as she watched him

disappear into a room. The gentle caress seared her, branded her as his.

But would he ever claim her?

Chapter Fifteen

Her fingertips traced the warmth still lingering on her lips. He'd kissed her. Not a passionate, "I want you" kind of kiss, but a sweet, loving gesture that said "I care." The poignant moment stretched as she considered the implications of that single little kiss.

He cared. Whether he wanted to admit it or not, he cared. And if he cared, then love could follow. Not the same love from their teenage years. They were adults now. Different than they'd been back then. And their love would be different. If he could love her. Her heart pounded loudly in her ears.

If they loved each other enough, surely they could find a way to make their lives come together. A nagging feeling that tried to rob her of the hope of happiness warned that love hadn't been enough once.

She wouldn't let doubt interfere. So much had happened, changed. She'd changed. She would find a way to make this work. She held her breath.

Maybe they were being given another chance.

Oh, God. Please, please. I want Josh to see that I can be a wife, a mother and *a doctor.*

In the morning, Josh showered and dressed quickly. He checked on Griff who still slept soundly. He paused outside of the guest room door. He considered waking Rachel up and asking her to leave, but decided a note would do just as well. After his fitful night's sleep, he didn't think seeing her before he left would be a good thing. He'd dreamed way too much last night. And all of his dreams had centered on Rachel.

Quietly he went down the stairs. He headed for the kitchen, but a movement in his peripheral vision stopped him in his tracks. He turned slowly, his whole body becoming alert to Rachel's presence, but when he actually saw her, he wasn't prepared for the sight.

Stunned pleasure surged through his veins and his mind screamed what his heart wanted to deny. She shouldn't be wearing his old football jersey, the hem flirting with her knees. She shouldn't be moving so gracefully, her lithe slender body flowing through controlled movements. She shouldn't be in his house at all.

He couldn't tear his gaze away. Somewhere in his foggy brain he recalled knowing the type of martial art she was practicing, but he couldn't think, let alone come up with the name.

Her fluid movements took her through a complete range of motion. Her capable hands, rigid and taut, slid through the air. Her legs gently carried her petite form in a wide arc, yet her feet barely left the ground.

"Good morning, Josh."

Even her voice flowed, graceful and calm. A shiver sent him into action. Averting his gaze, he began to pace, his heavy boots ringing hollow on the hardwood floor.

"You shouldn't be here," he said.

"Yes, I should," she replied firmly.

He shook his head. "No. When Griff wakes, you should go."

"You have a fire to put out, don't you?"

"The others can handle it."

He hated contemplating not going to the station, but he hated having her entrenched in his house even more because it was only temporary. He didn't want temporary.

He wanted forever.

She smoothly turned to face him, her hands competently cutting the air in front of her. "You'd hate that, Josh."

He stopped pacing and narrowed his gaze on her. "You think you know me so well, do you?"

A slight curving of her lips was her only answer.

"Rachel, I can't have you here anymore." He winced at the almost-desperate note in his voice. He ached all over, from his heart to his toes.

"Sure you can. You need me." She bent low at the knees, the hem of his old jersey riding up slightly to reveal firm muscle and curves. All the blood left his head.

"I don't need you," he said from between clenched teeth. He wanted her in the most base of ways but he did not need her. No way.

"Sure you do." She rose and rocked back on one heel. "You need me to stay with Griff."

"You're killing me here, Rachel," he choked out, and tried to pry his gaze from where his jersey pulled tight across her shoulders.

She paused midmotion. A graceful statue, a work of art. A feminine smile curved her lips. He couldn't imagine her cold or distant at the moment. She glanced at him knowingly.

He was surprised he didn't just vaporize on the spot. "Rachel."

"You didn't have a problem with me being here last night." She moved again, a slow sweeping arc from left to right, her hands twisting through space.

"I didn't have a choice last night. You fell asleep." He certainly had a choice now. But his resolve to make her leave was rapidly slipping and being filled with impossible thoughts. Thoughts about how nice it was to find her here, wearing his shirt. To have her in his house, willing to take care of his son.

"You said I could stay anytime."

He frowned. "I did?"

"You don't remember?"

"Well…I vaguely remember getting up in the night. But I don't remember what I said." He'd been concerned when he'd heard her bang into the hall table.

"Or what you did?"

He rocked back on the heels of his boots. "Did?"

She pulled her limbs together and executed a neat bow. When she straightened, a smile as bright as lightning lit her face. "You kissed me."

He blinked, stunned by her smile. Stunned by her statement. He searched his memory; a fuzzy image of Rachel standing in the soft light flowing into the hall came to mind. He'd kissed her good-night. "I did." He swallowed. That simple little kiss changed nothing. She still had to leave. Quickly. Before he got ideas about more kisses. "I'll wake Griff. We'll take you to your hotel."

"I've already arranged for the hotel to messenger my things over."

"Rachel."

"Josh."

He balled his hands into fists. "Why are you doing this? I thought you wanted to get back to your precious hospital and your big-city life as quickly as you could."

She cocked her head to one side, her smile still in place, only a little less sunny. "We made a promise and I intend on keeping it. Right now, you need help with Griff."

"I'll take him with me."

She rolled her eyes and walked toward him, her bare feet small and graceful. His jersey swished against her knees. She laid a hand on his arm. "Let me do this. Please."

He shouldn't. He should make her leave. But with those big, crystal-blue eyes staring up at him so imploringly, so…warm, he couldn't resist. He couldn't resist the pull she had on him. His poor battered heart sunk. "For Griff you can stay."

She patted his arm. "Good. Now off with you. You have a job to do."

He glanced up the stairs. "Do you want me to carry Griff down for you?"

"Don't worry. We'll manage."

Yes, but would *he* manage? Josh worried he was making a mistake. He worried that his son would be hurt, that his own heart would not survive the next few days.

He worried he was losing his mind to allow her to stay. But she was right; he couldn't take Griff with him. He rationalized that another day couldn't cause any more damage than had already been done. So he allowed her to bustle him out the door. He'd deal with how to get her out of his life and his heart later. There was always later.

Rachel finished cleaning up the last of the mess she'd made while fixing dinner. The dark cabinets and gray speckled counters were wiped clean. The round kitchen dining table was set with four places. Fresh flowers in a jar added a sparkle to the room.

The aromas of warmed garlic bread and baked chicken with carrots and onions tempted her appetite. Where was Josh?

When he'd called earlier to check on Griff, he'd said he would be home around now. And when she'd said dinner would be ready and waiting for them, he'd sounded…put out. As if he didn't like the idea of her cooking. Did he think she couldn't handle the meal alone?

She chuckled. She'd put together a fancy feast. In fact, she'd found the domestic task shockingly pleasant. She would prove to Josh that she was not only skilled in healing but in the domestic arts, as well.

The whole day had been pleasant. She and Griff had watched a movie, he'd taught her how to play chess and she'd taught him how to play solitaire. They'd laughed and talked about sports, school and dreams.

Her maternal instincts that had kicked in days before were blooming full force, and she found this form of caretaking appealing.

As a doctor she was responsible to care for bodily injuries, but not emotional well-being. Fix 'em And Move 'em Out was the motto of the E.R. She'd always thought that was best for her. No attachments, no hassles. No risking of her heart. Always staying focused on making sure her mother hadn't died in vain. Her heart soared to know that she'd accomplished what she'd set out to do.

Now she was free to take the risk with Griff. And she was willing to take the risk with Josh, too. She'd come a long way in a short time. She smiled and glanced upward. *Is this part of Your plan, God?* She hoped her assumption was on target. There had to be a way to make Josh see that she could be a part of their lives.

The back door opened, startling her. She whirled around as Josh stepped through the doorway. He filled the frame; his towering presence made the air crackle with enflamed energy.

She loved to see him in his uniform. Loved the way the fabric hugged his muscles and the muted green color brightened his hazel eyes.

This morning when he'd come downstairs and watched her do her exercises, she'd had a hard time concentrating, because she'd only wanted to stop and stare at him like a hormone-driven teen.

She swallowed back the urge to throw her arms around him and welcome him home the way a wife would. She wasn't his wife. The hope that one day she might be his wife made her smile. "Hello."

He stared at her in silence as if he couldn't quite believe what he was seeing. "Hello," he said, his tone cautious.

Had her expression given away her thoughts? She schooled her features to impassive politeness. She'd have to tread slowly with him. Let him get used to the idea of having her around. "Dinner's ready when you are."

He glanced around. "Wow, great." He hesitated, then moved farther into the room, closer to Rachel. So close that she could feel heat radiating from his big body.

"Where's your dad?"

His expression darkened. "He's staying at the station."

Though she didn't comment, she had a feeling she knew why Rod had stayed away. She smiled inwardly and reached to take Josh's jacket from him.

Their hands brushed, electricity shooting through her. Her gaze flew to his. He regarded her warily, his gaze searching her face.

She blinked and stepped back. *Slowly, remember. Don't spook him.* If lightly touching his hand put him on guard, what would an all-out kissing assault do?

She fought back an uncharacteristic giggle tickling her throat. Assaulting a man with her kisses. That was so unlike her. But this wasn't just any man. This was Josh.

What would he do if she kissed him again? Her blood sizzled with anticipation. She just might have to find out.

"This is awesome, Rachel," Griff exclaimed around a mouthful of chocolate brownie.

Josh watched his son with relief. He loved seeing the life shining from Griff's gaze. The ugly dark lump on Griff's forehead reminded Josh the situation could have been much worse.

And he was thankful for Rachel's stoic presence. Her ability to remain calm, to think in the midst of a crisis. Her willingness to stay with Griff, despite Josh's objections. She touched Josh deeply.

"Would you like another, Josh?" Rachel asked, her voice smooth and satiny.

She held out the pan, her smile pleasant and her eyes amiable. She was a confusing mix of cold and hot.

When she'd first come back to town, he'd have sworn there was no heat in the perfectly sculptured icehouse surrounding her. But he'd seen glimpses of the woman beneath the ice, a woman who was open and friendly, gracious and kind. He didn't know what to make of the contrasting elements of Rachel. He looked at the chocolate concoction. "No, thank you. Three's more than enough."

"They met with your approval?"

"Yes." Was she fishing for a compliment? Interesting. "You're a wonderful cook."

A soft hue of pink touched her cheeks. She looked pleased.

Griff chimed in. "This is great, huh, Dad? Wouldn't it be great to have Rachel here all the time?"

Josh's heart dropped to his toes. This was what he'd been afraid of. That his son would get ideas, get more attached. "Son, this has been nice. But Rachel's life's in Chicago. She'll be returning tomorrow or the next day."

Griff scrunched up his face. "Why?"

"The fire will be under control and Grandpa and I will be able to come home."

Griff shook his head. "No. Why does her life have to be there? Why can't it be here?"

Groaning inwardly, Josh glanced at Rachel. Why wasn't she helping him out with this? She'd gone motionless, her expression rigid and frosty. He frowned and turned back to his son. "Griff, Rachel's a doctor in Chicago."

"She could be a doctor here," Griff insisted.

Josh gritted his teeth. "Griff—"

"Couldn't you, Rachel? Couldn't you be a doctor here? Couldn't you live here with us? We could be a family," Griff implored, his eyes shining with unshed tears.

Josh clenched his fists. His son's heart was going to be broken. Anger—at himself for allowing this and at Rachel for wheedling her way into their lives—made his pulse pound.

And still she sat there cold as ice. Unfeeling and uncaring that she was destroying his son's young heart. He didn't even want to think about his own heart. Right now all that mattered was Griff. Josh needed to do damage control. "Son, please. Let's talk late—"

Then she moved, cutting off what he was about to say.

She leaned forward, her hand reaching to Griff.

His son clung to her. Her expression was no less icy, but sparks of heat danced just beyond the cold. Would he ever be able to figure her out? "Griff, I'd love to stay. But that's something your father and I need to discuss."

Floored, Josh sat back in his chair. She had no right to get his son's hopes up. No right to suggest there was some way for them. What about her precious career? What about her life in Chicago? He couldn't allow himself to give in to the spurt of hope her words produced.

If he did, he'd never recover.

Enraged by Rachel's suggestive remark, Josh abruptly stood. "Griff, this is something we'll discuss later. Right now you need your rest."

"Aw, Dad," Griff complained, his gaze darting between the two adults.

"Go on, Griff. Your dad's right."

Josh couldn't look at Rachel. He had to concentrate on his son. Had to get him out of there to a safer place. He picked Griff up and strode from the room.

"Dad, are you angry?"

Trying to control the wrath raging in his heart, Josh said carefully, "I'm upset."

"Why?"

Climbing the stairs, Josh wondered how best to answer that question. He decided on the direct and honest approach. "Because I'd like Rachel to stay, too, but she can't. She's a doctor and that will always be her priority."

Griff frowned, seeming to think over his father's words. "But she could be a doctor and still be in our family. Kevin's mom's a lawyer and she's still part of their family."

"That's different," he responded through a throat tight with aching. He ached for his son, for himself. He ached because he didn't want Rachel to leave.

But she couldn't stay. He couldn't play second fiddle to her career, knowing one day she might decide she no longer wanted to do both. And he'd be the one she'd give up.

He laid Griff on his bed.

Griff settled himself back on the pillow. "Why's that different?"

Josh sighed. "Because it just is. Rachel lives in the big city. She'd never be content here."

"Sure she would."

"But that's not what I want," Josh said harshly. He smoothed hair back from Griff's bruise, careful not to put pressure on the lump. "If I remarry, I want someone who would be content to be my wife and your mother."

Griff stared at him for a long moment, then his little jaw set into a determined line. "When I get married, my wife can be anything she wants to be."

Griff's simple, profound statement hit Josh hard, knocking the breath from his lungs.

He realized it wasn't about Rachel's career choice. It wouldn't have mattered if she'd become a dentist, a teacher or an accountant. As long as her career, her dream, was more important than his love, he couldn't risk his heart. He couldn't measure her commitment to him and he needed concrete assurance.

Josh gathered his son close to his chest. "I love you, Griff."

"I love you, too, Dad."

He left Griff with the bedside lamp on and books to read.

Squaring his shoulders, Josh knew what he had to do. It was time to tell Rachel to leave. Not tomorrow, or the next day, but now. Her presence was too confusing, too painful. For both Griff and himself. He was tired of hurting, tired of feeling that ache take root in his soul.

The healing process would take time, but he would heal. They would heal together, he and his son. They didn't need Rachel.

The thought left him feeling cold and empty, reassuring him that he was making the right choice. Because without Rachel in his life, he would be empty and cold.

He stepped into the kitchen to see Rachel holding the phone receiver to her ear. She had her back to him, with one finger she traced patterns in the woodwork on the wall.

"Yes, of course. I do realize the importance of my position and I'll be back to…I understand, Doctor. Yes, I will take care of the situation. A few days at the most."

Josh didn't need any further confirmation that sending Rachel away now was the right thing to do. He and his son couldn't withstand the torture of having her around for a few more days.

A noise behind Rachel announced Josh's presence. She turned in time to see him stalking away. She finished her call and hung up.

With a sigh she leaned against the wall. The chief of staff of Cook County Hospital in Chicago wanted to know when she would be returning. She'd bought some time because she needed time to sort out the future, but she also knew she had a responsibility to the hospital. She would go back to resign and help make the transition easier for a new attending.

But right now finding Josh was more important.

She hesitated before stepping into the living room. She was in trouble. This confrontation had come faster than she had wanted or expected. But life always worked out the way it did for a reason. God was in control and if His plan was for them to have this out now, she'd meet the challenge head-on. As always.

Logical and sound reasoning. Challenging questions. Unemotional. Those were the buzzwords that she had to remember. Now to keep her emotions in check and give Josh a rational argument for why they could work, why she could now stay in Sonora and be a doctor here. Why she could be his wife.

If only she had done some research by calling a female colleague and finding out how she managed to raise a family and be an effective doctor. No matter. She was going into this discussion armed with her love and force of will as her weapons. She had to convince Josh that she could be wife, mother *and* doctor.

Tread slowly.

A wild thought ran through her mind. She wanted to kiss him. Wanted to touch him, feel the connection to him she felt every time they touched. She shook her head. That approach wouldn't work. She almost giggled again, thinking how he'd reacted in the kitchen by the mere brushing of their hands. No, coming in with lips blazing wouldn't be the best way to start what was going to be a draining and lengthy discussion.

Drawing herself up and taking a fortifying breath, she sedately glided into the room and stopped at the end of the couch. Josh sat with his long legs stretched out in front of him and his big body taking up one end of the couch.

How to begin? "I think your son and your father have been doing a little matchmaking," she stated quietly.

He laughed slightly. "You just now noticed?"

A wry smile touched her lips. "I suspected it. I suspected Rod and Mom G. were up to something, but I was surprised by Griff's manipulations. He's a smart boy."

"Too smart for his own good."

She wondered what they'd discussed when he'd carried Griff upstairs. "I hope you weren't too hard on him for trying to bring us together."

He stared at her through hooded eyes. "I don't want him to get hurt," he stated flatly.

"Then maybe we should discuss his suggestion." Her voice sounded even, but inside she quivered with hope and dread. Hope that he'd want her love, dread that he wouldn't. Hope that they'd find a way to make them a family, dread that logic and reasoning wouldn't work.

He regarded her steadily. "Discuss?"

"Yes." She sat on the couch, keeping a safe distance

away. If she touched him, she wouldn't be able to keep her emotions from showing.

"All right. Let's discuss. What kind of game are you playing?" His voice was low and tinged with a sharp edge.

"There's no game." She understood his confusion. Her own awakening needs and feelings bemused her.

"Rachel, you can't waltz into our lives, getting our hopes up when you have no intention of staying."

The indefinable undertone to his words prepared her for battle. She jumped into the fray with both feet. "I could see myself staying here."

A tawny brow rose. "Oh?"

"I mean…" What did she mean? How did she express the contentment she'd felt the past two days? How did she express the love expanding in her heart? How did she stay unemotional when she wanted to throw herself in his arms and declare her love and ask him to love her back?

She drew herself up, collecting her composure. "I mean, I've enjoyed being here. I've enjoyed caring for your son." She swallowed then went on steadily. "I've enjoyed caring for you."

In the waning light of evening, his hazel eyes searched her face.

She rushed on. "Twelve years ago we were both young and we loved each other with an immature love. Neither of us was willing to compromise. We both dug in our heels and hurt each other."

His expression intensified, laying claim to her heart. "We did hurt each other. And I'm sorry for that."

"Me, too." She clasped her hands together to keep from reaching out to him. "We're older now, more mature. We've had time to learn to compromise. We've had time to figure out what we want in life."

She paused and drew strength from the conviction in her heart. "I know what I want in life, Josh. I want you." She gestured with her hand, encompassing the house. "I want this. I love you, Josh. Do you think you could love me?"

Chapter Sixteen

The heat in his gaze threatened to scorch, to enflame Rachel beyond endurance.

"Loving you, Rachel, was never the problem."

He loved her. She couldn't breathe for the joy bubbling in her heart. She trembled with the effort to contain her emotion. "You're right, love wasn't the problem. It was us. We each had set ideas of how we wanted our lives. I needed to be a doctor."

"And I've always wanted a wife who'd be passionate about me, about our life together."

"You could have that, Josh. With me."

"Could I?" His gaze narrowed and one corner of his mouth curved with cynicism. "What happened to 'my career's my priority. God wants me to make a difference'?"

Being slapped with her own words popped her little bubbles of joy. "I do believe God wants me to make a difference and my career *has* been my priority."

"So, you've had a miraculous change of heart?"

She stiffened. *Stay unemotional.* "In a way. God has been working on me ever since I returned home." If Josh heard the hitch in her voice as she said the last word he didn't indicate it. She swallowed, stunned to realize she was indeed home.

"Right. And how long will playing house be enough for you?"

"That's not fair, Josh."

"No, it's not fair. Life's not fair. But then again God never promised life would be fair."

The bitterness in his voice made her cringe. How could she get through to him? "These past few days here have made me realize that I've been too…" She trailed off, searching for the right word.

"Obsessed?"

She frowned. "No. Focused."

"And just where's the line, Rachel?"

"Line?"

"The line between doing God's will and obsession?"

She bit back her stirring anger. "I haven't been obsessed. I've been committed and focused."

He stood and moved to the fireplace. For a long moment he stared into the empty grate. Finally he pivoted, his gaze riveting. "What drives you, Rachel?"

Her mother's lifeless body flashed across the screen in her mind. Gut-wrenching pain followed the image. Her instinctive reaction was to push the pain to the far corners of her soul, but the need to tell him stopped her.

Maybe if she spoke of her mother's death, he'd

finally understand. Mustering every ounce of courage she possessed, she rose. "Do you really want to know?"

He folded his arms across his chest as if to protect himself from her. "Yes, I do."

Rachel swallowed several times before she could find her voice. "I was six when my mother died."

His expression softened. "I know. She died of a heart condition."

"She did have a heart condition when she died, but that wasn't what killed her."

"What do you mean?"

Rachel took a deep breath and slowly exhaled, careful to keep her voice unemotional. "She'd been under a doctor's care for a long time. Some days she was bedridden, other days she was like everyone else's mom. Normal." She stared out the window, her gaze trained on the big oak tree with the swing. She remembered the heat of that summer's day and the fear. "Mom was having a good day. We'd been shopping for school clothes when she started having trouble breathing."

Her chest grew heavy with remembered panic; she fought against letting the memory affect her. "We'd hurried from the store, our purchases forgotten. Mom drove, weaving all over the road and I was so scared we'd have an accident. We arrived at the hospital in one piece. The orderlies took her away. A nurse led me to a waiting area." She closed her eyes, unsure if she could tell the rest.

Josh moved, his warm hand covered hers. "Rachel, if it's too painful you don't have to tell me."

His compassion gave her the strength to continue.

"I need to tell you." She squeezed his hand. "To make you understand. I saw her, Josh. Lying on the table so still and pale. Machines screaming, the doctors frantic." The horror of the day haunted her dreams.

"Her heart failed," Josh stated, as if that explained everything.

"No," she cried. "Her heart didn't just fail, the doctors failed."

"Rachel, you of all people should know life's uncertain. Your mother had a bad heart and she died from it."

She yanked her hand from his grip. She'd heard those words before. The doctors, the social workers, her shrink. Useless anger dripped from her words. "You sound like everyone else. My whole life people have tried to make me believe that lie, but I know what happened."

"What did happen?"

She clenched her fists. Hating the anger and bitterness roaring to life again. "When the nurse wasn't looking, I went into the room. I saw them. I heard the doctor's words. He'd said, 'This shouldn't have happened.'"

"What shouldn't have happened?"

Rachel drew herself up. "Whatever mistake cost my mother her life."

"Do you have proof that they made a mistake?" he asked gently.

"I have my memory." It was all the proof she needed.

Josh laid a hand on her arm. "The memory of a scared six-year-old."

"Don't patronize me, Josh."

"I'm not. It's sad to think you've carried this burden with you your whole life. Why didn't you ever tell me?"

Lifting one stiff shoulder was all she could manage. "I tried. Your knowing wouldn't have changed anything. I still would have left to become a doctor."

"Yeah, but at least it wouldn't have hurt so bad." His expression turned rife with contrition. "Maybe I would've…"

"Waited?" Tears of regret stung her eyes. "I'm sorry, Josh. I was young and focused on my goal. We can't torture ourselves with what ifs. All that matters now is the future. Our future. Do you understand now why I had to become a doctor? Why making a difference was so important? I wanted to save others from the pain and rage of knowing a mistake cost them the life of their loved one."

"Yes, I understand." He backed away, the physical distance not nearly as wide as the emotional distance he'd just created.

His glittering hazel eyes bore into her. "But you have to understand where *I'm* coming from, what *I* need. Apparently we both have mother issues. The day I watched my mother walk away from her family to pursue her dream, I swore I wouldn't settle for less than a woman who would put her family first."

She closed her eyes, her heart screaming in agony over his loss. "You wouldn't have to settle for less, Josh. Not with me. Not ever. Don't you know that?"

"No. I don't." His tone was as coarse as sandpaper. "I don't know that one day you won't decide you've made a mistake. Decide that life wasn't fulfilling enough here. That I wasn't enough."

Her chest threatened to crack wide open. "That wouldn't happen."

"Dad didn't think it would happen, either. He tried to keep her, promised her anything if she'd stay. But she couldn't do both. She wanted her art more than she wanted us. She loved her art more than she loved her son."

The hurt so evident in his eyes tore at her soul. She reached out a hand. "I'm sure that's not true."

He jerked away. "Why weren't we enough for her?"

Behind the handsome exterior, she glimpsed the little boy who hurt with unspeakable torment. His mother's bitter betrayal had scarred the boy and the man. Her heart broke right down the middle, the two sides twisting in anguish. "I don't have an answer to that."

His eyes closed as if the pain were too excruciating. "I don't want to be hurt again, and I don't want my son hurt. I can't have you in our lives if we aren't your priority."

She stared up at him, tears filling her eyes. His words about Andrea came rushing back: *If I'd loved her enough. Been enough.* Josh took the weight of the world upon his broad shoulders, hefted the responsibility for other people like a heavy cloak. She'd thought he'd been wallowing in self-pity when he'd made that statement, but now she realized he owned the sentiment. "Not enough" was branded across his heart by his own hand.

He had no idea how much more than enough he was. *Dear Lord, I don't know how to reach him.*

Digging deep for her last vestige of strength and courage to do the one thing she hated most, she laid her heart and her emotions bare, vulnerable and exposed, before this wonderful man whom she loved with every fiber of her being. "I am who I am, Josh. A woman who loves you, wants to be with you and who's also a doctor. You can't ask me to give up a part of myself.

"God gave me a gift to heal people. I'm good at what I do. I find great satisfaction in my work. But I believe God has been trying to teach me that there can be more. If you take me, you take the whole package. I'm not saying it'll be easy, but if we work together, we can find a way. In time we'll both adjust."

His expression was heartbreaking in its intensity. He seemed to consider her words; conflicting emotions played across the hard planes of his face. Finally he shook his head. "I can't, Rachel. I can't take the risk. I don't have it in me."

Anguish, deep and exploding, nearly sent her to her knees. She gathered her control tightly, taking the composure that had served her so well over the years and wrapping it around her like cocoon. "A wise woman once told me that happiness lies beyond what you think's possible. You only have to have enough faith. God will take care of the rest."

A spasm of regret crossed his face. "I have plenty of faith in God. It's me I don't have faith in."

"Oh, Josh."

He stepped back, away from her outstretched hand. "It won't work, Rachel. I don't ever want to feel that way again."

Her hand dropped to her side. A spurt of anger gripped her. "So you'd rather be alone than take a chance on me?"

"That's the way it has to be. It would be best if you left as soon as you can." He walked past her and out the front door.

A scream of soul-searing pain tore at Rachel's insides as she watched him disappear into the night. Her legs could no longer hold her upright; she slowly sank to the floor.

Raw and bleeding inside, Rachel fought against despair. They would never find a way together if he wasn't willing to fight for it.

God, tell me what to do.

How could Josh think he wasn't enough? Enough for what? Her? Did he not trust her that much? Her mouth twisted wryly. *What have I done to earn that trust? Except lay my love down like a gauntlet, daring him to pick it up.*

Loving you, Rachel, was never the problem.

A spark of hope leapt to life. He loved her, even if he didn't want to admit it. He just didn't trust her not to break his heart.

His mother's betrayal had damaged Josh's perceptions and his ability to trust with faith. What could she do to rebuild that trust? To build his faith in her?

The answer that roared to her mind sent her doubling over. She couldn't defame her mother's memory; she couldn't give up medicine. Being a doctor defined her, made her who she was. If she walked away from that, what would be left?

Josh's wife.

A woman of faith.

Lord, what do I do? I thought You were giving us a second chance.

Understanding flooded her mind and a gentle peace settled over her.

"I do trust you, Lord." She spoke softly, reverently. "I want both. But if I have to choose, this time I choose Josh."

Josh stared at the moon's reflection wavering in the pool's water. He felt like such a fool. Rachel had offered him his heart's desire—her love—and he'd walked away. He loved her and she loved him. Why couldn't that be enough?

Because deep inside, fear laid claim to his heart.

Fear that his love wouldn't be enough. Fear that Rachel would one day walk away like his mother had. Fear that he couldn't survive her departure from his life.

Father, why am I so consumed with fear?

He closed his eyes with weary pain. Fear wasn't of God. God was love and light and hope. And yet, fear twisted in his heart.

Rachel's words floated back to him on the evening breeze.

A wise woman once told me that happiness lies beyond what you think's possible. You only have to have enough faith. God will take care of the rest.

Faith. It all came down to faith. Faith in God, faith in himself and faith in Rachel.

Faith's being sure of what we hope for and certain of what we do not see.

"God, forgive me for not having enough faith in You. Please, Lord, take my fear." He whispered his plea to the night sky.

"Josh?" Rachel approached and stopped beside him.

He stiffened, bracing himself for her goodbye. He didn't want her to say goodbye. But he wasn't free of the fear. A touch, like the delicate kiss of a snowflake on his arm, drew his attention.

"Are you okay?"

Rachel's sweet voice, so full of concern, wrapped around him. He tried to speak, to say he wasn't okay, he'd never be okay without her, but the constriction of his throat muscles wouldn't allow sound to travel from his body.

She withdrew her hand. "I'm not going to let you do this," she said. Her voice now held an edge of steel.

He looked at her. In the moonlight shining on her beautiful face he could see traces of her tears. Tenderness filled him, crowding the fear until he thought he'd choke on it. She'd cried because of him. He didn't want to make her cry, didn't want to hurt her. He loved her.

Her voice softened. "You're so full of anger and hurt. I can understand why you're afraid to trust me, to trust anyone. What your mother did was wrong. She shouldn't have abandoned you. But she made a choice and you have to live with the result of that choice.

"Now *you* have a choice, Josh. You can choose to hold on to the bitterness and the pain or you can forgive her."

He drew back. Something ugly and hateful twisted in his soul. "For…give her?" He could barely get the words out. "You want me to condone what she did?"

Compassion and sadness filled her eyes, lighting the blue depths like beacons in the night. "Not condone her actions, *forgive* her actions. Those are two very different things."

"No, they're not. Not in my book."

"In God's book they are."

"How can you say that?"

Her eyes narrowed slightly. "Do you believe the Bible is truth?"

"Of course," he said indignantly.

"Do you believe that your sins are forgiven?"

"Yes." He snapped the word.

"We need to work on your perceptions," she stated quietly.

"What are you talking about?"

"Do you think that when God forgives you He says, 'that's okay. I know you didn't mean it. Go back to what you were doing'?"

He frowned. What she said didn't seem right, yet wasn't that forgiveness? "I don't know. I think so."

A sweet smiled touched her lips. "When God forgives, He takes our sin and removes it as far as the east is from the west. Then He expects us to move on with our life, not looking back and *not* repeating the sin. He also demands that we forgive those who've sinned against us."

He blinked, trying to wrap his mind around her words. "But how do I forgive her? I don't even know where she is."

"Oh, Josh. She doesn't have to know." She moved closer, her slender hand taking his, the gesture unbearably kind. "When God forgives, it's for us. When we forgive, it's for God. Forgiveness frees us to have a relationship with God and...with others."

"Frees us?" Could what she said be that simple and so hard all at once?

"It'll take time. I'm not saying that if you say you forgive her you'll magically be healed. But have faith in God. Pray for your mother, pray for the strength to forgive. In time the little boy inside of you—" she placed her hand over his heart "—he will be able to let go of the awful stuff. And you, the man, will be able to trust and love."

Josh's mind resisted; the pain was too much a part of him to believe it could be so easily set aside. Thinking of her anger and bitterness toward those she held responsible for her mother's death, he asked, "Have you forgiven the doctors?"

There was a softening in her eyes. "I'm beginning to, thanks to you."

"Me?"

"My mother died in the E.R. at Sonora Community. And until two days ago, I'd never set foot back in there. I didn't believe I ever could. That's why I'd never wanted to practice medicine in Sonora."

Her softly spoken words floored him. He'd never made the connection, never realized the depth of her pain. "I'm so sorry, Rachel. I never..." He widened his eyes as a horrible thought occurred to him. "I asked you to go in there."

She nodded, a confident smile playing at her mouth. "Yes, you did, and I'm grateful. Because if you hadn't,

I would have never known that my life's work had made a difference, that my mother hadn't died in vain. I've faced my demons and have been set free. I want the same for you, Josh. You will find freedom in forgiveness."

Pride for the woman she'd become filled him, restricting his breathing. He thought over her words. Could forgiveness release the fear? Could he learn to love without being afraid to lose that love? "I don't know if I can, Rachel."

Her gaze seemed to frost over, like the car windshield after a winter's night. "Do you love me, Josh?"

She took a few steps away. Suddenly she was distant and untouchable again. She kept doing that, hiding behind an icy wall.

He realized with a start that *was* what she was doing. Hiding.

All the times he'd thought her cold and unfeeling, she'd been hiding. Hiding emotions that made her vulnerable. Hiding her feelings from him.

Inside the wondrously beautiful ice sculpture was a warm and loving woman waiting to be freed.

In forgiveness there was freedom, she said. Could he forgive his mother? Could he forgive God for allowing his mother to do what she'd done? His throat worked and his eyes burned as it dawned on him that deep down he blamed God for his mother leaving. *Oh, Lord, forgive me for blaming You.*

He gives us free will, Rachel had told him.

His mother made her choice. Josh now faced a choice to forgive and move on. His father had loved his mother enough to let her go. Josh hadn't understood until now how much courage that had taken. Did he have enough courage, enough love to let Rachel stay?

"Josh, I love you."

Rachel's tender words brought him out of his thoughts. She was so beautiful, standing there bathed in the full moon's brilliance. Light reflected off her dark hair, creating a shimmering glow that surrounded her. Her blue eyes were big and bright and cool with emotion. He'd been thickheaded not to realize before that when she was her coldest was when she was feeling the most.

She pulled in a breath. "I want to build a life with you. I want to earn your trust, make you know in your soul that I would never break my commitment to you. Love's a choice, Josh. Every day, it's a choice we have to make." Her voice echoed across the pool water, sounding brittle and frozen. "I choose you, Josh. And if giving up medicine's what it takes, I will."

"You'd hate that, Rachel. And then you'd end up hating me." He scrubbed a hand over his face. "I wish there were some way to measure commitment."

"The only measurable thing I can do to prove my love for you is to give up medicine."

Her words, so at odds with her icy tone, stopped his breath, trapping the air around his heart until he thought he'd pass out for lack of oxygen. She'd give up being a doctor for him. She'd make the ultimate sacrifice as a testament to her love.

He searched his heart, going over the things she'd said. Love was a choice to be made every day. Forgiveness brought freedom. Faith was believing and trusting in something you couldn't see but knew to be true anyway.

For him to find happiness, he had to step out in faith and trust Rachel.

In two long strides he closed the distance between them and took her in his arms. Her body felt rigid and straight in his hands. "Aw, Rachel. It's too much."

She tilted her head to look up at him. Her eyes glittered like icicles. "What?"

A slow, sweeping joy filled him. He breathed deep of the love at his fingertips. "It's too much, but more than enough."

She went impossibly colder.

A smile gathered at the corners of his mouth.

Her gaze narrowed. He felt the touch of frostbite and didn't mind.

"Why are you looking at me like a cat when he finds the key to a birdcage?"

His smile grew, and love, perfect love, drove out the fear. He caressed her cheek. "I'm smiling because I love you. And I won't let you give up being a doctor."

"You do? You won't?"

"Yes, I do. And no, I won't. You are who you are, Rachel. And I love every inch of you the way you are."

She blinked rapidly, but tears fell from her eyes anyway. The cold receded and a warm front moved in. "I promise you, Josh. You will always come first."

"I'll hold you to that promise," he said as his mouth moved closer, hovering, waiting.

She went on tiptoe and closed the distance into a heart-stopping, mind-melting kiss.

"Rachel," he said against her mouth.

"Hmm?"

"I'll need lots of these."

"Kisses of assurance," she stated huskily and recaptured his mouth.

"Rachel?"

"Hmm?"

"Will you marry me?"

She stilled, her lips turning cool against his mouth, her breath hitched. Then slowly the essence of Rachel fanned out around him, enflaming them both. Her head tilted back and indescribable joy reflected in her gaze. "Yes. I'll marry you. Only you."

Epilogue

Josh followed Griff through the double sliding-glass doors of Sonora Community Hospital's emergency entrance. Rachel stood behind the administration desk, her dark hair pulled back in a simple ponytail that brushed across the shoulders of her white coat.

"Hi, Mom," Griff called out as they approached.

She looked up from the report in her hand. Her eyes crinkled at the corners and her mouth curved upward into a welcoming smile that never ceased to move Josh deep down in his soul. Quickly she laid the file down before moving around the desk. Taking Griff in her arms, she held him close, as close as her protruding stomach would allow.

"How's she doing today?" Griff asked before kissing the mound that held his baby sister.

"Kicking up a storm," she commented, and met Josh's gaze.

The tender love in her blue gaze stirred his blood,

stoking the fire that always burned for his wife. In almost two years of marriage, the love between them grew more intense very day. "Are you ready for lunch?"

She hesitated. Old apprehension surfaced, catching him off guard. But he quickly squelched it. They both had lives outside of each other.

He was so proud of her and he respected the importance of the work she did. He could see the differences she made and knew about the lives she'd touched. And she supported his career, never once making him feel guilty for the time he put into the forestry service. They both carried the weight of responsibility on their shoulders, but as a couple, as a family, they would always come first.

Together, their love was enough.

"A quick lunch, if I want to get out of here early today to watch Griff's baseball game."

"Done." Easy contentment and satisfaction filled him. As they left the hospital, Griff skipping on ahead and their baby girl thriving beneath Rachel's heart, Josh sent up a prayer of thanks for bringing love back into his life.

* * * * *

Dear Reader,

I hope you enjoyed my first book with Steeple Hill. I'm very excited to be able to share Josh and Rachel's story with you. These two have been talking to me for a very long time now. They had to learn the power and freedom of forgiveness in order to find their way to a deep and lasting love. A love worth fighting for.

I used my childhood memories of Sonora as well as some creative license in constructing the backdrop for this story. If you ever get a chance to visit the gold counties of the Sierra Nevada, make sure you visit historic Columbia. I know you'll grow as fond of the area as I am.

May God bless you always.

Terri Reed

A SHELTERING LOVE

Do to others as you would have them do to you.
—*Luke* 6:31

To Robyn, friends forever. Thank you for all the times you listened. For all the times you were there when I needed you.

Thank you to author and retired social worker Delle Jacobs for so patiently answering all my questions. Any mistakes are purely mine.

Thank you to my editor, Diane Dietz, for believing in me and for the wonderful pep talk.

Chapter One

Here comes trouble.

Maybe some kids were beyond her help.

Claire Wilcox eyed the two teenage boys sauntering across the grassy park toward the shaded spot where she and fifteen-year-old Mindy were talking. Claire's gaze zeroed in on the taller, dark-haired boy with scraggly, shoulder-length hair and a thin face. The early April sunlight splintered off the earring dangling in his left ear. In his hands he carried a golden retriever puppy.

Behind the two boys, in sharp contrast, the purity of the majestic snowcapped peak of Mount Hood rose in the distance like a sentry, standing watch over Oregon's Willamette Valley.

She'd seen the dark-haired boy around town.

Some locals blamed last month's vandalism at the downtown theater on this kid. She didn't know his story, but she would soon if the opening of the teen shelter went as planned this coming July.

"Hey, Johnny, catch." The dark-haired boy suddenly tossed the puppy to his blond companion, who awkwardly caught the small dog.

Claire's heart pitched. She stalked forward, her hands clenched at her sides. "Hey! Don't do that!"

Johnny shoved the dog back into the hands of the taller kid.

"Do this?" He tossed the small dog back to his companion.

The puppy yelped and Johnny caught the little fluff ball, then held it at arm's length by the scruff of the neck. The kid's gray sweatshirt and faded jeans were dirty, as if he'd rolled or slept on the ground. His gaze darted away from Claire, his face flushing guiltily.

"Tyler, stop it," Mindy wailed as she moved to the side of the taller kid.

So this was Tyler.

Claire scrutinized the dark-haired boy in his red T-shirt with some rock band's logo on the front and ripped, dirty jeans. Mindy had said he was nice. He didn't look nice. He looked downright nasty. The kind of guy she would have fallen for at Mindy's age. The kind that would give any parent a heart attack.

Not her. She knew better. Everyone deserved a chance.

Claire understood the pain of the rebellious teens she was trying to help. She understood—had experienced the wounds of childhood. Wounds inflicted by those she should have been able to trust.

Teens like Mindy and Tyler stood on the cusp of adulthood, where the choices they made would affect the rest of their lives. By the grace of God, Aunt Denise had stepped in and helped Claire when she'd been at the point of no return. Not every teen was as fortunate.

If only Claire could get through to kids like these. Earning the right to be heard, to be trusted, would take time. Once The Zone officially opened, she hoped to make a difference in their lives. Give them a place to belong, to come to when it became too rough at home.

A safe haven.

But her only concern right now was for the animal.

She flexed her hands and willed herself to stay calm. With as much control as she could muster, she said, "Give me the puppy."

Tyler snorted and grabbed the puppy back from his friend. "You ain't the boss of me, lady."

"No, I'm not. You're the boss of you. But I don't think you're cruel, either, Tyler. Just let the pup go." Though she'd gentled her tone, anxiety wavered in her voice.

Tyler flipped his unwashed hair over his shoulder as his eyes narrowed. Claire met his challenging gaze dead-on. He wanted attention, wanted someone to trust, somebody to care. Well, she'd show him she cared and that she wasn't afraid or intimidated by him.

Most people in Pineridge would just as soon lock up these kinds of teens. The "throwaways." But Claire had different ideas. They needed help and understanding. And she could give that to them.

Tyler dropped his gaze first, affirming to Claire that he just needed some guidance, some boundaries. But when he lifted his gaze back to hers, she sucked in a breath at the malicious intent in his gray eyes.

"You want the dog?" His mouth curled up in a sneer. "Then you catch the dog."

Tyler flung the puppy upward. Fear clamped a steely hand around Claire's heart. The dog yelped again, its legs flailing in the air. She lurched forward, her arms outstretched, her hands ready to catch the dog. But she was too far away. Her feet stumbled on a rut in the grass. Her pulse pounded. The teens' snickering echoed in her ears.

Dear Lord, help!

A shadow crossed her peripheral vision. The air swirled with a rush of heat as a dark shape overtook her, passed her. She skidded to a halt.

A man.

He deftly caught the small pup and cradled the trembling dog against his black leather-clad chest. His big hands gently soothed the puppy with long strokes down its back.

The man was tall, well over six feet, wearing black leather down to his heavy boots. The ebony hair curling at the edge of his collar needed a trim and a few days growth of beard shadowed his square jaw. Tiny brackets edged his mouth and weathered little creases outlined his eyes.

But it was those dark orbs that sent her pulse into shock.

Though he stared down Tyler, she saw the hard glint of rage shining from the fathomless depths of his black eyes.

Tall, dark and dangerous. Nothing but trouble there.

Claire resisted the urge to back away. She'd learned

long ago that she was susceptible to the kind of guy that
sent good girls scrambling for cover. Claire wasn't a
good girl; she'd done some horrible things in the past.
Things she was ashamed of. But she'd turned her life
around and wasn't about to backslide.

Tyler scowled. "Hey, mister, that's mine."

"Not anymore." Anger punctuated the stranger's
words. His accent wasn't from the Pacific Northwest.

He thrust the butterball of a dog into Claire's arms.
His gaze flicked over her before once again settling on
Tyler. Claire shivered at the fury in those impenetrable
eyes.

She cuddled the puppy close. Its heart hammered
against its little ribs. She met Tyler's fierce glare. Animosity glowed bright in his eyes. She wasn't winning any
points with the kid. A long, tough road stretched ahead
if she wanted to help him. But she was up to the challenge.

"Time for you to leave, little boy," the man said. A
command, not a suggestion.

She groaned into the puppy's fur. Not the thing to
say to a teenage boy who was trying to grow up too fast.
Was the man deliberately trying to provoke Tyler? A
quick glance at the tall stranger confirmed what she
feared. His expression dared Tyler to react.

Tyler's chin jutted out in a mutinous gesture. "Who's
going to make me?"

The man didn't move a muscle, didn't say a word,
but the charged silence crackled with suppressed hos-
tility.

He'd have no trouble taking on an undernourished

fifteen-year-old, even one with the attitude of Godzilla. Why was the man still so enraged now that the puppy was safe?

Beside her, Mindy shuffled her feet, clearly uncomfortable with the situation. Wide-eyed, Tyler's friend looked between the intimidating man and Tyler. His hunched shoulders and the way he edged away from Tyler told Claire that the blonde would bolt at the first sign of a fight.

The fire in Tyler's eyes slowly turned to fear as the man stood there waiting, his expression intense and unyielding. She held her breath, hoping Tyler would take heed of his own internal warning system and leave.

He didn't.

"I'm not going. Not without the dog." Tyler's voice quivered slightly.

"You might want to rethink that idea."

The steely edge in the man's voice sent a ripple of concern down Claire's spine. Time for damage control. She couldn't let this male posturing go any further. Tyler was just a boy trying to survive in the world.

She stepped toward the stranger and laid a hand on his arm. The leather-clad muscles of his forearm bunched beneath her palm and shot little sparks of heat up her arm to settle in the middle of her chest.

Her hand tightened.

For a tense moment she thought the man wouldn't back down, but then he turned his gaze on her. The burning anger in his eyes slowly drained. Stark, vivid torment filled his expression.

Aching compassion welled within her, making the

need to heal, to offer comfort, tangible. She'd seen the haunted expression before, in the faces of teens who'd confronted the unimaginable and survived. But glimpsing the wounded soul of this man made tears sting the back of her eyes.

His eyes widened slightly, giving her the distinct impression that he'd somehow glimpsed her thoughts. Invaded her mind. She blinked rapidly, using her unshed tears as a shield against the threat of this man who twisted her up inside and made her forget to breathe.

Abruptly, he turned away, fixing his attention back on Tyler and giving her a moment to catch her breath. His body language relaxed slightly, giving her the signal that she could remove her hand from his arm. She did, her hand immediately turning cold.

"Go. Just go." The tired, ancient sound of the man's voice gave testament to the pain she'd seen in his eyes. "And don't come back."

Claire opened her mouth to protest, to say she wanted the teens to come, to know that they'd always be accepted at The Zone. But she met Tyler's gaze and the words died in her throat.

Hatred gleamed from his gray eyes. He brought his hand up and made a slicing motion across his throat. The stranger stiffened, all semblance of relaxation vanishing.

Tyler curled his lip and backed up. "Come on, let's blow this dump," he said, his chin jutting out once again.

Relief showed on the other boy's face. "Yeah, this is

boring." He didn't waste time retreating, gaining a large lead on Tyler as he headed west toward one end of the park.

Tyler kept backing up, his gaze darting between the man and Claire. "Mindy, let's go."

Claire put a hand on Mindy's slender arm. "You don't have to go. I can help you."

Mindy chewed her lip, her young face pale, scared. Indecision shone in her blue eyes.

"Mindy!" Tyler's demand made the girl jump.

"Don't go," Claire implored.

The puppy squirmed in her grasp and she loosened her hold. Mindy twirled her long, dirty brown hair around a finger, gave Claire an apologetic grimace and scurried after Tyler.

As Tyler's arm settled around Mindy in a gesture that Claire knew all too well, heaviness descended on Claire's shoulders. Billy had possessed her like that. Made her his property. She shuddered and repressed the memory. She was never going to allow herself to be that needy again.

"Lord, please protect Mindy," she murmured the prayer aloud.

Claire snuggled the puppy and turned to thank the stranger, but he'd walked away. His long legs carried him in the opposite direction of the teens, toward the parking lot at the east end of the park. The pocket-size Bible sticking out of his back pocket snagged her attention. Interesting.

She hurried after him, not wanting him to disappear without thanking him. In this day and age, not many people would have come to her aid.

"Hey, wait," she called.

He paused, glancing over his shoulder. When she caught up to him, he arched a black brow. His expression was less intimidating now, more playful. She swallowed.

Her first impression that he was good-looking had been marred by the anger hardening his features. She realized he was beyond good-looking and sliding straight toward gorgeous. Everything inside went on alert, like the quills of a porcupine sensing danger.

He raised both brows. Heat crept into her cheeks. "I wanted to say thank you."

"No big deal."

The soft rumble of his voice vibrated through her, sending tingles along her nerve endings.

He started forward again and she doubled her steps to match his lengthy stride. "But it was a big deal to this little guy…and to me."

One corner of his mouth kicked upward in an appealing way as he scratched the dog behind the ear. "You two take good care of each other."

Claire watched that big, strong hand stroke the yellow fur and envy flooded her. It had been a long time since a man had run his fingers through her hair. A long time since she'd allowed anyone close enough to touch her at all. But this was the wrong man to want that from.

She pushed aside her need for physical contact. "Where are you from?"

"That obvious, huh?"

She grinned. "Most Oregonians don't have an accent."

Both brows rose again. "Sure you do. You just don't hear it."

She pulled her chin in. "Really?"

He laughed and the sound warmed her all over. "Yes, really."

Bemused that she sounded as different to him as he did to her, she probed, "And you're from…?"

"Long Island."

"You're a long way from home."

His ebony eyes took on a faraway glaze. "Yes. A long way from home."

The loneliness in his voice plucked at her. "Where are you staying?"

His gaze came back to her, those dark eyes alight with an unidentifiable emotion. "I'm not."

Curiosity gripped her. "Where are you headed?"

He shrugged again.

A drifter. A twinge of sadness weaved through her curiosity. Did the pain she'd seen earlier drive him to keep moving, to drift through life? Looking at his tall, lean frame, she wondered when he'd eaten last. The familiar urge to help, to do *something,* rose within her.

"Could I make you lunch as a way of saying thanks?" She pointed to the gray two-story building at the north end of the park. "I live there."

He stopped, tilted his head to one side, and studied her. She gave him a smile of encouragement and tried to slow the pounding of her heart. This man with his dark good looks and bad-boy image was just the kind of guy to turn her crank. But she wasn't going to let her crank be turned again only to be left idling on the side of the road. Her smile stiffened.

"Don't you know you shouldn't talk to strangers, let alone invite them in?"

She barely stopped herself from rolling her eyes. She'd heard similar warnings from all the well-meaning people of Pineridge who thought she shouldn't open her heart and home to the teens.

Granted, this man was far from a teenager. But he posed a threat on so many levels that she would be wise to heed the warning. Wisdom was something she was still working on. "I run a shelter. Inviting strangers in is part of what I do."

"A shelter?"

"A teen shelter, to be exact."

"Why?"

She sighed. The infernal question seemed to be at the top of everyone's list of questions and asked in the same wary, derisive tone, though his held more edge to it. "The stigma of runaway teenagers is that they're crazy and out of control. But they're still just kids. Yeah, they're rough and tough and act horribly at times. But deep down most are scared, confused and need help."

"But why *you?*" He seemed genuinely interested.

It was on the tip of her tongue to tell him the unvarnished truth. Why she felt compelled to make him understand was a mystery. So instead she settled for her pat response. "I remember the anxiety and chaos of those teen years. If I can make a difference in someone's life, I know I was put on this earth for a reason."

"That's admirable."

His compliment pleased her, as did the almost wistful look on his handsome face.

"But woefully misguided." His expression hardened. "Thank you for the offer, but I should be heading out."

"Why are you in such a hurry, if you don't know where you're headed?"

He leaned toward her, his jet-black eyes probing and his decidedly masculine scent, full of leather and the outdoors, engulfing her senses. "You're tenacious."

Her spine stiffened and she lifted her chin. "Persistence is a virtue."

Amusement danced in his gaze. "*Patience* is a virtue."

Her cheeks flamed at being corrected. "I consider both to be virtues."

That appealing half-grin flashed again. "Both are admirable traits." His tone dropped to a deep and husky timbre that she found fully alluring. His accent rasped along her skin like a velvet caress. Her knees wobbled and knocked together. "We've established you have persistence, but do you have patience?"

Oh, yeah, she had patience. Hard-won and, at the moment, stretched taut.

Every instinct warned her that this man could endanger her vow to be self-sufficient with nothing more than his smile, let alone how his voice lulled her senses, and threatened to impair her judgment. He could make her want to lose herself in those dark eyes with one glance.

She didn't need or want a man in her life. Never

again would she allow herself to be vulnerable to the whims of a guy, to be used and abandoned, forgotten.

She stepped back, needing to put distance between them. She'd offered help. He'd said no. She needed to accept that. Time to stay focused and in control of her own responses.

"Be safe." Her voice sounded breathless. And she didn't like it.

This time there was no half-grin, but a full-blown, toe-curling smile that sent her blood zooming. He saluted and then sauntered to a low slung, shiny chrome-and-black motorcycle with the unmistakable winged insignia of a Harley.

He threw one long, lean leg over the seat, looking at home on the bike. He plucked a black, sleek-looking helmet from where it hung on the handlebars and put it on. A second later the bike came to life with a thundering rumble.

"Hey," she yelled over the noise of the engine and stepped closer.

He gave her a questioning look.

"What's your name?" She didn't know why it was important, but she needed to know.

His eyes widened slightly, then a slow smile touched his lips. "Nick."

His smile made her heart leap. He'd stormed into her life like a knight of old and performed a heroic deed, all the while putting her female senses into overdrive.

He flipped down the visor on the helmet and rolled away. She watched him turn the corner toward downtown Pineridge and then disappear from sight. It was a good thing he'd roared out of her life before she'd lost her head and done something embarrassing like drool.

"Well." She stood rooted to the ground for a moment as her heart resumed its natural rhythm. She held the puppy up and stared into his sweet little brown eyes. The puppy licked at her face. She laughed and hugged him close. Gwen was going to just love the little guy.

"Well, little Nick, you want to come home with me?"

Nick Andrews couldn't get the pretty blonde out of his head. The woman's heart gleamed in her baby blues and every subtle and not-so-subtle expression that had crossed her face.

Oh, she had courage, he'd give her that. Not many women—let alone men—would have stood up to those punks. She cared for those street urchins. But she might as well have worn a sign that said "Heartache Welcome."

She talked a good game, how they were just kids in need of some help. He didn't believe it.

Thankfully she wasn't his problem. No matter how attractive the package or how much he admired her spunk, he had enough to deal with. He wasn't exposing his heart to the pain of loss again.

He gunned the engine and took the exit out of Pine-ridge that dropped him onto Interstate 84 headed west toward Portland. As he jockeyed for a position in the traffic, a sharp urge to turn back assaulted him.

He frowned, convinced he was being paranoid.

Yet he couldn't shake the image of Tyler's slicing gesture.

Nah, the kid didn't have the guts to do anything serious. *Just throw a defenseless animal around,* a tiny voice inside reminded.

Nick's jaw tightened.

The kid was a bad seed. Nick had seen eyes like that before. The eyes of a killer.

Man, he'd have pulverized that kid in the park, would have gladly exorcised two years of bottled rage on the punk, if the blonde hadn't restrained him with her gentle touch.

He hadn't even asked her name.

Not my problem.

But yet…

He wove around a slow-moving truck. He shook his head, trying to rid himself of the nagging feeling he should turn back. Serena would have said it was God's nudging, but God had been quiet two years ago when a nudging could have saved her life.

So why would God start communicating with him now?

Twenty miles ahead the freeway split. He could either take the interstate exit for I-5 North heading toward Washington State and on up to Canada or he could take I-5 South toward California.

He was at a fork in the road, literally. Which way to turn? How far could he go to outrun the past? Where would he find peace? What had he done to deserve such punishment? How could he leave the blonde so unprotected?

"She's not my problem!" he shouted.

The words swirled around inside his helmet until they were sucked out by the rushing wind.

Chapter Two

"Here you go, little Nick." Claire set a plastic bowl full of water on the linoleum floor in the kitchen area. "Nick?"

The puppy had been sniffing around the kitchen floor moments ago. Now the little scamp was out of sight. Claire walked into the open area of The Zone. She looked under the Ping-Pong table that the Jordan family had donated, and behind the brown corduroy sofa she'd found at Goodwill. "Nick, here boy. Where are you?"

She wasn't equipped to care for a puppy. She needed dog food, a collar and a doghouse. Whew, the list was endless and could be expensive. She shrugged. Whatever was needed, she'd find a way to provide. She couldn't turn the dog out any more than she could a human.

"Ah, there you are."

The little fluff ball was snuggled up against a bright

yellow beanbag chair. Claire scooped him up and he licked her chin. "Thank you for the kiss. I wonder who you belong to. I'd sure be upset if I'd lost such a cutie." She snuggled her cheek into his soft fur. She'd have to make flyers and post them around town. Surely Nick's owners would be looking for him.

And if no one claimed him?

She would keep him.

She carried him back to the kitchen and set him down in front of the bowl. His black nose sniffed at the plastic rim and then, apparently deciding it was okay, he lapped at the water.

"Thirsty boy." Claire smiled at the ball of fur. Tenderness tightened her chest. She'd never had a dog before. She was excited by the prospect, but her internal monitor quickly warned not to expect to keep him. Somewhere out there were the little guy's owners.

She found a blanket in the closet under the stairs and made a cozy bed on the floor in the kitchen.

"Here you go, Nick," she said, picking up the puppy and setting him on the blanket. He walked in a circle, sniffing at the material.

A bump sounded from beyond the wall of the kitchen. Nick paused; his ears perked up. Claire walked to the window over the sink and peered out. Nothing on the grassy yard stretching to the woods that edged the property. She twisted her head, craning to see left, then right. Nothing.

"Probably a squirrel," she muttered to Nick. "You'll like chasing those when you're older." She wagged a finger at the dog. "I don't think you'll ever catch one, but if you do, don't bring it home. Wherever your home ends up being."

Nick plopped down in the middle of the makeshift dog bed and rested his head on his paws.

"Look at the size of your paws." She shook her head. "You're going to be a big one, aren't you? Just like your namesake."

The image of the tall, dark man sitting on his gleaming motorcycle made her flush again. He was the stuff dreams were made of. A modern-day knight coming to the rescue. But she didn't need to be rescued. She could take care of herself.

What was his story? Where would he end up?

There was something compelling about his dark eyes. She'd seen pain and intelligence, rage and mischief there. The way he'd smiled at her when he'd said his name was enough to make any woman's knees weak. The man was too handsome. But not in a pretty boy way or even a *GQ* way. The angle of his nose, the jut of his whiskered chin and the planes of his cheeks could have been sculpted by a master's hand.

She gave a wry laugh. *Well, he had been, you dolt.* God had done a nice job on Mister Nick. On the outside to be sure, but on the inside…?

A man who stepped in when he saw trouble was a rarity indeed. A man who carried a Bible with him out in the open even rarer. Was he a man after God's own heart?

She'd never know. He was long gone now, just a wonderful memory of a guy on a bike who'd offered his help and wanted nothing in return. Definitely a rarity.

A man like Nick would be hard to resist. Good thing she wouldn't face that temptation again.

With a quick glance to make sure the puppy still slept, Claire headed for her office—a small room located in the front of the house. It was an ideal spot to work and still be able to keep an eye on the main area of The Zone.

The bedrooms were all upstairs and she'd taken the largest of the five bedrooms at the far end of the hall. Gwen's room was at the top of the stairs while the other three rooms were in various degrees of readiness for taking on more teens. Not that Gwen was a teen any longer. She was a college student now with a part-time job—a far cry from the strung-out, skinny orphan Claire and Aunt Denise had first brought home.

Having Gwen come into their lives solidified Claire's desire to start a shelter. She'd decided to open it here in Pineridge because no such facility existed in the area.

But there would be soon.

Claire sat at her desk and rummaged through files and notes. There was still so much to do before she could officially open. More government hoops to jump through, the community to convince and teens to build trust with.

And a puppy to care for. She compiled a list of needs for Nick. Just in case she was unsuccessful in finding his owners, she wanted to be prepared. Then she went to work on her plans for The Zone.

The clock ticked by another hour.

The hairs on the back of her neck raised and chills raced down her spine. Something wasn't right.

The loud shrill of three fire alarms pierced the quiet. Heart pounding with dread, she jumped from the chair and raced into the living room. A gray haze hung in the air, stinging her eyes and burning her lungs.

Fire!

"Nick!"

She raced toward the kitchen. Smoke billowed from beneath the crack in the back door and through the open window over the sink, filling the room with frightening quickness. She heard the puppy whimper, but she couldn't tell from where.

She dropped to her knees like she'd been told to do in elementary school. She crawled across the floor toward the kitchen. The heavy smoke swirled around, making it difficult to see.

The puppy's blanket was empty. She crawled out of the kitchen. "Nick!" she called again, taking in smoke. She winced as her lungs spasmed. In the laundry room she found the puppy huddled in a corner, its little body shaking.

"Here, boy." Claire scooped the pup up and cuddled him close.

Claire crawled toward the front of the house while holding Nick in one hand. She breathed in. Coughed. Her lungs burned. She caught her hand on the leg of a chair and went down on her elbow, her knees scraping on the floor. Nick yelped as she tried to catch herself with the hand that held him.

The smoke became dense, more intense. The front

door seemed a mile away. Somewhere in the closet under the stairs was a fire extinguisher. She'd get Nick out, come back for the extinguisher and put out the fire.

She crawled forward again, laboring to breathe. Tears streamed down her cheeks. The puppy whimpered.

"It'll be okay, Nick. Dear Lord, please let us be okay."

She coughed, her breaths coming in short, shallow gasps. Her stomach rolled. She paused, waiting for the dizziness to pass. It didn't. She forced herself to continue on despite the effects of the smoke. Her survival instinct pushed her, urged her to keep crawling away from the source of the smoke.

Her wrist gave out, forcing her weight down hard on her elbow, sending pain up her arm. Her head fell forward to smack against the hardwood floor. Spots of light popped in front of her eyes.

She couldn't stop, she had to keep going.

Where was the man in black leather when she needed him?

Flames shot from the back of the house.

Nick's heart slammed against his ribs as he stopped his bike at the bottom of the cement stairs leading to the front door. He set the kickstand and jumped off his bike. He rushed up the porch steps and burst through the front door.

Smoke billowed around him, stinging his eyes. His gaze zeroed in on Blondie crawling toward the door with the puppy clutched to her chest with one hand, while she balanced with the other hand.

She lifted her head, her eyes wide. The puppy squirmed out of her grasp and ran past Nick's legs and down the steps.

Nick scooped up Blondie and carried her to the front yard where he gently laid her down on the grass. She opened her mouth to say something but coughed instead. He rolled her to her side as she spit out black soot between taking in gulps of air.

Relief surged through Nick. He'd finally given in to the urgent, nagging feeling that he should turn back. And a good thing, too. He patted her shoulder, offering her comfort as his heartbeat began to slow.

"You came back," she said in a hoarse whisper.

"Yeah," he acknowledged.

"The puppy?" she rasped, her eyes widening as she sat up and was momentarily gripped with another bout of coughing.

"He ran out. I'm sure he's fine."

She raised her gaze to her home. "My building."

The disappointment and hurt in her voice burned in his gut. This shouldn't have happened. He knew who was to blame. His fingers curled into a fist. He'd make sure they paid.

Seeing that the blonde was out of danger, he rose. He refused to consider why he felt the need to help her, why her distress tightened a knot in his chest. "I'll see what I can do."

He left her on the grass and went around to the back of the building where the smoke seemed to originate. Two garbage cans were on fire directly below an open window as well as the wooden slats of the back porch.

Pillows of black smoke rolled into the kitchen. The flames were licking at the back door and the ceiling of the porch, curling the gray paint and blackening the wood, which crackled and snapped.

Nick skirted around the fire to where a garden hose lay rolled on the ground. The faucet turned easily and water sprayed out. He aimed the spray on the door and porch since that would be where the damage would be most devastating.

Off in the distance the wail of a siren drew close, bringing hope of help. Within minutes firemen bustled about, waving off Nick and his efforts. He dropped the hose and headed back toward where he'd left Blondie.

He spotted her as he came around the corner and his chest tightened more. Grass clung to her hair, streaks of soot marred her creamy complexion and smeared her white blouse and jeans.

Two paramedics were tending to her. Or rather, trying to. She brushed away their attempts to get her into the ambulance. Nick stepped over a fire hose as he approached.

"No, I can't leave," she said as she dodged one EMT and snagged the arm of a passing fireman. "Do you know how much damage has been done?" Her voice rasped with the effects of the smoke. A purple goose egg formed on her forehead.

"Not yet, ma'am."

She dropped her hand away and the fireman continued on, giving Nick a nod as they passed each other.

The worried lines framing her mouth deepened and her eyes were troubled as she turned to face Nick. She closed the distance between them in a rush of steps. "Is everything ruined?"

The anxiety in her voice tore at his heart. He didn't want to care. He couldn't. "Hard to tell. The fire department will let you know. You need to go with the paramedics and let them check you out." He took her elbow and steered her back toward the ambulance.

"I need to find the puppy!" She doubled over, coughing.

He held fast as she tried to pull away from his hold on her elbow. "What you need to do is let them take care of you."

"But who's going to take care of things here?" She made a sweeping gesture with her hand. "I have to be here."

"Is there someone, a friend, a family member, you could call who could come?"

Two little lines appeared between her dark blond brows. "This place is *my* responsibility."

Was she a control freak or did she really not have anyone she trusted to help? What did it matter to him, anyway?

But it did matter. This happened because of *him*. His interference. He felt responsible for her. For her situation.

"I'll tell you what. I'll stay—make sure the police and the firemen have everything they need—while you go with the paramedics."

"You'll stay?" Big tears filled her eyes. She rapidly blinked them away.

That knot twisted another notch, warning him he

was getting too involved. But guilt was a stronger motivator than self-preservation. He owed her a debt because he'd brought this on her.

He gave her a reassuring smile. "I'll stay."

She sagged and allowed him to help her into the ambulance.

"Wait," she called as he stepped back. "You'll find the puppy?"

"Sure."

Her smile held gratitude. "Thanks. His name's Nick."

Their gazes held for a moment before the doors of the vehicle closed.

Nick stared after the ambulance. She'd named the puppy after him. Flattered warmth spread through him, heating his face. He was treading water in the deep end.

Not my problem?

He scoffed. "Yeah, right."

Claire sat on the gurney waiting for the emergency-room doctor to return. She swung her bare feet, picked at the cotton hospital gown and tried to ignore the noises from the other exam rooms.

She felt vulnerable and exposed, but mostly she was worried. Worried that everything she'd worked so hard for was ruined.

She chewed her lip, wondering if Big Nick had found Little Nick.

The corner of her mouth lifted at the memory of his expression when she'd told him the pup's name. He'd looked dumbfounded.

She still could hardly believe God had answered her prayers by bringing Nick back. When he'd come storming into The Zone she'd thought she was dreaming. Dreaming about a dark warrior who used his powers for good, not evil. Like some comic book character, except the strong arms that had held her so tenderly had been very real.

And the concern in his eyes called to her in a way nothing else could. It had been a long time since anyone had shown any real concern for her well-being. Oh, people had shown her kindness, but she often felt it came from obligation to her late aunt's memory rather than for herself.

The need to belong to someone rose sharply and she squashed it like an irritating fly. She couldn't allow herself to want anyone, to expect anything from anyone because expectations only led to disappointment.

More likely, Nick wouldn't stick around as he'd promised. She sternly steeled herself against any pain from hope. She wouldn't fret over it, wouldn't let it matter.

She was thankful he'd arrived when he had and that she hadn't inhaled too much of the smoke. The doctor had said her lungs might hurt for a few days and she'd probably have a headache from smacking her head on the floor, but otherwise she was in good health and could return home. He'd gone off to tell the nurse to discharge her.

But what would she be going home to?

Her stomach twisted. She had a pretty good idea who'd set the fire, but she hadn't told the police when they'd arrived because she wasn't a hundred percent certain.

She had to focus on moving forward no matter how much this incident set her back. She'd push through it, as always.

First she had to get back to The Zone. She didn't have money for a cab with her. She shrugged. She'd walk. She didn't relish putting on the smoke-scented clothes she'd arrived in, but she'd do what she had to.

The nurse pushed aside the curtain and stepped in. She was tall, African-American and very striking. Her black hair was pulled back into a fancy twist and her smile was kind.

In one hand she held a clipboard and in the other a brown paper bag, which she set on the counter. "The doctor says you can be released. I have a few forms for you to sign." She handed Claire the clipboard and pen.

Quickly looking over the form, Claire worried her bottom lip. She wasn't sure how the bill would be paid—if the insurance would cover it or not. She signed where appropriate and handed the clipboard back. She'd deal with the financial stuff later. "Where are my clothes?"

The nurse moved to the counter behind the gurney and picked up a clear plastic bag that contained Claire's dirty clothes. Wrinkling her nose, she said, "You're not going to want these anymore."

She set the bag down again and then grabbed the brown paper bag she'd brought in and handed it to Claire. "Your boyfriend brought you these. When you're dressed, come on out."

Claire blinked. Boyfriend? She opened the bag and pulled out her red polo shirt and fresh jeans. Embarrassed heat crept up her neck and settled in her cheeks.

Someone had gone through her things.

Nick?

A jittery panic hit her stomach like a spray of pebbles. He couldn't be her boyfriend. Not in a million years. She didn't need a boyfriend.

But she had to admit it felt good to have someone care.

Anticipation quickened her pulse. She put on the clothes. Finger-combed her matted mop of hair. Then sedately walked out from behind the curtain toward the administration desk.

Her nervous flutters fled, replaced with a melting warmth as Nick unfolded his long, lean frame from a chair and strode to her, reminding her of a dangerous panther stalking its prey.

And to her utter dismay, she realized she wanted to be hunted.

"The doc said you're okay," Nick stated by way of greeting as Blondie—Claire, he corrected himself—slowly drew nearer to him.

He'd waited to come until after the fire engines had disappeared and the investigators had finished scouring the area for clues to the arsonist. He'd answered the investigator's questions and told them what he could about Blondie and the teens.

She'd changed into the clothing he'd brought her. Smudges of soot stood out in stark contrast on her pale face. Her hair poked out in different directions with bits of green grass peeking out here and there. He stifled a smile.

She was adorable, vulnerable and in need of protection.

In need of help from someone other than him.

He'd get her settled safely, then leave.

She blinked up at him. "What are you doing here?"

"Came to get you. I didn't figure you'd have a way back. I hope the clothes are okay. Your roommate, Gwen, picked them out. She was pretty upset but I told her you'd call her as soon as you could. She had to get to work or she'd be here now."

"Thanks. I'm glad Gwen did the responsible thing and didn't come here." She tucked a strand of hair behind her ear. "How…how bad is the damage to the building?"

Anger flared in his gut at what those punks had done. "The porch is gone. You'll need a new back door."

They headed toward the doors of the hospital. "And the puppy?"

He slanted her a glance. "*Nick* is fine. I found him in the park chasing bees."

Ducking her head, she chuckled. "I hope you don't mind that I named him after you. I didn't think I'd see you again."

He held the door open. "I'm flattered."

To his amusement, her cheeks turned pink. "I guess I'll have to call him Little Nick. So I don't get you two confused." They walked in silence for a moment before Claire glanced back up at him. "Thanks," she said.

"For what?"

She stopped and tilted up her heart-shaped face. "I could have died if you hadn't rescued me."

The glint of admiration in her baby blues spread through him, making him think of knights, damsels in distress and fire-breathing dragons. Making him feel like a hero.

Stupid.

He was nobody's hero.

"You were almost to the door," he said.

"Why did you come back?"

"You wouldn't believe me if I told you." He ushered her to the parking lot where he'd parked her little green four-wheel drive Subaru.

"Try me." Her eyes widened. "Uh, thanks for bringing my car."

He lifted a shoulder as he unlocked the door and held it open for her. "Gwen gave me the keys—we didn't think you'd want to ride on the back of the Harley."

A gleam of longing entered her blue eyes. "Actually, I would have liked that."

He raised a brow. "Then I'll take you for a spin before I leave."

The hunger in her eyes set his blood to racing at full throttle on an open road, then abruptly she shook her head and wariness entered her gaze. "No, no. That wouldn't be such a good idea."

She climbed in the car and primly folded her hands in her lap.

Nick shut the door, grateful for the reprieve. The thought of her with him on his bike with her arms wrapped around his waist sent a shiver through him.

Not a good sign.

He wouldn't allow himself to become attracted, attached or anything else to her.

Gotta keep moving, he warned himself.

Chapter Three

Driving with Claire down Pineridge's main street, Nick surveyed the town with a jaundiced eye. Small-town America. He'd passed through so many over the last two years, they tended to blend together.

Redbrick storefronts with large, single pane windows lined both sides of the wide cement sidewalks. Every few stores sported a blue awning over the doorway. Nick barely glanced at the pedestrians moving at a sedate pace from shop to shop, going about their lives. He didn't want to consider an old man's frown or a young mother's smile. Didn't want to make a connection with anyone.

On both sides of the main street, about ten feet apart, stood a lone birch tree with a small square patch of dirt at its base. Kind of like himself, part of the whole, but separate.

On the west side of the main drag, cars parked between white angled lines. Red bricks indicated the crosswalks instead of painted lines. The street signs were tall, white posts with arrow-shaped slats and street names printed in bold black letters. The white posts rose out of large, round, colorful flowerpots. At each intersection, old-fashioned black metal lampposts added charm to an already charming community.

A family sort of town. A place to raise kids, watch summer parades and grow old in. A place he couldn't easily disappear into. A place where he didn't belong.

All the buildings were the same height. No high-power skyscrapers here. The perfect place for a woman like Claire, he thought, glancing over at her. Generous and kind. Open and friendly. A big city would eat her alive.

At the far end of town, he turned down the side street that led around the park.

The Zone came into view, a solitary structure flanked by empty lots. A lone police car sat at the curb in front. Nick parked behind the police car. Claire was out and up the cement front stairs before he had opened his door.

As he followed her inside, the puppy barked a greeting and raced to Claire. She bent and scooped him up for a quick hug. "Oh, you sweet little thing. I was so worried about you."

Nick's gaze focused on the officer rising from the couch. This guy had been here earlier. His uniform was starched and his badge shined. Not a single strand of hair was out of place. His young, clean-shaven face led Nick to guess the man to be in his early twenties.

The officer gave him an assessing once-over before focusing on Claire. "Good to see you're okay, Claire."

Nick didn't like the way the man said her name with such familiarity. And he didn't like that he didn't like it.

At least she didn't go all moonie-eyed. Not that he cared.

She set the animal back down. "Thanks, Bob. What are you doing here?" Without waiting for his reply, she walked toward the kitchen where most of the damage had been done by water. "Did the fire department say anything? How it started?"

Granting Nick a suspicious glance, Officer Bob walked to where she stood. "The fire started in the garbage cans. Whoever did this probably didn't expect the building to catch on fire. But it was sloppy work."

Nick stepped over to the counter and perched on a stool. "It was the teenagers from the park."

Claire's glare took him by surprise. "We don't know that for sure."

Officer Bob narrowed his gaze. "Which teenager?"

"Like I told the others, I came across two boys harassing Claire this afternoon in the park," Nick said to the officer, but his gaze was riveted on Claire. He couldn't figure out why she'd protect them.

Claire's gaze was direct and pleading. "I didn't see who did it."

Officer Bob cleared his throat. "Maybe *he* did it."

Nick's gut clenched. The unfounded accusation rankled worse than a bottomed out stock market.

What a lame, backwater-cop thing to say. Nick stared at the officer. Bob glared at him with more than just suspicion. Jealousy filled his hazel eyes. So that's how it was, Nick thought. Officer Bob had a thing for Claire.

"That's ridiculous, Bob. He saved my life."

"Maybe he set the fire to stage saving you."

Claire gave Nick a can-you-believe-this look and then rolled her eyes. "Tell him you didn't do it."

"I didn't do it," Nick stated flatly.

"See, there you go. He didn't do it." Claire put the puppy down and then heedlessly splashed through the thin layer of water on the kitchen floor to the sink.

Bob folded his arms across his chest. The stance only emphasized his thinness. "He's not from here, Claire. What do you know about him, anyway? He could be a serial arsonist, for all you know."

Nick snorted, gaining himself another glare from Bob.

She filled a bowl with water, her movements efficient and unhurried, then carried the bowl to the living room where she set it on the dry floor for the puppy.

She straightened and leveled a stern look on Bob. "I know he's from Long Island, that he's traveling through town, he carries a Bible in his pocket, he stopped to help me when he didn't have to and his name is Nick. That's all I need to know."

Nick blinked, touched that she'd so soundly defend him without really knowing anything more than she did. That she noted his Bible pricked his curiosity about her faith. She was too trusting and way too giving.

She needed a protector.

He wasn't about to apply for the job, but he had a feeling that old Bob would sure like to.

"I want to see some ID," Bob snarled at him.

Irritated to be the subject of the officer's suspicion, but grateful someone was watching out for Claire's interest, Nick dug his wallet out from the inside of his leather jacket and handed Bob his driver's license. "Did they find anything useful?"

"That's privileged information." Bob shot him a dark look. "I'm going to run this through the computer." He turned to Claire. "I'll be right out front if you need me."

She gave him a bland smile.

As soon as Officer Bob was out the door, Nick asked, "Why didn't you want him to know about the kids? You could have been killed."

Images flashed in his mind. The cloth shroud covering Serena's body. The blood stains on the sidewalk. The headstone at her grave site. His insides twisted with unspent rage.

"We don't know that they did it," she defended.

"And we don't know that they *didn't*. Come on, Claire. You know that kid's likely to do something."

"You heard Bob. *Whoever* did it was trying to scare me with some smoke. They weren't really trying to burn the place down."

"You could have passed out and suffocated if I hadn't come back!"

"*Might* have. And you did come back."

He shook his head. "You gonna wait until they seriously harm you before you make them take responsibility for their actions?"

"You don't know that they did it," she repeated, clearly exasperated and defensive.

"Then let the police prove they didn't do it."

"No! I'm not going to accuse someone without proof. If the authorities find clues that implicate them, then so be it. But I won't help them along."

"Instead you're going to wait for those punks to pull something else? Something worse?" Something like what had happened to Serena. He shuddered.

"I can take care of myself."

He scoffed. "Give me a break. Lady, you're a disaster waiting to happen." A disaster he wanted to avoid.

"Excuse me? I don't think you have any right to say that."

She was right. Nick stared at her. When had he lost his mind?

When he'd come within an inch of throttling a punk over a puppy and started this whole mess. He should be halfway to somewhere else by now, not here arguing with Blondie.

But the woman was intent on putting herself at risk. Responsibility weighed heavily on his shoulders, dragging him under.

What he wouldn't give for a life preserver right about now.

Pulsing with annoyance, Claire planted her hands on her hips and glared at Nick. "I have done perfectly well before you rolled into my life, thank you very much."

He spread his hands wide in a gesture of entreaty. "Hey, just stating the obvious. I've known you less than twelve hours and I've saved your bacon twice. Facts speak for themselves."

"My life is not a disaster."

"Ho!" Nick held up a hand, palm facing out. "I didn't say your life's a disaster. I don't know anything about your life. I'm just saying people will take advantage of you if you're not careful."

His words hit her like a slap upside the head. She'd been taken advantage of before. Billy had taken advantage. Used her. Squeezed her dry and then abandoned her without a second's hesitation.

But she was to blame for allowing him into her life, her heart. For needing him.

Well, she knew better now. She didn't need anyone. Certainly not a tall hunk with a blinding smile who threatened her resolve without even trying.

She had to send him on his way. Now. "Look, I appreciate your help. I thank God you were here, but feel free to go. I'm going to be fine."

"You won't be safe until the police find out who did this. What if next time Gwen's here? You willing to put her life in jeopardy, too?"

She frowned, hating the tremor of fear sliding along her limbs. As long as Gwen was under her roof, she was responsible to keep her safe, as well. "You're right. I'll mention to Bob that maybe Tyler might know something about the fire."

He gave her an odd look. "You and Bob an item?"

She pulled in her chin. "No. Not even. We've known each other since high school. His family lived next door to my aunt Denise. He's not my type, anyway."

One corner of his mouth kicked up. Her pulse did a little two-step.

"What is your type?" he asked.

Mysterious, gorgeous, a heartbreaker. Like you. The thought sent ribbons of heat winding through her bloodstream, warming her face. "I don't have a type," she stated firmly and spun away.

She walked to the back door where charred wood and curled paint spoke volumes. It could have been so much worse. A wave of helplessness hit her, threatening to overwhelm her. This was going to set her back both financially and time-wise.

She squared her shoulders. Somehow she'd manage. She always did with God's help. She didn't—wouldn't—need anyone else.

"It's really not as bad as it looks," Nick said.

She turned to see him rising from the stool. He shrugged out of his leather jacket, revealing a black T-shirt stretched taut over wide shoulders and well-defined muscles. His boots squished through the grimy water on the kitchen linoleum as he approached.

His tanned face bore traces of the sooty smoke that burned in her lungs. That explained why she was breathless. From inhaling too much smoke.

He stopped next to her, his attention on the wall. "Mop up the water. Replace a few boards. Sand and paint. It'll look good as new."

She sighed. If only it were that easy. "Did I thank you for saving me?"

Amusement gleamed in his eyes. "You did."

"Good. You should leave now."

He widened his stance. "You trying to get rid of me?"

She blinked. "Yeah, I am." She had to for her own

sake. "This isn't your problem and I'm not your responsibility," she said, her tone harsh.

A flash of something—hurt, maybe?—made his eyes seem impossibly darker. "That's what you really want?"

It wasn't. She felt safe with him around. Liked having him around. Which was exactly why he had to go.

"Yes, it's what I want."

He didn't say anything. Just stood there, tense and hard. His face became a mask of granite, the angles and planes unyielding. "And if I refuse?"

She swallowed and winced at the painful reminder of what had happened. She didn't have the strength to physically make him leave and she didn't know if she could find the strength again to ask him to leave. Not when all she really wanted was to have him hold her. To feel those strong arms around her. To have him tell her everything would be okay. To save her again if she needed it.

Weak.

"I can only hope you'll be a gentleman."

His mouth twisted into a harsh smile.

The front door to The Zone opened and Bob walked back in. He scowled as his gaze jumped from her to Nick and back. "You okay?"

Thankful for the distraction from this confrontation with Nick, she turned and smiled. "Yes, Bob," she said patiently.

She knew Bob was trying to be helpful—to show his concern for her—but it felt more like he was trying to control her.

"Mr. Andrews." He handed Nick's license back to him. "When are you moving on?"

Nick leaned against the counter. "When I'm sure Claire's safe."

Bob's scowl deepened. "I'll make sure she's safe."

"Excuse me." Claire waved her hands to get their attention. "I'm right here, remember, and I don't need either one of you to keep me safe."

"Until we apprehend who did this, you sure do." Bob gestured toward the burned wall. "We don't know they won't come back."

"On that we agree," Nick chimed, giving her a pointed look.

She blew out a sharp breath. She'd promised. "You might talk with a boy named Tyler. He could know something."

Bob pinned her with an intent stare. "I'll see what I can find out."

A knock drew Claire's attention. She left the two men and their meddling to open the front door. Surprised, she smiled at the brunette standing on the other side. "Hi, Lori. What—"

"I heard what happened. Are you okay? Rumor has it a handsome man rescued you." Lori Pearson, who she knew from church, peered over Claire's shoulder. "Is he in there? With Bob?" Lori's smile brightened considerably. "You poor thing. Two men."

Claire laughed with wry amusement. "It's good to see you. Please, come in." She stepped back so Lori could enter.

Lori paused. "You sure you're okay?" Genuine concern shimmered in her dark green eyes.

Flustered, Claire smiled. "Yes. I'm fine."

She didn't know Lori well enough to confide in her. To tell her that she was all jumbled up inside from her feelings about Nick and the fire.

She and Lori had met at a church gathering over a year ago. Lori seemed to find everything amusing. Claire enjoyed Lori's outgoing personality and positive view on life. Though at times Claire felt crowded by Lori.

Claire started to shut the door behind Lori when she heard her name. Peggy and Steve Jordan, followed by their three kids, thirteen-year-old Nathan, twelve-year-old Lisa and the youngest, at six, Matthew, hurried up the walkway.

Peggy came up the stairs looking fresh in rust-colored denims and a colorful peasant-style top with bell sleeves. Her waist-length chestnut hair was held back with a clip. She pulled Claire into a quick hug.

"I couldn't believe it when I heard what happened." She held Claire at arm's length, inspecting her. "You're not burned or anything?"

The display of affection pleased her. Claire stepped back. "No, I'm good."

Steve patted her shoulder. "If you need anything at all, you let us know." He was a big man with large muscles and a kind smile.

"Thank you." Claire moved aside so they could enter.

Nathan, as tall as his mother, ducked past her without a word. Lisa gave her a shy smile, and Matthew stared at her for a moment with his round green eyes and sweet expression. "You have grass in your hair," he declared before following his family.

Claire reached up and ran her fingers through her hair, mortified to imagine how she must look. She shut the door and took two steps when there was another knock. She quickly opened the door to find her aunt's best friend, Sandy Wellington and her husband, Dave.

"Hello, Sandy, Dave."

Sandy grasped her hand. Her short dark, graying hair curled becomingly to frame her round face. "Dear, we came to see that you're all right."

Dave stepped over the threshold. His silver hair was swept away from his forehead and he wore dark slacks and a blue oxford button-down shirt. "Sandy was beside herself when we heard the news."

"I'm okay. Really." She could see the doubt in Sandy's blue eyes. Claire smiled reassuringly. "Please, come in."

The Wellingtons were kind and thoughtful people. They had also been instrumental in helping Claire on the way to realizing her dream of The Zone.

She took a quick peek outside to make sure there weren't any other visitors before shutting the door.

The women and children had congregated at the edge of the kitchen, while the men had ignored the water to inspect the damage. Peggy Jordan shooed her children away, instructing them to go busy themselves. The oldest two went to the Ping-Pong table while Matthew sat in a beanbag chair to play with the puppy.

Claire's gaze landed on Nick. He leaned casually against the counter that separated the living room from the kitchen. Lori stood close by, smiling up at him. Something unfamiliar twisted in Claire's chest.

She started forward, trying to discern what she felt. The corner of Nick's mouth lifted at something Lori said. Claire's steps faltered. She realized with sickening clarity that she was jealous.

Nick only half-listened to the animated brunette in the pink blouse. His attention kept straying to Claire. Every time someone new entered, she acted as if she were unaccustomed to people caring about her, worrying over her. Why in the world wouldn't they? It was obvious these people were fond of her.

The Jordan family was friendly and he'd appreciated the way Steve had assessed him and then greeted him with a firm handshake. Mr. Wellington was honest in his wariness, had asked point-blank what his intentions were toward Claire, as if he were her father or favorite uncle.

He respected the man's forthrightness and had answered truthfully that he was passing through and had no designs on Claire—only that he wanted to make sure she was safe before he headed out again. His honesty had earned him a quick nod of approval and a pleased smile from Mrs. Wellington before they moved on to look at the damage with Officer Bob, who acted the tour guide.

The brunette—Lori, was it?—said something mildly amusing and he gave an obligatory smile. She put her hand on his arm, her fingers cool and inviting. He shifted out of her reach but smiled again to soften the rejection to her obvious interest. She was Claire's friend, after all. "How long have you known Claire?"

Lori sighed, clearly getting his hint. "For a while now." Her gaze turned speculative. "She's a hard person to get to know. Lots of walls up."

Nick raised a brow. He didn't see walls. He saw lots of open doors that invited trouble. He saw a woman protecting a puppy, protecting kids. "She seems pretty outgoing to me."

"Oh, don't get me wrong. She's definitely not the shy and retiring type. She's very sweet and giving, it's…" She pursued her lips in thought. "She doesn't talk much about herself. More concerned about others. Which is something I don't encounter often in my line of work."

"And what line of work would that be."

"I'm a hairdresser. Cheaper than a psychologist and you get nice hair."

He smirked and glanced at Claire. She looked tired, but her smile came quickly as she talked with the children before moving to where the adults had gathered in the kitchen. Mrs. Wellington had found a mop and was sopping up the waterlogged floor. Claire frowned before she bustled in and herded everyone into the living room. Then she traipsed right back into the kitchen, grabbed some sodas out of the refrigerator and began handing them out.

Not only did she need a protector, she needed a keeper. Someone to carry part of the burden she insisted on taking. He rolled his suddenly tense shoulders.

No way should that person be him.

Chapter Four

"Claire, dear. Stop fussing. We should be the ones serving you." Sandy took the soda cans from Claire's hands and put them on the counter.

"Thank you." Claire allowed Sandy to steer her away from the kitchen.

"You need rest. There's nothing that can't wait until tomorrow."

"But I really need to make some calls. Find out how soon someone can come to fix this mess," Claire protested.

Lori stepped up to flank her on the other side. "I can make your calls for you."

"That's sweet of you, Lori. But no." Claire's gaze darted between the two well-meaning women. "Really, you two. I can take care of things myself. I prefer it this way."

Lori shook her head, her brown hair swishing softly. "See. I told you," she addressed Nick. "Walls."

Claire's cheeks flamed. They'd been talking about her?

A soft, affable smile played at the corners of his mouth. His gaze traveled over her face, searched her eyes. She could feel the magnetism that made him so self-assured, so compelling. She blinked and quickly looked away before she succumbed to the pull he had on her.

"Lori, be nice," Sandy admonished gently, then she turned back to Claire. "What can we do to help you?"

Claire shook her head. "I don't know. Nothing at the moment, but if I think of something, I'll let you know."

Sandy frowned. "You really don't have to do everything on your own."

But she did. She couldn't rely on anyone. Wouldn't allow herself to. As long as she didn't have expectations of others, she wouldn't be disappointed.

Of course, she couldn't voice that thought, she didn't want to hurt their feelings. So instead she smiled politely and changed the subject. "How are Allie and Garrett? Will they be coming to visit soon?" Allie and Garrett were the Wellington's fraternal twins. They'd gone off to college last fall.

Sandy patted her arm with a knowing sigh. "Yes, they will be here this summer. I have an idea. Why don't you come home with us? You could stay in Allie's old room."

Claire dropped her chin. "Oh, no. I couldn't impose."

"It wouldn't be an imposition at all," Dave said as he stepped to his wife's side.

"Or you could come to our house," offered Peggy, as she and Steve joined the circle around Claire.

"That's sweet, but really…" she trailed off as panic flared. Things were spinning out of her control. Everyone meant well but she didn't want to need them. Didn't want to have to rely on anyone for anything.

Bob came around the group and stood beside Nick. The two men were so different.

Bob was good-looking, with his light brown hair and wiry build, in a very boy-next-door kind of way that appealed to some women. Not her, though. He was nice enough and they got along okay. He'd asked her out on several occasions over the years, but friendship was as far as their relationship could go. He just didn't do it for her.

She preferred Nick's near-black hair, dark eyes and towering muscular frame. His cool and dangerous demeanor appealed to her, making her pulse race and her brain sound alarms. He was the kind of man she didn't need in her life.

"You can't stay here alone." Bob pinned her with his hazel eyes.

Claire ground her back teeth at his high-handed tone. "I'm not alone. Gwen lives here, too."

Sandy piped up. "She can come to my house, too."

"Or she can stay with me," Lori offered.

Everyone started talking at once. Only Nick remained silent, his black eyes watchful. Her gaze slid away from him as she tried to reason with the people who were intent on arranging her life. She hated when people tried to arrange her life.

"Excuse me, everyone," Nick's voice, though low, rose above the chatter, effectively cutting off the noise. "Claire's been through a rough ordeal today. I'm sure she could use some time and space."

Surprised by his understanding, Claire's eyes widened.

"Of course." Peggy took her hand. "You let us know what we can do to help."

"I will. I promise." Claire's heart squeezed slightly at the woman's offer of help and friendship.

"Okay, kids, let's head out," Steve said as he took the puppy from Matthew and set him on the living room floor. He led his family out of The Zone.

Before they headed to the door, Sandy and Dave elicited a promise from Claire to call if she needed anything. Nick walked out with them.

Claire watched his retreating back with a frown and fought the ridiculous urge to cry. She'd asked him to leave, but she'd thought he'd at least say goodbye. There she went again—expecting something, only to feel hurt and rejected.

Would she ever learn?

Lori leaned in close, her gaze on Nick as well, and whispered, "He's certainly a prize worth holding on to."

Claire shook her head, feeling suddenly very tired. "You're too much the romantic," she whispered back.

Lori's eyes twinkled with mirth. "Bob, will you walk me to the shop?"

He looked surprised. "Why?"

"Because I asked you to, you big lug." Lori rolled her eyes. "Men." Then to Claire she said, "I'll check on you tomorrow."

She held up a hand as Claire opened her mouth to protest. "I know, but I'm coming, anyway." She wrinkled her straight nose. "It smells ghastly in here."

"I'll light some scented candles," Claire said.

"You shouldn't stay here," Bob said, his expression hard, concerned.

She tried for patience. "You sound like a broken record. This is my home. I'm not leaving. Besides, the damage is mainly outside. The water's only on the first floor and contained in the kitchen. I'll be fine."

"You are so stubborn." Exasperation echoed in his voice.

"Okay, time for us to go," Lori declared, linking her arm through Bob's. She gave Claire a meaningful look. "I'll talk with you later."

Too weary to argue, Claire nodded. "Fine."

Lori led a reluctant Bob out, leaving Claire alone.

Her lungs hurt and her throat felt like sandpaper. The place did smell and it looked horrible—all black and charred on the back wall around the door. But it was *her* place. The only thing she possessed worth anything. And someone had tried to wreck it. She blew out an angry breath. She wasn't about to let anyone destroy her dream.

A wet tickle at her ankle reminded her she now had one other possession. She bent and scratched behind Little Nick's ears. "Hope you don't mind that it's just you and me, little guy."

She straightened and moved toward the stairs when the front door opened and Nick walked back in.

A surge of happiness tore through her, catching her

off guard. She trampled down the giddy pleasure. "I thought you left."

"Sorry to disappoint you." His expression was unreadable but there was a tension in his body she hadn't noticed before.

"No. No disappointment. I'm glad to see you. I mean…I wanted to say goodbye."

"I came to get my jacket." He strode past her to where his leather jacket lay on the stool by the counter.

"Oh." A bubble of disappointment popped in her chest. He hadn't come to see her or to say goodbye.

He slipped the jacket on and crossed the room to stand a few feet from her. "I hear you might have a room to rent."

"You know of a teen in trouble?"

He gave her a sharp look. "I'd intended to stay awhile wherever I stopped this evening. My bike needs a tune-up. And now that it's getting late, I might as well stay in Pineridge. Steve recommended a mechanic a few blocks away."

Her heart pounded in her ears. He wanted to stay here? "That's not a good idea."

One side of his mouth curled up into a lopsided grin. "You'd be doing me a favor. And I could pay you by doing the work to repair the back of the building. That way you don't have to put any money out on expensive contractors and I can have a roof over my head. It would sure beat sleeping on the ground."

"There are hotels downtown. And a Motel 6 on the outskirts, just as you come off the freeway."

He shook his head. "I'll take my bedroll to the park."

"You can't do that. You'll get arrested."

"Your front grass will do."

"No. That's ridiculous."

Claire worried her lip, conflicted. On one hand she didn't like the idea of anyone invading her space. And he would definitely be an invader. But wasn't that the point of The Zone, to rent the rooms so kids wouldn't have to sleep on the ground? That was why Gwen lived with her, because she had nowhere else to go.

Nick wasn't a teen, but he obviously needed a place to stay for awhile. And apparently couldn't afford a hotel. She couldn't turn him out. She could only imagine the cost to his pride to have to ask for help. She knew her own pride held her back from asking anybody for assistance.

Yet, she couldn't shake a strong suspicion that somehow this was all just a ruse concocted to keep her under his protection. Why did he suddenly need his bike tuned up? You're being paranoid, she told herself.

Nick interrupted her thoughts. "I won't get in your way."

Heat crept up her neck. She was taking an awful long time to answer his question. Stalling, she asked, "You could fix the wall and the porch?"

"Yes. I've done carpentry work in the past."

Having him take care of the repairs would save her time and money. He was offering to work in exchange for room and board.

He needed a place to stay. She had it to give. Even though it wasn't a fair exchange. He would work harder than the rent she could charge. "I have a room. But I insist you let me pay you a small wage for the work."

He frowned. "Not necessary."

"It is to me." She wouldn't be a charity case. She'd use the money in the building fund for his wage, and insurance, she hoped, would pay for the repairs.

He considered her for a moment. "Okay. Deal."

He held out his hand. She slipped her smaller one into his. Warmth spread up her arm and wrapped around her senses. Looking in to his dark, commanding eyes, she felt the force of his attraction drawing her in. She sent up a silent prayer for strength to resist such a glaring temptation.

She was determined not to end up paying with her heart.

The strain of the day settled in Nick's neck as he lugged his saddlebag into The Zone. He'd taken his bike to the mechanic, a nice guy with an obvious love of Harleys. Nick had walked back to find Claire nowhere in sight and the front door unlocked.

Somehow he was going to have to get it through Claire's pretty head that safety was important. The quicker she learned that, the quicker he could leave.

He was relieved she'd agreed to let him stay, but the offer of a wage was too much. And so was Claire. Paying him to do the work appeased her stubborn sense of independence.

He would return the money she paid him with a little extra thrown in to help her cause when the time came for him to leave.

And he would leave. In the past two years he'd found that moving on was the only way to keep from going nuts.

But not until those punks were found and punished. Not until Claire was safe. He couldn't live with any more guilt.

Little Nick gave him a wet welcoming kiss when he'd opened the door, and now chewed at his shoes. He rubbed the pup behind the ears. "I'm counting on you to grow up to be a good guard dog."

Little Nick wagged his tail in response.

A noise on the stairs drew his attention. Claire, dressed in a light blue pullover T-shirt tucked into navy shorts, her blond hair pulled back into a ponytail, stood poised on the top stair. Her face was scrubbed clean of the soot from the fire and her blue eyes sparkled, reminding him of the Caribbean Sea on a clear day. Warm, inviting. A place you don't want to leave. He would make sure to keep their relationship on a purely superficial level. He couldn't afford to allow Claire to add another wound to his already battered soul.

He straightened as she came down the stairs.

"That didn't take you long."

"Caught the mechanic just as he was closing up. He seems to know what he's doing."

She flashed him a quick smile. "Do you want to freshen up?"

"Sure." He felt grimy and could use a shave. His jaw was beginning to itch.

"This way," Claire said over her shoulder as she headed back up the stairs.

He followed, his gaze appreciative of her feminine curves, her long athletic legs, trim ankles and dainty toenails painted a pale pink. She led him down the hallway past one closed door that she said belonged to Gwen and past two rooms that he could see would eventually be bedrooms, but at the moment were in disarray with boxes and mattresses propped against the walls.

She stopped at the fourth room. Stepping in, she flipped on the light.

From overhead, a soft glow illuminated the room, showing a twin-size bed made up with crisp white sheets and a dark green quilt folded at the foot of the bed. A mirror hung over a six-drawer dresser and a bedside table sported a brass lamp, the only other furniture.

She tugged on her lip with her teeth. "I hope you'll be comfortable. I only have twin beds in the rooms."

He quirked his mouth. He'd slept on a twin at his parents' house as a boy. His high-rise apartment on Lexington had had an oversize king. The apartment he'd shared with Serena. An ache throbbed in his chest. "I'll manage."

Claire ducked past him, moved to another open door and flipped on the light to reveal a bathroom decorated in pale blues and creams. "The shower gets fairly hot. Clean towels are in the cupboard under the sink. You can pile your dirty laundry by the door. I'll start a load before I go to bed."

"Great. Just like a hotel." Only here the proprietress was a leggy blonde with caretaking issues. The last thing he needed in his life.

Humor shifted in her gaze. "Bed-and-breakfast."

"Boarding house."

She grinned. "Teen shelter. Thus the twin beds. I hadn't planned on a full grown man sleeping here."

Nick's shoulders tensed. "You okay with me being here?"

"Yes, of course." Her cheeks reddened.

"If you're uncomfortable, I'll head to the nearest Motel 6."

She put her hand on his arm. Her warm touch soothed the tension gripping his insides.

"Really. I'm glad you're staying."

He searched her gaze, not sure what he expected to find. Certainly not the trust shining in her crystalline eyes. "You've done a nice job making this place homey."

Her smile was quick, grateful. "Thank you. I still have a ways to go. Especially now with the fire…" Her smile faltered momentarily, then she shrugged. "But now that I'm paying you to help, it will all come together."

"Are you always so optimistic?"

Her smile dimmed. "I try. It makes life easier to think positively rather than dwell on the negative. I'm not in control of the future or the past. The only thing I can control is my reactions, my choices."

"Right." He'd never been a success at letting go of the past. Even before Serena's death. Nor was he good at not trying to manage the future. Serena had called him obsessive. He was simply the way God made him.

"I can do all things through Christ, who strengthens me,'" she quoted softly.

"So, you are a believer?" That answered his question about her faith.

"Yes. And you are, too, right?"

His mouth twisted at her question. "I believe, but my faith isn't so strong these days."

That was an understatement. He didn't understand God. Didn't understand why He let bad things happen to good people. He definitely didn't understand why Serena had to die. Nick imagined he felt a lot like how Job must have felt.

Claire's eyes were troubled and concern radiated from her in waves. "Maybe coming to church with me on Sunday would help."

He liked her thoughtfulness. "Maybe. I don't know."

"The offer always stands. In fact, you don't have to come to my church. There are other churches in town. God doesn't care what building we worship in as long as we worship."

"I'll take that under consideration." Not liking the direction the conversation was headed, he changed the subject. "Tell me something. How do you expect homeless kids to pay rent?"

Her laugh was soft, husky, thrilling. "I don't. This isn't a business for profit. I plan to offer the teens who are serious about getting their life together a place to stay. Along with the room, comes responsibility."

"What kind of responsibility?" he asked.

"Helping out here, as well as working toward reconciliation with their parents. And if that isn't possible, then getting a GED and making a plan for the future. Finding a job. Going to school. Becoming a useful part of society. Most people just need someone to believe in them before they can believe in themselves."

"Impressive, but faulty. What about the ones that don't want to get their lives together? The ones that would rather steal, cheat and lie than earn an honest way in life?"

Two little lines creased between her brows. "Deep down, no one truly wants to live like that. And if someone doesn't offer these kids a way off the street, their souls wither and die. They feel that no one cares. So why shouldn't they lie, steal and cheat?"

He admired her earnestness. "One lone woman can't save all the homeless kids in the world."

Her chin went up. "No, of course not. But I can make a difference here in Pineridge. Be a safe haven for those that need it. Get to kids before they run to a place where they become just one more body lost in the crowd."

"Is that how you and Gwen hooked up? Was she a teen in trouble?"

She lowered her voice. "Yes. Gwen was living on the streets in Portland. Strung out on drugs and starving. But she's come a long way. All these kids need is someone to care. I will be their someone."

Respect for her tenacity and determination wound through him. She was a force to be reckoned with. He reached up and tucked a stray lock of hair behind her ear. "Lucky kids."

Her breath hitched and her eyes widened. She stepped back. "Uh, are you hungry?"

"Yes, I'm hungry." He liked the way her lips were full and a soft rose color. She had lips made for kissing. He wanted to kiss her, to somehow partake of her idealism, her faith. *Foolish fantasy.*

"Pizza okay?"

He forced his gaze up to meet hers, his brain suddenly sluggish. "Pizza?"

"I was thinking of ordering a pizza to be delivered since the kitchen's pretty much out of commission."

"Right. Pizza would be good." *And a cold shower*.

"What would you like?"

A long sweet kiss. "Pepperoni, cheese, whatever."

"Great." She stepped back and bumped into the wall. "I'll go call." She turned and fled, the door closing with a slight click behind her.

Nick dropped his head to the doorjamb. He had to get a grip. He shouldn't be thinking about kissing Claire. That would only lead to disaster. He would *not* allow himself to become attracted to her.

The sooner he got the work done and those kids caught the better. Then he could go.

Forget about The Zone being a safe haven. It wasn't for him. Not with Claire around.

Oh, my.

Claire leaned against the door. Her heart thumped in her chest, the rhythm as erratic as her thoughts. Her reaction to Nick was bad. Very bad.

But everything inside her wanted to throw open the door and invite Nick in.

She hadn't been this attracted to a man since…well, since Billy. And she and Billy had only been seventeen. Nick was a full-grown man with the entire powerful draw that went with maturity.

It wasn't that she didn't find men attractive. Bob

was good-looking, but he certainly never evoked this kind of response in her. There'd been a guy named Sean in college. Handsome, with a bit of an edge that had satisfied that wild streak in her, and a counselor at Young Life to boot. He'd seemed perfect. Aunt Denise had even approved, but Claire just couldn't let him in. The risk was too great, caring too dangerous.

There were other men in town. Single, available men who'd made it clear they wanted to date her. But she didn't want to date. Didn't want to ever be vulnerable to the whims of the male species again.

So why did she wish Nick had kissed her? It had to have been her imagination when she'd seen his eyes flare with interest, his head dip slightly, bringing his strong jaw and firm mouth closer.

She hurried to the side of the bed and knelt. She needed to spend some time with God, praising Him for his protection and asking Him for strength.

Because temptation would be sleeping just down the hall.

Chapter Five

The evening sun painted the sky with vibrant oranges and pinks. Claire loved this time of day when the world was winding down, becoming peaceful. If she listened carefully she could hear the first few crickets singing their nighttime serenade.

She sat on the front steps of The Zone with Nick, the doors and windows wide open because the acrid smell of smoke still permeated the air. But on the faint evening breeze, Claire did detect the soothing scents of the vanilla, bayberry and lavender air fresheners she'd placed around the inside of The Zone.

Little Nick frolicked in the grass and around the bushes, his body a flash of color against the greenery. Tenderness filled her chest. If Little Nick's owners claimed him, she would get another puppy.

Claire watched Nick devour his slice of pizza. He ate like a starved man. She offered him the other piece sitting untouched on her plate. "I'm not going to eat this. Do you want it?"

He slanted her a sharp glance. "You eat it. One measly slice isn't enough to keep you going."

Her natural reaction was to bristle at his censure and not eat, out of rebellion. She didn't like being told what to do. But the concern in his licorice-colored eyes belied her frustration. He wasn't trying to control her.

She picked up the slice of pepperoni pizza and bit into it. Okay, she was still a bit hungry. The approval in Nick's expression sent shivers along her limbs, making her want to preen under his warm regard. Pathetic. She concentrated on eating.

"So you never told me what made you come back," she said once she finished.

Nick wiped his hands on a napkin, his expression turning pensive, uncomfortable. "I had a strange feeling that I was supposed to."

Claire's spirit quickened. She kept her smile to herself. God had been watching out for her this day. "I'm glad you listened."

He gave her a sidelong glance before closing the lid on the pizza box. "There's enough left over for lunch tomorrow."

"Uh-huh," she murmured. His big strong hands captivated her attention. The sun had kissed them a golden brown. His nails were neatly trimmed. Her gaze traveled up his muscular forearms, past his biceps to his broad shoulders. She shouldn't be so attracted to him. He wasn't wearing black and leather now.

When he'd come down after his shower, her breath

had caught in her throat. He'd walked down the stairs looking like he'd just walked out of the pages of a magazine. Khaki pants, with little creases indicating where they'd been folded, and a white polo style shirt stretched taut across his chest. And he'd shaved.

His strong jawbone was now smooth. His dark hair was damp and combed back from his forehead, the ends curling gently at the collar of his shirt. Would his hair be soft and silky or coarse and thick? She itched to run her fingers through his hair.

She usually didn't go for the preppy look. But there was still an edge to Nick. Something wildly attractive that spoke to her, to the restless girl inside. She wanted to snuggle close and share his warmth.

Where was that puppy!

"What are you thinking?" Nick asked.

The heat of embarrassment flushed over her. "I was wondering about you. Wondering why you're here. Where's your family?"

His jaw tightened. Something dark slithered into his expression. She remembered his rage earlier. Remembered the haunted expression that had clawed at her.

My faith isn't so strong these days.

Something had happened to him, something bad. She ached inside. She wanted to help.

Abruptly, he stood and stretched out his hand. The glow from the porch light reflected off the hard angles of his face. "It's late. We both could use some rest."

She blinked, took his hand and allowed him to pull her to her feet, his grip strong and sure. She craned her neck to look up into his face. "I'm sorry if I offended you."

His expression softened. "You didn't offend. You have every right to wonder about me."

"But you're not going to tell me."

A slow smile touched his mouth. "Not tonight."

All right. His words were a promise. He'd tell her when he was ready. She could live with that. She had to earn trust before others would open up to her. She'd learned that in Young Life training. Ha! Who was she kidding? She'd *lived* it.

"Tomorrow you'll need to contact the insurance company. They'll want to come out and assess the damage. If you want, I could deal with them," Nick said.

"I can take care of it," she responded quickly.

He nodded. "I'll be here if you need me."

This was her responsibility. Speaking of which, she realized the puppy had disappeared. "Here, Little Nick, here, boy," she called.

The yard in front of The Zone wasn't big. Two green patches of grass edged both sides of a cement walkway, one Japanese maple tree, a lilac bush and a couple of unidentified bushes. She wasn't much of a gardener. "Here, boy," she called again.

Nick whistled between his teeth, one strong blast. A bush rustled, then a yellow ball of fur burst out.

Claire laughed. "That was good. I'll have to learn that."

Nick scooped up his namesake and handed him to her. "Do you have food for him?"

She gasped. "No. In all the chaos today I forgot to go to the store."

"Where's the closest one?"

"Through the park and left three blocks."

"I'll be back soon."

"Oh…" She wanted to say he didn't have to go for her, that she'd manage. But this wasn't about her. The dog needed food. She should be grateful. She *would* be grateful. "Thank you. I…we appreciate it."

He flashed her a grin, warming her as if the sun shone bright on her skin. She longed to bask in the glow, but knew if she did, she'd only end up with a bad sunburn for her folly.

"Be back soon. Lock the door." With those parting words, he strode away. She stood on the porch holding the puppy and watching him fade into the darkness.

She put the puppy inside the laundry room, closed the door, then picked up the leftover pizza and jumped in her car.

A half hour later, Claire slipped back inside The Zone. Thankfully, she'd made it back before Nick. There was no doubt in her mind that he'd have been standing at the door, arms crossed over that broad chest and his eyes sparking with anger, if he'd returned to find her gone. Relief pounded in her chest. She didn't relish explaining her errand because he wouldn't understand.

She noticed Gwen's coat hanging on the coatrack by the door. Better warn her about their unexpected houseguest. Claire went up the stairs and knocked on Gwen's door.

"Come in."

Claire eased open the door and as always was struck

by the color in the room. Gwen had painted one wall a deep burgundy. The other walls were covered with anatomy charts. Gwen wanted to become a doctor.

Gwen was colorful herself, with her long, bright red hair pulled to one side and plaited into a thick braid. She wore powder-blue velour sweats. Her amber-colored eyes smiled at Claire as her freckled face split into a grin.

Gwen bounded from her spot in the middle of her bed, causing several textbooks to crash off the sides, and launched herself into Claire's arms, hugging her and checking her for injuries. "You're okay? I called the hospital from work and they said you'd been released. But you weren't here when I came home. I thought…well, it doesn't matter what I thought because you're here."

Claire laughed and extracted herself from the nineteen-year-old's enthusiastic embrace. "I'm fine. Really."

Gwen nodded once sharply. "Good."

She went back to the bed, picked up her books and arranged them around her as she sat cross-legged in the middle and focused her attention back on her studies.

Typical Gwen. A burst of emotion and then back to business.

In the beginning when Claire and Aunt Denise had brought Gwen to live with them, the outbursts were wild, loud and dramatic. But keeping a job and going to school had forced the girl to learn to show her emotions in more appropriate ways.

Claire was proud of the young woman's growth. "Gwen."

Gwen lifted her head. "Yes?"

"We're going to have a guest for awhile."

She raised an auburn brow. "Oh?"

"Nick. You met him earlier, right after the fire."

"Ohhh," Gwen said, in a knowing way that grated on Claire. "Mr. Charming in black."

"He needs a place to stay and he's offered to repair the fire damage."

"Right."

Claire ignored Gwen's smirk. "Anyway. Just make sure you're not strutting around in hot rollers and your icky green mask."

Gwen laughed. "I will."

With that settled, Claire headed back downstairs and sat on the couch with Little Nick resting beside her. She closed her eyes and though her voice sounded raspy and her throat hurt a little, she sang softly.

A few minutes later a soft knock sounded at the door. Little Nick jumped to his feet and barked.

"Shhh, now, it's only Nick," Claire admonished as she went to open the door.

Nick gave her an irritated look. "You should always ask who it is before opening the door."

She drew back. "I was expecting you."

There was a disapproving set to his mouth as he moved past her. "You need to be more careful."

Claire didn't like the way her heart hammered in her chest or the panicky way her stomach contracted. She didn't need his approval. She shouldn't be feeling guilty. She didn't owe him anything. She didn't need him.

He fed Little Nick from the small bag of puppy food he'd carried in. "You okay?"

He stepped closer, oblivious to her inner turmoil. His masculine scent washed over her, making her aware of his size and appeal.

"Tired." *And too close to you.*

"It's been a long day."

She fidgeted. What was she supposed to do now? How were they supposed to proceed? She'd better figure it out quick if he was going to be staying there.

She paced away from him. They were adults; they had a business arrangement. There wasn't anything personal about it. She drew herself up. "Well, good night then."

"Good night, Claire." His smile was soft as he headed up the stairs, leaving her to deal with her grown-up loneliness.

And yearnings.

The day after the fire, Claire was awakened by voices. Through the foggy remnants of sleep, the voices sounded a long way off. But as she sat up and memory flooded in, she knew they were coming from inside The Zone. She glanced at the clock. Eleven in the morning. She never slept that late. And amazingly, she couldn't remember waking during the night. She must have been more exhausted than she'd realized.

She grabbed a long pink cotton robe and threw it on over her blue cotton pj's. Barefooted, she padded down the hall, past Nick's closed door to the top of the stairs. She paused to listen.

The unmistakable rumble of Nick's voice slid over her like fingers strumming a guitar. Each chord hummed through her. She struggled to quiet those accordant notes.

Other male voices joined in, though she couldn't make out their words. Cautiously, she padded down the stairs and peeked over the railing. At the large square coffee table, Nick and three men—Steve Jordan, Dave Wellington, and a man she didn't recognize—looked at some papers strewn across the flat surface.

"Nick?"

His smile of welcome sent tingles sliding over her skin. She pulled the robe tighter around her as if she could ward off the effect he had on her.

He stood up and moved to the foot of the stairs. "Sorry to wake you."

"That's okay. What's going on?"

"Volunteers to help," he said with a gesture toward the men staring at her.

She waved, before backing up a step to where she couldn't be seen. "Volunteers?"

He came up a few steps and shrugged. "I went to the hardware store earlier and they showed up wanting to help."

"But I'm paying *you* to do this." She didn't want anyone's charity. Or pity.

His expression hardened. "It will get done quicker with more bodies."

She searched his face, hoping to see something, anything that could reassure her that trusting him was a good thing. All she found was determination. "Fine."

"It'll be okay, Claire. I promise."

She lifted her chin. "Promises can be broken."

"Not by me, they aren't." He turned and walked away, his wide shoulders stiff.

Claire sank to the stairs. She wanted to trust that such a thing could be true. That he was a man who didn't break promises. Besides Aunt Denise, she didn't know anyone who didn't break a promise. And obviously, someone had broken a promise to Nick.

Her heart beat in her throat. Everything inside her wanted to heal him. Only she didn't know how. She had to get him to open up to her, trust her. *Lord, give me the wisdom, the words to say.*

She ran upstairs to get dressed. She had a man's mind to pick.

In her room, she threw on her old faded blue jeans and a purple top. She twisted her hair up and secured it with a clip. Grabbed her old Keds and some socks. When she came back downstairs, Nick and the other men were in the back. She rescued Little Nick from the laundry room and headed outside.

As she turned the corner, Nick saw her and smiled in greeting. She hugged the puppy close to her chest and watched as Nick excused himself from the other men. She put the puppy on the ground. He promptly scampered away.

"Have you called the insurance company?" Nick asked.

She started. "No. I'll go do that right now."

One side of his mouth quirked up. "Good idea."

She ran inside, found her insurance information and made the call. Her agent was understanding and said they'd send someone out right away.

When she went back out, Nick was alone, sitting on the porch with the puppy curled up at his side.

"Where'd everyone go?" she asked.

Nick tilted his head up to look at her. "Until we have the okay from the insurance company, we can't do much."

She sat down beside him. "The insurance adjuster should be here this afternoon."

"Great."

This was her chance to pick his brain, to get him to open up. "How long will your bike be in the shop?"

"A few days."

She ran her hand over the puppy's smooth coat. "How long have you been traveling?"

He glanced at her. "A couple of years."

"That's a long time. What made you decide to ride across the country?"

Her question sliced through Nick. He blocked out the grief welling up. He couldn't go there right now. He didn't know if he ever could.

He stood. "Hey, how about we run to a store where we can get some things for this little guy? I've heard that crate training is the way to go."

Claire blinked up at him, her clear blues showing disappointment. "Okay." She rose. "I also need to stop at the copy store and run off some flyers about him. I'm sure whoever owns this little guy is looking for him. Let me grab my purse." She disappeared inside with the puppy trailing behind.

A dull throbbing started behind his eyes. "Oh, Lord when will You ever grant me peace?"

He certainly wouldn't find peace with Claire wanting to know about his past. The only way he could handle the pain was by not dealing with it. If he wasn't careful, her stubbornness and determination would wear him down. He couldn't allow her in. Wouldn't allow himself to care about her.

"There you go, boy," Claire said as she put Little Nick inside his new crate. They'd decided to place the crate under a window in the living room where the puppy would get some fresh air.

The pet-store clerk had advised allowing the puppy to get used to his new bed by putting him in and leaving the door open so he could go in and out. The crate should become his refuge.

But for how long? One day, Little Nick's true owner would claim him.

She pushed aside the pang that thought caused.

Where was Nick? After setting up the puppy's crate, Nick had gone outside and not come back in.

Just as she was putting another load in the wash, she heard her name being called.

"Hello, I'm back here," she yelled loudly over the sound of water filling the washer.

Lori walked in wearing faded cut-offs, a yellow, flowered shirt and beat-up tennis shoes. Long tendrils of dark hair escaped from her ponytail. In one hand was a mop and in the other a plastic bag with what looked like cleaning supplies. "Hi. Who's that outside with Nick?"

Claire stared. "I don't know. What are you doing here?"

Lori smiled and lifted her hands, showing off her

items like trophies. "Came to clean. Sandy will be by later to help and I think Peggy said she'd stop in, too."

Claire shook her head. "You don't have to do this."

Lori lowered her arms. "I know I don't *have* to. I *want* to." She set the supplies down. "But first I want to know who that handsome man outside with Nick is."

Disconcerted by Lori's insistence, Claire followed her out into the afternoon sunshine. The warm air felt wonderful against her face. The clean scent of the lilac bush was a welcome reprieve from the smell of smoke. They followed the sound of voices to the back of The Zone. Nick stood a head or so taller than the Latino-looking man who introduced himself as Mario Benitto, the claims adjuster from her insurance company.

"Thank you for coming so quickly," Claire said politely, shooting Nick a curious glance. Why hadn't Nick informed her the man had arrived?

Lori nudged Claire in the side. "What?"

Lori gave her a pointed look.

"Oh." Amused, Claire said, "This is Lori Pearson."

The man smiled, showing white teeth as he extended his hand to Lori. "It's a pleasure to meet you."

Lori made a little noise in her throat. "Pleasure's all mine," she murmured beneath her breath.

Mario's eyes crinkled at the corners with good humor. Claire had the distinct impression he'd heard Lori's comment. The claims adjuster turned his light brown gaze to her. "I'll write up my report and send over the paperwork for you to sign."

"Oh. Okay."

Mario turned to Nick and the men shook hands.

"Ladies." Mario tipped his head with a smile that included Claire but his interest was clearly on Lori.

As soon as the man's car pulled away from the curb, Claire planted her hands on her hips and faced Nick. "Why didn't you come get me when he arrived?"

He drew his brows together. "I was just trying to help."

"You were trying to take over. This is my responsibility. I'm capable of dealing with the insurance company."

He held up a hand. "I didn't mean to step on your toes."

Lori backed up a step. "I'll just be inside." She hurried away.

"I'm glad to see you've got help," Nick commented quietly.

"I didn't ask her to come. She just showed up," Claire said quickly.

"I'm just saying, it's good of you to bless her by letting her help."

She tucked in her chin. "Bless her?"

His expression softened. His mouth curved up on one side. "Yes, bless her. 'It is more blessed to give than to receive.' She's given you her time and her energy. Don't rob her of her blessing."

Claire pondered his words. "So, you're saying I'm robbing you of your blessing if I don't let you help?" she asked slowly.

He raised a cocky brow. "Yes. That's what I'm saying."

She rolled her eyes. "I hate it when people quote Scripture to further their own agenda."

His expression turned contrite. "Look, Claire. I figured since you'd hired me to do the work, I should be the one to explain to the guy what needed to be done. I really didn't mean to upset you."

What he said made sense. Her initial indignation faded in the face of his sincere words. "I'm sorry I got upset. I'm so used to doing everything myself that I…"

"Have trouble giving up control?" he finished.

A wry laugh burst from her. "That pretty much sums it up."

She sobered and stared into his dark eyes, seeing kindness and understanding.

"There's no shame in asking for help."

She nodded, feeling herself lost in his gaze. "I guess I should go help Lori," she muttered.

"Probably."

But neither moved. Claire felt drawn to him and warning bells went off in her head. There was something about this man that lured her to him as if he were a bug light and she were some fluttery insect. Only she wasn't about to get close enough to get zapped. She knew up front this one was leaving. She backed away.

"Claire?"

Her name on his lips sent waves of warmth through her. "Yeah?"

"I've an errand to run. Can I borrow your car?"

"Oh, sure. Anytime." Then she hurried for the safety of The Zone.

Nick drove slowly through the side streets of Pineridge, his gaze alert and searching for the three errant teens. The runaways.

The tree-lined streets were quiet. The houses with their well-kept yards, a minivan here or an SUV there, all whispered tranquillity. Tranquillity he'd never get a chance to know, now that Serena was gone.

People who were in their yards or on their porches usually stopped whatever they were doing to watch him drive by—some stared with mild curiosity while others with wary suspicion.

He'd become used to the second type in the last two years—a man on a Harley attracted attention. Interest from some, mostly females, but the majority felt suspicion. So what was it about him in a green hatchback? He tightened his grip around the steering wheel of Claire's car and headed away from the nice suburban neighborhoods to more commercial areas.

He'd already stopped by the police department and had a word with Officer Bob. Bob had assured him the police were still looking for the teens, but without evidence there wasn't much they could do beyond keeping an eye on them.

Nick cruised into an industrial park bordered on either side by typical Oregon woods. Tall trees and thick underbrush. A hundred feet down the way, a boy emerged from between two buildings.

The blond kid from the park!

Nick sped up. The boy froze for a split second and then took off at a dead run through the dusty parking lot where he veered off into the thick woods. Nick threw the car's transmission into park, jumped out and took up the chase.

He crashed through the trees, but the kid had disappeared. Nick stopped. Bending at the waist, he braced his hands on his knees as he listened for noise to direct his search.

In the distance the faint hum of traffic underlined the sounds of the woods. A bird chirped to his left. The clickity-clack of a squirrel's nails as it climbed the bark of a nearby tree echoed through the woods. The faint rustling of leaves stirred by the slight breeze taunted him.

Nick straightened and made his way out of the trees. Back in the car, he drove around the buildings, looking for likely places the teens would hang out. On the backside of the lot several of the buildings were empty and boarded up.

There were any number of places for three runaways to hide.

Nick left, deciding he'd come back later, after dark. Because he didn't need proof that the kids had started the fire. His gut told him they had and he'd make sure the punks paid.

He owed that much to Claire.

Chapter Six

When Nick arrived at The Zone, Claire and Little Nick were playing in the front yard with a small rubber ball.

"Look, he fetches," she exclaimed with a big smile that lit her whole face.

"That's great," Nick replied, but his gaze never strayed off Claire.

She'd changed into a summery dress with little strappy sandals that allowed her pink-tipped toes to peek out. Her sleek blond hair was parted on one side and held back by a fancy clip.

She looked young and fresh, but the sparkle of wonder in her eyes lodged a knot in his throat. It called to a part of him he'd buried beneath so much bitterness he'd almost forgotten wonder and awe existed.

Shaken, he sat on the stair beside her. "Have you ever had a dog?"

She shook her head. "Aunt Denise had cats. What about you?"

He laughed, remembering. "My sister and I had an assortment of pets through the years. Dogs, cats, guinea pigs, rats. A python that drove my mother to hysterics. We once had a tortoise named Speedy."

Her interested gaze trapped his. "That's so cool. One of Aunt Denise's cats had kittens and she let me keep one. A black ball of fur that slept on my pillow until we realized I was allergic to cats. All watery eyes and runny nose. It wasn't pretty."

He shared her chuckle, though he couldn't imagine her not looking pretty. "What happened to your aunt?"

Claire's small, slender hands smoothed her skirt over her knees. "She died of lymphoma."

He covered her restless hands. "I'm sorry."

"Thank you."

"How old were you?" He rubbed the back of her warm hand with his thumb.

"Just finishing my last year of college. It's been two years now."

The same amount of time since he'd lost Serena. They shared the connection of having lost someone they loved. His heart throbbed. "Was she sick long?"

"No. It hit fast." She extracted her hand and stood. "Are you hungry?"

He pushed himself off the stair, acknowledging her need to change the subject. He felt the same. "Yes, food would be great. Leftover pizza?"

For some reason she flushed. "Uh, no, uh, I was thinking…maybe Chinese tonight. Or we could go to the hamburger joint where Gwen waitresses."

"Whichever."

She scooped up the puppy and hurried inside.

Nick waited on the steps. He scanned the park across the street even as he told himself to keep a distance from his very pretty and sweet hostess.

Over the next few days, Claire watched with equal doses of amazement and annoyance as Nick took charge of the men who'd volunteered their labor. He organized and smoothly created a team effort. They'd brought in equipment and lumber. The back of The Zone was dismantled and the frame for the new door was up.

After their conversation about the insurance company, Claire allowed Nick to handle the situation. She signed where he'd indicated and appreciated the way he kept her informed. She'd struggled with letting him take charge, but she was smart enough to acknowledge he was doing a great job.

Unfortunately, she hadn't done a bang-up job of getting inside his head. Whenever they were alone and she had the opportunity to find out more about him, she felt tongue-tied and scattered. She had to get a grip.

Today, she vowed, would be different.

The day was sunny. Perfect Oregon weather. The kind that made unsuspecting people want to move to the state. Only, when the rain hit for days on end, they'd soon realize how precious and rare the sunny days were.

She found Nick in the back, using a power saw to cut boards. She sat on the grass. Little Nick chewed on a toy at her feet.

Nick had taken off his shirt, revealing long, lean muscles beneath tanned skin. His beauty was distracting. She'd sought him out for a reason, but she hesitated to speak for fear she'd startle him. Saws made her nervous. All that noise. That sharp blade.

"You having a good day?" he asked without turning, effectively dismissing her fear that she'd distract him.

"I am. You've done a wonderful job so far."

"Wasn't just me."

"I know." He was so quick to give credit away. She liked that. "How come you know so much about building and things?"

He lowered the board he was cutting and went to the pile of lumber. He picked up several, discarded them and then finally settled on one, which he took to the saw. "My father owns a hardware and lumber store," he finally answered.

She smiled at his back. "On Long Island?"

"That's right. It started out a real mom-and-pop operation, but he's expanded. Some of the big conglomerates have offered to buy him out because he has a great location for the area. But he's not ready to retire. Mom's ready for him to, though. She'd like to travel, but the business is Dad's baby. He's devoted his whole life to making it a success."

"At your expense?" she ventured, wondering if that was the deep hurt she sensed in him.

His glance was razor sharp. "No. He's a great dad. To both me and my sister."

Envy twisted inside her. Ugly and dark. She envied

him that his parents were still together and that he thought his father had been a good dad. She envied that he had a sibling. Someone to confide in, share childhood memories with. She envied that he had family to love. "What's your sister's name?"

"Lucy. She's a fireball just like her namesake, Lucille Ball. My mom really liked the Lucy and Desi show. I'm lucky they didn't name me Desi." He finished with the board, laid it on the ground next to the others, and then turned off the saw.

"Were you named after someone?"

He nodded as he came to sit beside her. "After my grandfather, on my mom's side."

"Did you know your grandfather?"

"Sure." He slanted her a glance. "Didn't you know your grandparents?"

Claire shook her head. "My mom's parents live in Arizona. I saw them once when I was ten, but they weren't real warm people. And my dad and Aunt Denise's parents passed away when I was a baby."

"What happened to your parents?"

She took a deep breath. "My parents divorced when I was twelve and I came to live with Aunt Denise."

Nick noticed the strained tone of her voice. "Why not with one of your parents?"

She plucked at the grass. "Just didn't."

Did that mean neither of her parents had wanted her? Or she hadn't wanted them? Nick's chest tightened. "I'm sorry. That must have been tough, being away from both parents."

"I suppose," she said noncommittedly.

The sadness in her eyes cried out to his soul. He didn't want to take on her pain, too.

The silence stretched. His curiosity got the better of him. "Did you grow up here, Claire?"

"No."

"Where?"

"Portland," she said finally.

"Are both your parents still there?"

"My dad died in an accident on the job the year I graduated from high school." She lifted a shoulder in a careless gesture. "Don't know about my mother."

He turned to fully face her. "I'm sorry for your loss. You don't have contact with your mother?"

"Nope," she said, a bit too cheery. "It's for the best."

"How can not having contact with your mother be for the best?" He stared at her intently. "Is it your choice not to see her?"

She was tempted to look away, but instead unflinchingly held his gaze. "At first it was, but then after my father died, I contacted her. We talked on the phone and she made it clear there was no room in her life for me. She asked me not to contact her again."

She cleared her throat, hating how her mother's rejection still hurt. "Now, you know about my family. I'd much rather hear about yours." She could see he wanted to press, but she headed off his unspoken questions with a question of her own. "You're close with your grandfather?"

His mouth quirked at the corner. "All my grandparents, actually. The whole family, both sides, gathers every Sunday after church for dinner at our house."

"They *all* live on Long Island?" she asked.

He nodded. "Pretty much. Two sets of grandparents, aunts and uncles, tons of cousins. I lived in Manhattan for years, but always came home for the weekends."

She couldn't fathom that. "Do you miss your family?"

A dark shadow flickered in his eyes. "I do."

Her earlier suspicion was on target. His pain definitely had something to do with his family. "When was the last time you saw them?"

His gaze slid away. "A year and a half ago."

"That's a long time."

He grunted.

"Did you come out west for a job or something?"

His expression closed. He gave a negative shake of his head.

"What made you leave?" she probed.

What could drive such a steadfast and determined man away from the family he obviously adored? If she'd had parents like that, a family…she pushed the dark thought away.

"It's complicated. My parents wanted me to take over the hardware store. I couldn't do that."

"Ah. Bigger aspirations?"

He frowned. "Don't get me wrong. The business is great. For my dad. I had different dreams."

"What are your dreams?"

When his gaze came back to her, she sucked in a breath at the guarded expression darkening his eyes. "I'm not going there, Claire."

He'd set a boundary, she respected that. But still…

Realization struck with lightning-bright clarity. He was a grown-up runaway. God had brought him to her for a reason. He had saved her so she could save him. She liked a good challenge. "Does your family even know where you are?"

With one hand he rubbed at his neck. "I drop them a line once in awhile."

"Did you have a fight, is that why you left?" she pressed.

Blatantly ignoring her question, he stood and picked up the cut boards, his muscles bunching in a fascinating way. He carried the boards to the side of the building, leaving her alone.

She picked a blade of grass and split it in the middle. Nick's refusal to follow in his father's footsteps would obviously divide a family.

Aunt Denise used to say a family was only as strong as the threads binding them. Nick had said he missed them. That they were good parents. By the sound of it, he had a close-knit family. Nick's threads were weakened, but not severed, which gave her hope that the bond could be strengthened. If she could convince him to contact his parents, the haunted look might leave his eyes.

And she'd have the satisfaction of knowing she'd helped him do something she'd been unable to do for herself.

Two days later, Nick returned from an early morning walk around the perimeters of The Zone looking for any evidence that the kids had returned. The empty lots on either side of The Zone's boundaries showed no signs of disturbance. So far his search for the teens hadn't yielded much.

Just that one brief glimpse of the blond kid.

Nick had gone back to the warehouses several times, but to no avail. He'd look downtown again today. The teens had to surface at some point, unless they'd left town. One could hope.

His stomach clenched at the sight of Claire coming down the walkway from the front of The Zone. The heels of her brown sandals clicked on the cement. An ankle-length denim skirt covered her long legs.

The blue tank showed off her slender arms and graceful neck. Her blond hair shimmered in the afternoon sun. He hadn't noticed before the streaks of red highlights, making her more strawberry blond.

In her hands, she carried a brown leather purse and a hooded gray sweatjacket. She really was very lovely. He liked that she didn't feel the need to hide behind layers of makeup and overly styled hair.

"Where are you headed?" Nick asked.

She turned her head, sending her hair sliding across her shoulders. "I'm going to the bank."

"Anything I could help with?"

For a moment there was eagerness in her eyes, but she quickly shook her head. "I've got everything under control."

And there it was. She liked being in control of her life to the point that accepting, let alone asking for help, was seen as some kind of weakness. It made Nick sad to think she lived her life so self-confined.

"Mind if I walk with you?" He fell in step with her. "I want to check on my bike."

She relaxed, a teasing light appeared in her clear eyes. "Miss riding out on the open road?"

He made a noncommittal noise.

Strangely, he wasn't missing the "open road." He attributed the lack of restlessness to the distraction of rebuilding the back of The Zone. Once he was finished he was certain his memories and pain would push him on.

They walked through the park and down the main street. He enjoyed the companionable way she chatted about what she'd seen on the local news channel that morning. It felt natural to be with her as if they'd known each other for a long time.

As they passed by the hardware store, the owner, Mr. Hanson, waved a greeting to Nick through the window. They'd struck up a friendship once the older man had realized how much Nick knew about hardware and carpentry. Mr. Hanson had even offered Nick a job, much to Nick's amusement.

Nick didn't need a job or money. At least not yet. He'd made wise choices in the stock market for both himself and his clients before Serena's death. And after…he'd sold or given away everything they'd had. He lived off the interest in his bank account.

A fat lot of good that was to his empty heart.

As Nick and Claire approached the open door of Tessa's Bakery, Nick slowed and touched Claire's arm to indicate he wanted to go in. The spicy smell of cinnamon bread that mingled with the sweet scent of pastries made his mouth water, but the response seemed mild compared to the way his pulse jumped when Claire smiled her approval of their unexpected stop.

Tessa Burke came to the counter as they stepped inside. She was a slightly plump woman in her early fifties, with a wide smile and twinkling gray eyes. "How are you two today?"

"Good, thanks." Nick helped himself to a sample of cinnamon bread. "How's Timmy?" Tessa had told Nick all about her grandson during an earlier visit.

Tessa's eyes lit up. "He's great. Thank you for asking. He turns four next week."

"Wow, four. That's a milestone." Nick handed Claire a piece of bread.

As she took the morsel from him, her fingers brushed his, the contact almost causing him to drop the bread before she fully had hold of it. She popped the piece in her mouth and made an approving sound. "This is delicious, Tessa."

The woman beamed. "This was one of your aunt's favorites."

"I remember," Claire stated as she snagged another piece off the platter on the counter.

"Could we have a loaf to go?" Nick slanted Claire a grin. "Breakfast."

She grinned back, her blue eyes twinkling. She nodded eagerly. He paid for the bread before they moved on.

They stopped at the foot of the concrete stairs leading into the bank. The large white square structure was impressive in its beauty. Tall white pillars flanked the double brass-framed doors. Multiple flower baskets hung from hooks along the overhang shielding the doorway from the elements.

"Sure you don't want me to come with you?" Nick asked as he propped a hip on the railing.

She waved her hand. "No, no. I wouldn't want to keep you from your bike."

With a little shock, he realized he'd been so engrossed in Claire's company that he'd forgotten to stop at the mechanic's shop. "I'm where I want to be."

She backed up a few steps. The sun cast shadows on her face, hiding her eyes. "I need to go in now."

"I'll see you later."

She turned and fled to the building.

He certainly was treading in dangerous water.

Claire finished her business at the bank and walked outside into the sunshine. She glanced around and chided herself for the little bubble of disappointment that Nick wasn't here waiting for her. She would have liked one of his strong shoulders to cry on, though she doubted she would have said anything had he really been waiting. She knew better than to look for comfort from others.

It had rankled her sense of self-sufficiency to ask the bank manager for an extension on her loan payments, only to be told politely, but firmly, no. Her stomach dropped. Somehow she needed to figure out a way to squeeze more money from her budget.

She walked down a side street behind the library and stopped at the small patch of grass with a picnic bench beneath a large old oak tree. Today the spot was empty, but this was one place the teens in town sometimes hung out. The place she and Mindy had agreed upon as a place for them to communicate with each other.

Claire pulled out a sheet of paper from her purse and wrote a note on it. She folded the paper into a small square and stuck the note in the pocket of the gray hooded sweatjacket she'd brought from her closet before laying the jacket on the table.

"Lord, make sure Mindy gets this, please."

Knowing she couldn't do any more for now, she headed toward Main Street.

Nick would be at The Zone by now. She was glad he hadn't asked any more questions about her need to help the teenagers. She didn't know why she was so reluctant to tell him. She'd dealt with it all during college. She'd have been hard pressed not to earn a degree in counseling without coming to terms with her own life.

Maybe she was afraid he'd look at her with the same disgust with which he'd looked at Tyler and Mindy. The same look her parents had worn the last time she'd seen them face-to-face.

No, keeping Nick in the dark about why she felt such a kinship with the teens was for the best. She needed to guard her heart and her past by keeping Nick at a distance.

From the hardware store's front window, Nick saw Claire round the corner from the side of the library and head back down Main Street. He hoped her meeting had gone well, but the pensive expression on her lovely face concerned him.

A fierce protectiveness grabbed hold of him with stunning intensity. He hated the thought of Claire suffering. Past or present. Hated more the idea that she'd suffer in the future. A certainty if she stayed on her present course.

He wasn't necessarily opposed to her idea of a teen shelter. In theory, The Zone could work. But for one lone woman to take on such a burden…it would only result in heartache for Claire. She was a woman who gave without conditions, without reservations.

An easy mark.

He felt the need to protect her not only physically, but also emotionally, which was a really bad thing, considering he didn't want to be responsible for anyone.

He'd do what he could before he left, but he had a feeling he was digging himself a hole.

Though at the moment, he needed her opinion about paint color for The Zone. Setting the paint supplies he'd gathered on the counter, he told the clerk he'd be right back and then headed out of the store to intercept Claire.

"Hey, beautiful," he said as he came alongside her.

She halted and her head jerked up. "Nick, you startled me."

"You were lost in thought."

Her pink lips curved into a half smile. "That's me, always thinking."

"Good thoughts, I hope."

Her eyes widened slightly, a faint reddish tinge colored her cheeks. She shifted her purse from one slim shoulder to the other. "Oh, you know. Just random thoughts."

He cocked his head. "Didn't you have a jacket with you earlier?"

She dropped her gaze and tucked a stray strand of hair behind her ear. "I…uh, left my jacket somewhere."

"Do you want some help finding it?"

She gave a small laugh. "No. I'm sure it's fine. Are you headed back to The Zone?"

"In a while. How'd it go at the bank?"

The corners of her pretty mouth tipped down. "Not as well as planned."

"What's going on? Can I help?"

Uncertainty crept into her expression. "I…" She shook her head and the uncertainty left. In its place was proud determination. "I'll manage. Just a little glitch."

He scratched his chin with his knuckle, trying to keep hold of his frustration. Her independence was a hindrance to anyone trying to get close to her, though he doubted she'd take kindly to that observation or agree with his assessment. Which he shouldn't be making in the first place. He didn't want to get close to her. "Would you help me match the color of paint for The Zone?"

Her eyes widened. "You're ready to paint?"

"Not quite, but I'd like to have everything gathered before we're ready to start."

At the hardware store, Nick led her to the paint aisle. Claire picked up one swatch after another, comparing colors and shades to the sample of The Zone's paint that Nick had brought with him. Finally, she settled on one. "This looks as close as we're going to get." She handed him the swatch.

His fingers closed around it and her hand. Their gazes met over the color swatch.

The flare of attraction ignited. He knew she felt it, too.

The longing and trepidation in her eyes tore at him. A deep ache welled up inside of him, urging him to pull her into his arms and chase away whatever driving force kept her so closed off. He tugged on her hand, drawing her near, and her eyes widened. But then, like a shade being drawn, her expression became remote, distant. He remembered Lori's words. A wall had definitely just gone up.

With polite gracefulness she extracted her hand. "I have work to do. I'm sure I'll see you later."

She walked out of the store. Nick stared after her, tempted to follow, but he stayed rooted to the floor. He was definitely digging himself in.

He just hoped he didn't dig so deep he couldn't get back out.

Chapter Seven

An hour later, as Nick left the hardware store, a figure emerging from around the corner of the library at the far end of Main Street grabbed his attention. The girl he'd first seen Claire with—Mindy, if he remembered correctly—stepped out onto the sidewalk. She seemed to be searching for someone. She had on the same jeans as before but she also sported a gray hooded jacket that looked familiar.

With one hand, he scratched his chin, the bristles of the day's growth of whiskers rasping roughly against his calloused fingers. That jacket.

In his mind an image of Claire flashed like a slide show. Her walking downtown, her long skirt brushing her trim ankles with a gray jacket tucked under her arm. Then later coming back from her appointment without the jacket.

Now Mindy had the jacket. He fisted his hands. Had she stolen from Claire? But when and how? At the bank?

I left it somewhere.

No. Claire had given it to the girl. Probably when Claire had been behind the library. She was still trying to protect them.

Nick hefted his supplies in his arms, partially covering his face, yet not so much that he couldn't see Mindy. He decided to follow her. See if she led him to the ringleader. Tyler.

Mindy started walking up the street. Nick walked parallel to her on the opposite side of the wide road. She didn't seem to be in a hurry. When she came to a garbage can on the corner of Main and Elm, she paused.

Nick stopped and, still using his bag of supplies for cover, pretended to study the newspaper stand.

Mindy leaned against the can. Her gaze shifting quickly side to side before she turned and reached inside the can. He frowned. What was she doing?

She grabbed something out of the can before hurrying down the side street with her prize. Nick quickly crossed the street, but by the time he got to the corner of Elm she'd disappeared.

He spun around and his gaze went directly to the garbage can. He stalked over to it and peered inside. A sick feeling descended over him, weighing him down.

He backed away and swiped a hand over his eyes as if he could wipe away the image of what he'd witnessed. It wasn't as if he'd never seen a homeless person take from the garbage. He'd lived in New York long enough to see many awful things. He'd ridden through enough other big cities to know how common homelessness was.

But never before had he felt anything.

He wouldn't think about what the girl had taken. It didn't matter. He wouldn't let compassion get to him.

Claire heard the front door open and close. Gwen was already up in her room studying, so it could only be Nick. The heavy, masculine footsteps going up the stairs confirmed that thought. She sat at her desk in her office, the financial records and budget proposal for The Zone spread out before her across the oak desktop.

Everything inside her stilled as she listened to Nick come back down the stairs.

Usually they ate dinner together. Take-out or sandwiches. Sometimes heading to the restaurant where Gwen worked. Claire really did enjoyed Nick's company, but tonight she'd felt too vulnerable with the pressure of her visit to the bank to dine with him. She'd been glad when he'd said Dave, Steve and the man she hadn't recognized, Gary Parks, were going out for dinner and wanted him to join them.

She'd needed to distance herself, control the urge to confide in him.

The footsteps stopped outside the office door, then she heard a soft knock.

"Yes?" she called.

"Are you okay?" His voice sounded concerned.

She smiled at the door. "Yes, thank you."

"I brought you something."

Curious, she untucked her bare feet from beneath her and padded across the hardwood floor. She opened the door. The light spilling out from her office cast shadows across Nick's tall form. In his hand he held a white bag.

"I didn't know if you'd eaten, but I brought you some pasta from Cannelli's."

His thoughtfulness touched her deeply. "That was sweet of you. Did you have a good time?"

"Yes, actually." He said it like he was surprised that he'd enjoyed himself. "We played darts, ate tons of food. It was a really good time."

He was making connections and she was pleased. Maybe soon he'd realize he needed to reconnect with his family.

He held out the bag. "Are you hungry?"

"Yes. I am."

She took the bag and opened it. The delicious aroma of basil and garlic wafted out from the foam container. There was even a fork and napkins in the bag. Her stomach grumbled its appreciation.

Nick chuckled.

She glanced up with a sheepish grin. "This smells great."

"Go ahead, eat."

She moved past him and sat on the bottom stair, then pulled everything out of the bag and laid it on her lap and said a prayer of thanks. She picked up the fork, ready to take a bite when she sensed Nick's studied gaze. He leaned against the open doorjamb of her office, his arms crossed over his chest. She froze. "What?"

His brows came together. "I saw Mindy today wearing your jacket."

Her pulse gave a leap and her heart smiled. God had made sure she received the jacket. That was good. "Did you?"

He eyed her, clearly not buying her innocent act. "What is it with you and those kids?"

"I have to build their trust somehow. One step at a time."

He scoffed. "You make it sound like you're trying to tame a wild animal."

"I've never thought of it that way, but yeah, I suppose. Each kid is different. It's tricky gauging what strategy to use."

"Have you worked with kids before now? Besides Gwen."

"I was a Young Life leader during college and I volunteered at a shelter in Portland."

"Is that where you met Gwen?"

She nodded. "Aunt Denise and I stumbled over her, literally."

"Is that what prompted you to open a shelter?"

She ducked her head. "Among other things."

He looked toward her desk. "What are you working on?"

She grimaced. "Trying to work up a feasible projected budget for The Zone."

"Having trouble?"

She made a face. "I never was any good with math, but I'm muddling through it."

"Let me look at them." He disappeared into the office.

She scrambled to her feet, leaving her food on the stairs, and hurried to his side at her desk.

Against the backdrop of her white walls, he was a splash of life and color in denim and a green-striped button-down shirt. She blinked, trying to rein in her galloping heart. He invaded her space. Crowded her senses.

He picked up one sheet of paper from the desk and studied it before turning to another. He sank down on her white wicker desk-chair. It squeaked beneath his weight. He seemed to lose himself in the papers, so she retrieved her food and sat on the short bench that she'd pushed up against the wall.

"Who are these budgets for?" he asked, finally.

She stopped chewing and quickly swallowed. "Well, I'm hoping to put together proposals for grant money. Someone suggested that would be the best way to raise funds."

Nick turned to look at her. "How have you raised funds so far?"

"Mostly word of mouth. Mainly, Sandy and Dave's mouths."

Nick didn't doubt that the couple would do all they could to help Claire even if she didn't want them to. He didn't envy the battle they must fight every time they tried. "They care about you."

She shifted on the bench, looking uncomfortable. "Sandy and my aunt were best friends."

He narrowed his gaze. "So you think they care because they feel obligated?"

Her chin rose, her gaze direct. "Why else would they?"

"Because *you,* Claire Wilcox, are a generous, caring woman."

A blush like a shadow crossed over her pale complexion. He watched her tidy up, putting the barely touched foam container back in the bag, folding the top of the bag over, her hands toying with the edge. It saddened him that she couldn't accept a simple compliment.

Okay. Not so simple considering she hardly knew him. He slowly began to notice his surroundings. The walls were stark white. The oak desk and the matching oak bench the only furniture. His gaze landed on the two pictures on the wall.

Angels. Beautiful creatures in charcoal drawings. He got up and moved closer to inspect one. There in the corner he read the signature of the artist, C. Wilcox. He smiled with amazement. "You did these?"

When she didn't answer, he turned around. She abruptly rose and stood in the middle of her small office. Her hands clutched the white bag. He could see her mentally withdrawing as she looked at him warily. "Just doodlings that Aunt Denise framed. It seemed a shame to throw them away when she'd put so much effort in framing them."

"They're wonderful," he said. He came to stand in front of her. "Don't sell yourself so short." He didn't mean for his words to sound as harsh as they did.

She drew herself up. "Thank you for dinner. You must be tired after working so hard all day. I won't keep you."

Nick fisted his hands in frustration. She was shutting him out again, keeping herself self-contained, closed off. He really shouldn't care.

"Walls imprison as well as protect, Claire."

She pressed her lips into a tight line.

Irked by her stubbornness, he stalked back to her desk and breathed deep to clear the irritation from his brain. His fists relaxed. He crossed his arms over his chest as he turned to face her, ready to meet the battle head-on.

"Would it be too much to ask for you to let me help with this?" He gestured with his head toward her desk. This was something he was good at. Something he could do for her that wouldn't further his attraction or the ridiculous need to break through her icy walls.

She pulled her lip between her slightly crooked teeth. "You don't have to. I can manage."

He gathered his patience. "I know you can manage. It would make *me* feel good to help you."

She blinked and cocked her head to one side as if weighing the truth of his words. "Really?"

He remembered their conversation earlier in the week. He'd told her it blessed others to give their help. She'd accused him of using Scripture to further his own agenda. He didn't have an agenda. "Yes, really."

"You know about budgets and stuff?"

He unfolded his arms and hitched a hip on the edge of the desk. At least she hadn't flat-out said no. "I know budgets and stuff."

Humor danced in her eyes and she visibly relaxed. "A man of many talents."

"Jack-of-all-trades."

She laughed. The deep throaty sound wrapped around him, teasing his senses, making him want to make her laugh again.

"Okay." She made a sweeping gesture with her hand. "Be my guest."

Scrambling to control the chaos inside of him, he sat down at her desk. He forced his concentration on the papers in front of him, though he was acutely aware of the woman staring over his shoulder.

Claire didn't know what to make of the feelings bouncing around her head and her heart. She felt like she'd been outwitted by the sincerity in his plea to let him help her. Every time she turned around, Nick was working his way under her guard. Or, according to him, the walls she had erected around herself. Ha! If he only knew what protection those walls afforded her.

A blessing, he'd said before.

But asking for help, accepting help, threatened her vow of self-sufficiency.

Yet, she wasn't feeling threatened. It kind of felt good to think he'd wanted to help her. That he would receive some pleasure or a blessing from doing so.

He dwarfed her little oak desk and wicker chair. His dark hair fell forward as he bent over the pages. His hand holding the pencil deftly manipulated the numbers. She peered over his shoulder, amazed by the way he brought the numbers to life.

"You know, this would be a lot easier if you had a computer," he said.

She pulled a face. "I know. It's on my to-do list."

He grunted and returned his focus to the papers in front of him. He asked questions. Wanted to see her bill statements and know what her expenditures were. She should have felt like he was invading her privacy, but she didn't. She gladly handed him any information he wanted. She couldn't believe how much time and energy he was saving her. She almost felt bad for using him so shamelessly.

Pulling out another file folder full of paperwork from the cardboard box that served as a file cabinet, she explained to him about the nightmare of laws and regulations and agencies she'd been dealing with and still dealt with. "Often one agency's requirements conflict with another's. But different agencies have different concerns."

He flipped through the pages and whistled through his teeth. "Wow, how do you keep it all straight?"

She shrugged. "You're looking at my file system."

He turned in the chair, hooking one arm over the back. "We need to perk up your office space a bit. A computer with Excel, a real filing cabinet, stackable file holders."

She pointed to the papers on the desk. "Put that in the budget."

His mouth quirked up. "What about staffing? Do you plan to hire help? And how many?"

She sighed. "Staffing is regulated by minimum licensing standards. Which is another headache. Eventually, I'll have to hire more workers. There's a minimum staff to client ratio. I don't need to worry about that until closer to the official opening. So for now, it's just me, but I don't plan on taking a paycheck."

He held up a hand. "You should take a paycheck."

"I'm not in this for profit," she argued. She wanted to help the teenagers, not make money off them.

His brows drew down. "I'm not talking profit. I'm talking about personal items that you won't be able to write off as business expenses."

"Oh." She twirled a lock of hair around her finger. "I never thought of that."

"So what other hurdles do you have to jump?"

He sounded interested and she willed her mind to work as she fell into his compelling gaze. "The facility must meet specific standards for a group home. I'll have to run through the hoops to meet the fire codes again after the repairs. I was planning on opening the doors at the beginning of July, but now, I'm thinking August."

He nodded encouragingly.

She continued. "And then there's funding. Thus the need for a feasible budget. Achieving nonprofit status helps because I can solicit donations and apply for grants."

His eyes lighted up. "I know about grants. For the proposals, you'll need to come up with a mission statement. Do you have one?"

Claire tucked in her chin. "Not off the top of my head."

He waved his hand. "Not a problem. We'll come up with something, preferably fifty words or less. The foundations you apply to will want a copy of your proposed budget and they'll want to know what specifically the money is for. Some foundations won't give money for operating expenses. They don't want the recipient to rely on them for their cash flow. Most corporations like to see the fruit of the donation, something tangible, which could be anything from computers to an art teacher. Or maybe in the case of The Zone, a shrink or a zookeeper."

"Hey, wait a second," she protested, her defenses kicking in. But then she saw the teasing glint in his eyes. "You," she huffed with a smile, liking that he teased her. Liking *him*.

His grin packed a high voltage punch.

Her stomach cartwheeled, and her heart added a few extra beats, emphasizing the effect he had on her. It wasn't just his looks that kicked her senses into high gear. There was a kindness in his dark eyes when he looked at her that made her feel special. She hadn't felt special in a long time.

Mentally kicking herself, she dropped her gaze to the desktop. She wouldn't get sucked in by this man. She just wouldn't.

"How do you know so much about grant writing?"

"My…" he paused, his hands stalling in the act of writing. "I knew someone who worked for a nonprofit ministry. I helped her write grants."

A twinge of jealousy for some unknown "her" assaulted Claire's senses. Of course, there'd been a "her." Probably a long line of them considering he was handsome and kind, a man full of honor. A man worth wanting.

She wasn't looking for a man. But if she were, Nick would fill the bill.

"Where are these from?" He flicked the tassels hanging from her lamp.

"The black-and-blue one is from Pineridge High, and the green and yellow from U of O." At his questioning look, she clarified. "University of Oregon." She held up a fist and pumped it. "Go Ducks."

"Ducks?"

"Hey, it's Oregon, the wettest state in the Union. We have Ducks and Beavers. And believe me, the two camps are divided with a deep rivalry."

"Did you live off campus or in the dorm?"

"Started in the dorm, but it was too…" she trailed off, unsure how to describe the close quarters, the girls with their boyfriends and their parents who cared. The loneliness. "I never really fit in."

"I didn't like the dorm life much, either," he said. "Too many people wanting to know where I was going, what I was doing. The parties were fun the first year or so but after that it became tedious."

She nodded. "I went to a few parties that first year." Did things she'd rather forget. "After that, I decided to get serious about school."

"It's paid off." He showed her his calculations. "I'm impressed, Claire," he declared. "You've done a really good job of accomplishing so much with such a small budget."

His praise warmed her battered soul like heat from a bonfire in the middle of winter.

She was impressed, too. He certainly knew what he was doing. There was more to this man than met the eye. "What school did you attend?"

"Columbia."

Very prestigious. "What was your major?"

"Economics."

"Ah. That's why you know so much about budgets. So, what did you do after school?"

He looked uncomfortable. "I worked on Wall Street for a brokerage firm."

She frowned, trying to put all the pieces together. "You worked on Wall Street, but your parents were pressuring you to come in to the family business?"

She couldn't decipher what she saw in his dark eyes. "No. My parents were proud of me. It wasn't until later that Dad asked me to come work with him."

"Later?"

He gave her an odd, guarded look, then glanced at the black leather watch on his wrist. "It's late. I should let you get your rest."

Her first impression of him as the bad boy on a Harley was being radically changed, yet she wasn't losing interest. Quite the opposite.

And that scared her.

Deep into the night, Nick lay stretched out on the too-short twin mattress trying to doze off. His mind was abuzz with admiration for Claire. Her dedication was over-the-top. She'd managed the funds she'd been responsible for so far. She'd made every penny count, had documented every gift and donation, which helped to determine The Zone's budget.

He shifted on the bed, trying for a more comfortable position. He didn't really mind being uncomfortable, though. Not if it meant keeping Claire safe.

Though he didn't know if he was going to be able

to keep *himself* safe from Claire. He was confident he could control his attraction to her. But her curious mind was always working. Probing. He saw the way she studied him after he'd told her about working on Wall Street. Like he were some intricate puzzle that she was determined to solve.

But the worse part was he'd almost told her about Serena.

Telling her would serve no purpose. Telling her would only stir up his pain.

A noise echoed in the quiet of his room. He stilled, listening. It was Claire again.

He glanced at the clock. 3:00 a.m. Right on schedule. Most nights she got up, walked past his room and went downstairs for a few hours. At first he'd thought it was for the puppy, but after the second night, Little Nick had been tucked into his crate before she'd gone to bed.

He sat up. He should go check on her, make sure she was okay. He didn't—it was too dangerous an endeavor.

So instead he prayed for her. And for himself. All the while hoping, but not really believing, that God would listen to him.

Chapter Eight

Claire paused outside Nick's door on Sunday morning. Her heart picked up speed and she suddenly felt shy and exposed. The man on the other side of the door was so much more than she'd ever expected or experienced.

He was fun and nice. She found his wry sense of humor enticing. His sharp wit and intelligence challenged her. There was so much to like about him. So, so much to be afraid of.

She strove for the indifference that had served her well over the years. She couldn't let herself care for a man who obviously disliked the kids she'd dedicated her life to helping, even if he was willing to help her with the grants and such.

She was asking him to church because it was the polite thing to do. Not from any wish to be with him. She knew she could just go on her own as she had the last two Sundays since he'd rolled into her life. But since he always showed up anyway, standing in the back as though he wasn't sure he should make himself at home, she decided it would be okay for them to go together. As friends.

She took a deep breath and rapped her knuckles against the wood.

The door swung open, startling her back a step. Nick stepped out, pulling the door shut behind him. He wore dark pants and a short-sleeve, button-down shirt. The vivid blue of the shirt contrasted nicely with his tan skin and dark hair. Each time she saw him, his appeal was stronger, more compelling, and robbed her of reasonable thoughts. Where was that indifference she'd tried to muster up?

"Good morning, Claire."

She cleared her throat. "Morning. I wanted to ask if you'd like to attend church with me."

He smiled and held up his Bible, the pocket-size one she'd seen that first day. The thing that had solidified her trust. "I was hoping you'd ask."

Pleasure and relief washed through her. Maybe his faith was stronger than he thought. "Great. We can take my car."

"How about we take my bike?"

Excitement flared. He'd brought the bike home a few days ago. It would cause a bit of a scandal if they arrived together on his Harley. The wildness inside her urged her to accept. But what about Gwen? She held up her index finger. "Just a sec."

She hurried to Gwen's door and rapped sharply before opening the door and peering inside. She couldn't help the relief running through her veins to find the room empty.

"She there?"

Claire pulled the door closed and whirled around saying, "No. She must— Oh!" She found herself nose to chest with Nick. He smelled clean and masculine and…she backed up a half step and bumped against the closed door.

"She must what?"

She swallowed. "Be singing today. Gwen occasionally sings with the band at church."

"Ah. She's already up and gone." He grinned. "So what about that ride?"

Excitement battered against her ribs. "That would be great."

"After you." He motioned toward the stairs.

Claire fairly skipped down, feeling giddy with anticipation. When they got outside, she was touched to see two helmets hanging from the handlebars. Nick plucked off the smaller of the two and handed it to her. "I borrowed it from Joe. The mechanic. It's his wife's."

She raised a brow, unexpectedly delighted by his forethought. "You were pretty sure of yourself."

He flashed her a grin that curled her toes. "I'd promised you a ride," he said.

"True enough." She put the helmet on. He helped her with the buckle. The intimacy of the act made her realize the depth of her fascination with him. And it wasn't just a physical attraction.

Not that that wasn't important. He was gorgeous to her in a way few men were—all tall, dark and alluring.

But the care he took with her, the tenderness he showed toward her, made her ache. No matter how hard she tried or how fast she worked at building her defenses up against him, the truth was she was starting to care for him.

And that was as terrifying a thing as sleeping in a dark alley on a snowy night.

But as long as Nick didn't know that she cared, then she wasn't really vulnerable to him. He wouldn't be able to use her feelings against her. He wouldn't be able to ply her head with false words of love and then pressure her to prove her love the way Billy had.

A little voice inside her head whispered that Nick wouldn't take advantage of her. He wasn't like that.

But she wasn't going to risk it. She'd keep her feelings tucked away safe where they'd never see the light of day.

Thankful she'd worn her royal-blue capri pants with her brown leather mules, she climbed on the bike behind him and settled herself a hand's length from his back.

She listened to his instructions of where to place her feet and her hands. As he told her to lean with him when he leaned and to sit straight when he sat straight, she decided she didn't want to think about her heart or the risks of caring. She wanted to enjoy this moment, savor the thrill of riding on the back of his Harley.

When the bike came to life beneath her, excitement shuddered through her at the same tempo of the rumbling engine. Nick twisted around to look at her. She nodded and offered him a wide smile, hoping he'd see how much this meant to her.

The twinkle in his eyes said he got the message.

Then they were off, rolling through town, the pace too sedate, but necessary. Claire waved at several people and giggled when they just stared. The ride wasn't nearly long or wild enough for Claire. In a matter of minutes, they pulled into the Community Church's parking lot.

People were filing through the church's open doors. The building was beautiful with its white steeple, black bell tower and, colorful stained-glass windows.

She slid off the bike. Nick took the helmet from her and hooked it on the handlebars.

"Thank you," she said as he turned to offer her his arm.

"Later we'll take a more scenic ride."

Her heart thumped at the prospect.

Inside, they found a seat near the Jordan family. Soon the congregation was singing with the music director. Claire enjoyed listening to Nick's deep voice and noted with pleasure that he knew the songs. The other two times he'd come to the church, he'd been too far away for her to hear him.

When Gwen stepped up to the microphone, Claire smiled with pride for the once rebellious, feisty girl who had turned into a beautiful young woman with a bright future.

The worship service ended and the pastor, a man in his midforties, stepped to the podium. Claire liked Pastor Gary. He was real and humble. His sermons always touched her, as if God were speaking directly to her.

Pastor Gary directed the congregation to Micah 6:8.

Claire absorbed the message, sensing God's presence and feeling His grace as Pastor Gary talked of three things God required of His people. To act justly, love mercy and walk humbly with God. God was looking for an ethical response from His people. In Claire's heart, she reaffirmed her vow to remain honest in all she did, to cherish compassionate faithfulness, and to be in submission to God and His word.

When the service ended and the final prayer given, Claire glanced at Nick. His expression was pensive.

"You okay?" she asked.

He blinked and then focused his attention on her. She liked looking into his deep dark eyes, so full of intelligence and compassion.

"I was thinking about The Zone."

"And what were you thinking?"

"To generate community support, you need to generate community awareness. You can do that by getting the community involved."

She cocked her head to the side. "How do I get the community involved?"

"Create a task force of people willing to brainstorm and implement some fund-raising ideas that could involve the community at large."

"How do I create a task force?"

He smiled. "Ask people to help."

Easier said than done. "Like who?"

"Mrs. Wellington, Lori and Peggy Jordan. I'm sure they'd jump at the chance to help out."

And be blessed. She smiled ruefully. "You're right, they would."

"Mrs. Wellington is over there." He pointed in the direction of the large maple where several ladies had gathered to chat.

She bit her lip. Ripples of panic kept her feet planted to the ground. This was going to be hard. How did she ask for help and still be self-sufficient?

"I'll come find you in a bit," he said, giving her a little nudge, forcing her feet forward a step, before moving away through the crowd of churchgoers congregating on the church grounds. She saw several heads turn to watch him as he headed toward the pastor.

Determined not to be distracted by Nick, Claire shifted her gaze away. She wanted to do as he suggested and ask for help for The Zone, but she just didn't know if she had it in her. She liked Nick's idea. And it wasn't like she was asking help for herself. It was for the cause.

Though the rationale helped, she stumbled and sputtered as she approached each lady and told her what she needed.

An hour later, a task force had been assembled, consisting of seven women. Claire was grateful for all the ladies' enthusiasm. They decided to head to the bakery for coffee and pastries while discussing ideas, but first Sandy insisted she and Nick accept their invitation for dinner that night. Promising she'd talk with Nick about that, Claire headed off to find him.

She found Nick deep in conversation with Pastor Gary. The two men stopped talking when she approached.

"Hello, Claire," Pastor Gary said. He was of average height and athletic, with medium brown hair and a sweet demeanor that made him look younger than his midforties.

"Pastor Gary, that was a wonderful message today."

He inclined his head. "I'm glad you thought so. How are things coming with The Zone?"

She slanted a glance at Nick. "They're progressing nicely."

"Good, good. I'll keep you in my prayers. And if the church can do anything, you let me know. We're here for you, Claire."

"Thank you," she said, meaning it.

"If you'll excuse me, I see my wife beckoning." Pastor Gary walked away.

"You ready?" Nick asked, his dark eyes warm like rich coffee.

"Actually, I'm headed to Tessa's Bakery with some of the ladies to discuss The Zone."

Nick's smiled showed his approval. "That's great."

She preened. "I'll catch a ride back with Lori."

"Good enough. Later, then."

"Okay." She started to walk away but then turned back. "The Wellingtons asked if we'd join them for dinner at their house tonight."

Nick's dark brows flickered briefly in surprise. He hesitated.

"It's no big deal if you don't want to. I'll tell them you have other plans," she offered, thinking he was looking for an out. She didn't know why he'd be uncomfortable with the Wellingtons.

He seemed to decide. "Dinner at their house would be fine."

"You sure?"

"Yes."

Her gaze was captured by his dark intense eyes. He radiated a vitality that pulled at her like a magnet. She placed a hand at the base of her throat as she backed up, trying to break the magnetic force spinning her sense.

"Okay then. I'll see you later," she said.

He inclined his head.

She hurried to join the group of ladies waiting on the sidewalk. She glanced back and watched Nick walk to his bike. A part of her wanted to ditch the ladies and go with him. She forced herself to turn away even as the rumbling purr of the bike's engine raced up her spine.

She needed to stay focused on The Zone, not on her feelings for Nick, which would only lead her to disappointment.

Nick opened the throttle and let the bike scream down the empty back roads on the outskirts of Pineridge. The countryside was lush and green. The trees—evergreens, oak and ash—majestic in their beauty. It felt good to have the wind biting at him. To feel the power of his machine beneath him.

His mind raced with thoughts of Claire, of his intense feelings for her. He struggled with how to define them, how to box them up. He enjoyed the time spent with her. He loved the way she rose to a challenge, the way she offered help without judging. She was so sweet and kind. So stubborn and closed-off.

Giving and honest, yet so fragile. He wanted to protect her, to cherish her.

But he had no right to such feelings. He'd had someone to cherish and protect once. Yet he'd failed Serena. He didn't want to put himself in a position to fail again. He didn't want to hurt Claire. It was time to move on.

The repairs to The Zone would be done in a matter of days. Claire now had people she knew were willing to help her. He admired that she'd stepped out of her comfort level to ask for help for The Zone. All she needed was a little push and some confidence. He was gratified to think he'd had something to do with her achieving some self-assurance. Maybe that was God's purpose for bringing him here.

Claire would be okay now. The unruly teenagers hadn't been anywhere near The Zone as far as he could tell, but just to be on the cautious side he'd speak with Officer Bob and make sure he kept an eye on her.

Nick squelched the sting of jealousy that thought brought.

A few more days and he'd be ready to leave, to move on. Only now, he'd have not only his grief and anger to contend with, but also the ache of leaving Claire behind.

Claire stood on the doorstep of the Wellingtons with Nick at her side as if they were a couple. She felt nervous little flutters in her belly.

They weren't a couple.

And though they seemed to have fallen into a

friendly, comfortable pattern over the last few weeks, she sure didn't want anyone, including herself, getting any far-out ideas that she and Nick were an item.

Nick leaned over her shoulder to ring the doorbell. His warm breath stirred the little hairs exposed at the nape of her neck by her French twist. She shivered.

"Cold?" he asked and dropped an arm around her shoulders. His big, calloused hand smoothed over her arm.

Stunned by the gesture, her pulse jumped. But instead of moving away from him like she knew she should, she leaned into his wide chest. "I'm good," she murmured, her voice sounding strange, breathy.

The door opened. Dave Wellington, looking comfortable in khaki shorts and a Hawaiian-print shirt, smiled his greeting as his gaze swept over them. "Hello, you two. Welcome."

Claire felt heat rising up her neck past the collar of her white, peasant-style blouse. She broke away from Nick and stepped into the house that was as familiar to her as her aunt's had been.

Nick followed her in and shook hands with Dave.

The hardwood floors of the entryway gleamed beneath a colorful Persian runner. Claire dropped her purse onto an oak side table beneath a gilded mirror. She glanced at her reflection and noticed her flushed complexion. She hoped no one else noticed, especially Nick. She didn't want him to know how he affected her.

Sandy appeared around the corner at the end of the hall. "Come on in to the dining room. Dinner's just about ready." She disappeared back around the corner.

"I'll go see if I can help," Claire said with a quick glance at Nick. He nodded his encouragement.

She walked away as the two men began to talk of sports and such.

We are not a couple, she told herself firmly.

"What can I do to help, Sandy?" Claire asked as she entered the well-appointed kitchen.

Granite tile countertops and dark wood cabinets lined the walls. Sandy pulled out a covered dish from the oven. The aromas of garlic and paprika wafted in the air.

Sandy pointed with one oven-mitted hand toward a large cherry wood hutch. "Would you mind grabbing a trivet and put it on the dining table?"

"Sure." Claire went to the hutch. She noticed a small gold-framed picture on the top shelf, and reached out to touch the images. In the photo, Sandy and Aunt Denise stood with their arms around one another, smiles on their faces.

Claire traced her finger over Aunt Denise's face. Her white-blonde hair shimmered in the June sun. Claire had taken the picture with the camera her aunt had given her for graduation. "I miss you," she whispered.

"I miss her, too, you know," Sandy said quietly from behind Claire.

Blinking back her grief, Claire plucked a square-shaped trivet from the top of a stack and moved to the table. She set it down. "She'd appreciate all you've done for me."

Sandy's brow flickered. "I wish you'd let me do more."

"You do plenty," Claire reassured her. "Should I call in the men?"

Sandy's gaze searched her face. "You like him."

Claire ducked her head. "Should I fill the water glasses?"

Sandy tsked. "You know, it's okay to have feelings for people, Claire. For you to have feelings for Nick. He seems like a good guy. Dave has only good things to say about him. I know Denise would have approved."

Claire knew the older woman meant well. "He'll be leaving soon, Sandy. I can't…I don't want to…" *get hurt.* She waved her hand. "It just wouldn't work." *We are not a couple.*

But later, after they'd eaten and sat on the back porch for coffee and dessert, Claire had the weirdest longing she'd ever experienced.

As she sat next to Nick, their chairs close enough that his jean-clad knee pressed against hers, she wondered what it would be like to be married. To have someone in her life who knew her so well.

She watched the way Sandy and Dave communicated verbally with terms of endearments and little inside phrases that indicated a level of intimacy Claire had never known. She watched the way their affection for one another showed in the little gestures. A hand being held. Sandy offering Dave a bite of her pie, since he'd declared he was dieting. The way they looked at each other with love and life.

She'd been around the Wellingtons since she was fifteen, but she'd never noticed them as a couple. Until now.

Her attention moved to Nick and she watched him

with rapt fascination. He was so at ease, so personable. He kept the conversation going with talk of world events, sports and politics.

And what endeared her to him most was the way he kept her included. Asked her opinion as if really interested in the answer.

When the night wore down and they were leaving, it seemed natural for her to slip her hand into his as they walked back to the car after much hugging by Sandy and Dave.

It wasn't until they were at The Zone that she remembered to remind herself that they weren't a couple—could never be a couple. Couples expected things from each other, needed each other to complete the unit. Couplehood was not for her.

She whispered a quick good-night and fled to her room.

Light seeped out from beneath the edge of Nick's door. He wasn't asleep. Claire breathed a sigh of relief that was short-lived as a wave of panic hit her. She'd spent the last twenty minutes trying to banish her thoughts about Nick and couples and marriage.

She'd settled on a plan of action. Help Nick mend the rift with his parents and fulfill the purpose God had for bringing him into her life. Once that was accomplished, she could send him on his way and she'd go back to being self-sufficient and alone without him.

She frowned as that last thought brought a twinge of pain. That was what she wanted, wasn't it?

Mentally shaking away that thread of thinking, she

said a quick prayer, asking for support. She knocked on the door.

"Come in," Nick called.

She opened the door. He sat on the bed with his broad back propped against the wall. He wore a white cotton T-shirt and light gray drawstring shorts. Dark hair covered his athletic legs stretched out in front of him.

She sucked in a quick breath.

He looked good, comfortable and appealing. And Claire realized she'd probably made a big mistake by not waiting until morning.

She swallowed and tried to find her voice. "I brought you something."

He raised his brows and set aside the book he was reading. A Bible. Her heart smiled at the knowledge that even in his pain, Nick still sought the Lord.

He swung his legs to the side and stood. She moved forward and held out the pack of stationery—plain cream paper with gold edging that her aunt had once given to her.

His gaze flicked to the stationery, then to her face.

She offered him a smile. "I was thinking you might want to write to your parents. Let them know you're all right. They could even write back to you here."

A thoughtful expression crossed his face, though she could see a shadow lurking in the dark depths of his eyes.

"I think it might help you," she ventured, wishing he'd say something.

"You're all about helping people, aren't you," he said dryly.

She blinked, unsure whether he was making fun of her or not. "I like to help."

"Makes you feel good," he stated.

She drew in her chin. "Yes, I guess so. I never really thought about that."

A slow smile formed on his well-shaped mouth. "You have a good heart, Claire."

Warmed by his words, she smiled back. He reached out to take the stationery packet and their fingers connected. She released her hold. The last thing she needed was more fuel for her unwanted attraction.

"Thank you, Claire."

She squirmed slightly under his knowing gaze, but was thankful he'd accepted her attempt to help. She only hoped he'd use the stationery and write to his parents. "You're welcome."

He cocked one eyebrow. "Was there something else?"

"Uh, no."

His mouth quirked up as if he knew exactly the effect he had on her.

She backed up. "See you in the morning."

She left, shutting the door firmly behind her. With his tempting-as-chocolate grin imprinted on her brain, she undoubtedly would have another restless night's sleep.

Chapter Nine

Three days later, Claire listened and didn't hear the noise of construction that had greeted her every morning for the past few weeks. A bird chirped outside her window as if he sensed her good humor. She stretched, then threw off the covers and quickly dressed.

Last night after dark Nick had announced that the work was done and she'd have her kitchen fully back today.

With a light step, she hurried from her room to view the repaired wall, new back porch and door. From the inside she couldn't even tell there'd been a fire. She rushed out the new back door and down the steps with Little Nick nipping at her heels.

Standing in the middle of the backyard, she looked at the gray building. It looked great. Gone were the saws and piles of wood, both old and new. Nick had even swept the walkway of the sawdust debris.

Her heart swelled with gratitude for all he'd done. He'd worked so hard to finish the job and keep the cost under what the insurance would pay. She was also thankful he'd given her the push she needed to ask for help. The committee had agreed on a picnic-basket auction as The Zone's first fund-raiser.

Nick had made her see how much others wanted to be asked and how much people were willing to give.

She glanced up at the cloud-dotted sky. "Thank you for bringing Nick into my life."

Now she needed to thank Nick and let him know what a blessing he'd been. Not that she was attached to him or anything. Just grateful he'd roared into her life when he had. A little bubble of sadness escaped, reminding her that he would eventually leave. She'd deal with his departure when she had to. Not today. Today was too beautiful.

She looked around for the puppy and spotted him digging under the lilac bush.

"No digging," she admonished with a wag of her finger. He ran over and pawed at her shins. She bent down and scratched his head, thankful no one had claimed him.

Little Nick followed closely at her heels as she went back inside. She put him in his crate and walked up the stairs to Nick's door. She knocked lightly.

"Come in."

She opened the door and froze as he straightened from zipping his saddlebag closed. He was wearing his black leather motorcycle riding clothes. He looked like he had the day they first met. Had that only been a month ago?

"What are you doing?" Her stomach rolled with the implications of his actions, his clothes.

He shrugged. "Time to move on."

A shivery, panicky feeling grabbed her, squeezing tight. "You didn't say anything about leaving last night."

He threw her an odd look. "The repairs are done, Claire."

"Yes, but…" Her heart raced in her ears. "You're not staying for the auction?"

His dark brows rose. "That's two weeks away." He picked up his bag. "There's no reason for me to stay, is there?"

A reason for him to stay? Her mind worked frantically, looking for something to hold on to, a plausible reason to ask him to stay because she wasn't ready for this to happen. She hadn't had a chance to deal with it. She hadn't helped him with his parents. "Sandy and Dave will want to say goodbye. Everyone will want to say goodbye. You can't just up and leave. That's not fair."

He moved toward her. The scent of man and leather swirled around her, tantalizing in the depth of emotion and memory the scent evoked. A sense of safety remembered, cherished. His arms around her, carrying her out of harm's way. His kindness, his honor.

"And you, Claire? Do you want to say goodbye?" He ran a knuckle down her cheek.

"Yes. No. I mean. I want…" Her lungs contracted, trapping her in-drawn breath. The world spun, sending her off balance, out of control. She hated this feeling. Hated the need welling up, threatening to drown her.

She wanted him to stay. She wanted him to *want* to stay. And she'd willingly beg for his attention.

The air left her chest in a rush like the tie on a balloon coming undone. She'd promised herself she'd never go to this place again. This vulnerable, needy state.

She'd feared he'd use her feelings against her. But she was using them against herself. Disappointment and anger clogged her throat. Filled her soul.

She stepped back, away from the protective shelter of his presence, away from the feelings crushing her heart.

She had to put an end to this. To whatever it was between them. She swallowed the bitter pill of her own expectations and forced a smile. "I wanted to thank you for all your hard work. It was a blessing you came when you did." She strove for an indifference she didn't feel. "You can leave when you want."

Forcing her legs to move at a sedate pace, she went down the stairs, uncrated Little Nick and led him outside to the park across the street. She followed as he raced ahead through the grass. She was on the far side of the park when she heard the growl of Nick's Harley. She didn't look back nor did she wipe at the tears streaming down her face.

Nick cruised down Main Street without really seeing Pineridge. He'd seen the hurt darken Claire's blue eyes. Had heard the reedy tenor of her voice that betrayed her feelings.

He wanted to apologize for letting their relationship

ever seem more than it was. He'd tried to keep his distance. Tried to stay unemotional and detached, but that had proved impossible. There was so much about Claire to like. To care about.

And the other night at the Wellingtons, he'd become painfully aware how thoroughly she'd melted the ice around his heart.

He'd imagined a future with her. As he'd observed the love between Sandy and Dave, he'd ached to have a spouse to share his life with, to grow old with. And that scared him. He didn't want to risk the pain and the grief of loss again.

So it was time to leave.

But Claire was right about one thing. He shouldn't leave without properly saying goodbye to the people of Pineridge. The community had embraced him, accepted him and made him feel again. A lot of that had to do with Claire. She'd set the tone. He pulled off to the side of the street and parked, but didn't move.

Beneath his breath, he muttered, "Lord, I don't understand what You want of me. I live my life the way I think I should according to Your word and then You let it all crash down around me. So I try again to seek You and I land here. But to what end? For more pain? To hurt Claire?" He shook his head. "I don't get it. When will You give me peace? That's all I'm asking for, Lord. Some peace."

"Hey, Andrews," a masculine voice called.

Nick twisted around on the seat toward the sidewalk. Officer Bob walked toward him, his clothes pressed and his badge shining. Nick removed his helmet and hung it on the handlebars. "Officer," he acknowledged.

"Went by The Zone this morning. Good work."

Nick hid a smile at the grudging tone of Bob's praise. "I had help."

"So I've heard."

Nick raised a questioning brow at him.

Bob seemed flustered. "You know how people talk. You and Claire have been a hot topic."

Nick shot him a sharp glance. Bob held up a hand. "Hey, everyone loves Claire. No one wants to see her get hurt."

"Good. Then you'll keep an eye on her?"

Bob's gaze narrowed. "You leaving town?"

Nick nodded. "After a few goodbyes."

He considered Nick for a moment then conceded. "Sure, I'll keep an eye on her." His expression turned rueful. "If she'll let me."

Nick almost felt bad for the guy. He knew Claire wasn't interested in the young officer. At least not in a romantic way.

"Don't let me keep you from your job, Officer." Nick stuck out his hand. After the slightest hesitation, Bob accepted Nick's handshake.

"You know where you're headed?" Bob asked, his tone a bit more congenial.

He shrugged. "North, maybe."

"Well, good luck." Bob gave a curt nod and then ambled away, leaving Nick with an unnerving twinge of possessiveness toward Claire.

Rationally, Nick knew the other man would do his

best to protect Claire, but would he make her smile, make her laugh? Would anyone be able to breach the walls she'd constructed to keep everyone at arm's length? Walls Nick had tried to scale and at times thought he'd conquered. But now he had to leave Claire with her barricaded life. He had to keep moving.

Nick headed into Tessa's bakery to start the goodbyes. Something he'd never felt the need for in the last two years until he'd met a blue-eyed blonde named Claire.

Nick waved one last time to Sandy and Dave Wellington as he left their modest two-story home in a residential neighborhood on the east side of town. He liked the older couple and was thankful Claire had such caring people in her life. But seeing them made him realize he couldn't leave things the way they were between him and Claire.

He'd hurt her. Plain and simple. Her indifference wasn't real. It was her defense. Against him. Guilt stabbed at him. She did care for him. As a friend, at least. He hoped it wasn't more, because there couldn't be more.

He headed back toward town, back toward The Zone. He owed her an apology and a proper goodbye.

As he turned the corner and The Zone came into view, his gaze zeroed in on the slashes of red marring the side of the building. Anger and worry burned in his gut. Bringing the bike to a halt, he noticed Claire sitting under the tree, her knees drawn up and her head resting on her folded arms.

She looked up at him as he approached. His heart

wrenched at the sight of her red-rimmed eyes and tear-stained cheeks. He rushed to her side and hunkered down. "Are you all right?"

She blinked. "What are you doing here?"

He captured a tear with the pad of his finger. "I came back to apologize and to say goodbye."

Her dark blonde brows drew together. She pulled away from his touch. "You don't owe me an apology."

Her withdrawal stung. He needed to make it right. "I do. I shouldn't have let you think my staying was more—"

She cut him off with a raised hand. "Don't even go there. You did what you said you were going to do. Now, say your goodbye and ride away." She flicked her hand at him.

His jaw tightened with frustration. She didn't give an inch. "I'm not going anywhere."

She jumped to her feet, her blue eyes blazing. "Excuse me? What's that supposed to mean?"

He slowly rose. His temper hung by a thread. *"Hello."* He gestured to the wall. "Those punks came back. You think I'm going to leave you while they're still out there running loose?"

"Oh, yeah, I'm terrified of red spray paint. Please." She placed her hands on her hips. "I don't need a hero. I don't need you. I can take care of this myself."

He ignored the unexpected hurt her words caused. He clenched his fists. "You *should* be terrified, Claire. And thankful it was only spray paint and not some deadly stunt like the last time. You don't know that next time they won't come back with a gun."

Terror stormed through his veins.

God had sent him here for a reason, all right. To stop those kids and somehow he'd lost sight of that. He wasn't going to let anything happen to Claire. He stalked away, heading for his bike.

"What are you doing?" she called after him.

Grabbing his helmet, he sat and turned to stare at her. She looked like an angel from one of her drawings. Sunlight flittered through the tree branches, kissing her strawberry-blond hair with shimmering gold. Her blue eyes captivated him. Drew him in and made him aware that he was failing miserably at staying emotionally detached.

"I'm going to teach those punks a lesson they won't forget."

God was giving him another chance to protect the woman in his life. No matter how tenuous that position. He wasn't going to blow it a second time.

Claire's insides clenched with dread. "Wait!"

She ran after Nick's bike as he roared away, but stopped abruptly. There was no chance she'd catch him. Thank goodness he didn't even know where to look. Did he?

She ran back to The Zone, grabbed her keys and jumped in her little car. Too late to follow him, but she could head him off, if he did know where the kids hung out.

She didn't understand his rage, or the vengeance so obvious in his attitude. She'd seen it that first day and now it was back.

She pressed the gas pedal, pushing the car as fast as she dared.

She couldn't let him go half-cocked into a situation where someone could get hurt. Where *he* could get hurt.

"Please, God, don't let anything bad happen."

Anger, thick and hot like lava, boiled in Nick's blood. He drove to where he'd seen the blond kid. The industrial park. They had to be somewhere. Why not here? The warehouses were less visible with more hiding spots.

Nick drove slowly past the empty buildings. Another warehouse set back farther from the paved road on a gravel drive caught his attention.

Wooden planks boarded the windows. A chain lock looped around the handle of the door. Across the front of the building were the words "Pineridge Storage Company" in faded green lettering. A desolate feeling squeezed in on the anger burning in his gut. This seemed a likely spot.

Leaving his bike in the shade of a tree, he walked around the building looking for an opening. He found a hole in the wall on the side of the structure. The scuffs in the dirt and the smudges of handprints on the wall made him think this opening was well-used. He bent down and peered in, but saw only blackness.

Tires crunching on the gravel drew his attention. He peered around the corner. Claire's green Subaru pulled to a stop and the driver's door flung open. She stepped out.

He shook his head, exasperation tightened his jaw.

He shouldn't be surprised to see her. She'd probably known all along where the teens hid out. Serena had been just as headstrong. His heart contracted painfully in his chest.

He forced away the grief and concentrated on Claire.

She spotted him. Her mouth pressed into a firm line and with purposeful strides she moved toward the building, toward him. He met her before she could see the opening.

"Claire, you shouldn't be here."

"No one should be here," she stated abruptly.

He took her by the elbow and steered her back toward her car. "You need to leave."

She jerked out of his grasp. "Don't think you can manhandle me because you're bigger and stronger."

He drew back in surprise. "I would never physically hurt you, Claire."

The sparks of anger receded in her eyes and she took a deep breath, letting the air out in a steady stream. "I overreacted. I know you wouldn't intentionally hurt me."

But he had hurt her. Unintentionally.

He fought the urge to wrap her in his arms and shield her from the world. He was in deep enough as it was. "Maybe all this business with the teens is finally catching up to you."

"Maybe." She looked to the building. "What do you intend to do if you find them?"

He ran a hand through his hair. "I don't know. Scare some sense into them, I guess."

She turned her gaze back on him. The pain in her

eyes clawed at him with searing intensity. He had no shield to protect himself from her. "Most of these kids have suffered from abuse, neglect, starvation. You honestly think bullying tactics will work?"

He set his jaw against the plummeting sensation of getting sucked into her pain, which threatened to undercut his anger. "I have to do something, Claire."

"Why? What personal vendetta are you trying to carry out here?"

Her pointed question blasted a hole right through his heart with satellite-guided accuracy. He clenched his back teeth. "Someone has to protect you."

"This isn't really about me, though, is it?"

Guilt wrapped greedy fingers around his lungs, forcing the air out and refusing to allow any in. He spun away.

He couldn't do anything about the past, he was realizing that now. But he could do something about the future. Claire's future—and her safety. He'd do whatever it took to make it clear she wasn't to be messed with.

Even stay?

No! That wasn't a possibility. There was too much at stake—his heart, Claire's life. The vortex of pain endangered them all.

He couldn't stay, but he could make sure these kids didn't bother her again.

He stalked back to the hole in the building with Claire dogging his heels. "Stay out here."

Her expression told him clearly what she thought about that.

He bent down and slipped through the opening.

He waited a moment as his eyes adjusted to the dimness. The room had high ceilings and bare walls with exposed beams and the concrete floor was littered with debris and dirt. The smell of neglect clogged his throat.

Claire followed him through the opening. "I don't think anyone's here," she whispered. "Let's go."

She was still trying to keep him away from the teens.

He pointed to a big sliding door on one wall. At his back, Claire grabbed a fistful of his shirt. Nick picked his way through the rubble of broken Sheetrock, wood and metal to stand by the door. Several footprints tracked in the dirt in front of the door.

Bracing himself, with Claire still behind him, he slowly slid the door open.

An inner signal cautioned him to tread with care. He stepped back and over a few steps so he had a better view of the inner room. Claire stepped in tandem with him, staying behind him, allowing him to shield her.

A horrific thought crept into his brain. What if they did have gun? The possibility was within the realm of his experience with teenagers. They didn't respect life—theirs or anyone else's.

A shadow crossed his peripheral vision. A second later something launched at him. Claire's scream echoed inside his head. A shoulder rammed into his solar plexus. He absorbed the impact, compartmentalizing the pain. He wrapped his arms around the body and squeezed, lifting the smaller person off the ground.

A toe connected with his shin. He gritted his teeth

and squeezed harder. "Knock it off!" he roared to the squirming boy in his arms.

"Let go!"

Nick did, loosening his hold, and the boy fell to the ground with a thump. The boy, Tyler, scrambled to the far corner where Mindy and the blond boy stood wide-eyed and visibly trembling.

Claire touched Nick's back. "You okay?"

"Yes." As he stared at the teens, took in their lean faces, the filth, the condition of the place, his stomach rolled. This was no place for teenagers to be living, but that's exactly what it was to them—home. The makeshift cardboard beds, the empty take-out cartons piled in one corner. So that's what Claire had done with their leftover pizza and Chinese food.

On the floor by one of the beds, a soup can held a handful of wildflowers. Pity rose, sharp and choking. Nick's gaze snagged on a partially hidden spray can with red smudges.

He squared his shoulders and trampled down any softening. "We need to talk."

Tyler stood and faced him. "We have nothing to say to you."

Nick begrudgingly admired the kid's courage. "Too bad, because I do. Let's get something straight. I don't want to hear any lies or excuses. I know you vandalized The Zone today. And I'm pretty sure you set the fire." One look at Mindy's guilt-ridden face confirmed his suspicion.

"You can't prove anything," Tyler countered.

"We'll see what the police think."

That was the only course of action to take. Claire was right. No matter how much he'd like to threaten the teens or make them pay, he couldn't. They'd suffered far worse than he could ever hope to dish out. But the authorities could do something. Get them help. Keep them away from Claire.

"You can't turn them in."

His gut clenched. He stared at Claire in disbelief. "Not this again."

"You don't understand." Unshed tears glistened in her eyes.

That vortex of pain had a powerful draw. "Then make me understand."

"The authorities can only do so much. They'll be sent to juvenile detention and then back to their homes or to foster homes. They'll only run away again."

"That's right," Tyler interjected. "I'm not going back there."

Nick frowned. "That's not my problem."

She clutched his arm. "It's everyone's problem. Especially if you're a believer."

He shook his head as more bottled-up rage spurted through him. So many times his parents had pushed for him to let go of his anger and forgive that kid, claiming God would want him to. They'd pushed and pushed until he couldn't take it and he'd left. "Don't even try to lay that guilt trip on me."

She gave him a pained expression. "It's not about guilt. It's about doing what's right even if it's uncomfortable. About showing compassion, even when it's undeserved."

She cut the air with her hand. "No. Especially when it's undeserved. It's about loving the unlovable. Jesus calls us to love as He did."

A desperate plea for understanding shone bright in her eyes. "I've been where these kids are. I've lived this."

His mind reeled from her words. It wasn't possible. Not Claire. Not sweet, nurturing, soft-hearted Claire.

"What do you mean you've lived this?" He stared at her in shock, trying to reconcile her words with what he knew of Claire. No. This couldn't be true.

Chapter Ten

She waved away his question. "These kids aren't criminals." The conviction in her voice set Nick's teeth on edge.

Whoa! Back up. He wanted to know about her. All the time they'd spent together, discussed The Zone and the work she wanted to accomplish, and she'd kept hidden an important piece of information.

He forced himself to concentrate on the issue at hand. "You don't think destroying property and putting your life in danger isn't criminal?"

"If I believed turning them in would change anything for them, I'd do it."

A knot of wrath lodged itself in his chest. "It isn't for them, it's for you. Your safety. Shouldn't they pay the consequences for their actions?"

Like the punk who'd killed Serena. That kid should rot for eternity in jail, but because of the kid's age he'd be set free one day.

"Yes, of course. It's just…"

His hands clenched at his sides. "Coddling them isn't the answer, Claire."

She straightened. "Not coddle. Guide, mentor. Lead them down the right path."

"You're too idealistic for your own good." He made a sweeping gesture toward where the teens stood and stared at them. "Kids like these just want to destroy."

Her expression turned scornful. "You are so clueless. You have no idea what it's like to be alone and scared. Desperate. Digging through the trash to eat. To have everyone treat you like scum. To have the people who should protect you just as soon beat you or…or worse."

He flinched. Had the "worse" been done to her? His stomach churned, but he resisted allowing her to diminish his anger with her dramatic words.

"And you want to send them to juvie." As she pointed a finger at him, tight lines formed around her mouth. "I don't mean to be disrespectful of the system, but you want to put kids who still might have a chance in with harder, meaner kids. What do you think they're going to learn?"

She raised a mocking brow. "Huh? I'll tell you. They're going to learn to be harder and meaner and come out angrier. Then you're talking about the kids who use guns, the kids who grow into criminal adults. The prisons are full of them."

Anger and grief surfaced, taunting him as he stared into Claire's shimmering eyes. He rejected her words. Wouldn't let her bleeding heart affect him.

Lord, what am I suppose to do now?

He ran a hand through his hair. Unbelievable. She had been one of *them*. One of the kind who'd robbed him of his love. His life.

What was he doing here? He should be miles away by now, not facing off with a blue-eyed blonde over some runaways.

He leveled a hard look on the teens. "This is the way it's going down. You want a get-out-of-jail-free card? You be at The Zone in one hour. The three of you are going to clean up the mess you made. I'll find jobs for you to do to work off the debt you owe Claire. And no drugs. If there's even the slightest hint that you're using or have brought drugs with you, you go to jail."

"Hey, I'm not…" Tyler began, but stopped short as Nick took a step forward.

Mindy put a hand on Tyler's arm, much the way Claire had done to Nick that day in the park. Tyler turned toward her, and she shook her head, exerting some unseen female power.

"Thank you, Nick."

Claire's softly spoken words drew his attention away from the teens and deepened his frown. The gratefulness, the admiration in her voice, ripped a hole in his heart. He held up a hand. "Don't."

He didn't want either of those things from her. He wanted nothing from her. Pressure built in his chest. Only her safety. "Leave with me now, Claire, and let them make their choice."

He couldn't keep the edge out of his voice or his words from being a challenge. A demand. A plea.

She stared at his hand and then turned her gaze to the teens. They stared at her mutely.

After a tense moment, she straightened. Lifting her chin, she narrowed her eyes at the three kids. "Trust me—come to The Zone. I know what you're going through. I've been there. I can help. Please, come."

She placed her hand in Nick's. The pressure holding tight to his chest eased and tenderness filled him. He squeezed her hand and led her out of the building.

Claire dropped his hand and wrapped her arms around his waist.

"Hey, what's this?" He placed his hands on her shoulders.

She beamed up at him. "Just because."

Looking down into her smiling face, feeling her slender arms hugging him, he felt a jolt of emotion he couldn't identify. Then slowly, calmness seeped in, taking the edge off his anger. He rubbed her shoulders as he tried to come to grips with the caring that invaded his heart. "I hope you won't be too crushed if they don't show up."

Her smile turned rueful, determined. "They'll show up even if I have to drag them there myself."

He frowned. "Claire!"

Her expression became playful. "Kidding."

She gave him a quick squeeze then moved away from him and started walking toward her car. He followed, wishing he could believe her. Claire was a fixer, a caretaker.

A runaway.

His gut clenched. He pushed the horror aside. She

wasn't like the others, the troublemakers. The killers. She'd turned her life around.

But how many lives had she ruined in the process?

Claire picked up the ball Little Nick had dropped at her feet, then tossed it away. The puppy's short legs scrambled as he chased the ball across The Zone's small yard.

She was aware of Nick's intense gaze, could feel his unspoken questions. She couldn't believe she'd blurted out that she'd been a runaway.

The look on his face had cut her like the pointed end of a switchblade. The way she'd known it would.

He wouldn't—couldn't—understand. He'd had a home. A loving family. She'd only been able to dream about those things and vow to offer that kind of care and concern to other runaways.

She glanced at her wristwatch. Only twenty minutes left for the teens to show up. Anxiety twisted inside of her.

If they didn't show, Nick would go to the police. So far he'd displayed compassion and mercy by not contacting the authorities, but she doubted he'd see it that way. He was so intent on judging and condemning all runaways. All teens.

Why?

If she had an ounce of wisdom in her, she'd give up trying to solve the puzzle of Nick. But she didn't know if she could do that.

As she wandered to the edge of the walkway and stared off in the distance toward the road that led to the warehouse, doubts filtered in. The kids weren't ready to trust them. They needed more time, more guidance, to help them realize they could make good choices.

She spun on her heel and nearly tripped over Little Nick. He dropped the ball from his mouth. She kicked it and paced back to the stairs where Nick sat, his pose casual, unconcerned. She briefly met his gaze, his eyes inky and observant, before turning and walking the short distance down the walkway again.

She glanced at her watch. Fifteen more minutes. Where were they? A bird flew across the cloudless sky, a black streak that disappeared behind the towering evergreens of the park. If the kids didn't show by ten after, she was going to go get them.

"Claire."

"Hmm?"

"Come sit down. Your pacing isn't going to make them come any faster."

She acknowledged the truth in his words with a ruefully toss of her head. "I'm too antsy to sit."

"You can't control this, Claire. They're going to do whatever they're going to do."

She narrowed her gaze, chafing against his words because she knew he was right. "You hope they don't show. Then you can turn them in."

A muscle tightened in his jaw. He wasn't so unconcerned. "It doesn't matter what I hope."

"They're just kids. I should have stayed. They need me to help them."

He raised a brow. "Maybe they need the opportunity to earn your trust."

Where did he get off sounding so confident and sure of what the teenagers needed? He didn't have a degree in psychology, hadn't been through the Young Life training. Had never lived the lives of these kids. He didn't even like them.

Yet, something inside her wanted to let him be the one to bear the burden, to be the one to take responsibility. The temptation to let him rose and she hated the weakness in herself. She would not need him.

She took a deep breath, concentrating on his words about control and the simple truth that somehow she'd let it slip away. She wasn't in control and neither was Nick.

All she could do was pray the kids would show up on their own. That God would speak to their hearts.

It was hard to wait. Hard to release the worry and anxiety.

She wanted to ask Nick why he hated the teens so much, but she knew that if she did he'd ask about her past, about being a runaway. A dicey subject at best. One better left alone.

The puppy pawed at her shins, the ball forgotten. She sat on the step next to Nick and stroked Little Nick's yellow coat as he lay down beside her. She resisted the urge to check her watch again.

Then Nick's hand on her knee sent her thoughts scattering. Her gaze lifted. His attention zeroed in on three people walking down the road toward them. Her heart leapt with relief. God had answered her prayers. The kids were coming.

"I knew they'd come," she boasted.

One corner of his full mouth twisted upward in a mocking grin. "Didn't you just."

Heat stole up her neck and settled in her cheeks. She lifted her chin. "Okay, maybe I doubted it. A little."

He laughed. The dry, brittle sound scraped along her nerves. The first battle had been won, but the war to save the teens had just started.

Would Nick be an ally or an enemy?

"So, we're here," Tyler said with a large dose of insolence lacing his words as he and the other two teens stopped in front of The Zone.

Nick struggled with the desire to grab Tyler by the scruff of the neck and shake him. Instead, he flexed his fingers and leveled a stern glare on the three teens. He decided against commenting on their timing. "Follow me."

He led them to where he'd set up the leftover paint and clean brushes near the side of the house. He pointed toward the supplies. "There you go. Get started."

Defiance lit up Tyler's eyes, but the other two headed over without hesitation. Nick raised a brow. Tyler shrugged and turned away to join the other two. Nick let out a heavy breath, thankful the situation hadn't turned into another stand-off with the kid.

Claire stepped up beside him. "We can't let them go back to that warehouse."

A burst of anger tightened his gut. His gaze slid to her. The light of battle shone bright in her eyes. "And what do you suggest we do with them?"

She blinked up at him as if he should already know

the answer to that question—which he had a sinking feeling he did.

"They'll stay here. Won't take me but a few minutes to make the beds in the two rooms, clear away a few boxes."

He grimaced, his mind rebelling against sleeping with the enemy underfoot. "I had a feeling you were going to say that."

"What would you have me do, Nick? They've come this far, trusted this much. I can't send them back out there."

The dusty warehouse with the makeshift beds and that pitiful tin can full of flowers flashed in his mind. "Yeah, I know."

She gave him a smug, sidelong glance. "You're a good man, Nick Andrews."

He snorted. He was insane to be getting so mixed up and entangled with them all. Now how was he going to leave Claire and Pineridge when the teens would be sleeping at The Zone?

That evening, Claire prepared a simple meal. Baked chicken with potatoes and carrots. A sprinkle of dill over the top. Nothing fancy, but one of her favorite recipes from Aunt Denise.

"Can I do anything?" Mindy asked. She stood at the threshold of the kitchen, uncertainty written across her face.

Claire appreciated her manners. She understood the girl's uncertainty, could still remember how she'd felt when she'd first come to live with Aunt Denise. The same way Gwen had been when she'd first come to live with Claire and her aunt. Unsure of her role, wanting to belong but afraid to hope she would.

Mindy was opening a door, hoping to be admitted. The girl wanted to be helpful, be a part of something. Claire understood that deep down they all wanted to belong. "Would you set the table? The plates are in the cupboard by the fridge and glasses are above the sink."

Claire walked to the edge of the living room and called to the boys lounging on the floor. "Johnny, Tyler."

Tyler ignored her.

Johnny jumped up. "Yes?"

"Wash up for dinner, please. Restroom's over there." She pointed to the open door under the stairs.

Knowing it was best to assert her authority from the get-go, Claire wiped her hands on a dishtowel and strode all the way into the living room. She stopped in front of the TV. To her astonishment, Little Nick was stretched out on his back and Tyler's hand was gently stroking the puppy's soft underbelly.

The urge to snatch the puppy away gripped her with a fierce hold, but she forced it down. She wanted Tyler to feel trusted so he'd learn to trust her.

"Tyler. The polite thing to do when someone talks to you is to acknowledge them."

He stared at her knees. "What?"

"Are you hungry?" she asked, patiently.

He lifted a shoulder in a careless shrug.

"Well, I can't force you to eat. If you would like to

join us, please wash up in the bathroom and then come to the table."

She stared at the teen. The hard lines in his face belonged on an adult, not a fifteen-year-old kid. His clothes were filthy. She'd have to do something about that.

When she'd been arranging the rooms upstairs, she'd found a box of clothes Sandy had given her that had once belonged to her twins. There had to be some jeans and T-shirts in the boxes that would fit the teenagers. Maybe decent clothes would help Tyler feel more civilized.

The back door opened. Nick walked in, bringing with him a high level of energy that buzzed in the air and made Claire shiver with awareness. He wore black twill pants that hugged his body attractively, and a black T-shirt. He looked as dark and dangerous as a caged panther she'd once seen at the zoo.

Tyler shifted in the beanbag chair. His gaze darted to Nick and then to the front door. Claire had the distinct impression that if she weren't in his path, Tyler would make a break for the door.

Standing her ground, Claire smiled at Nick. "I hope you're hungry. We're just about to eat."

Nick glanced at Mindy and then Tyler. "I'm not hungry."

Johnny stepped out of the bathroom and froze. Claire frowned. All this tension made for a really bad beginning. She touched Tyler's arm. He flinched away as if he expected her to cuff him upside the head. Claire's heart twisted. "The bathroom's free. Why don't you go wash up?"

He scowled with his chin jutting out and marched past her to the restroom. He closed the door with a snap.

She ushered Johnny into the kitchen. "Why don't you help Mindy with the glasses? There's juice and milk in the fridge." To Nick she said, "You can wash up at the sink. If you prefer not to sit at the table, fill your plate and eat where you'd like."

His dark brows drew together. "Claire, I—"

"It's okay." She understood that he didn't feel the same about the teens as she did. She understood that this was a hard transition for them all. What she didn't understand was Nick's continued anger.

Nick filled his plate and then headed out the back door. Claire felt a stab of sadness and disappointment but she quickly smoothed over the little wound in her heart. She couldn't expect anything from Nick. He wasn't going to be a permanent fixture in her life. She should just be thankful he hadn't turned the kids in.

Claire wished Gwen hadn't had to work tonight. Claire could have used an ally.

Dinner with the three teens was silent and fast. By the way the kids slammed their food down, she figured it had been a long while since they'd had a decent meal. Satisfaction surged through her. She was making a difference in their lives. Just as she had in Gwen's.

As they were finishing the meal, Nick returned. He rinsed his plate and sat on the stool at the counter off to Claire's left, perched like a huge eagle waiting for its prey.

Claire explained the house rules to the kids. No

swearing, no drugs. On Sundays everyone attends church. Each person would be expected to clear their own plate, make their bed and pile their laundry by the door. "When we're done eating you can each pick through the boxes of clothes I have upstairs. And find something to wear while I wash what you have on."

Johnny and Mindy finished and without a fuss picked up their plates, carrying them to the sink. Tyler started to leave the table without his plate. Nick cleared his throat, prompting Tyler to glower at him as he picked up his plate. Claire was thankful for Nick's support, only she wished he'd be less threatening about it.

Upstairs, she showed the teens the boxes of clothes. They dug through them with enthusiasm.

Claire gave out towels and washcloths from the bathroom cupboard. "Mindy, why don't you shower first and then the boys can take turns."

"Do you have shampoo?" Mindy asked eagerly.

Claire laughed. "Yes. And conditioner."

"Yay!" Mindy took the clothes she'd decided on and hurried to shower.

Soon all the kids were showered and dressed. Claire carried down their dirty clothes in a basket. In the laundry room, she started the tub filling with water and then pulled a pair of jeans from the basket. She hesitated as she reached to check the pockets. She didn't want to invade their privacy, but she also didn't want to stick something in the wash that could ruin the clothes or worse yet, the machine.

Cautiously, she checked the pockets of the jeans.

Empty. She breathed a sigh of relief as she stuck them in the washing machine's tub. She checked the next pair. She found the folded note she'd left for Mindy.

"Thank You again, Lord," she whispered as she put the jeans in the tub.

The next pair of jeans was grubbier than the others. Tyler's, she thought. Wary, she checked the pockets. She found some change, a guitar pick and a stack of small square sheets of thin paper that she recognized from her days on the streets. Zig-Zags. Used legally to roll tobacco cigarettes. Used illegally to roll a joint.

She tossed the squares away. This wasn't enough proof to convict Tyler of using. But it did indicate he bore watching closely. At least she hadn't found a syringe or a pouch of cocaine. She threw the jeans in the wash.

A little while later, she was bustling around the kitchen making popcorn when Nick came up behind her. Though he didn't touch her, she felt his regard like a warm caress. "You're good with them."

She turned and found herself one popcorn bowl's length between them. "I know what they need."

"Because you were once one of them?" his low, deep voice washed over her, drenching her senses.

She knew he wouldn't let it lie. "Yes. Because I once was a runaway."

He leaned closer, pressing the bowl into her ribs. "Why didn't you tell me before?"

Her mouth went dry. "I…I don't know."

His whiskered jaw tightened. "Tell me now."

She heard the footsteps of the teens coming down the stairs. "Not now."

The two boys entered the living room. They stopped when they saw Claire and Nick in the kitchen. She called to them. "There's a stack of movies in the video case. Why don't you two pick a good one we can all watch?"

She turned back to Nick and smiled brightly. "Come watch a movie with us."

His lip curled. "I'd rather not." He grabbed a handful of popcorn and left through the back door.

Once again.

Claire sighed.

Chapter Eleven

A noise awoke Nick from a nightmare. Sweat trickled down his forehead. He wiped it away as the images of Claire, hurt and bleeding, faded from his mind, leaving him uneasy.

He didn't like the idea of the teens so close.

A quick glance at the clock gave him a pretty good idea who had made the noise. 3:00 a.m. Claire's nocturnal wanderings. But he didn't trust the teenagers, so he got up. After pulling on his jeans and a T-shirt, he left his room.

He stopped in front of Mindy's room and listened. Nothing. He moved to the door of the room the two boys shared. Silence.

He'd heard Gwen return from work hours ago. No light shone from beneath her door.

Downstairs, Claire, dressed in light gray sweat pants and a U of O sweatshirt, was curled up on the bright yellow beanbag chair with a book in her hands and a small pool of light spilling over her from the standing lamp.

She looked up as he approached, her eyes wide, lips parted in surprise. "I didn't mean to wake you."

"You didn't." He sat next to her on the couch. "Have you always had trouble sleeping or is it me being here?"

Her gaze softened. "I've always suffered from insomnia. Reading helps me relax enough to go back to sleep."

He wouldn't allow himself to think about Claire relaxed and sleepy. "What are you reading?"

She held up the book so he could read the cover. A majestic castle surrounded by rolling green hills set off center of a couple, dressed in medieval garb, gazing into each other's eyes. The titled slashed across the top in gold script. Something to do with the Highlands.

She smiled. "A romance. My aunt got me hooked on them."

Fanciful stuff. Serena had enjoyed medical thrillers. "My mom and Lucy read those." He leaned forward. Telling himself he was just trying to help, he offered, "When my mom can't sleep, my dad rubs her shoulders. Most times that's where people hold their tension."

She held his gaze. "Really?"

"Really." He was standing in quicksand and sinking fast. But as he stared into her eyes, saw her wariness and a glimmer of interest, he realized he'd gladly dive in headfirst if in doing so he could give back to her a tenth of what she gave out.

She'd amazed him yet again this evening when she'd

clucked over those three lost chicks upstairs like a mother hen. Oozing maternal nurturing and kindness, yet firm in the way she dealt with them. Seeing to their needs without being condescending.

She hadn't even chastised him for his gruff refusal to participate in the dinner she'd prepared or to watch TV with them as if this were a normal situation for them all. It hadn't sat well with him.

She should have expected, demanded, more from him. Not that he would have given it. He didn't know what to make of her or his jumbled-up emotions about her. Rubbing her shoulders, touching her no matter how innocent his intentions, would be tantamount to playing with matches. They could both get burned. He wouldn't allow himself to be affected by her in any way. And if he repeated that often enough to himself it had to be true.

Right?

He cleared his throat. "On second thought, maybe hot chocolate would be good."

Claire stirred milk in a pot at the stove on medium heat with a wooden spoon. She hummed softly to herself as she watched Nick measure out generous scoops of powdered chocolate mix into two large mugs. They moved around the kitchen in such a cohesive way, as if they'd been doing it for years. She enjoyed the comfortable and relaxed way he made her feel, yet it made her heart ache with a yearning. She forced the feeling away, because yearning, hoping, expecting, were all bad news for her.

"Tell me what happened after your parents divorced."

She stiffened, and stopped humming. Tension gathered between her shoulder blades. The need to share welled up like a geyser about to blow. Would he understand? Could he? Would it change anything? Maybe. Maybe she could make him understand that the teens needed compassion and mercy.

Resuming her stirring, she started at the beginning. "My parents were young, still in high school, when my mother got pregnant with me."

Her voice sounded hollow, detached to her own ears. "They married. My dad took a job on the docks. My mother resented being stuck at home with a baby. She never let me forget that I was a mistake, unwanted. My dad tolerated me as long as I stayed out of the way. I became very good at staying out of the way."

Slowly, he turned to stare at her. "They were abusive?"

Her mouth twisted with bitter humor. "Depends what you consider abusive. Did they lock me in a closet? Tie me to a chair? Break my bones? No. I had food on my plate and a roof over my head."

Her throat tightened with memory, but she forced herself to remain detached. Only one way to find out if Nick could handle her past. "I bounced back and forth for a while between them. My mother changed everything about herself—her hair, her clothes and her job. She met a doctor and they got married the next year.

"My dad wanted to take a job on a fishing boat in

Alaska, something he'd always talked about, but because the custody agreement stated he had to have me half of each month, he couldn't. And he blamed me.

"I hated the bobbing back and forth. Hated them for not wanting me." She stopped, afraid she sounded whiny. Self-pity had no place in her life.

His hand covered hers around the spoon. She looked into his face and saw only tenderness in his eyes. Her spirit felt cared for, her tongue felt loose. Extracting her hand from beneath his, she moved to a cupboard and brought out a jar of cinnamon, giving herself a moment to gather her courage to finish her tale. "On my four-teenth birthday, my parents fought over who had to have me. I think they thought I wanted a party or some-thing." She blew out a mocking breath and moved to where the mugs sat on the counter. "I told my parents a friend from school had invited me to her house for the weekend. They were ecstatic."

The bitterness crept into her voice despite her attempt not to let herself become emotional. As if she could rid herself of the past, she gave a violent shake of the spice jar, dumping the rust-colored powder into each mug. In her peripheral vision, she was aware of Nick as he came to stand beside her. He put the pot of steaming milk on a trivet on the counter and then stepped closer.

He slid her hair to the side and lightly brushed his fin-gertips on her shoulder. "Stray cinnamon," he murmured.

She set the jar down. "Thank you."

Her breath hitched as she felt a featherlight kiss on her head. Tears burned at the back of her throat.

His breath, warm and minty, fanned over her cheek. "Did you go to a friend's?"

Afraid to say the rest, she shook her head. His knuckles grazed her jawline. "You're so beautiful, Claire. Not just the outside, but inside where it matters."

Tears sprang to her eyes at his words. "I ran away."

"Ahh, sweet Claire," he said. His mouth hovered close to her cheek. If she turned her head a little, she could find his lips with her own. She held herself still.

"Tell me," he coaxed before his lips grazed her cheek. She closed her eyes against the torture of having him so close, so within reach, yet so unreachable.

"Uh-huh." The negative response was all she could manage.

He shifted, but then she realized he'd captured her hand and was tugging her close. She kept her gaze downcast.

"Did you run away to your aunt's?"

She shook her head and dropped her forehead to his chest. "My parents didn't miss me for two weeks. From what I was told they started asking around for me, but it was a good month before they contacted the authorities. By then I was in Seattle. A year later, I…"

She closed eyes against the memories. "I lived on the streets, dug through trash looking for food, begged from anyone who looked my way."

She'd gone this far, she might as well tell the rest. "I hooked up with a guy I thought needed me. But he didn't. I was the one who needed him. I made a bad choice. Several, really. I gave him my heart, my body. Allowed myself to get sucked into drugs."

She made a face as shame washed over her. "By the grace of God I never became addicted. The place where…where my boyfriend and I were staying was raided. He escaped and I was picked up by the police. The female officer took an interest in me when my parents didn't want me back. She contacted Aunt Denise, who took me in."

"Did you ever see your boyfriend again?"

"No."

He brought her captured hand up between them and slid his other arm around her back. She let her shame dissolve as she relaxed into him; his heart beat music in her ear. God had forgiven her for her foolishness even though she had a hard time forgiving herself.

It felt so good to be held, to have human contact. She understood why God had said it wasn't good for mankind to be alone. Human touch could bring peace and comfort.

Nick's deep voice filled the air as he began to softly sing. She melted further into his arms. She recognized the song. It was one of her favorites from Michael W. Smith's *Worship* album. She let the words wash over her, agreeing in her spirit that God would draw her close and never let her go.

As Nick's voice faded with the last refrain of the song, she wanted to tell him how grateful she was for his presence, for his soothing voice, but she didn't want to shatter the quiet of the moment with words.

When he started with a new song, her heart contracted painfully in her chest. The simple lyrics of the worship song spoke deep to her soul. He sang the song through the way it was written, the way she'd sung it a thousand times. Then he sang it again and changed the words, inserting her name for the pronoun I, making the song a prayer for God to open the eyes of her heart. To show her His power and love.

The tenderness of the prayer moved her deeply. Tears streamed down her cheeks. The last word of the chorus hung in the air, then seemed to swirl away, leaving a peaceful silence that wrapped around Claire, making her feel safe and cared for.

She must have sniffled or something, because he eased back. With the calloused pads of his fingers, he raised her chin so their gazes met. There was compassion in his eyes and tenderness on his face.

And she knew what she wanted.

With her free hand she reached up to touch his strong jaw. His day's worth of stubble tickled her palm.

His eyes grew darker and his breath hitched. "Claire," he said, his voice hoarse and rife with warning.

Her head told her to heed the warning. Her heart told her to take the risk. For ten years she'd been listening to her head. Tonight she was going with her heart. She went on tiptoe, moving cautiously, because if he showed any sign that he wasn't receptive, she'd retreat.

Tentatively, she touched her lips to his, felt the firmness and warmth.

The kiss was one-sided.

Then he breathed out her name and his lips yielded, molding to hers. She lost herself in the embrace. The sensations ran through her, reminding her of the time she'd fallen out of a tree. Dizzy, free and breathless. Anticipating the crash.

With agonizing clarity, she felt him disengage, pulling away, leaving her to face the landing alone.

He dropped his forehead to hers. "You're too generous, Claire."

Then he stepped back, his gaze bleak, his expression grim. "I can't do this. You deserve so much better than this. Than me."

Claire didn't know what she deserved, but she certainly knew what she wanted.

Nick.

And that terrified her. Because wanting could only lead to needing, which in turn led to expectations. And she knew where expectations led.

To a place she had no intention of going.

Eventually Nick would leave. He'd made no promise to stay. She had no choice but to shore up her defenses around her heart.

Being vulnerable to anyone was not something she could allow.

Nick sat on the twin bed in his room and stared at the stark white wall, but all he could see was Claire. Her big blue eyes wide with trust and hope. Her pink lips parting.

Oh, man. He'd made a mess of things.

He wasn't in the market for hurt again. He'd had his quota, enough to last the rest of his days. The hole Serena's death left in his heart, his life, could never be filled.

He wasn't any closer to understanding why God had brought him to Claire. He'd thought he was here to protect her from the teens. And he'd done such a great job, they were sleeping next door. With a groan, he laid back and sought the oblivion of sleep.

The morning came way too early for Nick, and with it a deep need to move, to get on his bike and feel the rush of wind biting at his skin, to see the world as a blur of color rather than details.

He dressed, putting his riding gear back on. He needed to get away from Claire, from the teens and the constant torment of remembering.

He stepped into the hall. The doors of the other rooms were closed. Moving quietly, he headed toward the stairs. Just as he arrived at the landing and was about to step down, Gwen's door opened.

She blinked at him through a fiery mass of red hair that engulfed her impish face. "Hey," she said.

"Good morning," he replied in a low voice.

She hefted her book bag onto her shoulder and shut her door.

"After you," Nick said, indicating she should proceed him down the stairs.

Little Nick stirred inside his crate. Gwen stopped and scratched his little snout through the crate before going outside. Nick followed her out. "You off to school?"

"Yeah. It's chem day."

He raised a brow. "What are you studying to be?"

She adjusted the bag on her shoulder. "I'm going into medicine. Thought I'd be a doctor, but now I'm thinking a physician's assistant."

"Why?"

Intelligence glowed bright in her amber eyes. "Less headache. Still get to do the doctoring but don't have the whole business aspect to deal with. I just want to help people."

Interesting. Another runaway who wanted to turn around and help others. Nick silently saluted Aunt Denise for her influence on Claire and Gwen. He would have liked to have known the woman. "Do you need a ride to school?"

"Bus stop's just down the road. I can study on the way." She started walking. "See ya later."

"Later."

Nick walked around to the back of the building where he kept his bike and pushed it a half block down the road before starting the engine and roaring away.

Two hours later, he was back. Though he felt invigorated, he wasn't refreshed the way he usually was after a ride. His mind was heavy with thoughts of Serena and the runaways. And Claire.

He parked his bike and went inside. He stopped at the sight of the teens sitting quietly at the table eating breakfast. Claire bustled about the kitchen, her graceful movements unhurried, her hair flowing free about her shoulders catching glints of sunlight.

The whole scene squeezed at his heart. He'd once hoped for a family. For children sitting at his table, his wife welcoming him with a warm smile as she offered him food she'd lovingly prepared.

But that wasn't to be. God had let some kid take away his chance for that kind of life. Serena had been ripped away from him as punishment for his greed. There were moments when he wished he'd died instead of her.

But he wasn't dead. And this wasn't his family.

He hardened his heart against the uselessness of his thoughts and moved forward, his boots echoing on the hardwood floor.

Mindy's eyes widened and she quickly shifted her attention toward Claire as if seeking refuge from him. Johnny stilled, his fork frozen half to his mouth while his eyes widened. Tyler's thin shoulders stiffened but he made a grand show of ignoring Nick by shoveling in his food at a rapid pace as if Nick might swoop down on him and take his plate away.

If being the bad guy kept the teens in line, Nick would gladly fill the role.

Claire stood by the counter that divided the dining area from the kitchen. Her wide smile didn't reach her eyes or so much as waver as she assessed him. He resisted the urge to squirm.

She lifted a brow. "Breakfast?"

He couldn't sit with the kids, couldn't bring himself to share a meal with the source of his pain. He shook his head.

She held his gaze for a beat. He couldn't decipher the emotion lighting her eyes. She spun away. Her movements turned jerky, angry.

He frowned. Ignoring the teenagers and their now curious stares, he walked to Claire. He laid a hand on her shoulder, stilling her action. "Why are you angry?"

"I'm not angry. What makes you think I'm angry?"

She slammed the dishwasher door shut, rattling the dishes inside.

"Is this about our conversation last night?"

She turned on the faucet and scrubbed a pot. "No."

"Then what has you so upset?"

"Nothing." She turned off the faucet and dried her hands. "What are your plans, Nick?"

He narrowed his gaze. "My plans?"

She faced him squarely. "Plans. Like, are you staying or leaving?"

He glanced at the group huddled at the table, their avid gazes fixed on him. He didn't trust them, couldn't leave her to their mercy. "Staying."

"For how long?"

He didn't know.

Feeling like he was walking into a trap, he shrugged. "As long as needed."

A cold smile twisted her lips. "I don't need you."

His chin came up and he tried to belie the sting her words caused. "Until we figure out a game plan for them—" he jerked his thumb toward the teens "—I'm staying."

"Why?"

He leaned in close so only she'd hear his words. "I don't trust them."

She leaned closer still, her breath tickling his ear. "Let them earn your trust."

Her fresh scent assaulted his senses, stirring a yearning in him he'd just as soon not have. A yearning to taste her kiss again. To bury his hands in her hair and feel her soft skin rasping against his calloused hands.

He straightened. She stepped back as color darkened her cheeks. Was she remembering their kiss?

He gave a negative shake of his head, not sure he was saying no to her statement or to his thoughts. Her gaze dropped but not before he saw the disappointment in her eyes. He didn't like the way her disappointment tempted him to relent.

Moving past him, she said to the teens, "When you're done eating, please take your plates to the sink." Then she walked through the living room and stomped upstairs, leaving Nick alone with three wary teenagers.

Now what was he supposed to do?

Claire took out her exasperation and frustration on the toilet bowl she was cleaning. Men!

When she'd awakened and found Nick gone, she'd assumed he left for good. Her heart had twisted in agony, but she told herself it was for the best. That a man with as much baggage as he carried would only drag her down.

But it had still hurt.

And she'd stuffed that ache down deep with all the other disappointments in her life and chastised herself for wishing he'd stay.

Then he just waltzed back in and she realized he'd only gone for a ride. She hated the joy that leapt in her soul. The joy turned quickly to anger directed at herself. When would she learn?

She finished the bathroom and went downstairs to make sure no mayhem had transpired after she'd left Nick alone with the three teenagers.

The teens were fine, she saw with relief. Mindy and Johnny were playing Ping-Pong and Tyler was slouched on the yellow beanbag watching TV. Little Nick was his constant companion.

"Where's Nick?" she asked.

"Out front," the boy named Johnny responded as he slammed a shot across the table.

Mindy deftly shot the white ball back at him.

Contentment unfurled inside Claire's chest. This was what she'd envisioned. Teenagers enjoying the place, feeling safe and secure. As time went on they would open up and trust her.

If only that would happen with Nick. But after this morning, she was too afraid to hope. For anything.

The days seemed to fly by. Claire couldn't believe how much work it was having three teens underfoot 24/7. Doing triple the amount of laundry. Triple the amount of food to feed three growing youths, plus a grown man. She felt like she spent half the week at the grocery store.

She hadn't realized how much Aunt Denise had done for her and Gwen. Or how self-sufficient Gwen had become over the years.

Claire kept expecting her bank account to run dry with all the extra expenses. But for some reason the bank's balance and her balance didn't match. The bank's balance was always higher. But she didn't have a spare moment to sit down and calculate the discrepancy.

On Sunday she took the teens to church with her.

Though the teenagers had grumbled, she reminded them of her house rules. She was certain once they got involved in the youth group, they'd want to attend. Nick had shaken his head when she'd asked if he were going with them. But halfway through the service, she glanced back and there he was, leaning against the wall looking intimidating and imposing.

They never talked about his appearance at church. Or the fact that he stayed away from the teens. She'd thought after hearing her story and understanding why she wanted to help the teenagers, he'd have softened some. He hadn't. The few times she asked him about it, he deflected her questions. Very neatly. She realized he was good at that.

Four days before the auction, Claire, wearing her twill khakis and a striped shirt, headed outside in search of Nick. He was tinkering with his bike.

The three teens were out front, as well. Mindy threw the ball for Little Nick while Johnny hung close to Nick, watching him. Johnny seemed to do that a lot. She wondered if Nick noticed how much the boy wanted his attention. Tyler, on the other hand, stayed as far from Nick as possible. Nick didn't even try to hide the simmering anger in his eyes every time he looked at the kid.

Claire stopped next to Nick. He glanced over his shoulder and then stood. His expression was welcoming. "Hi."

"Hi. I'm off to Sandy's."

Panic replaced the welcoming light in his eyes. "You're not leaving me alone with them."

She pursued her lips. Legally, she shouldn't since he wasn't an employee and wasn't licensed to provide care to anyone. But since The Zone wasn't officially open for business yet, she decided to consider the teenagers and Nick as guests.

She hoped to help them all reconcile with their parents, because deep inside she truly believed in the idea of family, but if reconciliation wasn't possible... well, she'd deal with that dilemma later.

She had to leave soon or she'd be late. "I'm confident you can handle things here. Find something for them to do."

She leaned closer so only he could hear. "Try to get them to open up to you."

His stricken look gave her a second's doubt about the wisdom of charging him with such a delicate task. "Pray. God will strengthen you," she whispered.

His nostrils flared and those dark eyes glared at her.

Claire backed up. "Hey, Mindy. Do you want to come with me?"

The girl's face lit up. "Sure."

Claire heart squeezed a bit. All these kids really wanted was someone to care.

But what about Nick?

Her gaze strayed to him. What did he want? And could she help him find it without losing herself in the process?

Chapter Twelve

"That's a good idea, Mindy," Claire declared with enthusiasm.

The young girl ducked her head with a pleased smile. Claire knew she'd made the right decision in bringing Mindy with her to the fund-raising committee meeting at Sandy's house.

They sat in the living room on blue chintz couches and matching overstuffed chairs. The soft taupe-colored walls coordinated well with the dark beige carpet. Like Sandy, the living room was well put together and cozy, evoking a sense of welcoming.

Lori, Sandy, Peggy Jordan and the pastor's wife, Mary, welcomed Mindy and kindly included her in the planning for the spring picnic basket auction.

Mindy blossomed under the warm regard of the ladies. She wasn't nearly as tentative as she'd been at first.

Anticipation mingled with anxiety in Claire. She

didn't want to hope for a lot, yet she couldn't quite muster up indifference. She wanted this event to be a success. Yet, she sternly told herself not to get her hopes up about the picnic because a fall from lofty heights always hurt.

As the ladies discussed the decorations, Claire thought about Nick and the two boys. He'd insisted on staying, so she'd decided to let him take some of the responsibility. And in truth, it was a relief to be able to take Mindy with her.

Away from Tyler's influence, Mindy might open up and say why she'd run away. Most people assumed kids ran away from some kind of abuse. Claire often found herself falling into that trap because of her own experience. But there were no telltale signs to watch for, no indicators that screamed abuse.

A kid could have been spoiled rotten by parents who never could get a handle on their child's behavior and when the parent finally set a boundary, the teen reacted. Some ran, some lashed out.

Or a good kid could get hooked up with the wrong type of friend. Peer pressure combined with hormones made for a crazy and sometimes dangerous mix.

Mindy seemed to have a good head on her shoulders. Claire had a feeling there was something ugly involved. Whatever it was, Claire would help Mindy deal with it.

"Thanks for coming with me today," Claire said on the way back to The Zone.

Mindy beamed. "I had a great time. Mrs. Wellington is so nice."

"Yes, she sure is. She and my aunt were best friends."

Silence met her comment. Claire thought through all the training she'd had, forming a plan to get Mindy to open up. She settled with a direct approach. "Does your mother have a friend like Mrs. Wellington?"

Mindy glanced over. "No."

"It's too bad she doesn't have anyone to lean on now that you're gone. She must be awfully lonely," Claire said in a conversational tone.

"She's got her boyfriend," Mindy muttered.

Claire winced at the bitter undertones. "You jealous?"

Mindy scoffed. "I hate that pig."

Now they were getting somewhere. Claire kept her tone low, unthreatening. "Does he hurt your mother?"

Mindy shrugged and turned away.

"Has he hurt you?"

When she didn't answer, Claire gripped the steering wheel. *Stay calm.* She didn't want to push too hard and lose what little ground she'd gained. "No one has the right to hurt another person. Especially when they're bigger and stronger."

Still silence. Claire tried another tactic. A personal one. "My father used his fists when he'd get angry or drunk. Or both." She shuddered at the memories assaulting her. Thankfully, time and distance had lessened the impact of her childhood.

Several minutes stretched by before Mindy shifted. Her shoulders shook and Claire realized the girl was silently crying. Claire quickly maneuvered the car through the traffic and entered the parking lot of the local elementary school. She stopped and turned off the car.

She put a hand on Mindy's shoulder, offering her comfort. The young girl swiveled around, allowing Claire to put an arm across her thin shoulders. Words tumbled out of Mindy.

Claire hung on to both the girl and her own repulsion as the nature of the abuse became apparent. Her mother's boyfriend hadn't hit her, he'd molested her.

Sickened and angry, Claire found her voice. "Did you tell your mother?"

Mindy wiped a hand across her nose. "She didn't believe me. She said I must have misunderstood what he did." Mindy's eyes pleaded with Claire. "It wasn't right what he did to me."

"No, honey, it wasn't right. Your mama needs to know exactly what happened." Claire resolved to make it right even if she had to drag the boyfriend to jail herself.

Claire started the car and headed back to The Zone. She needed to talk about what she found out, needed help processing the information. For the first time since her aunt's death there was someone whom she wanted to confide in.

Nick.

Nick squatted next to his Harley. With a rag he wiped down the pipes, bringing the chrome to a gleaming shine. It was an excuse, really—something to do while keeping an eye on the two teens.

He'd set them to weeding the yard. Amazingly, Tyler had only rolled his eyes once before doing as instructed. Johnny, Nick discovered, was eager to please. The boy had finished one section and asked for an inspection. Warily, Nick had gone to check out the boy's work.

"Good job," he'd commented and noted with mild surprise the pleasure lighting up the boy's eyes at the simple praise. It made Nick wonder more about the boy, made him mad that he wondered.

He paused as he heard quiet footsteps behind him. He glanced over his shoulder.

Johnny stood there. His eyes devoured the bike, reminding Nick of his own youth when he'd been fascinated with motorcycles but his mother had put the kibosh on having one any time he'd brought up the subject. The first thing he'd done when he'd graduated from college was buy his dream bike.

"Cool bike," Johnny said when he met Nick's gaze.

"That it is." Nick stood, wiped his hands on his jeans. His gaze swept the area, stopping on the target of his search. Tyler had moved to the area around one of the laurel bushes.

"What's it like to ride?"

Nick brought his gaze back to Johnny. "It's pretty cool."

Johnny nodded, his eyes gleaming with wistfulness. Nick averted his gaze. "My dad had a bike. Not nearly as tricked out as yours but it was cool. I never got a chance to ride on it."

Nick frowned, not liking the twinge of understanding running through him. "Did your mom make your dad get rid of it?"

The light in the kid's eyes dimmed. "No. Mom was okay with the bike." The kid shrugged. "Dad just took off on it one day and never came back."

That grabbed Nick's attention. "How long ago?"

Johnny shrugged. "A year or so."

Nick saw the burn of pain in Johnny's eyes that said he wasn't as nonchalant as he sounded. Nick would've bet the kid knew exactly how many days, if not hours, his father had been gone. Nick didn't even try for tact and went for the obvious. "And your mother? Did she beat you?"

"Mom? No." Johnny kicked at the dirt, his gaze now downcast.

Nick really didn't want to know. Didn't want to care. *Not my concern.* But for Claire's sake he asked, "Then why'd you take off?"

Johnny jammed his hands into his front pockets. With his shoulders hunched, he looked even younger than sixteen. "Easier on Mom."

Nick raised a brow. "Easier, how?"

Johnny slanted a quick glance in Tyler's direction, before replying, "She's got my two sisters to look after plus her job at the bank. I just was in the way."

Nick crossed his arms over his chest. "Does she even know you're alive?"

"Huh? Of course."

"So you've talked to her since you ran off."

The kid frowned. "Well. No. But I mean…"

Nick shook his head in disgust. "Man, you need to

call her. Let her know she only needs to be mourning your absence, not your death."

By the horrified expression in Johnny's eyes, Nick guessed the boy never thought about his mother thinking the worst. Nick inclined his head. "The phone's waiting."

Johnny spun on his heels and raced inside, slamming the door behind him.

Nick let out a heavy breath. *Andrews, you're a hypocrite.* Time to break out that stationery Claire had given him. But what would he say to his parents?

The hairs on the back of Nick's nape rose a split second before he heard Tyler demand, "What'd ya do to Johnny?"

Nick pivoted to face Tyler. The teen's eyes glittered angrily. His hands were fisted and jittery. Nick narrowed his gaze. Interesting. Tyler was ready to brawl with him in defense of Johnny. Maybe runaways had their own code of honor. Nick could respect that. Even though looking at the kid stirred up painful memories, igniting the anger that never seemed to extinguish itself.

Nick wasn't about to defend himself to Tyler, nor was he going to break Johnny's confidence by revealing what they'd talked about. Really, he'd just as soon Tyler took a swing at him. But knowing that it would upset Claire, he deliberately relaxed his stance and shrugged. "When you gotta go, you gotta go."

Tyler's challenging gaze wavered slightly with doubt.

Nick diverted his attention. "Since you're so good at painting, I have some signs that need to be made."

Nick walked away and a few seconds later Tyler followed. Nick explained to him what they were after. Signs to advertise the spring picnic basket auction.

Tyler gave a curt nod before organizing the supplies. Nick watched with interest the way he lined each can of paint up, laid out the different-size poster board that Claire had brought home one day last week. The kid seemed to be assessing the situation, approaching it like a puzzle.

Tyler glanced over his shoulder. "What?"

Nick held up his hands, palms out. "Nothing. I'll be in the house if you have a problem."

Tyler turned back to his task as if Nick had already disappeared.

Nick walked inside with a frown. He didn't get that kid. Didn't want to. All he had to do was remember Serena, and that a punk like the one out front killed her. He wasn't going to let anything bad happen to Claire.

Johnny was sitting at the counter with the phone to his ear. From the pained expression on his young face, Nick surmised the conversation with Johnny's mother was pretty heavy.

"Yeah, Mom. I know. I'm sorry." Johnny dropped his head into his free hand. "Aw, Mom, don't cry again. I'm okay. I'm here at this…" Johnny looked at Nick.

Nick nodded his encouragement.

"I'm at this shelter place. In Pineridge. No, Mom. Please." Johnny rolled his eyes. "They're real nice here." He listened for a few moments. "Okay, hold on." He held the phone away from his ear and grimaced. "She, uh, wants to talk with you."

Nick's solar plexus spasmed, forcing the air from his lungs as effectively as a punch to the gut. He wasn't qualified to speak to the mother of a runaway. Where was Claire? He slowly took the phone. "Hello?"

"I sure hope this is legitimate because if it isn't, I'll have you in jail so fast your head will spin. I want my son home," the female voice on the other end of the line snarled.

A mama bear defending her cub. Obviously, she hadn't considered her son a burden. Nick cleared his throat. "Mrs...?" He looked expectantly at Johnny.

"Kent," Johnny supplied.

"Kent," Mrs. Kent snapped at the same time.

Nick took a deep breath. "Mrs. Kent. The Zone is a teen shelter run by Claire Wilcox. She—"

"I want to speak to her," Mrs. Kent interrupted.

"She's in a meeting at the moment but the second she is able, I will have her call you."

"Well, who are you?"

Grimacing, Nick wasn't sure how to answer that. "I...I help out Claire."

"How do I know you haven't kidnapped my son for some depraved purpose?"

He could tell she was working herself up. He tried for a soothing tone. "Why don't you contact the Pineridge Police Department? Ask for Officer Bob Grand. He will vouch for The Zone."

"Believe me, I will."

The sound of the front door opening brought welcome relief. Nick waved Claire over with a sharp flick of his wrist.

Into the phone he said, "Could you hold on one moment, please?" He covered the mouthpiece with his hand as Claire approached, her eyes questioning. "Johnny's mother."

Claire's eyes went wide and a soft "Ohhh," escaped her parted lips. Her gaze swung to Johnny. He gave her a half smile and half grimace.

Still holding his hand over the mouthpiece, Nick extended the phone to her. "You've got to reassure her that he's okay and explain who you are. Her name's Mrs. Kent."

Claire's eyes narrowed. "What's the scoop?"

Not waiting for Johnny to respond, Nick explained, "He ran because his dad took off. Thought his mom and sisters would be better off without another mouth to feed. His mom's not so happy."

Without batting an eye, she took the phone. "Hello, Mrs. Kent. My name is Claire Wilcox and I run The Zone, a teen shelter here in Pineridge."

Winded as if he'd run the New York City marathon, Nick left Claire to her work and headed for his bike. Johnny wasn't such a bad kid, after all.

Score one for Claire and The Zone.

The back roads on the outskirts of Pineridge were becoming familiar to Nick. He'd found a mile-long stretch of flat road where he could wind up the engine and let go full throttle. Though the road wasn't a curved track and there were no fans cheering, he felt the same exhilarating rush of adrenaline as if he were flat-track racing.

Short-lived.

Temporary.

Unlike Claire.

There was nothing temporary about her. She was the kind of girl his mother would approve of. The kind of woman Serena would have liked. The kind of woman who deserved forever.

He didn't have forever in him. Not anymore.

He took comfort in knowing he'd been up-front with her. Neither one of them had illusions that he was staying for good.

He parked his bike near the front cement stairs leading into The Zone. The most heavenly smell drifted out the door as he walked in. The scents of savory spices evoked memories of family dinners. All the laughter, the contentment. He yearned for hearth and home. Things he'd denied himself for the past two years.

Little Nick barked as he raced to greet him. Nick petted the dog. Dodging wet kisses, Nick realized the small animal had worked its way into his heart. Better a puppy than a blue-eyed blonde.

Claire paused in the act of serving dinner. Her hair was caught back in a barrette at the nape of her graceful neck. Her jeans embraced her gentle curves. A flash of skin showed at her midriff where her tank top rose as she leaned forward to dish out the wonderful-smelling casserole in her hands. The warmth in her eyes and her smile trapped the air in his lungs.

"Hello." Her greeting was equally warm. "Have a good ride?"

"I did." The invigorating ride had cleared his head

and his heart for a moment. He savored such moments. "That smells wonderful."

She grinned wider. "Hopefully it will taste good. Mindy and I made it up."

His gaze raked over the three teenagers sitting at the table. Tyler had his elbows on the tabletop, his face averted from Nick. Johnny poured himself some milk. Mindy gave him a tentative smile. "That was nice of you to help out," Nick said to the young girl.

Her smiled grew and she ducked her head.

Claire patted his arm. "Go wash up."

He shrugged out of his leather jacket and hung it on the coatrack by the front door, then went to wash his hands. When he came out of the bathroom, he noticed Gwen had joined the group at the table. A thick braid hung down her back and an open textbook lay in her lap. She glanced up as he approached and waved a quick greeting before returning her attention to her book. Claire handed him a full plate of casserole, salad and bread and offered him a fork and a napkin.

"Thank you," he said.

"What would you like to drink?"

"A bottle of water would be great." He tracked her movements to the fridge, his gaze drinking in the sight of her. She came back and handed him a cold bottle. On the outside of the plastic container, her prints showed in the condensation. Small, delicate hands.

She sat at the table, leaving him standing alone. He was tired of being alone.

Tonight he would join Claire's world. He just hoped he survived the visit.

He sat in the empty chair and enjoyed the surprised look on Claire's pretty face. "So, what happened while I was out?"

She looked at him, her expression the epitome of bliss. "Nothing."

Sunset filled The Zone with radiant rays of orange and gold that shone through the windows, casting long shadows across the furniture as Claire descended the stairs. The Zone was finally quiet after the ruckus of dinner and TV. Now the kids were safely tucked in bed.

Interestingly enough, Tyler's response to her mothering wasn't what she expected. She'd thought he'd rebel with loud words and angry actions when she came in to say lights out. He'd scowled at her fiercely, turned over and faced the wall without another word. Obviously, his gruff demeanor was a defense against the world. That gave her hope. He wasn't unredeemable.

She still couldn't get over Nick joining her and the teens for dinner at the table. The atmosphere had been reasonably amicable. Nick had drawn Johnny out with talk of motorcycles. Mindy had even ventured into the conversation. Gwen had closed her book and engaged, as well. The only blight had been Tyler's smart-mouthed comments and Nick's smoldering anger every time he looked at the boy.

But she wouldn't let that ruin the good that had been done that day. She was ecstatic that Nick had done way beyond what she could have ever expected or hoped with Johnny.

Admiration and affection unfurled in her chest. Nick had somehow managed to get Johnny to not only open up, but to call and reconcile with his mother. It took a man relating to a young man to accomplish that. She was so thankful Johnny's history didn't include abuse and neglect. Just a misguided attempt to help his mother.

A soft glow illuminated the window in the new back door. She headed in that direction and peeked through the door's square, curtainless window.

Nick sat on the top stair, his shoulders hunched. Little Nick lay beside him chewing on a bone. Her brows drew together until she realized Nick was furiously writing on the stationery she'd given him.

Yes! She couldn't help the satisfied grin on her face. This was an important step in mending whatever broken fence separated Nick from his parents. She was so proud of him. Now, if she could only ferret out his dreams.

Claire moved away from the window. She didn't want Nick to think she was spying on him. She sat on the couch, slipped off her shoes and tucked her feet beneath her. Closing her eyes, she silently talked with God, telling him about the day and how grateful she was for all of His blessings.

A little while later, the back door opened and Nick stepped in. His presence filled The Zone with the contrasting elements of calmness and energy. Her senses went on heightened alert. Awareness like a homing beacon tracked him to the living room.

Little Nick leapt onto the couch and into her lap,

licking at her face. "Oh, yes, I love you, too," she said while dodging his kisses.

Nick sat on the couch a mere cushion's space away. Her pulse quickened. His scent, masculine and clean, enveloped her as she breathed in.

"So…quite the day," he said, his voice a low rumble she felt in her chest.

She set Little Nick back on the floor while trying to control her attraction to Nick. "Yes. It's been an amazing day. For both of us." She proceeded to tell him about Mindy's revelations. Every time her gaze met his, her heart skipped a beat.

Nick whistled low through his teeth. "That's rough. What are you going to do?"

She plucked a lint ball from the edge of the couch and rolled it between her index finger and her thumb. "Contact the proper authorities and her mother." She grimaced, knowing the battle that lay ahead. "I'm praying her mom will wake up and see the truth."

"Are you sure she's telling the truth?" he asked as he stretched an arm across the back of the couch.

"Yes. I believe her." She studied his arresting face. His strong jaw, shadowed by a manly beard, made her itch to feel the burn of his whiskers. His tanned skin stretched taut over his finely sculpted cheekbones. Those dark eyes that entranced her. She enjoyed looking at him.

He reached for her hair, gently twining a lock through his fingers. The intimacy of the gesture caught her off guard with a jolt. She fought back the urge to scoot closer and snuggle up against him. Like a married couple.

She swallowed. "I…I promised Mrs. Kent I'd bring Johnny home tomorrow. They live about forty-five minutes away in Beaverton. The poor woman was beside herself with worry. She'd thought something horrible had happened to him. In this day and age, I don't blame her."

Nick nodded empathetically. "If you don't mind, I'll take Johnny home."

"Really?" Claire tucked her chin and stared at Nick. A little dumbfounded with surprise, she said, "Uh, sure. You know where my keys are."

A mischievous gleam entered his eyes. "I think the bike would be better."

"Oh." Understanding dawned. Tenderness exploded in her chest. "Much better. He'll be thrilled."

Nick grinned and her heart thumped against her ribs with all kinds of hopes and needs and wants. But she couldn't muster up her defenses. Nick was systematically removing the barricade she'd erected around her heart without even realizing he was doing so. She was going to have to find some cement left within her to resist his powerful pull.

Obviously, there were some lessons she had trouble learning.

Chapter Thirteen

The next morning dawned with dark clouds threatening rain. Spring in Oregon. One minute nice and temperate and then the next moment the rains appeared, giving the soil and vegetation a cleansing drink. Though the state needed the rainwater to keep the greenery lush, Claire didn't like the idea of Nick and Johnny astride a motorcycle on wet pavement.

The mood was somber as Johnny said his goodbyes. Mindy sniffed back tears but smiled gamely as she hugged her friend.

Tyler's hooded eyes observed everything from where he stood at the bottom of the stairs. He didn't come close and wish Johnny well. "Whatever," had been his response to Johnny's earlier goodbye.

Claire gave Tyler a worried glance. For all his supposed indifference, he had to be feeling something. She looked back to where Johnny was climbing on the back of Nick's bike with a huge grin. The helmet Claire had worn fit the boy well.

Her gaze locked with Nick's. Her own concern reflected in his eyes. Would Tyler act out over this? She squared her shoulders and gave Nick a quick shake of her head and mouthed, "It'll be okay." She was confident she could deal with whatever Tyler tried to dish out.

Nick's eyes narrowed as he looked from her to Tyler and back. "You call Bob if you need anything. I'll be back in a few hours."

She should have bristled at his protectiveness. Instead, she found it touching. "I will. You be careful." She glanced up at the swollen clouds.

"A little rain won't hurt," Nick murmured.

She nodded, taking his assurance at face value. Of course, he'd have ridden in the rain before. She hugged Johnny one last time then squeezed Nick's arm.

His lopsided grin made her lungs stall. Then he started the motorcycle. The rhythmic rumble vibrated right through her. "I never got my second promised ride."

"When I come back."

She grinned. "I'll hold you to that."

He and Johnny rode away. Claire watched until they were out of sight, her heart squeezing slightly. She sighed. Oh, baby. She was in deep trouble, because already she missed Nick and couldn't wait for him to return.

Expectations only lead to disappointments.

It's okay to have feelings for people, Sandy had said.

Her feelings for Nick were complicated and unclear. She wasn't ready to examine them too closely. She didn't know if she ever would be.

"Claire?"

Mindy's voice pulled Claire from her thoughts. Gathering her weak resolve to not hope for anything from Nick, she focused her attention on the young girl.

"Yes?"

"Will you call my mom?"

With a smile, Claire looped her arm around Mindy. Pride that she was helping the girl so soon filled her chest. They walked inside together with Tyler bringing up the rear, and Claire was glad to have something else to concentrate on other than her growing feelings toward Nick.

Feelings that terrified her.

Claire first informed social services of the crime against Mindy and then called Mindy's mother. The conversation turned heated. Shari Vaughn didn't want to believe her daughter had been molested. It wasn't uncommon for parents of molested children to resist the truth because in acknowledging what had happened, they had to admit they'd been unable to protect their child.

Mindy had been reluctant to talk with her mother and Claire hadn't pressed. She assured the girl they weren't giving up. It would take time.

Mindy retreated to her room. Tyler lounged in front of the T.V. with Little Nick in his lap. Wanting to give Mindy space and not up to the challenge of delving into Tyler's psyche, Claire decided to do laundry.

After changing her own sheets, she took a fresh set of twin sheets out of the cupboard in the bathroom and went to Nick's room.

As had become her routine on every third day, she laid the fresh linens on the corner of his neatly made bed. She knew tomorrow she'd find the dirty sheets piled tidily on the floor by the door. She tried not to think about how uncomfortable he probably was sleeping on the twin mattress. Not once had he complained.

She went down the stairs with her load. As she passed the coatrack by the front door an envelope lying on the floor caught her attention. A piece from the stationery she'd given Nick. She snatched up the envelope. It was sealed and addressed to Mr. and Mrs. Andrews, Long Island, New York. It must have fallen from his jacket pocket.

Whatever rift lay between him and his parents wouldn't be healed with him clear on the other side of the country. His parents deserved to know he was alive and well. They deserved to know what he'd written.

She dropped the basket off in the laundry room and went to her desk where she put a stamp on the corner of the envelope. Stacking Nick's letter with her other outgoing mail, she was confident Nick would thank her later.

The late afternoon sun appeared after the morning showers. The golden rays brought steam rising from the leaves of the plants and heightened the scent of moist earth. Claire loved to breathe in the fresh, crisp air after a rain shower. She stood on the new back porch contemplating how a patio table and chairs would fit on the square expanse of wood.

She heard the low rumble of Nick's motorcycle. Her heart did a little thump in her chest as he rounded the corner on the paved path, stopping his bike close to the porch steps.

He smiled. "Are you ready for that ride?"

Excitement bubbled and pulsed in her veins. Yes, she wanted to sit close to Nick and wrap her arms around his waist as the wind whipped by. But she couldn't. She shook her head as she quelled the rebellious chorus of groans going on in her head. "I can't."

He raised a brow. "Why not?"

"I can't leave." But, oh, she'd like to.

"We won't go far." The smoothness of his deep voice contrasted with the rough rumbling of his Harley.

"What if they need something?" She had to be there for the teens. She'd brought them to The Zone—she couldn't go off and play, leaving them alone.

He contemplated her for a moment. "How about we ride around the park? I'll even let you drive," his silky voice challenged.

His suggestion sent her pulse spinning. "I wouldn't know the first thing about driving one of these."

He held out the extra helmet. "It's easy. Like driving a car." His eyes took on a roguish gleam. "Besides, I'm not going to let you ride this alone."

She still hesitated.

"Come on, Claire. You deserve to play," he coaxed.

"We'll stay close by?" The eagerness in her voice betrayed her inner conflict.

His infectious grin was irresistible and drew her down the stairs. "We'll never lose sight of the building."

Heady anticipation had her reaching for the helmet. She slid it on her head and buckled the clasp under her chin. Nick scooted back and patted the seat in front of him. She swallowed down her giddy excitement and tried for decorum, but couldn't stop the silly grin on her face.

She climbed on the Harley and looked over her shoulder at him, waiting for her lesson. His broad chest rested against her back as he leaned forward. He guided her hands to the handlebars. His big, warm hands closed over hers on the black grips, making concentration difficult.

"Right hand has the front brakes. Squeeze gently," his deep voice intoned, causing her to shiver at the thrill of sitting so close, so intimately with him. He applied pressure to her hand and demonstrated the squeezing of the brake lever.

"Left hand works the clutch." Again he demonstrated with her hand trapped beneath his—she ridiculously felt sheltered and secure.

With his right foot, he nudged her foot onto the pedal. "Rear brake. When you brake to stop, use both in tandem. Rear brake won't completely stop you and the front alone will send you flying over the handlebars."

She absorbed that. She had no wish to go head over heels onto the pavement.

He reached down and tucked her left foot under a small bar. When he straightened, he said, "Left foot works the gears. We'll stay in first. Squeeze the clutch and press your foot down at the same time just like in a car. Right hand twists the throttle back slightly until you're ready to open her up."

"Whoa. Much more complicated than I'd imagined." She tried to remember his instructions.

He laughed. "You'll do fine." He shifted on the seat behind her. "You ready?" he asked, his breath tickling her exposed neck below the helmet.

Trepidation hammered in her ears. She nodded.

"Okay. Clutch, gear, throttle."

She tried the sequence. She usually didn't have a problem with coordination, but as she pressed and squeezed and twisted she felt awkward and clumsy. The bike lurched and died. Her heart jumped in her throat. Nick's laugh vibrated against her back. He started the engine again.

She glanced back at him. The enjoyment on his face and the encouragement in his eyes affected her deeply. This man had brought so much into her life. So much she hadn't realized was missing. He'd brought fun, joy and companionship when for so long her life had been about achieving her goal. About staying safely behind her walls.

"Try again," he said.

She blew out a breath. Okay. She could do this. How hard could it really be? She tried again. The bike lurched but didn't die this time.

"Throttle," Nick's voice commanded.

"Oh, yeah. All three. At the same time. Right."

She tried again, this time rolling the rubber-coated throttle back as she worked the clutch and the gear. They moved forward, startling her into squeezing the front brake. The sudden jarring stop bounced her on the seat.

Nick's arm came around her waist, steadying her.

"Again," he said.

She tried again. Again. And again until she thought she'd scream with frustration. Sweat trickled down her neck. Then, finally, she managed to coordinate her limbs and they moved slowly forward.

"Take us to the road," Nick suggested.

She did. Nick let her be in control as she drove the Harley down the street. When they came to the intersection, he leaned closer, pressing himself flat against her as he helped her steer the bike in a wide arc. He released his hands from her and straightened. Cool air rushed between them as she drove the bike back down the street.

"Use both brakes when you're ready to slow and stop," he instructed.

She pressed with her foot and squeezed with her hand and they slowed to a stop in front of The Zone. Gwen, Mindy and Tyler stood on the front porch. Gwen and Mindy clapped and ran down the walkway to them. Tyler remained on the porch, his arms crossed over his chest and a bored expression on his face.

Claire reached up and took off the helmet. She met Nick's glittering gaze. "That was fun."

"Yes. It was." The underlying tone lacing his words captivated her. Made her aware of herself as a woman and him as a man. A couple. Her heart stalled.

"Can I have a ride?" Mindy asked, her eyes wide and her expression eager.

Grateful for the intrusion of reality, Claire slipped from the seat. Nick scooted forward on the seat and indicated for Mindy to climb on the back. He took her for a ride around the park.

"You two are good together," Gwen commented.

Claire tracked Nick. "We're…friends."

"Right."

At the disbelief in Gwen's tone, Claire shifted her gaze to the young woman at her side. "Really. We're just friends."

Gwen's jewel-colored eyes twinkled. "If you say so." She checked her watch. "Ohhh, got to go get ready for work." She disappeared inside.

Claire returned her attention to Nick. There couldn't ever be anything more between them. Could there?

She turned her mind away from that thought. There was no use in hoping, expecting more. Life didn't work that way. Not for her.

The last few days before the auction were a whirl-wind of activity, with people coming and going from The Zone. Claire felt like a revolving door. The fund-raising committee worked endlessly on publicity and decorations.

Pastor Gary offered his services as the auctioneer. Bob stopped by several times offering his help, but Claire knew he was keeping an eye on Nick as well as the teens. Bob had made a habit of checking in ever since Mrs. Kent had called him.

Tyler was still sullen and uncommunicative. Claire noticed he had a certain artistic flare that came out in the most simple of paint projects. He'd done a great job on the signs for the auction.

She'd tried to talk to him about his creativity, but he'd shot her down with a smart remark before withdrawing to his corner of the living room. She'd let it go. If she pushed he'd bolt altogether.

She'd resorted to asking Mindy if she knew anything about Tyler's background. She learned the boy's father was in prison for manslaughter, leaving him at the mercy of his crack-addicted mother, who used lit cigarettes and a thick belt to control her child. Tyler had been taken from his mother and placed in foster care. Mindy had shrugged and said that didn't work out so he ran. Claire's heart cried for Tyler. She had to figure out a way to help him.

The day of the auction arrived with a beautiful cloudless sky. The evergreen-scented air was ripe with anticipation that Claire felt deep in her bones. It seemed even the two teens felt the invigorating impatience. They rose early, dressed and helped Nick set up the chairs in the park across the street.

It had been decided to set up the auction in the park, using the gazebo for the auctioneer, with tables in front to display the many baskets.

Claire's own basket sat on the table with the other thirty-six baskets donated for the auction. She'd found a white wicker, oval-shaped basket with a high handle at the antique store in town. Mindy had helped her decorate it with purple ribbons and silk flowers.

For the fare inside, Claire had dug out some of her aunt's favorite recipes. Spicy fried chicken, dill-and sour-cream potato salad, blueberry turnovers, hot-and-smoky baked beans and green apple slices with French brie. Gwen had also added a gold foil box of chocolates.

People started arriving at the appointed hour and soon the festivities were under way.

"Do I hear sixty? Remember folks, this is for The Zone," Pastor Gary said smoothly into the microphone from his perch in the gazebo.

"Eighty," called a man at the back of the crowd.

Claire strained to see over the anxious ladies standing off to the side of the gazebo. Ah, Steve Jordan was bidding on his wife's basket.

"We have eighty. Do I hear ninety?"

"I'll take that for one hundred." An older man sitting next to his striking, silver-haired wife raised his hand.

Claire's gaze swung to Steve, who was silently communicating to his wife. Claire watched the exchange as an odd yearning rose, squeezing at her chest. The couple didn't need words, just facial expressions and hand gestures Claire guessed came from years of togetherness.

She'd never experienced that kind of connectedness, that oneness only couples who truly loved each other had. She'd read about such stuff in novels and caught glimpses of it here and there, mostly between Sandy and Dave Wellington. But it was for other people, not her. Yet...

She fingered the envelope in her pocket as her gaze sought out Nick. She found him leaning casually against a tree off to the side of the festivities.

Across the crowd their eyes locked. His magnetic draw reached out to her and a maelstrom of heat flooded through her, quickening her breath and burning her cheeks.

She had felt that oneness. She'd felt that connection with Nick. She hadn't recognized it, nor understood the implications of such a phenomenon.

Deep in her heart she realized she loved him.

The thought staggered her. She clutched the back of the chair in front of her. She loved Nick.

But a gulf existed between them.

She didn't understand what drove him, what inspired such rage to fill his eyes when he looked at Tyler. She didn't know what haunted him and brought that desolate expression to his face when he didn't realize she was watching.

She wanted to shrug off her feelings. To smash the love down with the indifference and detachment that had served her so well over the years. But the feeling expanding in her chest had a life of its own and wouldn't be denied.

Walls imprison as well as protect, Nick had said.

There was truth to that. She'd tried to stay emotionally safe, had tried to keep her feelings under wraps for many years, and still ended up with the pain of loneliness. She just hadn't recognized the pain.

Until Nick roared into her life.

Still, she forced her gaze away from Nick as she tried to deal with this devastating revelation.

"Sold to the gentlemen in the front."

Claire rounded up her thoughts and focused on the proceedings. Her breath caught somewhere between her lungs and her throat as her basket was brought to the podium.

"Let's see." Pastor Gary flipped over the card with the information on it. "This beautiful, romantic basket is donated by our own Claire Wilcox. Filled with goodies for two."

Romantic? Claire smiled wanly at the sea of faces turning her way. She hadn't thought in terms of romance but, yeah, she supposed the basket had a romantic flare.

"We'll start the bidding at twenty. Do I have twenty?"

"Claire."

She turned to find Mindy's tear-stained face peering at her from around the side of the gazebo. She hurried to her. "What's wrong? Are you hurt?"

The girl shook her head. "Tyler's gone."

Claire blinked. "Gone? What happened?"

Mindy wiped at her nose. "I told him…I want to go home."

A surge of joy, of satisfaction ran rampant through Claire. Yes! This was what she'd been gently pushing for ever since she'd met Mindy. Even though Claire hadn't been able to bond with her own mother, she was happy that Mindy would be able to. Shari Vaughn had called several times, having finally accepted the truth.

Claire wrapped her arms around the teen. "I'm so proud of you." She leaned back to look into Mindy's face. "It's going to be okay."

"But I feel bad for Tyler. He doesn't have anyone.

He can't go home and I don't think my mom would let me bring him home."

Claire sighed and hugged the girl again. "We'll look for Tyler, I promise. We'll find a way to make it better for him. Okay?"

Mindy gave her a watery smile. "Okay."

Keeping an arm around Mindy, Claire led her toward the front of the gazebo. "Let's go see if anyone bought my basket."

Her basket was still on the podium. Pastor Gary pointed to the side. "The gentleman bids five hundred. Do I hear six?"

Claire's mouth dropped. Five hundred dollars for her little basket? Who on earth would do such a thing? She went on tiptoe trying to see who was bidding. All she saw was a sea of faces, some she recognized, others she didn't.

"I have six from the back. Do I hear seven?"

Claire searched the rear of the audience but she missed who'd made the bid. Her gaze tripped over Nick, where he still leaned up against the tree, his arms folded across his chest, his expression neutral.

A movement in her peripheral vision caught her attention. Bob raised his arm. Her eyes widened. She didn't know what to feel about that. Flattered, but Bob? Why would he do that? She prayed he didn't expect to share it with her. Hopefully he'd decided that The Zone was a good thing.

"Seven it is." Pastor Gary looked toward the back of the crowd. "Do we have eight?"

Claire scrutinized the crowd of people. Steve Jordan

was back there but he didn't make a move. She recognized the owner of the hardware store but he didn't move.

"Eight, we have eight. How about nine?"

Claire stared at the pastor. She hadn't seen anyone make a move or say anything. Who was bidding? There was a pregnant pause then, slowly, Bob lifted his hand. Claire pushed her way through the throng of ladies so she could get a better view. Lori nudged her with an elbow and gave her a grin.

The pastor smiled and inclined his head. "We have nine from the gentleman in the front. Are we going to go for a thousand?"

Claire scanned the crowd and snagged on Nick as he flexed his wrist, holding up two fingers. Ripples of excitement washed over her skin.

"Two?" Pastor Gary questioned. "Are you bidding two thousand?"

Nick nodded. Claire gasped. No way!

"The bid is two thousand." The pastor looked to Bob. Bob shook his head. "Two thousand going once. Two thousand going twice. Sold to the gentleman in the back."

There was an excited buzz through the crowd. Claire smiled feebly at the women surrounding her; their voices seemed far away as her gaze met Nick's. He gave her a slow grin that left her breathless.

A seed of hope began to sprout, taking root through the thick layer of dashed expectations surrounding her heart.

Chapter Fourteen

Two thousand for a picnic basket? At least Bob hadn't won it.

As Claire made her way through the crowd, Nick found he couldn't work up much regret for his actions. She was lovely and generous and kind, this woman who took such pains to make a difference in the lives of those around her. His respect for her grew every day.

Claire had overcome an abusive childhood, had survived life on the streets and now strove to make a safe haven for at-risk and displaced teens.

The tide of anger that ebbed and flowed within him broke, slicing a path straight through his heart. A bitter burn simmered in his veins. Regardless of his feelings for Claire, he had to end this now before either of them got hurt. He couldn't risk having another woman ripped from his life.

His faith wouldn't survive. He wouldn't survive.

"That was very generous of you, Nick," Claire stated as she stopped in front of him.

His intentions had been less than noble. She'd realize that soon enough. "Claire, let's take a walk."

As Claire fell into step with Nick, an uneasy chill pricked her skin. She rubbed her arms. They walked away from the crowded gazebo farther into the park. The scent of cut grass rose up from the ground with each step.

She glanced at Nick. How could he afford the two thousand for her basket when she'd thought he couldn't afford a hotel?

Her mouth twisted with wry amusement. His request to stay had been a ruse to keep her from being alone and unprotected, after all.

And strangely, she didn't mind. Having him around gave her a peaceful sense of security she'd never known before. And left her breathless, because he'd never promised to stay.

His somber, almost sad demeanor confused her. She worried her bottom lip. Had something happened? Did he know that Tyler had run away again?

"It went really well today," Nick stated.

"It did," she agreed. "Better than I could have imagined. The only blip on the happy meter is Tyler taking off."

His brow flickered briefly with surprise. "That's for the best. Make sure you mention that to Bob."

Claire frowned. She just didn't get it. He knew what Tyler had endured, yet he couldn't give the boy an inch. "Why should I tell Bob?"

Nick stopped walking. He stood tall and stiff. Unreachable. He looked as if he were holding a raw emotion in check. The effort thinned his lips and hardened his jaw. His eyes were hooded, as if he were deliberately trying to keep her out of his thoughts. "It's time for me to leave, Claire."

Her stomach dropped. She'd known this was coming. She expected it, but after realizing that she loved him, she couldn't fight the choking hurt crawling up her spine and settling in her throat. It was too late to pull out her detachment shield for protection. By letting herself love him, she had set herself up for more than mere disappointment.

"Where will you go?" she forced the words past the constricting lump in her throat. Her world was spinning out of control. She'd become used to him. Used to the laughter and light he'd brought into her life.

He looked toward the blue sky. His broad shoulders moved in a shrug. "I haven't decided. It doesn't matter. Anywhere."

Anywhere away from her. Agony gripped her soul. "You could stay."

He gave a terse shake of his head. "No." He ran a hand through his hair. His fingers left grooves in their wake. "I need to find peace. I have to go."

He grazed his knuckle down her cheek. She closed her eyes against the yearning his touch evoked. "You'll be okay, Claire. You're surrounded by people who love you and who want to help. Those teens aren't a threat to you anymore. There's no need for me to be here."

"But there is," she protested. "I…" She swallowed

back the trepidation that told her not to go down this road. That warned she was destined for heartbreak and disappointment.

If she didn't say something, if she just let him walk away she'd be disappointed in herself.

He'd taught her it was okay to need people. That she didn't have to fear her expectations. It was okay to feel. The good and the bad. Her heart pounded so hard against her ribs she figured that any second, one would snap. "I need you."

That was as close to a declaration as she could come.

His face softened and he closed his eyes as if in pain. "I can't," he said in a harsh, raw voice. "You can't."

When he opened his eyes, the haunted hollowness of those dark depths stabbed at her.

"I'm sorry." The resignation, the defeat in those two words uttered so low she barely heard them, slammed into her like a train.

Tears stung her eyes as he took her hand and pressed a folded piece of paper into her palm. She unfolded the paper and stared. A cashier's check. Her knees threatened to buckle as the staggering amount registered. Ten thousand dollars.

"What is this?"

"A donation. A gift. It's whatever you want it to be," he said almost desperately.

"I don't want it." *I want you.*

His expression hardened. "Do what you will with it."

With long, purposeful strides he left her standing in the middle of the park holding his check, while her heart bled.

She looked over to the gazebo where the auction must have ended, because people were milling around, talking, laughing. A faint numbness hovered around the edges of the pain gripping her insides. Her detachment shield was ready. All she had to do was pick it up and cloak herself with indifference.

She knew how to mask the pain.

She started walking, slowly at first, then quicker as determination overtook the hurt.

No way was she going to let Nick off that easy. He couldn't roar into her life, turn it upside down and make her love him, and then think he could just roar out again without explaining why. Her business with Nick Andrews was not finished.

If she had her way, it was only beginning.

The Zone was quiet and still as Nick gathered his things together. He wondered where Tyler had taken off to. Would he go back to the warehouse or leave the town altogether? And how was Mindy taking Tyler's absence?

He jammed his clothes into his bag.

They are not my concern.

Yet…he should swing through nearby Beaverton to see Johnny, at least. The kid's father had up and disappeared without saying goodbye.

But I'm not the kid's father. I'm nothing to him and he's nothing to me.

Nick could use Tyler's disappearance as another excuse to stay. He could use the excuse that Claire needed him to protect her. But those excuses had lost their power. If he stayed it would be because of Claire. If he stayed he'd be opening himself up to the risk of losing her.

He heard light footsteps coming up the stairs. Claire.

He wiped a hand over his face, trying unsuccessfully to wipe away the memory of the hurt and disappointment in her clear moist eyes.

I need you.

The words echoed in his heart, kindling to his already burning anger. He didn't want her to need him. He didn't want to need her.

He didn't want to love her.

"Seems like we've done this routine before." Claire's voice held a hard edge.

He braced himself as he turned to face her. She was leaning in the doorway with her arms folded across her chest. Her eyes bright and narrowed with determination.

"Yes, well. There won't be a repeat performance."

"No, I don't suppose there will be. But don't you think it's time to fess up and tell me what's eating away at you? I know it's more than just not wanting to go into your father's business. You can barely contain your rage when you're around Tyler. What is it with you and him? If for no other reason, appease my curiosity."

More than curiosity motivated her to press. She wanted to help, heal him. She didn't have that power. No one did.

But she did deserve the truth. He steeled himself against the wave of grief rising up to cut off his air supply. "A teenager, a runaway, killed my wife."

She made a shocked little gasp. "Oh, Nick. I'm so sorry."

She reached out to him. He jerked back.

Hugging herself, she asked in a soft voice, "What happened?"

He tightened his jaw, not wanting to say the words, to dredge up the nightmare his life had become. "I was working late one night." His lips twisted wryly. "Later than usual. I can only guess Serena needed something from the store."

He fisted his hands, feeling the consuming rage fill his soul. "I'd told her a million times it wasn't safe to be out too late at night by herself, but she was so confident that she'd be okay. She was headstrong and stubborn."

His throat contracted, he had to work to keep going. "She was in front of the store when two rival teens started fighting. One pulled out a gun." He swallowed. "Witnesses say she was caught in the middle between the two when the boy opened fire, emptying the chamber."

Claire's whole posture and attitude changed, softened. Tears gathered in her eyes. Her face took on that "let me make it better look" she'd used with the kids. He averted his gaze as she came to him. He was powerless to stop her from wrapping her arms around his waist. He took a shuddering breath. Her comfort hurt. She couldn't make it better.

A moment of silence stretched. She stepped back, then she said in a voice tight with emotion, "That must have been devastating. Are you angry that she defied you?"

"No," he said vehemently. "It wasn't her fault."

She sniffed and took a deep breath. "But you can't hold the actions of one teenager against all of them. Just because a child, a teenager, runs away doesn't automatically make them a criminal."

A bitter laugh escaped. "There you go again, protecting them."

"I'm not trying to protect anyone, Nick. I'm trying to help *you*."

Her expression implored him to understand. He didn't. "You can't. No one can."

"Is that what you told your parents? Is that why you took off on your motorcycle, because you wouldn't let anyone help you?"

"They were smothering me with their concern. They wanted—" His fist clenched. "They want me to forgive that kid. I left because I wanted to find some peace. I just want to make sense of all this."

She moved closer and laid a warm hand on his arm. Her touch comforted, yet stirred up so much turmoil at the same time he felt a physical ache. "Sometimes life doesn't make sense. We just have to make the most out of our lives."

"How can I make the most of my life when I'm being punished for wanting a good life? I'd worked so hard to make a successful career, a stable future for us. It was all for nothing."

Her grip tightened. "You aren't being punished. God doesn't work that way."

The conviction in her voice echoed through the tiny room.

He let out a sharp breath. He'd heard that enough

after Serena's death. His parents, his pastor, his friends.

No. It had to have been his greed, his grasping for more that brought on God's wrath.

Her determined gaze tore through him. "My aunt once told me that in times of tragedy and hardship, we face the temptation to make God our adversary instead of our advocate. God's not trying to hurt you.

"And yes, He has punished people who were acting in deliberate disobedience, but that's not you. The fact that you still seek Him in the middle of your pain is a testament to your faith."

A sharp stab of misery pierced his soul. "But I can't find Him."

Her hand reached up to touch his cheek, the gesture tender and heartbreaking. "He's here, Nick. Waiting, under all the anger and hatred. He's waiting for you to rest in His love."

Nick zipped his bag and her hand fell away. The ache continued as her words bounced around his head. His heart.

She held out an envelope to him.

"This came in this morning's mail for you," she said.

He stared at the rectangular paper with narrowed eyes. Slowly he reached for it. "This is from my parents. How…?"

"I mailed your letter."

He frowned as the air left his lungs. "I'd thought I lost it."

"I found it. Mailed it."

Remembering what he'd written to them made his

muscles tense and his gut tighten more. He'd told them about Claire, about the fire and the teenagers. He'd confessed his growing feelings for Claire.

He ripped open the envelope and pulled out a sheet of paper. Another folded envelope fell out and landed at his feet.

He read his mother's flowing script. A viselike pressure built in his chest. He shifted his gaze away from his mother's words to the envelope on the floor.

When would his punishment end?

Claire watched the color drain from Nick's face. His hand trembled and released the letter. It fluttered to the floor, landing so that it covered the second envelope.

Concern arced through her, battering her already wounded soul. "What is it?"

He shook his head, his features harsh, his eyes grim.

She took a hold of his hand. He felt cold to her touch. "Nick?"

He jerked away from her. His eyes glittered with fierceness. "You can't fix me. I'm not one of your projects."

She drew back. Was that how he saw her work with the teens, as a project? Her rational side said he was lashing out, directing his anger at her because she was handy. She tried for a gentle tone. "Let me help you."

His laugh was dry, brittle. "So you can feel good? Sorry, but I can't accommodate you." He kicked at the letter. "Or them."

He pushed past her and through the door.

Stung, she stood rooted to the spot as the echo of his steps slowly faded with the slam of the front door.

She picked up the letter and unopened envelope. Tears rolled down her cheeks as she read the letter, the plea from his mother for him to return, to please read the enclosed letter from the teenager who'd killed Serena—his wife.

The rumble of Nick's bike rattled Claire's composure. He was right. She couldn't help because he alone held the power to choose forgiveness.

With a sob, she ran down the stairs and out the door. She planted herself in front of his bike in the gravel driveway.

"Get out of the way, Claire."

She moved to his side where she leaned close so her words would be clearly heard. "Walls imprison as well as protect. You'll never find peace as long as you're shackled by unforgiveness. You'll never be free to live again. To love again."

She shoved the unopened envelope into his chest and kept pushing until his hand reached up to clasp her wrist.

He pulled her nearer until his mouth was close to her ear. His warm breath fanned over her cheek, drying her tears. "You're wrong."

She turned her head and pressed her lips to his and put all the love and care and hope she had within her into the kiss.

Abruptly, she broke away.

His confusion showed in his eyes. Her heart beat furiously. She wanted to continue to lecture, to teach him and guide him to forgiveness. But deep down she knew she was done. It was all up to him now.

His choice.

She turned and walked away, feeling as if her heart was caving in on itself within the walls of her rib cage. When he revved the Harley's engine and she heard the tires crunching on the gravel as he drove out of her life, she sank to the stairs of The Zone.

"Lord, he's in your hands now. I pray you'll help him because I couldn't."

Chapter Fifteen

Claire was wrong.

As the miles zipped by on Interstate Five South, another little fissure of air blew through Nick's confidence. The first crack had opened up when she'd turned her head and kissed him.

More fissures burst through the protective layer he'd erected around his heart until the holes bled into each other, creating a gaping abyss. As he left the Portland area behind, his unease grew. Grief and oppressive condemnation settled heavy on his shoulders, making the muscles tighten and contract.

He tried to shake it. Tried to shake off the echo of Claire's words. He rolled his shoulders and the envelope sticking out of the inside pocket on his jacket stabbed at him. He jerked.

The bike wobbled, making his stomach lurch. He merged into the slow lane of the freeway and then took the next off-ramp to the frontage road. He found a gravel turnout in the brush, a place that looked to be a cop spot.

Maneuvering the bike as far out of the way as possible, he shut off the engine and removed his helmet. Something wasn't right.

Riding always took the edge off his grief. He always felt the anticipation that up ahead he'd find peace, like some sort of burger joint with a drive-up window where he could just order some calm, some sanity, as an antidote for the chaos and slicing pain of losing Serena.

But that was before Claire.

Sometimes life doesn't make sense. You have to make the most of your life.

"What life?"

He'd had a good life once. An enviable life. A wonderful marriage, a satisfying job and lots of friends. A sharp ache of loss tightened his throat.

He yanked out the envelope. "Gone. All because of this kid."

Hatred breathed fire into his soul, but quick on its tail was Claire's soft, imploring voice taking him back to that day when they'd found the three teenagers.

They're going to learn to be harder and meaner and come out angrier.

Her words were like a knife gutting his midsection, laying open his fears, his pain. Would Serena be dead if someone had tried to help the kid who had killed her? Now that boy was in jail learning to be harder, meaner. Nick had never thought about the boy beyond his own hatred. Never wondered what drove the teen to use a gun that day.

Nick hadn't cared.

Until now.

The envelope burned in his trembling hand. He slipped a finger under the seal and ripped it open. The sound of tearing paper mingled with the raggedness of his breathing.

Feeling like he was on the pinnacle of some high cliff, he withdrew the folded letter.

He didn't want to do this. Didn't want to have this kid become more than just an object of his rage. But he couldn't stop the masochistic need to read the letter. He flipped open the page. Large, scrawling words in an uneven cadence filled the lines.

Nick read the letter once quickly. His throat closed against the boulder-size knot forming in his chest. He read back through the lines, his gaze stumbling over the three words that brought a burn to the back of his eyelids.

"Please, forgive me."

He mentally scrambled away from the edge of the cliff. He crumbled the letter in his hand and threw it into the bushes. "Never!"

Then as if she were standing right next to his bike, he heard Claire's words ringing in his head. *You'll never find peace as long as you're shackled by unforgiveness.*

He started the engine with jerky movements and in a spray of gravel, pulled out onto the road.

He'd had everything he could want.

You'll never be free to live again. To love again.

Serena, dear sweet Serena. She didn't deserve to die.

"Was I too greedy, too materialistic, Lord?"

You aren't being punished. God doesn't work that way.

"If I'm not being punished Lord, then why? Why did You let this happen?"

Sometimes life doesn't make sense.

He pulled over onto the shoulder of the road again and sat, his bike idling. The breathless, teetering-on-the-edge-of-a-long-fall feeling came over him, urging him to search his heart.

The last few weeks played themselves over in his head. Claire. Brave, determined, walled-up Claire.

So full of life, so compassionate.

So afraid to be hurt.

I need you.

Nick closed his eyes as he tumbled off that cliff. For two years he'd held on to his hate and anger to keep from feeling, to keep from hurting.

And one cute blond lady with the courage of King David shamed him for his lack of faith, his lack of mercy.

One beautiful woman with the wisdom of King Saul demonstrated God's love in a tangible way.

With one former runaway he had found peace.

He opened his eyes and resolve settled in. He checked the traffic and made a U-turn. Found the gravel turnout again. It took a few moments to find the letter in the bushes. When he did, he spread it out, smoothing the wrinkles, before carefully folding it and tucking it into his pocket.

Knowing he had to make things right with his

parents, he was back on the freeway headed east. He could only hold a prayer in his heart that Claire would give him another chance to claim her love when he returned.

Claire stood outside of The Zone and watched Mindy run into the arms of her mother. Shari Vaughn was a petite brunette with big eyes and a sweet smile.

Rough roads lay ahead, but the case agent who had been assigned to Mindy had assured Claire that Shari had indeed gotten rid of the abusive boyfriend. The man would be brought up on charges and Mindy would have to testify against him.

Shari was going to make a fresh start for her and her daughter in Yakima, Washington, where Shari's parents lived. Mindy was excited and nervous, but Claire knew it was for the best.

Mindy dragged her mother forward. "Mom, this is Claire."

"Hello." Claire extended her hand.

"Thank you, again," Shari said as they shook hands.

"My pleasure." Claire put an arm around Mindy, giving her a squeeze. "When you get settled, drop me a line, okay? Let me know you're all right."

Mindy turned into Claire's embrace and gave her a fierce hug. "I'll miss you."

Claire fought the tears gathering at the corners of her eyes. "I'll miss you, too. But I'll always be here if you need me."

Mindy stepped away and wiped her nose on the sleeve of the gray hooded sweatjacket. "You'll help Tyler?"

Claire nodded, not sure how she was going to manage that when he'd disappeared from town.

"Bye," Mindy said as she linked arms with her mother and walked to the blue four-door sedan Shari had arrived in.

Claire waved as the car pulled away. She heaved a contented sigh as she walked back inside. "Another successful ending. Lord, keep watch over her."

Inside The Zone an eerie silence wrapped around her, making the dull ache in her chest more acute. She found Little Nick curled up in his crate. She lifted him to her chest and hugged him close.

She missed Nick.

It'd been a week since he'd rolled out of her life, taking her heart with him. It was just her luck that when she'd come to terms with needing someone, he'd up and leave.

Over the course of the next month, amid the plans for The Zone's official opening, which had to be pushed back from July to mid-August, Claire finally located Tyler. The teen had made his way to neighboring Troutdale.

Per Bob's instructions, she went first to the police station where an Officer Nyguen had given her directions to a park where Tyler had last been seen. Once she found him, she was going to drag him back with her. The boy was self-destructive and in need of some guidance.

She found the wooded park easily. Since it was summer, the park was filled with kids and parents. A large wooden play structure dominated one end of the park with swings, monkey bars and a wobbly bridge.

Claire got out of her car and scanned the area. Her gaze snagged on a group of kids beneath a large oak tree at the far end of the grassy field. She couldn't be sure, but she thought the tall kid with his back to her was Tyler.

Mindful of the children, she worked her way around the play area. She crossed the grassy field, ducking a Frisbee, and jumping out of the way of a running black Labrador.

As she advanced on the group of boys, they fell into silence. Tyler spun around. "Wh…what are you doing here?"

Leveling a pointed stare at him, she said, "I could ask you that same question."

"Wow, man. This your mother?" a tall freckled kid with splotches of acne, asked.

An older, tougher-looking boy whistled through his teeth. "Hot. Definitely, hot."

Claire ignored them, but was amused to see Tyler shoot the rude offender a glare. She grabbed him by the hand and pulled him with her away from the influence of the boys. He jerked out of her grasp, but continued walking with her. Oh, he challenged her patience.

She gazed at him sternly. "Why'd you leave?"

His thin shoulders moved in a careless shrug beneath the red T-shirt he wore. He needed a bath and some food. Her heart twisted.

"A goodbye at least would have been nice," she said, keeping her tone even.

"Didn't think it mattered."

Claire knew that feeling, intimately. She put her hand on his arm, stopping him. "Tyler, you matter."

He scuffed his foot in the dirt and wouldn't meet her gaze.

"I want you to come back with me."

He looked up, his chin jutted out, his expression stubborn. "No."

She frowned. He was going to make her work for it. She was a trained counselor and all the methods and arguments forming in her head weren't worth the price of a warm blanket in the dead of winter if the boy didn't want to change.

I'm not one of your projects.

At the time she'd thought Nick was lashing out at her, but now she realized, his words were a truth she'd ignored.

Let them make their choice, Nick had once said.

Free will, the Bible called it.

She stared at Tyler, seeing beyond the attitude to the pain he so desperately tried to hide. He so reminded her of Gwen. The way she'd been at first.

Claire couldn't make Tyler seek help any more than she could make Nick choose to forgive. It had to come from within them.

Both Tyler and Nick needed to want to change their lives and be willing to do what was necessary. No matter how difficult.

"The Zone's open and waiting for you, Tyler. Anytime. There's no shame in asking for help."

She walked away. All she could do now was pray, and rest in God's love.

* * *

August fifteenth arrived with excitement and fanfare. The whole town, it seemed, came out for the official dedication of The Zone.

Claire bit at her lip as her gaze scanned the crowd. A bittersweet longing for Nick engulfed her. He should be here to help celebrate. He'd done so much to help make this a reality. But more than anything, she longed for his steady presence. She felt so alone and lonely. She missed Nick's companionship. She missed confiding in him. And she missed hearing his booted steps echoing through The Zone.

Every time she heard the low rumble of a motorcycle, no matter how distant, she held her breath, hoping Nick would roar back into her life.

She'd finally figured out the discrepancy between her check register and her bank balance. She'd found the checks she'd given to Nick for his weekly wages neatly stacked in one of the dresser drawers in his room. He'd given her so much, but not the one thing she really wanted. His heart.

Today, she decided, she'd stop hoping and start living her life without him.

She stood on the front steps of The Zone with Pastor Gary and the mayor of Pineridge. A microphone had been set up for them to say a few words. The crowd spilled off The Zone property, filling the street and part of the park.

The mayor, a dark-haired man in his late fifties with a thick mustache, looked impressive in a well-tailored suit and polished shoes. He spoke with the even, smooth tones of a politician. "The Zone is a needed asset to our community. The youth of Pineridge will find a safe and friendly environment when they venture in. The town council and I would like to thank Claire Wilcox for her willing and compassionate heart."

Applause rose, bringing heat to Claire's cheeks. The mayor handed her the microphone. Holding it tightly so her trembling hands wouldn't bob the thing against her mouth, she searched for words to express her pleasure at having her dream realized. "There are so many people who have made this a reality. I couldn't have seen this through on my own. I want to thank you all for you support, encouragement and your prayers.

"I want to dedicate The Zone to my Aunt Denise, who was my anchor when I was a teen. I..." she trailed off as her gaze landed on a tall dark-haired man who moved his way through the crowd toward her.

Nick.

Her heart tripped, skipped and stopped, only to trip and skip again. She handed the microphone to Pastor Gary and hurried down the steps. Jostling her way through the crowd, she met him in the middle amid a sea of people and curious stares.

"You're here," she breathed out in a rush.

His grin was devastating. Welcomed. Loved. She wanted to wrap her arms around him. To tell him how much she'd missed him. But she held back as old fears buzzed around like little gnats drawn to sweet fruit.

He took her hand and pulled her through the crowd until they were standing on the edge where an older couple she'd never seen before, but would recognize anywhere, stood. Nick's parents.

His father stood as tall as Nick and had the same dark, watchful eyes, and the same hard line to his jaw. His mother was arresting, with jet-black hair swept up in a fancy twist and warm brown eyes that regarded her with interest.

"Mom, Dad. This is Claire. Claire, Victor and Olivia Andrews."

In a bit of a daze, Claire shook hands with Nick's parents.

"Nick has told us so much about you, I feel I already know you," Olivia stated warmly in that east coast accent that Claire had come to love in Nick.

"Thank you for everything," Victor Andrews said with meaning.

She barely heard him. All she could think, all she could see was Nick. "You went home."

The warmth of his smile echoed in his voice. "I did."

Awed and pleased, she could only smile wider. If he went home then…

She blinked. Then what?

"Why are you here?" Her breath stalled in her lungs with possibilities. Was he back to stay? Just to visit? Could she dare hope he'd come for her?

He captured her hand, his grip sure and strong. "Mom, Dad. Excuse us."

"Of course, Son."

His father's knowing tone confused Claire. All of this confused her. "Where—"

"I'll answer all your questions. I promise."

She allowed Nick to lead her farther away from the throng of people to a quiet spot behind a flowering rhododendron.

"I came back, Claire, because I don't like being shackled. I want to live again."

Her mouth went dry. She swallowed. She had to ask because she had nothing to lose. She had no expectations. Only hope. "Are you free to live again?"

"Yes. I went to see that kid." His dark gaze held compassion. "You were right, Claire. If someone had reached out to that kid…"

Tears gathered at the corner of her eyes. "And what about love?"

He reached up to caress her cheek. His tender expression captivated her. "I found love, right here, Claire."

Her breath hitched. "You did?"

He nodded. "I love you, Claire."

Her heart beat so fast and hard she thought it might burst from her chest. Only hope. Only love. A wave of joy washed through her. There were no doubts, no hesitation. "I love you."

"Good." And his lips descended onto hers, warm and tender. She lost herself in the melding of their breaths, the sweetness of love.

"You're going have to marry her if you keep that up."

They jerked apart. Claire gaped at the kid standing a few feet away. Tyler. Same jutting chin, same challenging gaze, same attitude.

She held her breath as she turned her gaze back to Nick, dreading to see the hatred and rage. But his eyes crinkled at the corners with amusement. Her heart melted into a puddle at his feet. He truly was free.

"You've got that right, my friend," Nick said. His hands gently framed her face. "Claire, will you marry me?"

One question still burned on her heart. "What about The Zone?"

The corners of his mouth rose. "I thought we made a good team."

She blinked back her tears of joy. "We did."

His thumb rubbed across her bottom lip. "We do," he corrected. "You still haven't answered my question."

Full-fledged happiness exploded within her and the tears fell in earnest. "Yes. Oh, yes."

Her heart sang a song of praise as she slipped into the shelter of Nick's loving embrace.

Thank You, God, for answered prayers.

Epilogue

Twenty-month-old Rebecca Andrews lifted her chubby finger toward the end of the room. Her yellow sundress rode high and showed off her ruffled diaper cover. "Mommy, yook! Dare Tiyer!"

"Yes, sweetie. There's Tyler," Claire whispered to the raven-haired toddler squirming in her father's lap.

On the stage at the front of the auditorium, Tyler Riggs, wearing a blue gown and matching square hat with a gold tassel, extended his right hand to the principal of Pineridge High School and reached for his diploma with his left hand. The tall teen flashed a grin at the audience as he held up the scrolled paper in a victory salute. His once scraggly hair now sported a hip style that Claire's hairdresser friend, Lori, swore was all the rage with the young hunks in Hollywood.

"What a goof," Gwen remarked with a wide grin of her own, as she clapped loudly from her seat on the other side of Claire.

Claire met her husband's gaze over the head of their daughter as they clapped with enthusiasm. The pride and love swelling in Claire's chest reflected in Nick's dark eyes.

Tyler had matured and was fast becoming the man Claire knew he could be. The man God wanted him to be. With Nick's help, Tyler had formulated a plan for his future. Two years at Mount Hood College, then off to Eugene to study architecture at the University of Oregon.

That wasn't to say the last three years had been easy. Tyler had come to live with them at The Zone and the adjustment had been tough on all of them at first, despite the love that grew daily between her and Nick.

Thankfully Sandy and Dave had become parenting mentors to Claire and Nick and had assured them that Tyler's attitude and actions were typical for his age, regardless of the scars left by his childhood.

With firm boundaries and love, they weathered the storm of building trust and respect. Claire was proud not only of Tyler, but of her husband, as well. Nick had proved himself to be an excellent father figure for Tyler.

She put her hand on her growing abdomen, her gaze going to little Rebecca. And an amazing father for their own children. Their legacy.

Every day she thanked God for the gift of Nick. With their marriage she gained a wonderful, loving husband, a child she adored, another due to arrive in four months and caring in-laws. She never imagined she could be so happy.

God had blessed The Zone, as well, with donations

and support from the community. She and Nick had had the opportunity to help many teens over the last few years. She'd never forget any of them or the richness they'd brought to her life. And God willing, there would be more. She still kept in contact with Johnny and Mindy. The first two success stories of The Zone.

Johnny was headed to Portland State in the fall. And Mindy and her mom, Shari, were leaving for Florida to be near Shari's sister's family. Mindy promised to write as soon as they were settled. She hoped to get a job at Disney World while she attended the local community college in Orlando.

And then there was Gwen. Claire glanced over at the woman who'd become like a younger sister. Gwen's long red hair fell over her shoulder in her traditional braid and her bright rust-colored blouse accentuated her amber eyes. Claire was proud of her and would miss her when she left at the end of the month to start her new job as a physician's assistant in Seattle—a long way from the streetwise kid that had come to live with her and Aunt Denise.

Claire was so grateful for the blessings in her life. Her husband and children. Gwen. Tyler. The teens.

The Zone had become what she'd envisioned. A safe haven for kids in need. A place for them to go to when running away seemed like the only option. She was making a difference.

She leaned over and kissed the top of Rebecca's head.

"How about me?" Nick asked, his eyes filled with tenderness. The collar of his royal blue polo shirt was bunched up in Rebecca's fist. His strong hands held their daughter with the utmost gentleness, steadying her as she stood with one sandal-clad foot on each of his khaki-covered thighs.

Deep abiding love filled Claire's heart and brought tears to her eyes. Nick had made a difference in her life. One that could have only come from God. "Always."

Their lips met and Claire sighed with contentment.

* * * * *

Dear Reader,

Thank you for reading my second novel with Steeple Hill Love Inspired. I hope you enjoyed Claire and Nick's journey as they overcame the pain of the past to discover *A Sheltering Love*.

As I did the research for this story, I was touched by the plight of homeless teens. The many stories I read brought me to tears. And I discovered homelessness among the youth in this country is reaching crisis proportions in every city in every state. Young people are routinely sleeping in parks, abandoned buildings, alleys and doorways. Lacking guidance, many turn to drugs, crime and violence. Without intervention the street culture becomes home and family.

But there are many, like Claire, who've stepped up to the plate and are trying to make a difference by supporting their local teen shelters.

May God bless you always,

REQUEST YOUR FREE BOOKS!

2 FREE INSPIRATIONAL NOVELS
PLUS 2
FREE
MYSTERY GIFTS

YES! Please send me 2 FREE Love Inspired® novels and my 2 FREE mystery gifts (gifts are worth about $10). After receiving them, if I don't wish to receive any more books, I can return the shipping statement marked "cancel". If I don't cancel, I will receive 4 brand-new novels every month and be billed just $4.24 per book in the U.S. or $4.74 per book in Canada, plus 25¢ shipping and handling per book and applicable taxes, if any*. That's a savings of over 20% off the cover price! I understand that accepting the 2 free books and gifts places me under no obligation to buy anything. I can always return a shipment and cancel at any time. Even if I never buy another book, the two free books and gifts are mine to keep forever.

113 IDN ERXA   313 IDN ERWX

Name	(PLEASE PRINT)
Address	Apt. #
City	State/Prov.	Zip/Postal Code

Signature (if under 18, a parent or guardian must sign)

Order online at www.LoveInspiredBooks.com

Or mail to Steeple Hill Reader Service:

IN U.S.A.: P.O. Box 1867, Buffalo, NY 14240-1867
IN CANADA: P.O. Box 609, Fort Erie, Ontario L2A 5X3

Not valid to current subscribers of Love Inspired books.

**Want to try two free books from another series?
Call 1-800-873-8635 or visit www.morefreebooks.com**

* Terms and prices subject to change without notice. N.Y. residents add applicable sales tax. Canadian residents will be charged applicable provincial taxes and GST. Offer not valid in Quebec. This offer is limited to one order per household. All orders subject to approval. Credit or debit balances in a customer's account(s) may be offset by any other outstanding balance owed by or to the customer. Please allow 4 to 6 weeks for delivery. Offer available while quantities last.

Your Privacy: Steeple Hill Books is committed to protecting your privacy. Our Privacy Policy is available online at www.SteepleHill.com or upon request from the Reader Service. From time to time we make our lists of customers available to reputable third parties who may have a product or service of interest to you. If you would prefer we not share your name and address, please check here. ☐

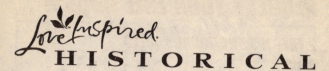

HISTORICAL

INSPIRATIONAL HISTORICAL ROMANCE

This delightful anthology celebrates the timeless institution of motherhood, in all its shapes and forms. Written by two bestselling Love Inspired Historical authors, these novellas are about two young women who find love, marriage and family in the American West during the nineteenth century.

Look for

In a Mother's Arms

by

JILLIAN HART
VICTORIA BYLIN

Steeple
Hill®

Available in April wherever books are sold.

www.SteepleHill.com

LIH82809

Love Inspired
SUSPENSE
RIVETING INSPIRATIONAL ROMANCE

WITHOUT A TRACE

Without a Trace: Will a young mother's disappearance bring a bayou town together...or tear it apart?

WHAT SARAH SAW
by MARGARET DALEY
January 2009

FRAMED!
by ROBIN CAROLL
February 2009

COLD CASE MURDER
by SHIRLEE MCCOY
March 2009

CLOUD OF SUSPICION
by PATRICIA DAVIDS
April 2009

DEADLY COMPETITION
by ROXANNE RUSTAND
May 2009

*Available wherever books are sold,
including most bookstores, supermarkets,
drugstores and discount stores.*

Steeple
Hill®

www.SteepleHill.com

LISWATLIST